ALSO BY
LAIRD BARRON

Not a Speck of Light

=stories=

=LAIRD BARRON=

Not a Speck of Light: Stories
Copyright © 2024 by Laird Barron
Print ISBN: 979-8-218-03606-5

Cover Art & Illustrations by Trevor Henderson
Cover Design by Michael Bailey
Interior Design by Todd Keisling | Dullington Design Co.

"In a Cavern, in a Canyon" previously appeared in *Seize the Night: New Tales of Vampiric Terror*, edited by Christopher Golden, *Gallery Books* 2015; "Girls Without Their Faces On" previously appeared in *Ashes and Entropy*, edited by Robert S. Wilson, *Nightscape Books* 2018; "Mobility" previously appeared in *WHAT THE #@&% IS THAT?: The Saga Anthology of the Monstrous and the Macabre,* edited by Douglas Coen and John Joseph Adams, *Gallery/Saga Press* 2016; "The Glorification of Custer Poe" previously appeared as "The Beatification of Custer Poe" in *Shades of Blue and Gray: Ghosts of the Civil War*, edited by Steve Berman, *Prime Books* 2013; "Jōren Falls" previously appeared in *Come Join Us by the Fire, Volume 2,* edited by Theresa DeLucci, *Tor Nightfire* 2021; "The Blood in My Mouth" previously appeared in *The Madness of Cthulhu, Volume Two*, edited by S.T. Joshi, *Titan Books* 2015; "Nemesis" previously appeared in *Primeval: A Journal of the Uncanny, Issue 1,* edited by G. Winston Hyatt, *Blood Bound Books* 2013; "Soul of Me" previously appeared in *The Burning Maiden Anthology, Book 2,* edited by Greg Kishbaugh, *Evileye Books* 2016; "Fear Sun" previously appeared in *Innsmouth Nightmares: Lovecraftian Inspired Nightmares,* edited by Lois H. Gresh, *PS Publishing* 2015; "Swift to Chase" previously appeared in *Adam's Ladder,* edited by Michael Bailey and Darren Speegle, *Written Backwards,* 2017; "Don't Make Me Assume My Ultimate Form" previously appeared in *Cthulhu Fhatgn!* Edited by Ross Lockhart, *Word Horde* 2015; "American Remake of a Japanese Ghost Story" previously appeared in *There is No Death, There are No Dead: Tales of Spiritualism Horror,* edited by Jess Landry and Aaron French, *Crystal Lake Publishing* 2021; "Strident Caller" previously appeared in *Whispers from the Abyss 2: Horrors That Were and Shall Be*, edited by Kat Rocha, *01 Publishing,* 2015; "Not a Speck of Light" is original to this collection; "Tiptoe" previously appeared in *When Things Get Dark: Stories Inspired by Shirley Jackson,* edited by Ellen Datlow, *Titan Books* 2021; "(You Won't Be) Saved by the Ghost of Your Old Dog" previously appeared on Laird Barron's author site, 2021

Bad Hand Books
www.badhandbooks.com

For Jessica M.

At first it seemed a little speck,
And then it seemed a mist;
It moved and moved, and took at last
A certain shape…

—Samuel Taylor Coleridge

TABLE OF CONTENTS

I
BLOOD RED SAMARITANS

IN A CAVERN, IN A CANYON

Husband number one fondly referred to me as the Good Samaritan. Anything from a kid lost in the neighborhood to a countywide search-and-rescue effort, I got involved. If we drove past a fender-bender, I had to stop and lend a hand or snap a few pictures, maybe do a walk-around of the scene. A major crash? Forget about it—I'd haunt the site until the cows came home or the cops shooed me away. Took the better part of a decade for the light bulb to flash over my hubby's bald head. He realized I wasn't a Samaritan so much as a fetishist. Wore him down in the end and he bailed. I'm still melancholy over that one.

Lucky for him he didn't suffer through my stint with the park service in Alaska. After college and the first kid, I finagled my way onto the government payroll and volunteered for every missing person, lost climber, downed plane, or wrecked boat scenario. I hiked and camped on the side. Left my compass and maps at home. I wanted to disappear. Longest I managed was four days. The Feds were suspicious enough to send me to a shrink who knew his business. The boys upstairs gave me a generous severance check and said to not let the door hit me in the ass on the way out. Basically, the beginning of a long downward slide in my life.

Husband number three divorced me for my fifty-fourth birthday. I pawned everything that wouldn't fit into a van and drove from Ohio back home to Alaska. I rented a doublewide at the Cottonwood Point Trailer Park near Moose Pass, two miles along the bucolic and winding Seward Highway from Cassie, my youngest daughter.

A spruce forest crowds the back door. Moose nibble the rhododendron hedging the yard. Most folks tuck in for the night by the time Colbert is delivering his monologue on Comedy Central.

Cassie drops off my infant granddaughter, Vera, two or three times a week or whenever she can't find a sitter. Single and working two jobs (hardware cashier by day, graveyard security at the Port of Seward Wednesday and Friday), Cassie avoided the inevitability of divorce by not getting married in the first place. She kept the dumb, virile fisherman who knocked her up as baby-daddy and strictly part-time squeeze. Wish I'd thought of that. Once I realized that my nanny gig was a regular thing, I ordered a crib and inveigled the handsome (and generally drunken, alas) fellow at 213 to set it up in my bedroom.

On the nanny evenings, I feed Vera her bottle and watch westerns on cable. "Get you started right," I say to her as Bronson ventilates Fonda beneath a glaring sun, or when a cowboy rides into the red-and-gold distance as the credits roll. She'll be a tomboy like her gram if I have any influence. The classic stars were my heroes once upon a time—Stewart, Van Cleef, Wayne, and Marvin. During my youth, I utterly revered Eastwood. I crushed big time on The Man with No Name and Dirty Harry. Kept a poster from *The Good, The Bad, And The Ugly* on my bedroom wall. So young, both of us. So innocent. Except for the shooting and murdering, and my lustful thoughts, but you know.

Around midnight, I wake from a nap on the couch to Vera's plaintive cry. She's in the bedroom crib, awake and pissed for her bottle. The last act of *High Plains Drifter* plays in scratchy 1970s Technicolor. It's the part where the Stranger finally gets around to exacting righteous vengeance. Doesn't matter that I've missed two rapes, a horsewhipping, Lago painted red and renamed HELL… all those images are imprinted upon my hindbrain. I get the impression the scenes are *always* rolling down there against the screen of my subconscious.

I am depressed to recognize a cold fact in this instant. The love affair with bad boy Clint ended years and years ago, even if I haven't fully accepted the reality. Eyes gummed with sleep, I sit for a few seconds, mesmerized by the stricken faces of the townspeople who are caught between a vicious outlaw gang and a stranger hell-bent on retribution. The Stranger's whip slithers through the saloon window and garrotes an outlaw. I've watched that scene on a dozen occasions. My hands shake and I can't zap it with the remote fast enough.

That solves one problem. I take the formula from the fridge and pop it into the fancy warmer Cassie obtained during a clearance sale. The LED numerals are counting down to nothing when it occurs to me that I don't watch the baby on Sundays.

The night in 1977 that my father disappeared, he, Uncle Ned, and I drove north along Midnight Road, searching for Tony Orlando. Dad crept the Fleetwood at a walking pace. My younger siblings, Doug, Shauna, and Artemis, remained at home. Doug was ostensibly keeping an eye on our invalid grandmother, but I figured he was probably glued to the television with the others. That autumn sticks in my memory like mud to a Wellington. We were sixteen, fourteen, eleven, and ten. Babes in the wilderness.

Uncle Ned and I took turns yelling out the window. Whenever Orlando pulled this stunt, Dad swore it would be the last expedition he mounted to retrieve the "damned mutt." I guess he really meant it.

Middle-school classmate Nancy Albrecht once asked me what the hell kind of name was that for a dog, and I said Mom and Dad screwed on the second date to "Halfway to Paradise," and if you laugh I'll smack your teeth down your throat. I have a few scars on my knuckles, for damn sure.

Way back then, we lived in Eagle Talon, Alaska, an isolated port about seventy miles southwest of Anchorage. Cruise ships bloated the town with tourists during spring, and it dried up to around three hundred resident souls come autumn.

Eastern settlers had carved a hamlet from wilderness during the 1920s; plunked it down in a forgotten vale populated by eagles, bears, drunk Teamsters and drunker fishermen. Mountains and dense forest on three sides formed a deep-water harbor. The channel curved around the flank of Eagle Mountain and eventually let into Prince William Sound. Roads were gravel or dirt. We had the cruise ships and barges. We also had the railroad. You couldn't make a move without stepping in seagull shit. Most of us townies lived in a fourteen-story apartment complex called the Frazier Estate. We kids shortened it to Fate. Terra incognita began where the sodium lamplight grew fuzzy. At night, wolves howled in the nearby hills. Definitely not the dream hometown of a sixteen-year-old girl. As a grown woman, I recall it with a bittersweet fondness.

Upon commencing the hunt for Orlando, whom my little brother Doug had stupidly set free from the leash only to watch in mortification as the dog trotted into the sunset, tail furled with rebellious intent, Dad faced a choice—head west along the road, or troll the beach where the family pet sometimes mined for rotten salmon carcasses. We picked the road because it wound into the woods and our Shepherd-Husky mix hankered after the red squirrels that swarmed during the fall. Dad didn't want to walk if he could avoid it. "Marched goddamned plenty in the Corps," he said. It had required a major effort for him to descend to the parking garage and get the wagon started and pointed in the general direction of our search route. Two bad knees, pain pills for said knees, and a half-rack a day habit had all but done him in.

Too bad for Uncle Ned and me, Midnight Road petered out in the foothills. Moose trails went every which way from the little clearing where we'd parked next to an abandoned Winnebago with a raggedy tarp covering the front end and black garbage bags over the windows. Hobos and druggies occasionally used the Winnebago as a fort until Sheriff Lockhart came along to roust them. "Goddamned railroad," Dad would say, despite the fact that if not for the railroad (for which he performed part-time labor to supplement his military checks) and the cruise ships and barges, there wouldn't be any call for Eagle Talon whatsoever.

Uncle Ned lifted himself from the back seat and accompanied me as I shined the flashlight and hollered for Orlando. Dad remained in the station wagon with the engine running and the lights on. He honked the horn every couple of minutes.

"He's gonna keep doing that, huh?" Uncle Ned wasn't exactly addressing me, more like an actor musing to himself on the stage. "Just gonna keep leanin' on that horn every ten seconds—"

The horn blared again. Farther off and dim—we'd come a ways already. Birch and alder were broken by stands of furry black spruce that muffled sounds from the outside world. The black, green, and gray webbing is basically the Spanish moss of the arctic. Uncle Ned chuckled and shook his head. Two years Dad's junior and a major league stoner, *he'd* managed to keep it together when it counted. He taught me how to tie a knot, paddle a canoe, and gave me a lifetime supply of dirty jokes. He'd also explained that contrary to Dad's Cro-Magnon take on teenage dating, boys were okay to fool around with so long as I ducked the bad ones and avoided getting knocked up. *Which ones were bad?* I wondered. Most of them, according to the Book of Ned, but keep it to fooling around and all would be well. He also clued me in to the fact that Dad's vow to blast any would-be suitor's pecker off with his twelve-gauge was an idle threat. My old man couldn't shoot worth spit even when sober.

The trail forked. One path climbed into the hills where the undergrowth thinned. The other path curved deeper into the creepy spruce where somebody had strung blue reflective tape among the branches—a haphazard mess like the time Dad got lit up and tried to decorate the Christmas tree.

"Let's not go in there," Uncle Ned said. Ominous, although not entirely unusual as he often said that kind of thing with a similar, laconic dryness. *That bar looks rough, let's try the next one over. That woman looks like my ex-wife, I'm not gonna dance with her, uh-uh. That box has got to be heavy. Let's get a beer and think on it.*

"Maybe he's at the beach rolling in crap," I said. Orlando loved bear turds and rotten salmon guts with a true passion. There'd be plenty of both near the big water, and as I squinted into the forbidding shadows, I increasingly wished we'd driven there instead.

Uncle Ned pulled his coat tighter and lit a cigarette. The air had dampened. I yelled "Orlando!" a few more times. Then we stood there for a while in the silence. It was like listening through the lid of a coffin. Dad had stopped leaning on the horn. The woodland critters weren't making their usual fuss. Clouds drifted in and the darkness was so complete it wrapped us in a cocoon. "Think Orlando's at the beach?" I said.

"Well, I dunno. He ain't here."

"Orlando, you stupid jerk!" I shouted to the night in general.

"Time to boogie," Uncle Ned said. The cherry of his cigarette floated in midair and gave his narrowed eyes a feral glint. Like Dad, he was middling tall and rangy. Sharp-featured and often wry. He turned and moved the way we'd come, head lowered, trailing a streamer of Pall Mall smoke. Typical of my uncle. Once he made a decision, he acted.

"Damn it, Orlando." I gave up and followed, sick to my gut with worry. Fool dog never missed an opportunity to flirt with danger. He'd tangled with a porcupine the summer before and I'd spent hours picking quills from his swollen snout because Dad refused to take him in to see Doc Green. There were worse things than porcupines in these woods—black bears, angry moose, wolves—and I feared my precious idiot would run into one of them.

Halfway back to the car, I glimpsed a patch of white to my left amidst the heavy brush. I took it for a birch stump with holes rotted into the heartwood. No, it was a man lying on his side, matted black hair framing his pale face. By pale, I mean bone-white and bloodless. The face you see on the corpse of an outlaw in those old-timey Wild West photographs.

"Help me," he whispered.

I trained my light on the injured man; he had to be hurt because of the limp, contorted angle of his body, his shocking paleness. He seemed familiar. The lamp beam broke around his body like a stream splits around a large stone. The shadows turned slowly, fracturing and changing him. He might've been weirdo Floyd who swept the Caribou Tavern after last call, or that degenerate trapper, Bob-something, who lived in a shack in the hills with a bunch of stuffed moose heads and mangy beaver hides. Or it might've been as I first thought—a tree stump lent a man's shape by my lying eyes. The more I stared, the less certain I became that it was a person at all.

Except I'd heard him speak, raspy and high-pitched from pain; almost a falsetto.

Twenty-five feet, give or take, between me and the stranger. I didn't see his arm move. Move it did, however. The shadows shifted again and his hand grasped futilely, thin and gnarled as a tree branch. His misery radiated into me, caused my eyes to well with tears of empathy. I felt terrible, just terrible, I wanted to mother him, and took a step toward him.

"Hortense. Come here." Uncle Ned said my name the way Dad described talking to his wounded buddies in 'Nam. The ones who'd gotten hit by a grenade or a stray bullet. Quiet, calm, and reassuring was the ticket—and I bet his tone would've worked its magic if my insides had happened to be splashed on the ground and the angels were singing me home. In this case, Uncle Ned's unnatural calmness scared me, woke me from a dream where I heroically tended a hapless stranger, got a parade and a key to the village, my father's grudging approval.

"Hortense, please."

"There's a guy in the bushes," I said. "I think he's hurt."

Uncle Ned grabbed my hand like he used to when I was a little girl, and towed me along at a brisk pace. "Naw, kid. That's a tree stump. I saw it when we went past earlier. Keep movin'."

I didn't ask why we were in such a hurry. It worried me how easy it seemed for him and Dad to slip into warrior mode at the drop of a hat. He muttered something about branches snapping and that black bears roamed the area as they fattened up for winter and he regretted leaving his guns at his house. *House* is sort of a grand term; Uncle Ned lived in a mobile home on the edge of the village. The Estate didn't appeal to his loner sensibilities.

We got to walking so fast along that narrow trail that I twisted my ankle on a root and nearly went for a header. Uncle Ned didn't miss a beat. He took most of my weight upon his shoulder. Pretty much dragged me back to the Fleetwood. The engine ran and the driver side door was ajar. I assumed Dad had gone behind a tree to take a leak. As the minutes passed and we called for him, I began to understand that he'd left. Those were the days when men abandoned their families by saying they needed to grab a pack of cigarettes and beating it for the high timber. He'd threatened to do it during his frequent arguments with Mom. She'd beaten him to the punch and jumped ship with a traveling salesman, leaving us to fend for ourselves. Maybe, just Maybe it was Dad's turn to bail on us kids.

Meanwhile, Orlando had jumped in through the open door and curled into a ball in the passenger seat. Leaves, twigs, and dirt plastered him. A pig digging for China wouldn't have been any filthier. Damned old dog pretended to sleep. His thumping tail gave away the show.

Uncle Ned rousted him and tried to put him on Dad's trail. Nothing doing. Orlando whined and hung his head. He refused to budge despite Uncle Ned's exhortations. Finally, the dog yelped and scrambled back into the car, trailing a stream of piss. That was our cue to depart.

Uncle Ned drove back to the Frazier Estate. He called Deputy Clausen (everybody called him Claws) and explained the situation. Claws agreed to gather a few men and do a walkthrough of the area. He theorized that Dad had gotten drunk and wandered into the hills and collapsed somewhere. Such events weren't rare.

Meanwhile, I checked in on Grandma, who'd occupied the

master bedroom since she'd suffered the aneurysm. Next, I herded Orlando into the bathroom and soaked him in the tub. I was really hurting by then.

When I thanked Uncle Ned, he nodded curtly and avoided meeting my eye. "Lock the door," he said.

"Why? The JWs aren't allowed out of the compound after dark." There weren't any Jehovah's Witnesses in town. Whenever I got scared, I cracked wise.

"Don't be a smartass. Lock the fuckin' door."

"Something fishy in Denmark," I said to Orlando, who leaned against my leg as I threw the deadbolt. Mrs. Wells had assigned *Hamlet*, *Julius Caesar*, and *Titus Andronicus* for summer reading. "And it's the Ides of August, too."

My brothers and sister sprawled in the living room front of the TV, watching a vampire movie. Christopher Lee wordlessly seduced a buxom chick who was practically falling out of her peasant blouse. Lee angled for a bite. Then he saw, nestled in the woman's cleavage, the teeny elegant crucifix her archeologist boyfriend had given her for luck. Lee's eyes went buggy with rage and fear. The vampire equivalent to blue balls, I guess. I took over Dad's La-Z-Boy and kicked back with a bottle of Coke (the last one, as noted by the venomous glares of my siblings) and a bag of ice on my puffy ankle.

The movie ended and I clapped my hands and sent the kids packing. At three bedrooms, our apartment qualified as an imperial suite. Poor Dad sacked out on the couch. Doug and Artemis shared the smallest, crappiest room. I bunked with Shauna, the princess of jibber-jabber. She loved and feared me; that made tight quarters a bit easier because little sister knew I'd sock her in the arm if she sassed me too much or pestered me with one too many goober questions. Often, she'd natter on while I piped Fleetwood Mac and

Led Zeppelin through a set of gigantic yellow earphones. That self-isolation spared us a few violent and teary scenes, I'm sure.

Amid the grumbles and the rush for the toilet, I almost confessed the weird events of the evening to Doug. My kid brother had an open mind when it came to the unknown. He wouldn't necessarily laugh me out of the room without giving the matter some real thought. Instead, I smacked the back of his head and told him not to be such a dumbass with Orlando. Nobody remarked on Dad's absence. I'm sure they figured he'd pitched camp at the Caribou like he did so many nights. Later, I lay awake and listened to my siblings snore. Orlando whined as he dreamed of the chase, or of being chased.

From the bedroom, Gram said in a fragile, sing-song tone, "In a cavern, in a canyon, excavatin' for a mine, dwelt a miner forty-niner and his daughter Clementine. In a cavern in a canyon. In a cavern, in a canyon. In a cavern, in a canyon. Clementine, Clementine. Clementine? Clementine?"

Of the four Shaw siblings I was the eldest, tallest, *and* surliest. According to Mom, Dad had desperately wanted a boy for his firstborn. He descended from a lineage that adhered to a pseudo-medieval mindset. The noble chauvinist, the virtuous warrior, the honorable fighter of rearguard actions. Quaint when viewed through a historical lens; a real pain in the ass in the modern world.

I was a disappointment. As a daughter, what else could I be? He got used to it. The Shaws have a long, long history of losing. We own that shit. *Go down fighting* would've been our family motto, with a snake biting the heel that crushed its skull as our crest. As some consolation, I was always a tomboy and tougher than either of my brothers—a heap tougher than most of the boys in our hick town, and tougher than at least a few of the grown men. Toughness isn't always measured by how hard you punch. Sometimes, most of the time, it's simply the set of a girl's jaw. I shot my mouth off with the best of them. If nothing else, I dutifully struck at the heels of my oppressors. Know where I got this grit? Sure as hell not from Dad. Oh, yeah, he threw a nasty left hook, and he'd scragged a few guys in the wars. But until Mom had flown the coop, she ruled our roost with an iron fist that would've made Khrushchev think twice before crossing her. Yep, the meanness in my soul is pure-D Mom.

Dad had all the homespun apothegms.

He often said, *Never try to beat a man at what he does.* What Dad did best was drink. He treated it as a competitive event. In addition to chugging Molson Export, Wild Turkey, and Absolut, Dad also smoked the hell out of cannabis whenever he could get his hands on some. He preferred the heavy-hitting bud from Mexico courtesy of Uncle Ned. I got my hands on a bag those old boys stashed in a rolled-up sock in a number-ten coffee can. That stuff sent you, all right. Although, judging by the wildness of Dad's eyes, the way they started and stared at the corners of the room after he'd had a few hits, his destination was way different than mine.

Even so, the Acapulco Gold gave me a peek through the keyhole into Dad's soul in a way booze couldn't. Some blood memory got activated. It might've been our sole point of commonality. He would've beaten me to a pulp if he'd known. For my own good, natch.

Main thing I took from growing up the daughter of an alcoholic? Lots of notions compete for the top spot—the easiest way to get vomit and blood out of fabric, the best apologies, the precise amount of heed to pay a drunken diatribe, when to duck flung bottles, how to balance a checkbook and cook a family meal between homework, dog-walking, and giving sponge baths to Gram. But above all, my essential takeaway was that I'd never go down the rabbit hole to an eternal happy hour. I indulged in a beer here and there, toked some Mary Jane to reward myself for serving as Mom, Dad, Chief Cook and Bottle Washer pro-tem. Nothing heavy, though. I resolved to leave the heavy lifting to Dad, Uncle Ned, and their buddies at the Caribou Tavern.

Randal Shaw retired from the USMC in 1974 after twenty years of active service. Retirement didn't agree with him. To wit: the beer, bourbon, and weed, and the sullen hurling of empties. It didn't agree with Mom either, obviously. My grandmother, Harriet Shaw, suffered a brain aneurism that very autumn. Granddad passed away the previous winter and Gram moved into our apartment. By day, she slumped in a special medical recliner we bought from the Eagle Talon Emergency Trauma Center. Vivian from upstairs sat with her while I was at school. Gram's awareness came and went like a bad radio signal. Sometimes she'd make a feeble attempt to play cards with Vivian. Occasionally, she asked about my grades and what cute boys I'd met, or she'd watch TV and chuckle at the soaps in that rueful way she laughed at so many ridiculous things. The clarity became rare. Usually she stared out the window at the harbor or at the framed Georgia O'Keefe knockoff print of a sunflower above the dresser. Hours passed and we'd shoo away the mosquitos while she tunelessly hummed "In a cavern, in a canyon, excavatin' for a mine" on a loop. There may as well have been a **VACANCY** sign blinking above her head.

After school, and twice daily on weekends, Doug helped bundle Gram into the crappy fold-up chair and I pushed her around the village; took her down to the wharf to watch the seagulls, or parked her in front of the general store while I bought Dad a pack of smokes (and another for myself). By night, Dad or I pushed the button and let the air out and she lay with her eyes fixed on the dented ceiling of the bedroom. She'd sigh heavily and say, "Nighty-night, nighty-night," like a parrot. It shames me to remember her that way. But then, most of my childhood is a black hole.

The search party found neither hide nor hair of Dad. Deputy Clausen liked Uncle Ned well enough and agreed to do a bigger sweep in the afternoon. The deputy wasn't enthused. Old Harmon Snodgrass, a trapper from Kobuk, isolated footprints in the soft dirt along the edge of the road. The tracks matched Dad's boots and were headed toward town. Snodgrass lost them after a couple hundred yards.

In Deputy Clausen's professional opinion, Randal Shaw had doubled back and flown the coop to parts unknown, as a certain kind of man is wont to do when the going gets tough. Uncle Ned socked him (the Shaw answer to critics) and Claws would've had his ass in a cell for a good long time, except Stu Herring, the mayor of our tiny burg, and Kyle Lomax were on hand to break up the festivities and soothe bruised egos. Herring sent Uncle Ned home with a *go and sin no more* scowl.

"How's Mom?" Uncle Ned stared at Gram staring at a spot on the wall. He sipped the vilest black coffee on the face of the earth. My specialty. I'd almost tripped over him in the hallway on my way to take Orlando for his morning stroll. He'd spent the latter portion of the night curled near our door, a combat knife in his fist. Normally, one might consider that loony behavior. You had to know Uncle Ned.

"She's groovy, as ever. Why are you lurking?" The others were still zonked, thank God. I hadn't an inkling of how to break the news of Dad's defection to them. I packed more ice onto my ankle. My foot had swollen to the point where it wouldn't fit into my sneaker. It really and truly hurt. "Ow."

"Let's go. Hospital time." He stood abruptly and went in and woke Doug, told him, "Drop your cock and grab your socks. You're man of the house for an hour. Orlando needs a walk—for the love of God, keep him on a leash, will ya?" Then he nabbed Dad's keys and took me straightaway to the Eagle Clinic. Mrs. Cooper, a geriatric hypochondriac, saw the RN, Sally Mackey, ahead of us and we knew from experience that it would be a hell of a wait. So Uncle Ned and I settled into hard plastic waiting room chairs. He lit a cigarette, and another for me, and said, "Okay, I got a story. Don't tell your old man I told you, or he'll kick my ass and then I'll kick yours. Yeah?"

I figured it would be a story of his hippie escapades or some raunchy bullshit Dad got up to in Vietnam. A tale to cheer me up and take my mind off my troubles. Uh-uh. He surprised me by talking about the Good Friday Earthquake of '64. "You were, what? Two, three? You guys lived in that trailer park in Anchorage. The quake hits and your Dad's been shipped to 'Nam. My job was to look over you and your mom. Meanwhile, I'm visiting a little honey out in the Valley. Girl had a cabin on a lake. We just came in off the ice for a mug of hot cocoa and BOOM! Looked like dynamite churned up the bottom muck. Shit flew off the shelves, the earth moved in waves like the sea. Spruce trees bent all the way over and slapped their tops on the ground. Sounded like a train runnin' through the living room. Tried callin' your mom, but the phone lines were down.

"I jumped in my truck and headed for Anchorage. Got part way there and had to stop. Highway was too fucked up to drive on. Pavement cracked open, bridges collapsed. I got stuck in a traffic jam on the Flats. Some cars were squashed under a collapsed overpass near the inlet and a half-dozen more kind a piled on. It was nine or ten at night and pitch black. Accidents everywhere. The temperature dropped below freezing. Road flares and headlights and flashing hazards made the scene extra spooky. I could taste salt brine and hysteria in the air. Me and a couple of Hells Angels from Wasilla got together and made sure people weren't trapped or hurt too bad. Then we started pushing cars off the road to get ready for the emergency crews.

"We were taking a smoke break when one of the bikers said to shut up a minute. A big, pot-bellied Viking, at least twice the size of me and his younger pal. Fuckin' enormous. He cocked his head and asked us if we'd heard it too—somebody moaning for help down on the Flats. He didn't hang around for an answer. Hopped over the guardrail and was gone. Man on a mission. Guy didn't come back after a few minutes. Me and the younger biker climbed down the embankment and went into the pucker-brush. Shouted ourselves hoarse and not a damned reply. Mist was oozin' off the water and this weird, low tide reek hit me. A cross between green gas from inside a blown moose carcass and somethin' sweet, like fireweed. I heard a noise, reminded me of water and air bubbles gurglin' through a hose. Grace a God I happened to shine my light on a boot stickin' outta the scrub. The skinny biker yelled his buddy's name and ran over there."

Uncle Ned had gotten worked up during the narration of his story. He lit another cigarette and paced to the coffee machine and back. Bernice Monson, the receptionist, glared over her glasses. She didn't say anything. In '77 most folks kept their mouths shut when confronted by foamy Vietnam vets. Bernice, like everybody else, assumed Uncle Ned did a jungle tour as a government employee. He certainly resembled the part with his haggard expression, brooding demeanor, and a partialness for camouflage pants. Truth was, while many young men were blasting away at each other in Southeast Asia, he'd backpacked across Canada, Europe, and Mexico. Or, *went humping foreign broads and scrawling doggerel*, as my dad put it.

Uncle Ned's eyes were red as a cockscomb. He slapped the coffee machine. "I didn't have a perfect position and my light was weak, but I saw plenty. The Viking laid on top of somebody. This somebody was super skinny and super pale. Lots of wild hair. Their arms and legs were tangled so's you couldn't make sense of what was goin' on. I thought he had him a woman there in the weeds and they was fuckin'. Their faces were stuck together. The young biker leaned over his buddy and then yelped and stumbled backward. The skinny, pale one shot out from under the Viking and into the darkness. Didn't stand, didn't crouch, didn't even flip over—know how a mechanic rolls from under a car on his board? Kinda that way, except jittery. Moved like an insect scuttling for cover, best I can describe it. A couple seconds later, the huge biker shuddered and went belly-crawling after the skinny fellow. What I thought I was seeing him do, anyhow. His arms and legs flopped, although his head never lifted, not completely. He just skidded away, Superman-style, his face planted in the dirt.

"Meanwhile, the young biker hauled ass toward the road, shriekin' the whole way. My flashlight died. I stood there, in the dark, heart poundin', scared shitless, tryin' to get my brain out a neutral. I wanted to split, hell yeah. No fuckin' way I was gonna tramp around on those Flats by myself. I'm a hunter, though. Those instincts kicked in and I decided to play it cool. Your dad always pegged me for a peacenik hippie because I didn't do 'Nam. I'm smarter, is the thing. Got a knife in my pocket and half the time I'm packin' heat too. Had me skinning knife, and lemme say, I kept it handy as I felt my way through the bushes and the brambles. Got most of the way to where

I could see the lights of the cars on the road. Somebody muttered, "Help me." Real close and on my flank. Scared me, sure. I probably jumped three feet straight up. And yet, it was the saddest voice I can remember. Woeful, like a lost child, or a wounded woman, or a fawn, or some combination of those cries.

"I might a turned around and walked into the night, except a state trooper hit me with a light. He'd come over the hill lookin' after the biker went bugshit. I think the cop thought the three of us were involved in a drug deal. He sure as hell didn't give a lick about a missing Hells Angel. He led me back to the clusterfuck on the highway and I spent the rest of the night shivering in my car while the bulldozers and dump trucks did their work." He punched the coffee machine.

"Easy, man!" I said and gave an apologetic smile to the increasingly agitated Bernice. I patted the seat next to me until he came over and sat. "What happened to the biker? The big guy."

Uncle Ned had sliced his knuckles. He clenched his fist and watched the blood drip onto the tiles. "Cops found him that summer in the inlet. Not enough left for an autopsy. The current and the fish had taken him apart. Accidental death, they decided. I saw the younger biker at the Gold Digger. Must a been five or six years after the Good Friday Quake. He acted like he'd forgotten what happened to his partner until I bought him the fifth tequila. *He* got a real close look at what happened. Said that to him, the gurglin' was more of a slurpin'. An animal lappin' up a gory supper. Then he looked me in the eye and said his buddy got snatched into the darkness by his own guts. They were comin' outta his mouth and whatever it was out there gathered' em up and reeled him in."

"Holy shit, Uncle Ned." Goose pimples covered my arms. "That's nuts. Who do you think was out there?"

"The boogeyman. Whatever it is that kids think is hidin' under their bed."

"You tell Dad? Probably not, huh? He's a stick in the mud. He'd never buy it."

"Well, you don't either. Guess that makes you a stick in the mud, too."

"The apple, the tree, gravity…"

"Maybe you'd be surprised what your old man knows." Uncle Ned's expression was shrewd. "I been all over this planet. Between '66 and '74, I roamed. Passed the peace pipe with the Lakota; ate peyote with the Mexicans; drank wine with the Italians; and smoked excellent bud with a whole lot of other folks. I get bombed enough, or stoned enough, I ask if anybody else has heard of the Help Me Monster. What I call it. The Help Me Monster."

The description evoked images of Sesame Street and plush toys dancing on wires. "Grover the Psycho Killer!" I said, hoping he'd at least crack a smile. I also hoped my uncle hadn't gone around the bend.

He didn't smile. We sat there in one of those long, awkward silences while Bernice coughed her annoyance and shuffled papers. I was relieved when Sally Mackey finally stuck her head into the room and called my name.

The nurse wanted to send me to Anchorage for X-rays. No way would Dad authorize that expense. No veterinarians and no doctors; those were ironclad rules. When he discovered Uncle Ned took me to the clinic, he'd surely blow his top. I wheedled a bottle of prescription-strength aspirin, and a set of cheapo crutches on the house, and called it square. A mild ankle sprain meant I'd be on the crutches for days. I added it to the tab of Shaw family dues.

Dad never came home. I cried, the kids cried. Bit by bit, we moved on. Some of us more than others.

I won't bore you with the nightmares that got worse and worse with time. You can draw your own conclusions. That strange figure in the woods, Dad's vanishing act, and Uncle Ned's horrifying tale coalesced into a witch's brew that beguiled me and became a serious obsession.

Life is messy and it's mysterious. Had my father walked away from his family or had he been taken? If the latter, then why Dad and not me or Uncle Ned? I didn't crack the case, didn't get any sense of closure. No medicine man or antiquarian popped up to give me the scoop on some ancient enemy that dwells in the shadows and dines upon the blood and innards of Good Samaritans and hapless passersby.

Closest I came to solving the enigma was during my courtship with husband number two. He said a friend of a friend was a student biologist on a research expedition in Canada. His team and local authorities responded to a massive train derailment near a small town. Rescuers spent three days clearing out the survivors. On day four, they swept the scattered wreckage for bodies.

This student, who happened to be Spanish, and three fellow countrymen, were way out in a field after dark, poking around with sticks. One of them heard a voice moaning for help. Of course, they scrambled to find this wretched soul. Late to the scene, a military search-and-rescue helicopter flew overhead, very low, its searchlight blazing. When the chopper had gone, all fell silent. The cries didn't repeat. Weird part, according to the Spaniard, was that in the few minutes they'd frantically tried to locate the injured person, his voice kept moving around in some bizarre acoustical illusion. The survivor switched from French, to English, and finally to Spanish.

The biologist claimed he had nightmares of the incident for years afterward. He dreamed of his buddies separated in a dark field, each crying for help, and he'd stumble across their desiccated corpses, one by one. He attributed it to the guilt of leaving someone to die on the tundra.

My husband-to-be told me that story while high on coke and didn't mention it again. I wonder if that's why I married the sorry sonofabitch. Just for that single moment of connectedness, a tiny and inconstant flicker of light in the wilderness.

High noon on a Sunday night.

Going on thirty-eight haunted years, I've expected this, or something like this, even though the entity represents with its very jack-in-the-box manifestation, a deep, dark mystery of the universe. What has drawn it to me is equally inexplicable. I've considered the fanciful notion that the Shaws are cursed and Mr. Help Me is the instrument of vengeance. Doesn't feel right. I've also prayed to Mr. Help Me as if he, or it, is a death god watching over us cattle. Perhaps it is. The old gods wanted blood, didn't they? Blood and offerings of flesh. That feels more on the mark. Or, it could be the simplest answer of them all—Mr. Help Me is an exotic animal whose biology and behavior defy scientific classification. The need for sustenance is the least of all possible mysteries. I can fathom *that* need, at least.

A window must be open in my bedroom. Cool night air dries the sweat on my cheeks as I stand in the darkened hall. The air smells vaguely of spoiled meat and perfume. A black, emaciated shape lies prone on the floor, halfway across the bedroom threshold. Long, skinny arms are extended in a swimmer's pose. Its face is a smudge of white and tilted slightly upward to regard me. It is possible that these impressions aren't accurate, that my eyes are merely interpreting as best they can.

I slap a switch. The light comes on, but doesn't illuminate the hall or the figure sprawled almost directly beneath the fixture. Instead, the glow bends at a right angle and gathers on the paneled wall in a diffuse cone.

"Help me," the figure says. The murmur is so soft it might've originated in my own head.

I'm made of sterner stuff than my sixteen-year-old self. I resist the powerful compulsion to approach, to lend maternal comfort. Doesn't matter. My legs go numb. I stagger and slide down the wall into a seated position. Everybody has had the nightmare. The one where you are perfectly aware and paralyzed and an unseen enemy looms over your shoulder. Difference is, I can see my nemesis, or at least its outline, at the opposite end of the hall. I can see it coming for me. It doesn't visibly move except when I blink, and then it's magically two or three feet closer. What keeps going through my mind is that predator insects seldom stir until the killing strike.

"Oh my darlin', oh my darling, oh my darlin' Clementine. You are lost and gone forever, dreadful sorry Clementine." I hum tunelessly, like Gram used to after her brain softened into mush. I'm reverting to childhood, to a time when Dad or Uncle Ned might burst through the door and save the day with a blast of double-aught buckshot.

It finally dawns upon me that I'm injured and am sitting in a puddle of blood. Where the blood is leaking from, I've not the foggiest notion. Silly girl, *that's* why I'm dead from the waist down. My immobility isn't a function of terror or the occult powers of an evil spirit. I've been pricked and envenomed. Nature's predators carry barbs and stings. Those stings deliver anesthetics and anticoagulants. I've been speared through the gut and didn't even notice.

Have venom, will travel. I chuckle. My lips are cold.

"Help me," it whispers as it plucks my toes, testing my resistance. Even this close, it's an indistinct blob of shadowy appendages.

"I have one question." I enunciate carefully, the way I do after one too many shots of Jager. "Did you take my dad on August 15th, 1977? Or did that bastard skip out? Me and my brother got a steak dinner riding on this."

"Help me." The pleading tone descends into a lower timbre. A satisfied purr.

One final trick up my sleeve, or in my coat pocket. Recently, while browsing a hardware store for few odds and ends, I'd come across a relic of my youth—a black light. Cost a ten spot, on special in a clearance bin. First it made me smile as I recalled how all my childhood friends illuminated their funkadelic posters, kids as gleeful as if we'd rediscovered alchemy. Later, in college, black light made a comeback on campus and at the parties we attended. It struck a chord, got me thinking, wondering...

A little voice in my head, an angel on my shoulder, the manifestation of my extremely paranoid subconscious, had said: *you'll need this. You'll need this very soon.* And I bought it and kept it close.

Any creature adapted to distort common light sources might be susceptible to *uncommon* sources. Say infrared or black light. I hazard a guess that my untutored intuition is on the money and that thousands of years of evolution hasn't accounted for a pocket change device used to find cat piss stains in the carpet.

I raise the tube, nothing more than a penlight, in my left hand and thumb the toggle. For an instant, I behold the intruder in all its malevolent glory. It recoils from my beam, a segmented hunter of soft prey retreating into its burrow. A dresser crashes in the bedroom, glass shatters, and the trailer rocks slightly, and then it's quiet again. The moment has passed, except for the fresh hell slowly blooming in my head.

The black light surprised it and nothing more. Surprised and amused it. The creature's impossibly broad grin imparted a universe of corrupt wisdom that will scar my mind for whatever time I have left. Mr. Help Me's susurrating chuckle lingers like a psychic stain. Sometimes the spider cuts the fly from its web. Sometimes nature doesn't sink in those red fangs; sometimes it chooses not to rend with its red claws. A reprieve isn't necessarily the same weight as a pardon. Inscrutability isn't mercy.

We Shaws are tough as shoe leather. Doubtless, I've enough juice left in me to crawl for the phone and signal the cavalry. A quart or two of type-O and I'll be fighting fit with a story to curl your toes. The conundrum is whether I really want to make that crawl, or whether I should close my eyes and fall asleep. *Did you take my father?* I've spent most of my life waiting to ask that question. Is Dad out there in the dark? What about those hunters and hikers and kids who walk through the door and onto the crime pages every year?

I don't want to die, truly I don't. I'm also afraid to go on living. I've seen the true, unspeakable face of the universe; a face that reflects my lowly place in its scheme. And the answer is yes. Yes, there are hells, and in some you are burned or boiled or digested in the belly of a monster for eternity. Yes, what's left of Dad abides with a hideous mystery. He's far from alone.

What would Clint Eastwood do? Well, he would've plugged the fucker with a .44 Magnum, for starters. I shake myself. Mid-fifties is too late to turn into a mope. I roll onto my belly, suck in a breath, and begin the agonizing journey toward the coffee table where I left my purse and salvation. Hand over hand, I drag my scrawny self. It isn't lost on me what I resemble as I slather a red trail across the floor.

Laughing hurts. Hard not to, though. I begin to sing the refrain from "Help!" Over and over and over.

GIRLS WITHOUT
THEIR FACES ON

Delia's father had watched her drowning when she was a little girl. The accident happened in a neighbor's pool. Delia lay submerged near the bottom, her lungs filling with chlorinated water. She could see Dad's distorted form bent forward, shirtsleeves rolled to the elbow, cigarette dangling from his lips, blandly inquisitive. Mom scooped Delia out and smacked her between the shoulder blades while she coughed and coughed.

Delia didn't think about it often. Not often.

Barry F threw a party at his big, opulent house on Hillside East. He invited people to come after sundown. A whole slew of them heeded the call. Some guests considered Barry F an eccentric. This wasn't eccentric—sundown comes early in autumn in Alaska. Hours passed and eventually the door swung wide, emitting piano music, laughter, a blaze of chandelier light. Three silhouettes lingered; a trinity of Christmas ghosts: Delia; Delia's significant other, J; and Barry F.

"—the per capita death rate in Anchorage is outsized," Barry F said. "Out-fucking-sized. This town is the armpit. No, it's the asshole—"

"*Bethel* is the asshole," J said.

"Tell it on the mountain, bro."

"I'll tell you why Bethel is the worst. My dad was there on a job for the FAA in '77. He's eating breakfast at the Tundra Diner and a janitor walks past his table, lugging a honey bucket—"

"Honey bucket?"

"Plumbing froze, so folks crapped in a bucket and dumped it in a sewage lagoon out back. Honey bucket. It's a joke. Anyway, the dude trips on his shoelace…Go on. Imagine the scene. Envision that motherfucker. Picking toilet paper outta your scrambled eggs kills the appetite. Plus, cabin fever, and homies die in the bush all the livelong day. Alcoholism, poverty, rape. Worst of the worst."

"Please," Delia said. "Can we refrain from trashing a native village for the sin of not perfectly acclimating to a predatory takeover by the descendants of white European invaders?"

"Ooh, my girlfriend doesn't enjoy the turn of conversation. Sorry, my precious little snowflake. Folks weren't so politically correct in the 1970s. I'm just reporting the news."

"If we're talking about assholes, look no further than a mirror."

"Kids, kids, don't fight, don't derail the train," Barry F said in an oily, avuncular tone. "Anchorage is still bad. Right?"

"Wretched. Foul."

"And on that note…" Delia said.

"Haven't even gotten to the statistics for sexual assault and disappearances—"

"—Satanists. Diabolists. Scientologists. Cops found a hooker's corpse bound to a headboard at the Viking Motel."

"Lashed to the mast, eh?"

"You said it."

"Hooker? Wasn't she a stripper, though? Candy Bunny, Candy Hunny…?"

"Hooker, stripper, I dunno. White scarves, black candles. Blood everywhere. News called it a ritual killing. They're combing the city for suspects."

"Well, Tito and Benny were at the Bush Company the other night and I haven't seen 'em since…"

"Ha-ha, those cut-ups!"

"I hope not literally."

"We're due for some ritual insanity. Been saying it for months."

"Why are we due?"

"Planet X is aligning with the sun. Its passage messes with gravitational forces, brain chemistry, libidos, et cetera. Like the full moon affects crazies, except dialed to a hundred. Archeologists got cave drawings that show this has been a thing since Neanderthals were stabbing mammoths with sharpened sticks."

"The malignant influence of the gods."

"The malignant influence of the Grays."

"The Grays?"

"Little gray men: messengers of the gods; cattle mutilators; anal probe-ists…"

"They hang around Bethel, eh?"

"No way to keep up with the sheer volume of insanity this state produces. Oh, speaking of brutalized animals, there was the Rabbit Massacre in Wasilla."

"Pure madness."

"Dog mutilations. So many doggy murders. I sorta hate dogs, but really, chopping off their paws is too damned far."

"And on that note…!" Delia stepped backward onto the porch for emphasis.

"On that note. Hint taken, baby doll. Later, sucker."

Delia and J separated from the raucous merriment of the party. The door shut behind them and they were alone in the night.

"What's a Flat Affect Man?" Delia wore a light coat, miniskirt, and heels. She clutched J's arm as they descended the flagstone steps alongside a treacherously steep driveway. Porchlights guided them partway down the slope.

"Where did you hear that?" Sportscoat, slacks, and high-top tennis shoes for him. Surefooted as a mountain goat. The softness of his face notwithstanding, he had a muscle or two.

"Barry F mentioned it to that heavyset guy in the turtleneck. You were chatting up turtleneck dude's girlfriend. The chick who was going to burst out of her mohair sweater."

"I wasn't flirting. She's comptroller for the university. Business, always business."

"Uh-huh. Curse of the Flat Affect Men, is what Barry said."

"Well, forget what you heard. There are things woman was not meant to know. You'll just spook yourself."

She wanted to smack him, but her grip was precarious and she'd had too many drinks to completely trust her balance.

Hillside East was heavily wooded. Murky at high noon and impenetrable come the witching hour. Neighborhoods snaked around ravines and subarctic meadows and copses of deep forest. Cul-de-sacs might host a house or a bear den. But that was Anchorage. A quarter of a million souls sprinkled across seventeen-hundred square miles of slightly suburbanized wilderness. Ice water to the left, mountains to the right, Aurora Borealis weeping radioactive tears. October nights tended to be crisp. Termination dust gleamed upon the Chugach peaks, on its way down like a shroud, creeping ever lower through the trees.

A few more steps and he unlocked the car and helped her inside. He'd parked away from the dozen or so other vehicles that lined the main road on either side of the mailbox. His car was practically an antique. Its dome light worked sporadically. Tonight, nothing. The interior smelled faintly of a mummified animal.

The couple sat in the dark. Waiting.

She regarded the black mass of forest to her right, ignoring his hand on her thigh. Way up the hillside, the house's main deck projected over a ravine. Bay windows glowed yellow. None of the party sounds reached them in the car. She imagined the turntables gone silent and the piano hitting a lone minor key, over and over. Loneliness born of aching disquiet stole over her. No matter that she shared a car with J nor that sixty people partied hardy a hundred yards away. Her loneliness might well have sprung from J's very proximity.

After nine months of dating, her lover remained inscrutable.

J lived in a duplex that felt as sterile as an operating room—television, double bed, couch, and a framed poster of the cosmos over the fake fireplace (a faux fireplace in Alaska was almost too much irony for her system). A six-pack in the fridge; a half-empty closet. He consulted for the government, finagling cost-efficient ways to install fiberoptic communications in remote native villages. That's *allegedly* what he did when he disappeared for weeks on end. Martinis were his poison, Andy Kaufman his favorite (dead?) entertainer, and electronica his preferred music. His smile wasn't a reliable indicator of mood or temperament.

Waking from a strange, fragmentary dream, to a proverbial splash of cold water, Delia accepted that the romance was equally illusory.

"What is your job?" she said, experiencing an uncomfortable epiphany of the ilk that plagued heroines in gothic tales and crime dramas. It was unwise for a woman to press a man about his possibly nefarious double life, and yet so it went. Her lips formed the words and out they flew, the skids greased by a liberal quantity of vino.

"Same as it was in April," he said. "Why?"

"Somebody told me they saw you at the airport buying a ticket to Nome in early September. You were supposed to be in Two Rivers that week."

"Always wanted to visit Nome. Haunt of late career Wyatt Earp. Instead, I hit Two Rivers and got a lousy mug at the gift shop."

"Show me the mug when I come over for movie night."

"Honey pie, sugar lump! Is that doubt I hear in your voice?"

"It is."

"Fine, you've got me red-handed. I shoot walruses and polar bears so wealthy Europeans can play on ivory cribbage boards and strut around in fur bikinis." He caressed her knee and waited, presumably for a laugh. "C'mon, baby. I'm a square with a square job. Your friend must've seen my doppelgänger."

"No. What do you actually do? Like for real."

"I really consult." He wore a heavy watch with a metal strap. He pressed harder and the strap dug into her flesh.

"There's more," she said. "Right? I've tried to make everything add up, and I can't."

"Sweetie, just say what's on your mind."

"I'm worried. Ever have a moment, smack out of the blue, when you realize you don't actually know someone? I'm having that moment."

"Okay. I'm a deep-cover Russian agent."

"Are you?"

"Jeez, you're paranoid tonight."

"Or my bullshit detector is finally working."

"You were hitting it hard in there." He mimed drinking with his free hand.

"Sure, I was half a glass away from dancing on the piano. Doesn't mean I'm wrong."

"Wanna get me on a couch? Wanna meet my mother?"

"People lie to shrinks. Do you even have a mother?"

"I don't have a shrink. Don't have a mother." His hand and the watch strap on his wrist slid back and forth, abrading her skin. "My mother was a…eh, who cares what the supernumerary does? She died. Horribly."

"J—" Would she be able to pry his hand away? Assuming that failed, could she muster the grit to slap him, or punch him in the family jewels? She hadn't resorted to violence since decking a middle school classmate who tried to grab her ass on a field trip. Why had she leapt to the worst scenario now? Mom used to warn her about getting into bad situations with sketchy dudes. Mom said of hypothetical date rapists, if shit got real, smile sweetly and gouge the bastard's eye with a press-on nail.

The phantom piano key in her mind sounded like it belonged in a 1970s horror film. *How much did I have? Three glasses of red, or four? Don't let the car start spinning, I might fly into space.*

J paused, head tilted as if concentrating upon Delia's imagined minor key plinking and plinking. He released her and straightened and held his watch close to his eyes. The watch face was not illuminated. Blue gloom masked everything. Blue gloom made his skull misshapen and enormous. Yet the metal of the watch gathered starlight.

"Were you paying attention when I told Barry that Planet X is headed toward our solar system?" he said.

"Yes." Except…Barry had told J, hadn't he?

"Fine. I'm gonna lay some news on you, then. You ready for the news?"

She said she was ready for the news.

"Planet X isn't critical," he said. "Important, yes. Critical, no. Who cares about a chunk of ice? Not so exciting. Her *star* is critical. A brown dwarf. It has, in moments of pique that occur every few million years, emitted a burst of highly lethal gamma rays and bombarded hapless worlds many light years distant. Every organism on those planets died instantly. Forget the radiation. She can do other things with her heavenly body. Nemesis Star first swung through the heart of the Oort Cloud eons past. Bye-bye dinosaurs. Nemesis' last massive gravitational wave intersected the outer fringe of Sol System in the 1970s. Nemesis has an erratic orbit, you see. Earth got the succeeding ripple effect. Brownouts, tidal waves, earthquakes, all them suicides in Japan… A second wave arrived twenty years later. The third and final wave hit several days ago. Its dying edge will splash Earth in, oh, approximately forty-five seconds."

"What?" she said. "I don't get it."

"And it's okay. This is when *they* come through is all you need to understand. I'm here to greet them. That's my real job, baby doll. I'm a greeter. Tonight is an extinction event; AKA: a close encounter of the intimate kind."

Delia fixated on the first part of his explanation. "Greeter. Like a store greeter?" She thought of the Central Casting grandad characters stationed at the entrance of certain big box stores who bared worn dentures in a permanent rictus.

"Stay. I forgot my jacket." J (wearing his jacket, no less) exited the car and be-bopped into the night.

Stay. As if she were an obedient mutt. She rubbed her thigh and watched his shadow float along the driveway and meld into the larger darkness. Chills knifed through her. The windows began to fog over with her breath. He'd taken the keys. She couldn't start the car to get warm or listen to the radio. *Or drive away from the scene of the crime.*

Delia's twenty-fifth birthday loomed on the horizon. She had majored in communication with a side of journalism at the University of Alaska Anchorage. She was a culture reporter, covering art and entertainment for the main Anchorage daily paper.

People enjoyed her phone manner. In person, she was persistent and vaguely charming. Apolitical; non-judgmental as a Swiss banker. Daddy had always said not to bother her pretty little head. Daddy was a sexist pig to his dying breath; she heeded the advice anyhow. Half of what interviewees relayed went in one ear and out the other with nary a whistle-stop. No matter; her memory snapped shut on the most errant of facts like the teeth of a steel leghold trap. Memory is an acceptable day-to-day substitute for intellect.

Her older brothers drove an ambulance and worked in construction respectively. Her little sister graduated from Onager High next spring. Little sister didn't have journalistic aspirations. Sis yelled, *"Fake news!"* when gentlemen callers (bikers and punk rockers) loaded her into their chariots and hied into the sunset.

Delia lived in an apartment with two women. She owned a dog named Atticus. Her roommates loved Atticus and took care of him when she couldn't make it home at a reasonable hour. They joked about stealing him when they eventually moved onward and upward with trophy spouses and corporate employment. *I'll cut a bitch*, she always said with a smile, not joking at all.

Should she ring them right then for an emergency extraction? "Emergency" might be a tad extreme, yet It seemed a reasonable plan. Housemate A had left on an impromptu overnighter with her boyfriend. Housemate B's car was in the shop. Housemate B helpfully suggested that Delia call a taxi, or, if she felt truly threatened, the cops. Housemate B was on record as disliking J.

Am I feeling threatened? Delia pocketed her phone and searched her feelings.

Her ambulance-driving brother (upholding the family tradition of advising Delia to beware a cruel, vicious world) frequently lectured about the hidden dangers surrounding his profession. Firemen and paramedics habitually rushed headlong into dicey situations, exposing themselves to the same risks as police and soldiers, except without guns or backup. *Paramedics get jacked up every day. While you're busy doing CPR on a subject, some street-dwelling motherfucker will shiv you in the kidney and grab your wallet. Only way to survive is to keep your head on a swivel and develop a sixth sense. The hairs on the back of your neck prickle, you better look around real quick.*

Words to live by. She touched the nape of her neck. Definitely prickling, definitely goosebumps and not from the chill. She climbed out and made her way into the bushes, clumsier than a prey animal born to the art of disappearing, but with no less alacrity.

She stood behind a large spruce, hand braced against its rough bark. Sap stuck to her palm. It smelled bitter-green. Her thigh stung where a raspberry bush had torn her stocking and drawn blood. A starfield pulsed through ragged holes in the canopy. She knew jack about stars except the vague notion that mostly they radiated old, old light. Stars lived and died and some were devoured by black holes.

Nearby, J whooped, then whistled; shrill and lethal as a raptor tuning a killing song. Happy and swift.

He sounds well-fucked. Why did her mind leap there? Because his O-face was bestial? Because he loved to squeeze her throat when they fucked? The subconscious always knows best. As did Mama and big brother, apparently.

J's shadow flitted near the car. His whistle segued to the humming of a nameless, yet familiar tune. Delia shrank against the bole of the tree and heard him open the driver's door. After a brief pause, he called her name. First, still inside and slightly muffled (did he think she was hiding under a seat cushion?); second, much louder toward the rising slope behind him; last, aimed directly toward her hiding spot. Her residual alcohol buzz evaporated as did most of the spit in her mouth.

"Delia, sweetheart," he said. "Buttercup, pumpkin, sugar booger. I meant to say earlier how much I adore the fact you didn't wear makeup tonight. The soap and water look is sexxxxxy! I prefer a girl who doesn't put on her face when she meets the world. It lights my fire, boy howdy. But now you gotta *come here*." His voice thickened at the end. By some trick of the dark, his eyes flared dull-bright crimson. His lambent gaze pulsed for several heartbeats, then faded, and he became a silhouette again. "No?" he said in his regular voice. "Be that way. I hope you brought mad money, because you're stranded on a lee shore. Should I cruise by your apartment instead? Would your roomies and your dog be pleased to meet me while I'm in this mood? Fuck it, sweetheart. I'll surprise you." He laughed, got into the car, and sped away. The red taillights seemed to hang forever; unblinking predatory eyes.

The entire scene felt simultaneously shocking and inevitable.

Of course, she speed-dialed her apartment to warn Housemate B. A robotic voice apologized that the call would not go through. It repeated this apology when she tried the police, her favorite taxi service, and finally, information. Static rose and rose until it roared in her ear and she gave up. She emerged from cover and removed

49

her heels and waited, crouched, to see if J would circle around to catch her in the open. A coyote stalking a ptarmigan. Yeah, that fit her escalating sense of dread—him creeping that ancient car, tongue lolling as he scanned the road for her fleeting shadow.

The cell's penlight projected a ghostly cone. She followed it up the hill to her nearest chance for sanctuary, the house of Barry F. Ah, dear sweet Barry F, swinging senior executive of a successful mining company. He wore wire rimmed glasses and expensive shirts, proclaimed his loathing of physical labor and cold weather (thus, he was assigned to Alaska, naturally), and hosted plenty of semi-formal parties as befitted the persona of a respectable corporate whip hand—which meant prostitutes were referred to as *companions* and any coke-snorting and pill-popping shenanigans occurred in a discreet guestroom.

Notwithstanding jocular collegiality, Barry and J weren't longtime friends, weren't even close; their business orbits intersected and that was the extent of it. J collected acquaintances across a dizzying spectrum. Scoffing at the quality of humanity in general, he rubbed shoulders with gold-plated tycoons and grubby laborers alike. Similar to the spartan furnishings of his apartment, individual relationships were cultivated relative to his needs.

What need do I *satisfy? Physical? Emotional? Victim?* Delia recalled a talk show wherein the host interviewed women who'd survived encounters with serial killers. One guest, a receptionist, had accompanied a coworker on a camping trip. The "nice guy" wined and dined her, then held a knife to her throat, ready to slash. At the last second, he decided to release her instead. *I planned to kill you for three months. Go on, the fear in your eyes is enough.* The receptionist boogied and reported the incident. Her camping buddy went to prison for the three murders he'd previously committed in that park.

Which was to say, how could a woman ever know what squirmed in the brains of men?

As Delia approached the house, the porch light and the light streaming through the windows snuffed like blown matches. Muffled laughter and the steady thud of bass also ceased. At moments such as this, what was a humble arts and entertainment reporter to do? Nothing in her quarter century of life, on the Last Frontier notwithstanding, had prepared her for this experience: half-frozen, teeth chattering, absolutely alone.

Darkness smothered the neighborhood. Not a solitary lamp glimmered among the terraced elevations or secluded culs-de-sac. She looked south and west, down into the bowl of the city proper. From her vantage, it appeared that the entire municipality had gone dark. Anchorage's skyline should have suffused the heavens with light pollution. More stars instead; a jagged reef of them, low and indifferent. Ice Age constellations that cast glacial shadows over the mountains.

The phone's beam trembled, perhaps in response to her fear. She assumed the battery must be dying despite the fact she'd charged it prior to the evening's events. It oozed crimson, spattering the stone steps as if she were swinging a censer of phosphorescent dye. She barged through the front door without a how-do-you-do. Warm, at least. In fact, humid as the breath of a panting dog. Her thoughts flashed to dear sweet Fido at the apartment. *God, please don't let J do anything to him. Oh yeah, and good luck to my housemate too.*

She hesitated in the foyer beneath the dead chandelier and put her shoes on. Her sight adjusted enough to discern the contours of her environment. No one spoke, which seemed ominous. Most definitely ominous. A gaggle of drunks trapped in a sudden blackout could be expected to utter any number of exclamatory comments.

Girls would shriek in mock terror and some bluff hero would surely announce he'd be checking the fuse box straight away. There'd be a bit of obligatory ass-grabbing, right? Where were all the cell phones and keychain penlights? A faucet dripped; heating ducts creaked in the walls. This was hardcore Bermuda Triangle-*Mary Celeste* shit.

Snagging a landline was the first order of business. Her heels clicked ominously as she moved around the grand staircase and deeper into the house to its spacious, partially sunken living room.

Everyone awaited her there. Wine glasses and champagne flutes partially raised in toast; heads thrown back, bared teeth glinting here and there; others half-turned, frozen mid-glance, mid-step, mid-gesticulation. Only dolls could be frozen in such exaggerated positions of faux life. The acid reek of disgorged bowels and viscera filled Delia's nostrils. She smelled blood; smelled it soaked into dresses and dripping from cuffs and hosiery; she smelled blood as it pooled upon the carpet and coagulated in the vents.

Her cell phone chose that moment to give up the ghost entirely. She was thankful. Starlight permitted her the merest impressions of the presumed massacre, its contours and topography, but nothing granular. Her nose and imagination supplied the rest. Bile rose in her throat. Her mind fogged over. Questions of why and how did not register. The nauseating intimacy of this abominable scene overwhelmed such trivial considerations.

A closet door opened like an eyeless socket near the baby grand piano. Atticus trotted forth. Delia recognized his general shape and the jingle of his vaccination tags and because for the love of everything holy, who else? The dog stopped near a throng of mutilated party-goers and lapped the carpet between shoes and sandals with increasing eagerness. Next, a human silhouette emerged and sat on the piano bench. The shape could've been anybody. The figure's thin hand passed through a shaft of starlight and plinked a key several times.

B-flat? Delia retained a vague notion of chords—a high school crush showed her the rudiments as a maneuver to purloin her virtue. Yes, B flat, over and over. Heavily, then softly, softly, nigh invisibly, and heavily again, discordant, jarring, threatening.

I'm sorry you had to bear witness. These words weren't uttered by the figure. They originated at a distance of light years, uncoiling within her consciousness. Her father's voice. *The human animal is driven by primal emotions and urges. How great is your fear, Delia? Does it fit inside a breadbox? Does it fit inside your clutch? This house?*

The shape at the piano gestured with a magician's casual flourish and the faint radiance of the stars pulsed a reddish hue. The red light intensified and seeped into the room.

The voice in her head again: Looking for Mr. Goodbar *stuck with you. Diane Keaton's fate frightened you as a girl and terrifies you as a woman. In J, you suspect you finally drew the short straw. The man with a knife in his pocket, a strangling cord, a snub-nose revolver, the ticket stub with your expiration date. The man to take you camping and return alone. And sweetie, the bastard resembles me, wouldn't you say?*

Ice tinkled in glasses—spinning and slopping. Glasses toppled and fell from nerveless fingers. Shadow-Atticus ceased slurping and made himself scarce behind a couch. He trailed inky paw prints. Timbers groaned; the heart of the living room was released from the laws of physics—it bent at bizarre, corkscrew angles, simultaneously existing on a plane above and below the rest of the interior. Puffs of dust erupted as cracks shot through plaster. The floor tilted and the guests were pulled together, packed cheek to jowl.

There followed a long, dreadful pause. Delia had sprawled to her hands and knees during the abrupt gravitational shift. Forces dragged against her, but she counterbalanced as one might to avoid plummeting off a cliff. She finally got a clean, soul-scarring gander at her erstwhile party companions.

Each had died instantaneously via some force that inflicted terrible bruises, suppurating wounds, and ruptures. The rigidly posed corpses were largely intact. Strands of metal wire perforated flesh at various junctures, drew their bodies upright, and connected them into a mass. Individual strands gleamed and converged overhead as a thick spindle that ascended toward the dome of ceiling, and infinitely farther.

The shape at the piano struck a key and its note was reciprocated by an omnidirectional chime that began at the nosebleed apex of the scale and descended precipitously, boring into plaster, concrete, and bone. The house trembled. Delia pushed herself backward into a wall where normal gravity resumed. She huddled, tempted to make a break for it, and also too petrified to move.

There are two kinds of final girls. The kind who escape and the kind who die. You're the second kind. I am very, very proud, kiddo. You'll do big things.

Cracks split the roof, revealing a viscid abyss with a mouthful of half-swallowed nebulae. It chimed and howled, eternally famished. Bits of tile plummeted into the expanse, joining dead stars. Shoe tips scraped as the guests lifted en masse, lazily revolving like a bleeding mobile carved for an infant god. The mobile jerkily ascended, tugged into oblivion at the barbed terminus of a fisherman's line.

Delia glanced down to behold a lone strand of the (god?) wire burrowing into her wrist, seeking a vein or a bone to anchor itself. She wrenched free and pitched backward against a wall.

The chiming receded, so too the red glow, and the void contentedly suckled its morsel. Meanwhile, the shadow pianist hunched into a fetal position and dissolved. *Run along,* her father said. *Run along, dear. Don't worry your pretty head about any of this.*

Delia ran along.

A laska winter didn't kill her. Not that this was necessarily Alaska. The land turned gray and waterways froze. Snow swirled over empty streets and empty highways and buried inert vehicles. Powerlines collapsed and copses of black spruce and paper birch stood vigil as the sun paled every day until it became a white speck.

Delia travelled west, then south, snagging necessities from deserted homes and shops. Her appearance transformed—she wore layers of wool and flannel, high-dollar pro ski goggles, an all-weather parka, snow pants, and thick boots. Her tent, boxes of food, water, and medical supplies went loaded into a banana sled courtesy of a military surplus store. She acquired a light hunting rifle and taught herself to use it, in case worse came to worst. She didn't have a plan other than to travel until she found her way back to a more familiar version of reality. Or to walk until she keeled over; whichever came first.

In the beginning, she hated it. That changed over the weeks and months as the suburban softness gave way to a metallic finish. Survival can transition into a lifestyle. She sheltered inside houses and slept on beds. She burned furniture for warmth. However, the bloodstains disquieted her as did eerie noises that wafted from basements and attics during the bleak A.M. hours. She eventually camped outdoors among the woodland creatures who shunned abandoned habitations of humankind as though city limits demarcated entry to an invisible zone of death. The animals had a point, no doubt.

Speaking of animals. Wild beasts haunted the land in decent numbers. Domestic creatures were extinct, seemingly departed to wherever their human masters currently dwelled. With the exception of the other Atticus. The dog lurked on the periphery of her vision; a blur in the undergrowth, a rusty patch upon the snow. At night he dropped mangled ptarmigans and rabbits at the edge of her campfire light. He kept his distance, watching over her as she slept. The musk of his gore-crusted fur, the rawness of his breath infiltrated her dreams.

In other dreams, her mother coalesced for a visit. *Now it can be said. Your father murdered eight prostitutes before lung cancer cut him down. The police never suspected that sweet baby-faced sonofabitch. You were onto him, somehow.* She woke with a start and the other Atticus' eyes reflected firelight a few yards to her left in the gauze of darkness that enfolded the world.

"Thanks for the talk, Mom."

Delia continued to walk and pull the sled. Sometimes on a road, or with some frequency, on a more direct route through woods and over water. She didn't encounter any human survivors, nor any tracks or other sign. However, she occasionally glimpsed crystallized hands and feet jutting from a brush pile, or an indistinct form suspended in the translucent depths of a lake. She declined to investigate, lowered her head and marched onward.

One late afternoon, near spring, but not quite, J (dressed in black camo and Army-issue snowshoes) leaped from cover with a merry shriek and knocked her flat. He lay atop her and squeezed her throat inexorably, his eyes sleepy with satisfaction.

"If it were my decision, I'd make you a pet. You don't belong here, sugar pie." He well and truly applied his brutish strength. Brutish strength proved worthless. His expression changed as terror flooded in and his grip slackened. "Oh, my god. I didn't know. They didn't't warn me…"

Her eyes teared and she regarded him as if through a pane of water. Her eyes teared because she was laughing so hard. "Too late, asshole. Years and years too late." She brushed his hands aside. "I'm the second kind."

He scrambled to his feet and ran across fresh powder toward the woods as fast as his snowshoes could carry him, which wasn't very. She retrieved the rifle, chambered a round, and tracked him with the scope. A moving target proved more challenging than plinking at soda bottles and pie tins. Her first two shots missed by a mile.

Delia made camp; then she hiked over to J and dragged him back. He gazed at her adoringly, arms trailing in the snow. He smiled a broad, empty smile. That night, the fire crackled and sent sparks homeward. J grinned and grinned, his body limp as a mannequin caught in the snarled boughs of a tree where she'd strung him as an afterthought. The breeze kicked up into a chinook that tasted of green sap and thawing earth.

"Everything will be different tomorrow," she said to the flames and the changing stars. Limbs creaked. J nodded, nodded; slavishly agreeable. His shadow and the shadow of the tree branches spread grotesquely across the frozen ground.

The wind carried to her faint sounds of the dog gnawing and slurping at a blood-drenched snowbank. The wind murmured that Atticus would slake himself and then creep into the receding darkness, gone forever. Where she was headed, he couldn't follow.

"So, while there's time, let's have a heart-to-heart," Delia said to Grinning J. "When we make it home, tell me where I can find more boys just like you."

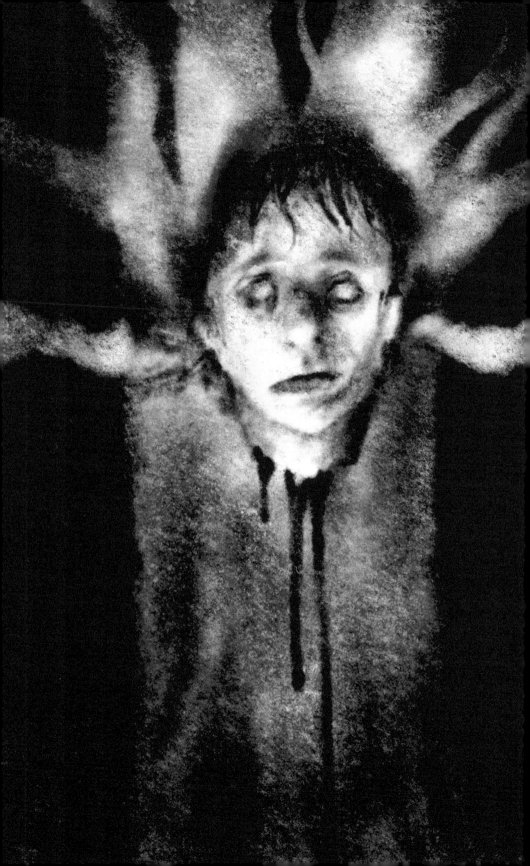

MOBILITY

*L*ife is hard in 40 million B.C. beneath the apple-green heavens. Something is always trying to eat the monkeys. A shadow ripples across the forest canopy to confirm this fact. The monkeys screech and scatter among the lush treetops. The black shape veers out of the sun in pursuit. It closes the gap at an astonishing rate.

Branches slap together and howlers howl. The shadow snatches a few of the slower troop (rending treetops as well) and glides away, trailing pitiful monkey screams.

The forest is still. Eventually, birds trill and buzz in a thousand tongues. The monkeys also call to one another and the survivors make their way back to the central group for commiseration. The troop settles. The monkeys return to cracking nuts and eating fruit and picking each other's nits. One watches the cloudless apple-green skies, although the memory of why soon fades.

*B*ryan murdered a squirrel a few hours into his eleventh birthday. Uncle so-and-so handed him a pump action air rifle for a birthday present and the kid shot the first animal he saw. Which happened to be a semi-tame gray squirrel nibbling an acorn on the sidewalk in front of Bryan's house. He pumped the action twenty or thirty times, aimed with his tongue sticking out, and squeezed the trigger. Lucky (?) shot blew that squirrel's eyeball to jelly. A little kid laboriously pedaling a tricycle witnessed the slaughter with a vacuous smirk. This was the brat who'd recently learned how to burn ants with a magnifying glass.

Bryan felt a little bit sick for a few minutes. The family cat, Heathcliff, also known as The Black Death, swooped in and nabbed the squirrel's corpse and Bryan forgot the whole thing.

The universe would have its vengeance. It had begun to wreak it eons before Bryan was ever born.

Snow fell on Providence all afternoon. Made a mucky slush of the walk from school. Bryan ordered baked tuna at the grill where Lovecraft had eaten whenever *Weird Tales* sent a check, which was sufficiently frequent to qualify as a special occasion. Came back to bite both of them in the ass.

Bryan stood a shade under six feet. Burly Scandinavian stock. Curly hair and precisely trimmed beard, colored blond out of a bottle. Forty-five years made him as good as any vintage LP. He didn't smile, but he didn't *not* smile, either. He'd worn his lucky cardigan to dinner. Black and white, separated by a jagged divide, animals fighting, the two wolves locking jaws. He'd worn a knit cap, black. He'd worn black and white knit gloves to match the sweater. He'd worn glasses, rimless. Not necessary, yet the coeds liked the look. The glasses said *philosopher, poet-wunderkind*; he was professor of Pawhunk Community College Nonfiction Writing department these past four years, so it seemed appropriate. He'd worn a gold band, although it signified nothing since he'd never married and never planned to (God help him if his fiancé, Angie, ever twigged to the truth). Merely a prop from his community theater stint. The coeds *liked* men with wedding bands. The band said, *I could fuck you if I wanted to, but I'm not gonna try, because well, look.* He'd worn buckskin pants. And moccasins. With fringe.

Angie, his eye-rolling girlfriend of a decade, served as the English Chair at Brown and good for her although he routinely mentioned she could do better and tried to ignore how her eyebrows shot up. Late that autumn, after much subtle manipulation on Bryan's part, they celebrated her birthday with a cruise to Nova Scotia. Serendipity! He wanted to research a nonfiction crime author who lived there anyway. Angie toured thrift shops and outlet malls while he spent the weekend plying the down-on-his-luck author, one Buford Creely, with booze and picking (pickling?) the fellow's brain about a sensational murder case from the 1960s and '70s. Thirty-nine missing persons, a secret grotto littered with skulls piled into pyramids and skulls on stakes. Unsolved, cops baffled, movie of the week fodder. The kind of lurid material the faculty at Pawhunk frowned upon, yet were stuck with in the infrequent event one of its professors girded his loins and took a stab at publishing.

The vacation arrangement worked out great, although Angie seemed moody after they returned to his apartment in Providence. Meanwhile, Bryan was positively energized and stoked to sequester himself in the spare bedroom (his den) for a week or two go at a new essay, which is exactly what he did.

This was the first evening they'd been together during that hectic stretch.

"Eat up, sport," she said, watching him put away another fork-load of the tuna. "You'll need your strength tonight."

"Oh, boy!"

She smiled, pure flint. "Got some bad news. Skylark Tooms passed away. Remember her?"

"Rich, attractive. Dad was a clothing designer or…?"

"She died in an industrial accident the other day. Burned alive. Like this damned steak."

"I'm sorry your friend is dead." Through a mouthful.

"Friend, no. We weren't close since school. It's been on the news. A whole port town was destroyed. Train derailment. Chemicals. Nobody can get close."

"Awful, awful." Another chunk of delectable, flaky tuna glazed in garlic and lemon. This bite almost lodged in his throat. It left a metallic aftertaste. Bryan's eyes smarted and he quickly sipped water to ease the lump in its passage.

"I'm over it. A shock is all." Angie appeared oblivious to his struggle, utterly consumed with her own concerns.

Bryan recovered. He signaled the waiter and ordered crème brûlée and a cup of black coffee. Delicious. "Did you want something?" he said, dabbing his lips with a cloth napkin, vaguely piqued she hadn't offered to do it for him like when they first dated. She'd acted the part of a depraved concubine then.

She smiled and shook her head.

After dinner, he called a cab to save them from another slog through the gloppy streets. Back at his place, he put *Boys in the Trees* on the stereo (antiquing for the win!) and broke out a bottle of kinda good wine. Angie watched from her perch on the arm of the leather couch, where he'd begged her pretty please not to sit a million and one times. Her manic pixie haircut, thick-rimmed glasses, and red lipstick seemed brutally severe. However, she rocked an angora sweater and tartan skirt combo and that made up for the rest.

He wiped his sweaty face with his sleeve. He pried the cork loose, poured half a glass and drank it while sorting his phone messages. Three—two from Mom, and the last from that drunken author Creely. Mom said, *I love you, why don't you ever return my calls*; Creely said, *Get in touch soonest, you got my number,* and hung up. From all the hooting and yelling in the background, the author sounded like he'd used a payphone at the local tavern.

Bryan's stomach felt the slightest bit queasy. He burped and the metallic taste returned. He did himself up with another quarter glass of cabernet sauvignon, glanced over his shoulder and saw that Angie remained poised and smiling as if she'd slipped on a reasonably lifelike mask of herself in one of her better moods. Ah, yes, he should pour her a stout one, keep her in that happy place.

Angie accepted the too-full glass without comment. She balanced it on her thigh.

"Your engagement ring," he said. "You're not wearing it."

"I'm not?" Again with the flinty smile.

His stomach burbled. He made his apologies and bee-lined for the bathroom. His reflection in the mirror was an ashen nightmare. He dropped his trousers and sat on the commode, head in his hands.

Angie knocked on the door. "FYI: I don't fancy you anymore, Bryan. Ten years in Chinese Hell should be considered time served. It's your turn on the spit."

Bryan would've retorted, but at that moment his guts began to convulsively evacuate their contents. He groaned.

She continued in a pleasant voice, quite unlike her customary tone. "Do you recall that dream I mentioned? The one where I was a knight traveling the land on a fearless steed and lopping heads with a talking broadsword? Probably not. That's the problem, Professor. Had it again last night. I am now convinced time has come to cut bait and pursue other life opportunities. You always say I can do better. Kudos. Kudos, you heartless motherfucker!"

His vision contracted. His breath whistled. He clutched his tightening chest and toppled face-first onto the tiles. The descent took forever.

"Don't be melodramatic. Whining isn't manly. I mean, hell, Bry. I'm the one who should be pissed. Ten goddamned years." She sighed and if Bryan hadn't simultaneously been suffocating and shitting himself, he might've imagined her pressed against the panel, wistfully tracing the grain with her nail, enacting the breakup scene that comes at the end of act two of every chick flick. "FYI, I've already met someone, so please do fuck right off and don't pester me with calls. We're flying to the Caribbean in a few hours."

Bryan clawed at the door in a doomed gesture. He vomited. Angie's engagement ring rode the sluice from his guts and floated in a puddle of bile and tuna under his nose. He blacked out and had a vision of lying helpless among reeds while giant herons pecked his liver to itty bits. Angie, clad in a shiny chainmail bikini, leaned upon her equally shiny broadsword and smiled contemptuously. She stroked the pommel with her thumb and said, "Who's sticking it to whom now, you silly bitch?"

"Collapsed lung," the beefy nurse said with supreme indifference. "You aspirated a shitload of vomit. Not good, bro."

Bryan woke, after a fashion, in a hospital bed with the monotone report in progress. Tubes clogged his nose and throat. Cottony wooziness softened the interior of his skull. No, aspirating a shitload of vomit did not sound good at all, he had to agree. He closed his eyes and had a foggy recollection of his eleven-year-old-self standing in the drive, pellet rifle in hand while the squirrel twitched its last.

The tops of the sycamore (sequoias?) trees rustled and monkeys screeched fearfully. A shadow blotted the sun. A ten-foot tall Martian descended from the belly of the mother saucer on a cold white beam. The Martian took his eleven-year-old-self's pulse while brandishing a shiny chromatic blaster in the other hand. *Nice shooting, Tex,* the Martian said via telepathy. *We hate those damned things where I come from.* Heathcliff snatched the squirrel and darted away. The Martian telepathically laughed with savage gusto and Bryan's nose bled.

"Go back to sleep," the beefy nurse said and snapped his fingers.

Bryan went back to sleep.

A few days and several sketchy diagnoses later, the beefy nurse said, "That's a wrap. You're officially mended. There's your clothes." He turned the light off as he left the room.

Darkness shifted to light. Bryan hobbled into his apartment on a set of cheap hospital crutches with no memory of how he'd arrived. His muscles and nervous system remained mysteriously at odds, causing spastic tics and farcical nightmares starring aggrieved monkeys and an endless green hell of jungle. His re-inflated lung felt seared and scarred. He wheezed at the slightest exertion.

The weekend dripped through his veins and cocooned him in a gray malaise that precluded research, much less actual writing. He possessed trace memories of whatever had scrolled ceaselessly across the television screen. His condition remained so moribund he only left five or six increasingly strident messages on Angie's answering machine. Between stretches of torpor, he obsessed about her and his new rival, picturing them on a Caribbean beach sipping rum and laughing at his misfortune.

On Monday, Frank Mandibole, a former college chum and infrequent confidante, rang. Mandibole said the situation sounded intolerable and that he'd be over right away with proper medicine. The man arrived within moments. He pranced through the door and laid his hand on Bryan's forehead. "Gracious! Not a moment too soon. Let's take a ride, get some fresh air in your lungs. Hang around sucking in Providence, you'll eventually go the way of Uncle Howard."

"I feel half dead, Frank."

"It's Tom. To-om! I don't go by Frank anymore. Try to focus on the positive. We'll throw a few things in a bag, and *wheee* all the way to Mom and Dad's house for some R and R."

Bryan didn't argue the point. While generally the same height and composition as his old self, Mandibole no longer precisely resembled the "Frank" of school days. He'd trimmed his hair and shaved off the mustache. His skin gleamed the way a doll's skin does. In fact, his features (and helmet hair) were decidedly action figure plastic. There'd been rumors of an accident. Obviously, he'd had work done. He wore a black and white cardigan that also seemed annoyingly familiar, yet not.

Bryan lacked the strength to protest the car ride. Anyway, how much worse could it be than lying around his apartment sloughing into eternity?

They hopped onto the interstate and cruised south, then west, into the wild lands of the Empire State. Mandibole's car had a rusty pink paint job. Compactly European, a tin can on bicycle wheels. Bryan didn't recognize the make or model, nor could he decipher the faded pennant on the radio antenna. Polka music burped and barked over the radio, interspersed with commentary that sounded Russian.

Mandibole said, "I've a theory regarding your illness. You're not superstitious—you gave up bowing to altars and thumping holy tomes, yes? Hang with me for a second. What if you're punishing yourself subconsciously?"

"Punishing myself for what?"

"For bailing on the Mormons. Unresolved guilt."

"All my guilt is resolved. I'm a confirmed atheist. Happily." Bryan massaged the swollen glands in his neck. Bundled in a parka, scarf, mittens, snow pants, and snow boots, he still shivered. The landscape stretched brown and bare on either side of the highway.

"Uh-huh. When I first met you, I knew something was amiss. Absolutely knew it. You were kind of head-shy. Ponder this: Leaving the fold, running off to college... Screwing, smoking, educating. Kicking indoctrination takes a stout heart and a dedicated support system. Nobody helped you, did they? You packed your bags and split the family homestead in the dead of night with nary a kiss-my-ass to anyone. Cold turkey off the LDS teat. Traumatic, right?"

"Of course, Fra—I mean Tom. I had a few dark days."

"Surely that left a scar."

"Not likely."

"Be realistic, friend. Unplugging from a cult is tricky. People who detach from rigid, hierarchal religious organizations are prone to depression, alcoholism, suicide, you name it. Botch the deprogramming and, well...Exhibit A in my passenger seat."

"Really, that's not related to my situation."

"If you say so."

"Getting away from the church meant getting away from my dad. That's a net gain, I assure you." A sense of déjà vu overcame Bryan. He recalled vivid fragments of this very conversation from years ago—he and Mandibole tossing darts at a college pub, blitzed on draft beer and sharing life stories. He tried to recall Mandibole's tale and drew a blank. The main thing that stuck in his mind was that his friend had been blond, taller, and cheerfully evasive.

"Daddy issues. Revealing, although not the nut of your predicament. *My* father worked for the FBI." Mandibole adjusted his glasses. Thick and square, straight from a 1960s NASA Control Room. "He vetted the suicide letter Hoover's boy sent to Martin Luther King."

"Suicide letter?"

"*The* suicide letter. The feds wrote a note detailing the reverend's alleged infidelities and gave him thirty-four days to 'do the right thing.' By which they meant blow his brains out. My dad proofread the letter, made revisions, and got it up to snuff."

The music changed and broadcasters argued in Spanish. Fields and barrens ceded to hills and forest. Sunlight ebbed. Mandibole made several turns that propelled them along dilapidated roads through increasingly rustic habitations. After the last town had disappeared from the rearview for the better portion of an hour, he pulled into a yard before a quaintly ramshackle two-story house. Some of the windows were boarded. The gutters were stuffed with twigs. A squirrel sat amid the twigs and glared. Bare-limbed trees encroached upon the yard, their roots exposed in the muddy soil. Patches of snow glowed like bone.

"This is the summer house. Mom and Dad lived here until 2010. I bolt here every few months and hibernate." Mandibole climbed out. He snatched up a stone and drilled the squirrel in the head. The creature fell, boneless, into the bushes. He chuckled and came around to Bryan's side. "Easy does it, pal. Bit of a climb, I'm afraid. Now, now, struggling only makes this more embarrassing. You're a bag of bones! Don't they feed you at the hospital?"

Bryan gave in and allowed himself to be carried like a bride along a flagstone path, up nine rickety wooden steps, across a covered porch, and into a foyer. The house smelled of dampness, algae, and unidentifiable spices. Tall ceilings and narrow passages, with nooks and crannies galore. Antique black and white portraits full of crabby subjects. The whole scene—Mandibole, the house and environs—could've been drawn by Gorey. Mandibole propped Bryan against the wall. He swooped around like a bat, clicking on lamps here and there. This pallid light pushed back the gloom and held it in tenuous abeyance. He hauled Bryan's suitcase and overnight bag in and stacked them near a dusty player piano.

"Kitchen's that way. Parlor is over there. The couch folds out into a bed. I advise against the stairs in your delicate condition. The cellar is absolutely off-limits. Phone is in the hall. Sometimes it works. No Internet, sorry."

Bryan summoned the strength to speak. "Why does the mailbox say Smith?"

"Eh? I didn't mean this place belonged to *my* parents. Here are your crutches. Okay? Okay! Got to run. Make yourself at home."

"Wait, you're leaving? I thought—"

"Hell yes, I'm leaving. I wouldn't stay in this creepy shithole for a million bucks. Weather is supposed to be warm tomorrow. You'll find the garden a tonic to cure your ills." Mandibole adjusted his fedora and ducked through the door. He called, "Remember, don't go down into the cellar. The amontillado isn't worth a broken neck."

As the motor's whine receded, Bryan tried to piece things together. Why had he agreed to lay up here in the boonies? He *hadn't*, not in so many words. Life caught him in a bore tide and swept him to this peculiar shore. He thumped his way into the kitchen and wearily rummaged through the tall pine cabinets and a deep, dark pantry. Dark because the light bulb was dead. Plenty of canned goods and pilot bread. Who ate pilot bread these days? He heated tomato soup and rustled a bit of not-too-moldy cheddar and a loaf of bread from the buzzing refrigerator. The fridge was an old, decrepit model; lime green exterior, pale and fluorescently-lighted interior. Spartan other than the cheese, a bottle of murky milk, and dubious items sealed in plastic containers. There were half a dozen eggs nestled on a side rack—four cream-colored hen's eggs, a pale blue pigeon egg, and a crusty black petrified egg. He took the lump of cheese and closed the unit, killed the pale, deathly light and the strident buzzing.

Yes, yes, soup and grilled cheese. He slumped at the kitchen table and ate every damned bite in defiance of his queasy guts. Ten minutes later, he puked onto the sixty-year-old linoleum. *Ting!* Went Angie's damned engagement ring as it rolled across the floor and into the shadows of the sink cupboards. Novocain numbness filled his mouth. He located his cell phone and tried to dial Angie. *Tried,* because the moment it powered on, the screen went into video mode and there she was on a beach blanket taking it doggy style from an oiled dude in sunglasses and a ponytail. Bryan cursed. He stabbed impotently at the face plate until it went black.

Those movies where the emaciated, ship-wrecked hero staggers along a beach, step by agonizing step? Such was Bryan's voyage into the parlor. He collapsed onto the sofa and surrendered to a tidal surf of terrors thudding against the break-wall of his conscious mind.

The administrative secretary at Pawhunk CC called him, or maybe he imagined it. Either way: "You're fired."

"I'm on sick leave!"

"We don't honor sick leave. Fired, squirrel-killer. Don't bother cleaning out your desk. We burned your shit."

Tom Mandibole emerged from the shadows and tip-toed across the parlor. His plastic features had altered to mimic those of Bryan's father circa Bryan's childhood.

Mandibole knelt in an uncannily mechanical series of motions. "If you devour the raw heart of an enemy, you gain his courage. But! If you consume his living brain, you acquire his memories. My gods, the Smiths were fusty!" He smiled and ran his wormy tongue up Bryan's left nostril; kept wriggling deeper.

Bryan gazed in terror at an enormous black form detaching from the sun. If words were possible, he would've cried, *What the hell is that?* Instead, he screamed and screamed.

The house seemed much cheerier by daylight. Its crooked edges were blunted, its remnant shadows less sinister. In some respects, the place reminded him of his childhood home—Mom in her flour-dusted apron, Pastor Tallen on the step wagging his finger, and the serial puppy murders, ritual suicides, and forced sodomy. Reminded him of how Dad sometimes hid under the bed while wearing Mom's nylon stocking over his face, and the homemade blood transfusion kit he unpacked when they played *Something Scary.*

Bryan managed to gain his feet after a bitter contest with the crutches, which were carved from the antlers of a stag. Their tips dug grooves in the floor as he maneuvered down the hall. His muscles ached, his head ached, and pain knifed him in the bowels. His breath gurgled and his throat constricted. His hands twitched with palsy.

Greatest blow to his vanity came from a direct, hard look into the mirror. Formerly shot with gray when left uncolored, his hair and beard were bleached white as dirty snow. Could this explain Angie's unceremonious decampment? Had it been his hair all along? Bryan made a mental list of his symptoms and feebly attempted to correlate them with various diseases. Epidemiology wasn't his area of expertise and thus he could only speculate as to whether he'd contracted AIDS, syphilis, hepatitis C, or something worse. It could always be something worse. He didn't speculate for long, however. Walking from parlor to bathroom and back again taxed him to the core. The notion of peeling off his musty, sweat-sticky clothes and taking a hot shower made him want to vomit again. That reminded him: Another sandwich?

Crazed, scotch-guzzling has-been author Buford Creely awaited him in the kitchen when, after hours or days had dragged past, Bryan made it there.

"You gonna die if you don't eat, kid." Creely slurred so it sounded like *eat a kid*. He wore a brown tweed jacket. His eyes were possum-red and glazed with cataracts from staring at crime scene photographs for too many years. The evil of the abyss and so forth. "Fuck it. You ate last week. We gotta do somethin' about your nerves. Gotta do somethin'. C'mere, squirrel-killer. You're fresh outta agency."

Bryan contemplated fleeing. He immediately lost his balance and fell. His right hand crutch spun across the floor. He feebly brandished the other at Creely. "How did—why?" Each word was a tooth pulled with tweezers.

"Eh, your dad sent me. Your old man, remember him? Was him did all them slasher killin's back when. The headless Horseman of Halifax. Didn't have the heart to break it to you earlier. Frank said you deserved the truth. Frank abhors a lie."

"Not Frank. Tom…"

"Who in blazes is Tom?" Creely knelt and cradled Bryan in his bony-flabby arms, lifted him to the kitchen table and set him there. "Relax. I know what you need. Hospital didn't help, did it?"

Bryan shook his head.

"Right, you need *real* medicine. Old medicine. See, kid, you can barely move. Gotta drop some weight." Creely smiled a boozy, reassuring smile as he unbuttoned Bryan's shirt and removed it with the tenderness of a father undressing his son. "On three, roll to your left." He counted and then turned Bryan over. "That hurt?"

"Yes!" Bryan said it as more of a protest rather than an assertion of fact. The fear of further pain, or worse, humiliation, provoked his anxiety. "Mr. Creely, Buford…You have to be careful. The spine is delicate."

"Nothin' to worry about, kid. You're already beyond fucked. Good news is, my family learned acupuncture from the Chinese. Fix you right up.." The old man banged cupboard doors and rummaged through shelf drawers.

Bryan mouthed the word acupuncture in horror with his cheek pressed against the tablecloth. In an act of great willpower, he lifted his head and looked over his shoulder. What he saw did not prove comforting. "Are those knitting needles?"

"Stifle yourself. Hold real still." Creely raised both arms and then hammered them downward.

The twin bolts of agony ripping through Bryan's lower back had a psychoactive effect. He departed his body. The kitchen windows transmitted a pristine white glow. White gradually dulled to rose, then crimson, then black. The blackness absorbed him. He sailed on a cosmic breeze until a pinprick of pale white radiance beckoned ahead. The candle flame steadied and brightened. Angie and her lover fucked on a white sand beach bordered by a black gulf of water. The man glanced at him: Mandibole wearing a shiny white shirt and a huge, cruel grin. Angie turned her head—also Mandibole's superciliously grinning face. Bryan's eyes popped open. Returned to the shabby, dim kitchen, he tried to scream but couldn't suck in sufficient air.

"Huh," Creely said. "Well, hell. Whoops, I guess." The author's footsteps clipped rapidly away. The front door slammed.

Blood pooled around Bryan's hips and dripped from the edge of the table. Enough blood that he felt as if he were partially afloat in a kiddie pool. He tried to lift himself and realized the darning needles had gone clean through the small of his back and into the wood of the table. He cried.

Snow fell against the windows and after a while it grew dark.

Light engulfed the room and gushed into his eyes.

"Ten years! Nary a tear. But now that you're nailed to a table, look at the waterworks. I mean, really." Angie circled. She had dressed in white and black earmuffs, a white and black pea coat, black pants, and white Wellingtons. "What a mess, what a bloody mess. Proud to wallow in your own gore, I suppose. Really showed me, haven't you?"

"Please help me."

"Addition by subtraction. Are you ready for that, squirrel-killer?"

"Angie. Please." Bryan's right arm refused to work. He feebly pawed with his left, supplicating a goddess of torment.

"Fine. Fine, Bryan. This doesn't mean we're back together." She sighed and yanked the needles free. "Oh, you asshole. This coat is ruined."

Air, and everything else, hissed out of him.

Winter had slunk into the mountains. A warm breeze shushed through the treetops and awakened Bryan by thawing his frozen, glaciated innerscape sufficiently for a stray thought to escape the merciless grip of entropy. Pine sap, grass, and perfume tickled his nose. He opened his eyes. Angie hunkered before him, pristine but for several drops of blood on her coat and galoshes.

"You're in a bad way," she said.

He'd been stripped naked. From the blackened thighs down, his body resembled an unearthed Egyptian mummy, or one of the petrified corpses of climbers that adorn the slopes of Everest. His feet had ballooned and split at the joints. The nails were gone. Pus seeped. He felt absolutely nothing. Oh, inside he screamed unceasingly, but it didn't hurt.

"Call an ambulance," he said. *Barely* said. His lips cracked. Possibly he'd only projected the thought at her.

"Are you crazy? The ambulance drivers around here are surely not. They wouldn't come within a mile of this creepy shithole for a million bucks. Nope, it's home remedy or death. Worse than death, actually."

"Ambulance," he repeated. How shiny and plastic her hair flowed in the light like mud, how shiny and plastic her lovely face seen through a muddy filter. Differently familiar, it provoked queasiness.

"Gangrene," she said. "On its way to your heart. My opinion is, your heart's *already* rotten. Nonetheless, I've a filial duty as your ex-fiancé. You made me call you Daddy often enough." Angie hefted a serrated cleaver. A relic from some Civil War surgeon's grim bag of atrocity tools. She poked his leg. "These have to come off. That's how you regain mobility. Give to get, sweetheart. I'll do the first, as a favor. After that, you're on your own." She set the teeth of the blade against his left thigh and began sawing. His flesh made small corkscrew piles on the floor. Only a dim tugging sensation reached his brain. He screamed anyway.

The femur cracked. Sweat dripped from the tip of her nose as she made several final strokes, gesticulating with the frenetic grace of a concert violinist. "Done!" Angie shoved the severed limb aside and wiped her brow. "Easy-peasy. You're a total dipshit with tools, I know, I know. Just… Do your best." She pressed the cleaver into his hands and, despite his cries of protest, assisted with getting a groove started. "Keep going, Bry. That gangrene will eat your innards if you fail. Ciao, stumpy."

He persisted, albeit sloppily, after she kissed his forehead and left. His hands, both of them swollen and plum-dark, operated independent of his delirious mind. There was something childishly compelling about the repetitive action of sawing—almost akin to the morbid pleasure in shooting a woodland critter or dismembering a bug, except he *was* the woodland creature in this instance; he *was* the bug. Amputation would free him from the trap, this sundew house.

Plop went the right leg onto the deck. Birds twittered encouragement.

Yes, this seemed a slight improvement. He dragged himself, hand over hand, inside and through the kitchen into the parlor. His body felt light, although the journey took several days if the rotating carousel of sun and moon could be trusted as a guide. He left a red trail through the parlor and to the box television. He clicked the television on and then rested. Some kernel within his dimming soul craved information from the outside world. It yearned for even the sterile contact of cathode rays. He crawled to the couch and lifted himself onto its bleached flower-pattern cushions. The TV played in jittery black and white. Static snarled. *Davey and Goliath. The Muppet Show. Mr. Rogers. Lamb Chop.* The actors spoke in Russian or Spanish or Slavic or the *click-click* buzz of hunting insects.

A dark-haired toddler pedaled a red tricycle into the room. The child wheeled close to the couch and stopped. His shiny hair and plastic features glowed with roly-poly good health.

"I know you," Bryan said in a perfectly clear voice. His breathing came easily. Still woozy, still full of pustulant anxiety (and pus), yet he grudgingly admitted that the compulsory mutilation had alleviated the worst symptoms of whatever disease gripped him. "Yes, you were there. I know you."

"As I know you," the child said.

"Wait. Who are you?"

"But you know. Feel better?"

"Yes. It's a miracle."

"Leeching is good for the soul. You aren't really better. Daddy said it's only temporary. You've got the gang-green."

The putrefaction of Bryan's hands had corrupted his arms to the elbows. He'd done his best to ignore this latest incursion of rot and enjoy the cartoons. Now the meddling kid had ruined everything. "What am I supposed to do? It's in my arms, for fuck's sake."

"Everything must go." The boy rolled over to the couch and handed Bryan a serrated penknife. "Daddy says to do a good job. Bye!"

The sky darkened and clotted and the windows became opaque with purple. Bryan sniffled bitter tears. He gripped the toy knife between his thumb and index finger and made the first, tiny cut. Better still.

Months oozed past. Years. Once his traitorous limb was severed, he dropped the knife and took a few breaths. Yes, better. Lighter. Addition by subtraction made increasing sense with a come-to-Jesus shock of epiphany. The next stage presented a challenge to his transcendence. Not wildly intelligent, but plenty clever, went Bryan's family motto as mumbled by drunk Dad.

He raised his remaining biceps to his mouth and bit in. Angel food cake, food of the gods.

"**I** am impressed. Truly." Mandibole retrieved Bryan's severed arms and studied them. "My grandfather trapped wolves along the Yukon. Leg-hold traps with nasty teeth. Those wolves, ah my. Rebellious critters chomped their own legs to get free. Humans really are animals with a fancy operating system, aren't you?"

Bryan concentrated on *Sesame Street.* He frowned when Mandibole clicked the screen dead.

The man dressed in a soot-tarnished three-piece suit. His profile could have been Bryan's father's during his prime belt-buckle-swinging-days. He clucked his tongue at the filth and grime; the holes in the ceiling, the windows melted to slag with age, mushroom beds where carpet once spread, the wasp nests, and termite-riddled beams.

"This joint sure went to seed," Mandibole said. "Stupid me. You're Bryan the Amazing Torso. I can hardly expect you to push a broom. You can't even wipe your own ass. Entropy. There's a secret to life. Entropy. Our dads are the gods of our puny universes, and yet even they are powerless beneath the cloddish tread of enervation and heat death."

"I'm at peace." Bryan's belly distended with a feast of his own muscle and marrow. Perfectly sated for the coming ages and divested of humdrum, mortal concerns such as fear and happiness.

Mandibole threw back his head and laughed. His helmet hair didn't stir, nor did his eyelashes flutter. "Not so fast, chum. Are you blind? The rot is in your chest. It's creeping toward your brain. We must act fast, else you're a goner. Or worse."

Bryan waggled his stumps with bewilderment. His serenity evaporated, replaced by petulant misery. "What do you expect of me, Dad? I can't chew my own damned throat."

"A bit more commitment would be nice. No matter." Mandibole leaned over and retrieved the rusty penknife. "I used to tie your shoes. In for a penny."

"Wait," Bryan said, too late. Despite years of accreted cynicism, he was profoundly surprised at how much blood remained, albeit momentarily, in his body.

Mandibole finished the job by twisting Bryan's skull until it popped free. He whistled as he carried his trophy into a lush garden amok with brambles and bushes. He offered Bryan's head to the dark and ominous tree that lorded it over the smaller plants of the kingdom. The tips of its thorny branches pierced Bryan's ears and lifted him until he hung like a piece of bleeding pomegranate, a gaping manikin skull.

Constellations drifted and the sky became green. The house went under the burgeoning jungle. Heat and steam and green, endless green. The pomegranates in the great tree possessed distorted faces. The newer heads, raw and brash could speak at first. A wrinkled and ruddy soul dangling next to Bryan said, "Ezra Tooms, goddamn you cretins! Ezra Malachi Tooms! I'm a rich man! A powerful man!"

A howler monkey descended from its leafy berth and plucked that shouting fruit-head and promptly chewed it to gushing smithereens. Such were the risks of making a scene in paradise. Not that it mattered. Sooner or later, the animal would crap, the seeds would grow, and in a hundred years or so, Mr. Tooms would again blossom on the vine, on this tree or another, sadder and infinitely wiser.

Later, as happened every epoch or two, the sun divided and a vast, Godlike hand extended with greedy eagerness. The monkeys gibbered and screamed and fled in all directions while the hand made itself a claw and tore loose swathes of canopy. Hundreds of monkeys, and squirrels, and bright-plumed birds, tumbled toward the sky, and became tiny silhouettes inhaled by the sticky maw of a child leaning over the colossal handlebars of his trike.

Bryan could do nothing except exult in this recurring terror. Tears of red juice trickled from his bulging eyes. He was gravid with seeds and they stifled his mindless protest. Whenever he screamed, red seeds dripped from his mouth, splattered upon the soil and found purchase.

Over time, inconceivably deep geological time, the sentient fruit of his tree and the trees of the surrounding jungle, multiplied. Each became a perfect version of himself, howling and gibbering in a mute, eternal chorus. Eventually, he grew to accept it. His multiplicities spread, inexorably across the infinite, and took root everywhere.

—*For Michael Cisco*

THE GLORIFICATION
OF CUSTER POE

1915, interior Alaska

S pring is far away.

Spring in Alaska is a time of thawin' mud and bitter green saplings and soon enough salmon ladderin' their way up the falls. The big snows draw back and reveal the carnage of winter: bones, white and worn, embedded in muck; skulls and ribcages and thighbones of them critters what breathed their last when nights was killin' cold and the Northern Lights danced the cruel red dance of a lowerin' scythe.

Cold is always and ever the watchword in this place, even when summer sun cooks hot enough to boil pitch and the mosquitoes swarm in their black millions. For the cold is present beneath the green and blue veneer. Cold is the point of a skewer fixed to stab.

Nights grow long in late September. Bull moose get to whackin' the hell out of one another as ruttin' season begins. Leaves twirl out a the trees after the first stiff blow. Stars wink through a rime of warped glass. Ice creeps down from the outer darkness and spreads a caul across the summits and glaciated valleys, cracks apart the planed slats of my shack. Shouts and gunshots, the chuckles of ravens on the wing, carry for miles, or not at all. The shadow of every cliff-side is the mouth of a tomb.

My marker, if'n I die where anyone can find me, will read: *Here Lies Custer Poe, Ramblin' Man at Rest.* But I reckon I won't get no gravestone. The wilderness will swallow me and spit out my guns and knives to rust back into the dirt. I'll be elevated in that death. Upraised and become one with the alkaline streams, bear shit, and deep-diggin' roots that tickle Old Scratch's bald head. My huntin' cry will echo on the wind that screeches down these valleys.

Another man might've changed his name after what I done in the war. Pappy surely did and he weren't even no soldier nor assassin. Rumor has it, the ol' man went by Ferris or some-such nonsense. Dunno whether to laugh or spit. Hell with him. I take a cussed pride in this here handle, its provenance. My kin sailed over from Europe in 1809 and their children eventually homesteaded an Ozarks Mountain valley. I come along around 1842, eldest among a squallin' and brawlin' clutch of fourteen brothers and sisters. We Poes trapped and hunted and brewed moonshine and was known far and wide as a mighty cantankerous clan that held onto a grudge like grim death. Four of my brothers were rubbed out in saloon fights and blood feuds. Two more died takin' on the blue-bellies. Mama gave up the ghost after droppin' the last of the litter and straight away Pappy got himself hitched to a sweet filly from Nashville. They sold the homestead and run off to Texas. Ain't heard a peep from him since.

I high-tailed it from my valley home when I was sixteen. Me and Pappy were at each other's throats and if it'd gone on, one of us woulda got himself planted in the back forty. So I lit out for greener pastures with nothin' but a sack of vittles, a muzzle-loader my grandpa give me for my eleventh birthday, and my coon dog, Thule. Been a ramblin' man ever since.

Speakin' of handles, folks in town got their own names for me— Ol' Man of the Mountain; Ol' Man Custer; Whitebeard; Creepy Pete; and White Fox…those last monikers stuck on account of my God-given talent to sneak through the woods on my trappin' rounds like a Comanche and the fact I'm old as the dust on the hills. There's codgers at the Wolftooth Saloon who'll swear I'm so sly that I can creep upon a perched grouse and sprinkle salt on its tail. Ain't sayin' they're wrong, either. Dress me in buckskins and mukluks and there ain't too many critters that'll hear me before I'm on 'em with gun, knife, or stranglin' wire. I do surely enjoy the feel of the wire in my mitts. Better than the bone handle of a knife, even. Oh, yes indeedy.

But, I'm getting' off the trail.

A reporter traveled from Seattle to visit me this past autumn, right before the first hard freeze. Imagine that! Tracked me all the way from the Ozarks where I was born to this bolthole in the Alaskan wilderness a few miles north of McCafferty Landing on the mighty Kuskokwim. Wet behind the ears lad named Johnston. I shoulda took it for an omen of ill. On the heels of that palaver the animals began whisperin' to me and the long shadows made peculiar shapes and moved against their own nature. There are words that shouldn't be uttered lest a man is ready to call down the attention of powerful forces.

See, the interview became my confession. Don't matter none that nobody will ever read it in any damned yellow rag. The Maker knows what lies in the heart of a man—and so does the Devil. Them words of mine stirred up revenants. Even so, it felt right liberatin' to come clean here in the twilight of my mortal span.

Wasn't me that truly interested Johnston. Nah, he was writin' an essay about infamous figgers of the war. Corrupt officers, mutineers, criminals and such. He aimed to make his fortune by bringin' this rogues' gallery to the modern public. I'd known the man he was after. Known the man, and what's more, laid him low. And so for the first time in almost fifty years I was asked the fateful question. Bein' an honest sort, I answered true.

H ere's what I told Johnston as we tucked into plates of lumpy dick and molasses while the wind knocked in the chimney:

Yeah, it was me who assassinated Mordecai Jefferson at the tail end of the War of Northern Aggression. Was the Captain really a bad man? A murderer and a horse thief? Sure, I reckoned so. A rapist and a drunk? Oh, indeedy. And had the Captain ordered the slaughter of farmers and the wanton sacking of their homes? Was it also true he killed his own men over petty grievances? All true, said I. Mordecai didn't require no grievance to do dirt to his comrades. He'd shoot a fellow through the gizzard just because the sky was blue and the wind fell out a the west. Everybody who knows anythin' about the war knows that Mordecai Jefferson collected scalps from the battlefield. He often skinned his enemies, at least the ones who'd made him mad. The Captain was a student of history, especially if it had to do with warfare. He was partial to a long dead Scotsman named William Wallace who'd done the same. Mordecai's standard was blazoned upon the flesh stripped from a platoon of Blue Belly regulars. His belt came from the hide of a Northern Colonel he'd captured in a burned-out farmhouse. The officer come forth under the white flag and Mordecai smiled and slashed off his head with a cavalry saber. Kept that molderin' skull as a paperweight on his camp desk.

All that said, my assassinatin' him was nothin' personal. The job sort a fell into my lap. Can't say who originally ordered the deed done—a faro dealer in Bridgeton took me aside and made the proposition, flashed a secret writ with the Confederate seal affixed neat as you please. The dealer said that the command came from on high. He also said that now I knew too much to refuse. So I didn't refuse. Anyway, for two hundred dollars and a bottle of Kentucky bourbon you could get me to set fire to my own ass, much less ventilate an irascible coot like Mord.

Tell you this, though: for the remainder of our bivouac in town, the awerdenty, vittles, and women were my treat. Mord wanted for nothin'. We whooped it up, boy. I sent my pardner off in grandiose style.

Upon week's end, Mordecai and I set to marchin' homeward alongside a wagon train. Long, wearyin' slog after all the commotion and clamor of battle. Comin' on to dusk our posse was fixin' to portage Gillis Crick. Never would be a better opportunity for murder, or so I reckoned. I waited until he turned to tether his big piebald in the rushes. Now, I had to be extra cautious on account Mordecai's reflexes were like a cougar's and he was mighty slick with a shootin' iron. Lined up my trusty Colt with the back of his skull and squeezed the trigger. A lick of flame shot from his hair and he dropped, dead as dirt. The piebald spooked and tore out of there. Galloped for three miles and we played Hob tryin' to catch him. A feller in Madison give me a Sharps 1851 rifle for that horse.

I didn't roll Mordecai over, or nothin'. Was a bad business puttin' down the poor ol' cuss; made me sick to my soul and I turned and walked away while the smoke still rose from his corpse. I heard tell from the drovers who packed him into a box that he didn't have no face left on account of the slug blowing it off, just a black and bloody hole. Didn't need the drovers to pass the news. I see that god-awful wound all the time, peepin' at me from the shadows. Blamed thing gives me the shivers. But Doc Green says it ain't unusual for a man my age to have a bit of water on the brain, ain't unusual for a man my age to see Death sneakin' along his backtrail.

Anyway. That was the end of the line for me. I got cashiered a few weeks later and sat out the final battles in one bucket of blood dancehall or another. Word got around that I'd smoked Mordecai and I decided it best to make myself scarce.

Used the last of my iron men for ship passage. I lit out for Alaska and never returned to the civilized world. Traveled all around this here northern territory for a passel of years. Haines and Skagway, Poorman and Ruby on the bitter Yukon, Kotzebue, and Nome. Oh, Lord, Nome ain't no place for an honest man. The women are hard, the whiskey harder, and in the summertime a cold wind blows from the sea and whips the dust along the flats past the seawall. Winters are mean enough to put icicles on your soul. I got shut of Nome quick as I could, lemme tell you.

I been a fisherman, trapper, placer miner, and sometime chief cook and bottle washer at line camps. I can hunt and skin and always seem to know the direction of true north whether the sun or the stars are in their heaven. I get by. Easy to get by when your needs are small and space is so wide. Some go mad here in the land of the midnight sun. Endless light and bugs all summer; eternal darkness of the pit come winter. It's the kind of place a man slips away to when he wants to vanish. The kind of place even God Almighty might forget to look. Maybe that's why nobody come after me to exact vengeance on Mordecai's behalf. Too damned much trouble. I lived real quiet and folks in this neck of the woods don't give a tin shit about what happened to grampa or grand-uncle Joe in Antietam or any of them other fields of slaughter. Here, I'm just one of many shiftless, wise-crackin' whitebeards scrabblin' in the hills.

Wasn't much else to tell my reporter chum. Johnston seemed a mite disappointed that my demeanor wasn't more fearsome, but he wrote it all down in his little book.

Like so many cheechakos who swagger north, the kid was a tadpole in a man's wilderness. Shaved his face smooth as a sow's ass. Bright-eyed and red of cheek, the rotgut hit him hard. Takes almost half a bottle to knock me sideways, but that reporter lad was skunk drunk after a couple of snorts. In hindsight, us drinkin' together probably made for a tragic mistake. Kid was in such an all-fired hurry to get back to civilization, he took down my testament and skedaddled before dawn lit up the mountains. Still soused, I reckon. The gods were against him, too. Like some kind a cursed magic, the first snowflakes blew in across the range that very mornin'. Snowed so damned hard I couldn't see the woodshed from the porch. Got trapped indoors for the better part of a fortnight.

The boy never was seen again. Missed the boat to Seattle. Constable Tom figgered he met with misadventure along the way from my shack to town. Them caribou trails are treacherous, mighty treacherous. What with the storm and the ice, well…his fate seemed clear. The kid took a tumble or got lost and froze. Either way, he was surely raven meat.

Maybe, maybe.

For my part, I ain't so sure Johnston slipped and fell into a crevasse nor wandered afield and ended his days in the manner of a moose calf et by wolves. There's bad men prowlin' these hills. Claim jumpers and assorted riffraff. And talkin' bears, evidently. Could be one a them done for him. In any event, lota folks go missing in these parts.

Sad; I kinda liked him even if he was a cheechako.

Weeks passed. It just kept gettin' colder and nastier. We was in for a winter the likes I ain't seen in a coon's age. Supplies was runnin' a mite low, so I strapped on my snowshoes and commenced the hike into McCafferty Landing.

Got me a jug of awerdenty at Jeb Parson's dry goods store. Lugged it with the flour, coffee, and sundries back to my shack over the mountain on Slawson River. There's gold in that there river. It's a shallow crick compared to the Kuskokwim, but it's fast and just a few years ago people set to cuttin' each others' throats each spring when the passes opened and the cheechako panners came a runnin' from the lower Forty-Eight. Every summer was a blood and thunder, rip-roarin' claim jumpin' summer. I eagerly awaited the party. Oh, yes indeedy. Course, it's quieted down a mite.

I made it back to my shack, kindled a fire and settled in for a spell. Built this shack in 1904. She's drafty. She leaks. Her floorboards hang over a cliff that plunges clear down to rocks and the gnashin' teeth of the river. Marten and mice rustle in the eaves. A rude and homely abode, but she's my castle.

So, there I was, shucked outta my duds and lyin' naked as a newborn but for a pair of holey, grimy socks, and sippin' off the neck of the jug and feelin' no pain. I've testified how miserable it gets in the north, well this beat all—cold as a witch's tit. I'd stoked the fire in the pot stove and warmed my toes near the flames and stared at the antlers and the smudged photographs hangin' from the walls. Didn't recognize no folks in the pitchers—none were of my kin, nor associates. Kept 'em up there all the same as I didn't have no pitchers of my own.

Custer.

My eyelids had almost shut. That strange, breathy groan might've been the wind in the spruce moanin' my name. I knew better. My heart did too. It plumb froze for a couple of ticks and I lay helpless as a baby in my cot. Something heavy moved along the porch and there came a scratchin' of long nails on wood. The front door creaked open and frigid air rolled into the cabin. I smelled the foulness of wet fur and rotten salmon mixed with the sharp, clean taste of spruce boughs and snow. A shadow fell across the wall.

I turned my head and beheld a bear halfway through the door. A big ol' brute, its shaggy black hide rimed in frost, bits of ice and snow caught in its clabbered jaws. Them fangs was crooked and dark as flint knives. Beady eyes flared red in the fire glow, rolled in the sockets to the whites and back again.

"Oh, shitfire," I said. My visitor had no business bein' awake and prowlin' the hills. It should've been snug in a cave and dreamin' of spring.

The beast swayed in place and growled. That growl sounded a lot like *Custer, I'm here for you, you sonofabitch.* Sounded like it wanted to say more, too. The Colt I brung home from the war was in my fist and I rolled onto my belly and shot the varmint four times (the other two bullets blew holes in the wall) and it slumped, the red light in its eyes coolin' right quick. Gods, the cabin stank of shit and piss and gun smoke and I nearly chucked my dinner.

Custer, the bear gurgled with its dyin' breath.

"Fuck you too, Mordecai," I said. My hand was shakin' so bad I dropped the pistol. Despite the bitter chill and the flakes of snow twirlin' about my head, my sight grew dim and I rested my eyes for a while in a whiskey faint.

I woke to three inches of windblown snow swishin' in the cabin and that damned bear goin' stiff in the doorway. The shack's windows were tiny as portholes, so I figgered the only way out was to cut my way through before the carcass froze solid. I pulled on my britches, rekindled the fire, and gave my skinnin' knife a few licks on the whetstone.

The bear had bit the dust all hunkered down, its massive shoulders wedged in the threshold. I reached as far as I could and let out its guts with a jerk of my Arkansas Toothpick. Blood did surely gush forth and dripped down through the knotty planks and painted the icy cliff face below. Had to work a mite fast. Dark was on the way, and maybe a blizzard. Then it'd be chilly enough to quick freeze hapless me.

I rolled my sleeves and set to yarding the guts into a pile on the floor. The bear's hide twitched and bunched along its shoulder, made a lump the size of my fist, like somethin' was slidin' around underneath. I helped myself to another snort of awerdenty, wiped my mouth, and poked the lump with the point of the knife. The fur flattened, as if whatever hid there had gone deeper inside. A small critter retreating into its burrow of flesh. My heart beat faster.

"Ah, Mordecai. You cagey ol' bastard." I'd heard the injuns in the southwest call men who change their shape skin-walkers. So, what did they call a man whose spirit inhabits corpses and animals and suchlike? Didn't really hold with such superstition as a rule, but Lord take mercy, I'd seen queer things aplenty durin' my time. If my long dead pal's immortal soul had ghosted its way into the body of an animal, that'd just be the latest development in a saga that got queerer by the day.

I gazed down at the growin' mound of guts and for a moment, I was a Roman prophet, lost in his bloody tale.

Half a lifetime ago when I first come to this territory, I rode with a sourdough named Victor Haagen. Scandinavian by way of Canada. Fellow had a hooked nose and hands that could choke a moose. He was a well-digger by trade. Victor gave up diggin' wells for placer minin' and pitched a teepee near Ophir. He taught me a thing or two about survivin' in the northlands. What berries to eat, where the ptarmigan roost, how to roll in the snow after you fall in a crick, the best way to toss an axe. He's the one who learned me how to snare, and for that I'm ever grateful.

Victor seldom spoke. I expect he had kin overseas, or east of the Yukon, maybe a wife and younguns, but as he didn't utter three words on a given day, the Lord alone knew the truth of it. Once in a while I'd go on a week-long trappin' expedition with him and we'd camp in one of the lean-tos he'd built along the way. We'd swill awerdenty and watch the sparks from the fire dance among the stars. If'n he got plenty soaked, the codger would take a pitcher from his pocket and press it against the breast of his buckskins and weep. I knew better than to try and peek at the pitcher, and sure as hell I wasn't keen to ask what had broken his heart in two. Nah, I liked my teeth where they sat and I kept my peace.

He surprised me once, though. This was after a long night of drinkin' in our customary silence. I'd drifted to sleep and had a dream wherein dead folks, some of whom I'd kilt, rose from their graves and assailed me with ghastly wails and clutchin' hands. I awoke with a groan to Victor starin' at me with a peculiar intent. He got a right mischievous gleam in his cloudy eyes, and he grinned, but more like a wolf grins. He said, "Custer, you cursed, ol' son. Yore demons ridin' you like a hoss."

I asked what he meant by that. Victor shrugged and mumbled somethin' in Yupik (he'd spent a few winters among the tribes). Course, this riled me and I demanded to know what the devil he meant. No use. Victor commenced to pourin' more awerdenty down his throat and pretty quick he collapsed, dead to the world. Frustrated, I took a notion to do the same.

Next mornin' Victor was nowhere to be found. He'd slipped away and left me a few supplies and ashes in the fireplace. Didn't make a damned bit of sense. Maybe the coot had gone round the bend after one too many seasons in the wild.

I only figgered much later that he didn't cotton to me. We weren't nowhere near as friendly as I'd thought, and never had been despite appearances. Nope, he was like a grizzled lobo who'd scented somethin' off about me, and it scared him. Scared him so bad, he pretended we was thick as thieves, smilin' to my face, all the while plannin' mischief. After that fateful night I didn't speak to him again. He stripped his teepee clean and departed the territory. Rafferty, the gent who runs the Wolftooth Saloon, claimed Victor returned to Canada. Jeb Parson told me a lawman had been spotted travelin' from village to village along the Kuskokwim. Parson figgered it to be a US Marshal on Victor's trail for some old business. Maybe a murder. I didn't peg my pal for no dirty dog bushwhacker and said as much to Parson. He just shook his head and informed me that rumor had it Victor shot a few folks in British Columbia, stole their vittles and the gold from their teeth. Whatever the case, none a us ever clapped eyes on the ol' boy again, that's certain.

Round about then that I first spied the shade of Mordecai Jefferson.

I'd decided to rest a spell after tyin' one on at the Wolftooth, so I lay me down on the Main Street boardwalk. Earlier that night Bobby Yu (a trapper from North Fork) had punched me in the jaw and I feared it might be broke. Twas pissin' rain and dark as a mineshaft but for a feeble glow comin' through the saloon window and the occasional flash of lightnin'. I didn't give a rip. My legs was done and my chin had gone numb. Somebody come along and lifted me out a the mud and propped me against the door of Parson's store. I laughed to imagine how I would look in daylight sittin' there all pretty, like one a them outlaw corpses people stacked along the walkway with signs around their neck.

Well, I happened to open my eyes from a nightmare about bein' scalped by a Blue Belly regular and a whipcrack bolt of fire whizzed across the sky and I beheld a figger lurkin' across the way in the alley between Magoon's Feed and what used to be the telegraph office. Good God Almighty, the vision nearly unhinged me: a man in tattered Confederate Gray. Faceless. Eyes, nose, mouth all one jagged wound oozin' gore. I knew it for Mordecai just the same. He waved at me.

Yeah, I was drunk and it was dark and thus when the light flashed again and Mord had vanished, I quickly dismissed the incident as a fever dream. The taste of puke lingered in my mouth for days, though.

The ghosts showed themselves a lot more after that. Mostly it'd be a shadow in the corner of my eye, or a suspicious arrangement of bushes, or a mirage when I'd slept too little and drunk too much. Mord's garbled voice would come to me through the walls of my shack as I lay in a stupor. He haunted my dreams and them badlands between sleep and wakin'. Whenever I was weakest, he'd come and mutter his laments.

That was all he could muster though. Just a phantom with a phantom's complaints. After the first shock of his grisly appearance, I never rightly feared him in that puny state. I didn't fear none of them.

You might be puzzled what I mean by "them."

Mordecai weren't the first man I murdered. Not by a long shot. He weren't the last, neither. I got myself a powerful taste for bloodlettin'. How many were there, over the years? God damn me if I can reckon for certain. Too many drunk trappers, miners, and dancehall gals to even count, so I don't bother. Some of those folks went a real hard way, not painless like my buddy Mordecai. There was stabbin's and shootin's that turned out wrong, and one or two who fought and struggled no matter how deep I tightened the stranglin' wire. Them's the revenants who come callin', hungry for vengeance, I expect. Mordecai weren't nothin' special, except bein' the maddest and the loudest of the bunch.

In some parts of this vast ol' continent, the natives speak of the *wendigo*. Dependin' upon the particular superstition, *wendigo* is a demon of the wastes that eats men and it can be bested with fire and steel like any other dumb beast. Other, darker, traditions suppose the wendigo is a shadow that stains the soul. Acts of terrible cruelty or violence make it bold and cause it to spread. Depravity, gluttony, malice, maybe a taste of cannibalism—these make a codger's heart beat faster and quicken the black sap within.

I'm thinkin' if the *wendigo* exists, it's likely that second thing. My mind wanders, see. I ramble. When I said I built this here shack in '04, what I meant was, I took possession of it from Calvin Buntline. These pitchers on the wall, those are Buntline's kin. Cal made the trip from Indiana when word come that they'd seen color along the Kuskokwim. He took me in one miserable night as I wandered the hills searchin' for a claim to stake. We drunk us a shitpot load of awerdenty and fell to arguin' over cards. I stuck him with my knife, watched the red run down his leg, watched his eyes change to glass. Don't know what possessed me to lean over and press my lips to his as he gasped his last, but I did and breathed it in.

Victor Haagen I did for with a wire snare. Seemed only right as he'd taught me how in the first place.

That reporter, the Johnston kid, him I took apart with a pickaxe, though I don't rightly recall the details. I only recall how my mouth sealed his at the end, and how the snow melted in his lashes like bits of diamond.

Ain't a one of my defeated foes seemed capable of enacting their desire to wrap cold dead hands around my throat. Nah, all they do is mope and bluster from the shores of Purgatory. Back when it all began I drank a jot more. Slept sound as a baby. In time the visions faded. Most nights I plumb forgot the whole mess.

Until the bear, that is.

Darkness closed in over the mountain and the snow fell thick as goose down through the spruce. I continued to skin the black bear. I peered into its eyes every now and again, lookin' for a spark of resumed life. A powerful sense of impendin' doom come over me and I half expected its jaws to snap shut on my arm. Somethin' stirred within that great, sodden bulk. This wasn't gas escapin' from guts, or death twitches. Nosir, nosir. I slid my knife under the ribs, drivin' inward till I was elbow deep and kept sawin' until the drippin' heart come free. For a moment it lay quiet and cool in my hands. Then, by God, it twitched, squirtin' dribs and drabs of blood through its slashed arteries.

Wisps of yeller steam twisted away from that quiverin' flesh with a teakettle moan. Them vapors moved against the risin' wind and wove themselves into the apparition of a man. A frail, and decrepit manifestation, to be sure. So pallid and thin it seemed about to drift apart at any moment. There floated Mordecai, a smoky void where his expression of wrath should a been. He moaned again, in tune with the wind as it rushed over the rocks and through the trees. That mournful keenin' went on and on. Finally I grew plumb weary of the game. I yawned and gulped him in. His yeller form disappeared down my gullet the way smoke goes sucked up a chimney flue.

I pushed the bear carcass out onto the porch and shut the goddamned door against the storm. Sliced that heart into strips and fried them in a pan. Man, it was sweet and bitter and good. A mite stringy, but not nearly as tough as I'd expected.

Not tough at all, in fact.

II
WANDERING STARS

JŌREN FALLS

In an homage to the countrified roots of their flown youth, Larry and Vonda Prettyman retired to a farmhouse on a big piece of property a few minutes southwest of Kingston, New York. Cornfields and blackbirds. Winding back roads and golden light reflecting from streams. Rural, yet within shouting distance of civilization.

Larry departed a career in heavy equipment sales for a Newark-based contractor. Vonda had managed a doctor's office in Queens. He'd spent the juiciest span of his life flying international business class and riding in the back of company cars. She'd burrowed into the metro art scene, routinely hosting parties for the lower-echelon literati. Between hectic careers, children, and encroaching age, they had gradually been worn to the nub.

Cashing in their 401Ks and moving to the country was just the tonic. He'd grown up in a Norman Rockwell-esque county of Western New York; she'd come of age in Ogdensburg, which was basically a woodsy suburb of Canada. To the surprise of those who never really knew them, the graying couple said their goodbyes with cool handshakes and dry pecks on the cheek, pulled up stakes overnight, and vanished into the ether.

Sunset and sunrise were cool and soft as a bruised apple. There was a garden, a copse of sycamore and pine, distant meadows, then low, heavily wooded slopes that built to an arm of the Catskills. Orb spiders crept out of the dewy grass and spun traps in the eaves. The grand dame of them built her silken death maze in the kitchen window overlooking the garden. Vonda snapped photographs and mentioned an essay she'd read. According to scientists, the web was actually an extension of the spider's mind. Vonda subscribed to eight or nine periodicals. Arts and crafts; popular science; modern art; a couple on film and literature and high-class pornography. The *Skeptical Inquirer* and *Fortean Times* rounded out her collection. She carefully removed the pages with her favorite articles and photocopied them at the library in Stone Ridge. She sent the pertinent items to the kids—girls in Arizona and Alaska; two boys in Montana. The girls promptly wrote back. The boys called on Thanksgiving and Christmas, or the day *after* Thanksgiving and Christmas, yelling season's greetings over a cacophony of children and barking dogs.

Larry leaned against the sink, abstractedly longing for a dog. The notion of a fluffy, warmhearted, nonjudgmental companion snoozing at his feet appealed to the peculiar loneliness gathering in his heart, as did the idea of leisurely strolls in the nearby forest and someone to woof at the door when the express delivery guys dropped packages. His parents had raised a border collie. Bought from a farmer who preferred blue heelers. He had shared many adventures with the dog. The dog's name escaped him.

"Hello, raccoon eyes." Vonda sailed in from stage left. She

poured a glass of water and studied him as she sipped. "I rolled over to a cold spot at 4 a.m."

"Something woke me." He'd surfaced from an incoherent, yet erotic dream, but wasn't about to admit it. "Guess I slept in the den." This might've been true.

"Something? Something, as in…?"

"I don't remember."

She regarded him speculatively.

"Maybe it was the farmer's dogs." He indicated the dairy farmer who lived nearby and kept a trio of blue heelers to safeguard his cows. The heelers patrolled the vast property, yodeling periodic alarms late at night.

She tapped her forehead and smiled. "A dream, perhaps? Lately, you're so…in the clouds."

"Am I?" He nodded, blandly affable to cover his discomfort with her perception.

A breeze whipped the spiderweb. The spider clung tight.

Afternoon shadows dappled the wall. Larry peered at the computer monitor, comparing prices for Wellington boots. Bemused by the sea of choices, he contemplated visiting the hardware store yet again. Perhaps the fifth time would be the charm. *Shop Local!* was an admonishment blazoned on seemingly every other business window. Mud season rapidly approached; the owner promised him new stock would arrive momentarily. Larry hoped "momentarily" came before the driveway and his favorite walking trails devolved to muck.

His mouse cursor hovered—

Directly overhead, something moved in the attic. He startled, his gaze dragged to the dim eggshell paint and the stained globe light fixture. A long, portentous silence followed, then an outburst of frantic scrabbling. His heart sank. The unthinkable had finally occurred. One of Vonda's squirrels had invaded the house. He blamed Vonda because every morning she filled bird feeders hanging from the crabapple tree in the backyard. She also scattered unshelled peanuts for the deer. This attracted every possible variety of avian and mammalian miscreant. Local feral cats once checked the smaller wildlife population. Coyotes subsequently roved through the neighborhood and put paid to the cats. In the absence of feline assassins, birds flocked, and heaps of squirrels too.

Accessing the attic via a loose ceiling panel in the closet, he pushed aside winter coats and awkwardly scaled a stepladder and pushed his head and shoulders through the opening, keychain penlight in hand. Rich, dusty gloom, redolent with the faint odors of decay, greeted him. The attic ran the length of the house, divided by a thin partition at the halfway point, which blocked his view. Not much to see, anyhow; exposed timbers that ribbed a sharply-peaked roof; shriveled puffs of fiberglass insulation; a cable attached to an industrial fan; and a low stack of boxes of junk.

One of the boxes lay toppled, spilling curios he collected during his journeys abroad. Paperweights and coffee mugs. Cheap pens. Photographs of him and his colleagues plastered, ties loosened, acting like clowns, hanging on the arms of burlesque dancers and cocktail waitresses. He'd chosen the attic as a likely spot to stash mementos. His wife wasn't enchanted with his former rambling man persona, whom she termed the Other Larry. Though the photos were nothing more than proof that boys-will-be-boys, he feared Vonda might get the wrong idea. When was the last time he'd visited his attic trove to indulge in nostalgia? Days? Weeks? In the early days of his retirement, he made frequent pilgrimages. The life of a salesman could be monotonous, yet he still missed the foreign nightclubs and karaoke bars, and the drunken camaraderie of fellow travelers.

He thrust his arm forward and scooped the items into the box and righted it. A mildew stain on the side had congealed into a leering visage he almost recognized.

Making another sweep, his light caught the edge of rotting wooden placard that had pitched to one side, and lay partially obscured by the box. Roughly the dimensions of a license plate, it was draped with cobwebs, withered moths, and the desiccated flap of a burst cocoon. Red, flaking kanji warned against disturbing or removing anything from the "waterfall site."

It took him back. He'd almost forgotten his lone tour of Jōren Falls in Izu, Japan, months prior to 9/11. Travel companions—jocular guys from advertising—egged him into swiping the sign to take home for a cool souvenir. How many martinis had they downed to uproot that homely, weathered little warning sign? He vaguely recollected sweating as he waited to clear customs the next day, hungover and mightily ruing his impulsiveness, yet embarrassed to "chicken out." The advertising guys were right, though—it *was* indeed a cool souvenir.

Larry gingerly laid the sign inside the box and rubbed at cobwebs that stuck to his fingers. He could've walked the beams and floor joists in a crouch if the spirit had moved him to investigate further. Which it did not. Observing neither the interloping squirrel nor any obvious entry point for the critter, he retreated.

"**C**all Roger," Vonda said at dinner. She meant Roger Miller, a friend and handyman who lived not far down the road. Roger had a solid decade on the couple, who were no spring chickens themselves. Vonda referred to him as Sundance's Hot Granddad, in honor of an ancient Robert Redford. Larry thought Redford resembled an unwrapped mummy. Admittedly, Roger had aged well.

Larry frowned at his plate. Autumn allergies were kicking in— nothing tasted right. "I could have a peek—"

"Don't fool around. You'll crash through the ceiling."

"As you say, dear."

He didn't regard himself as overweight. Beefy, perhaps. He walked daily along the road where it climbed a steep hill toward the neighborhoods of historic colonial homes. He also split two cords of firewood every autumn as insurance against the not infrequent power outages caused by winter storms. Nonetheless, Roger was inarguably lighter and spryer, despite pushing his late seventies. The fellow had shipped out to Vietnam in the Army. Plenty of unobtrusive crawling in the jungle during wartime. Lean, mean, clambering machine.

Larry morosely dumped peas onto the remnants of his potatoes. He topped the milk in his glass. He methodically ate the cardboard potatoes and then drank the chalky milk, looking his wife in the eye throughout.

"Oh, they'll burn your house to the foundation," Roger said on the phone later that evening. Yelled, really. His hearing had deteriorated. "Right to the ground. Bet your sweet bippy."

"Because they chew the wires," Larry said, hoping to sound authoritative. He considered Roger's blue-collar competence a form of black magic. Larry excelled at massaging bad news and wining and dining balky clients, but didn't know one end of a wrench from the other. That seemed like a personal failing.

"Yeah, that's how they keep their teeth short," Roger said. "Buggers don't mean any harm. Won't stop 'em from doing plenty, though. Gotta take action. The wiring in your house is probably subpar. None of the old places in this neighborhood are up to code."

"Actually," Larry said. "Vonda hired an electrician to inspect the attic. Two or three months ago. Upstairs hall light started turning on and off by itself. Guy didn't report any critters or damage." As a point of fact, the electrician had lingered in the attic for quite a while. Later, the fellow muttered a perfunctory report and then practically bolted to his van.

"Gotta be careful," Roger said. "Some fly-by-night jokers in this neck of the woods do a half-baked job and call it a cake."

"Sure, we're rubes from the city. Who wouldn't fleece us? You'll take a look?"

"Bright and early." Roger's deliberate cadence suggested he'd soaked up a skinful of Boone's. Since his wife Lucy's death, the old boy polished off more than his share. A real tragedy. On the other hand, as a widower divested of Lucy's infamous honey-do lists, his schedule was wide open.

"I'll be here. Considered going by the store to check on Wellingtons…"

"Good luck with that. I've an extra set in storage. What size you wear?"

"Thirteen," Larry said.

"Ha! Forget I said anything."

"Excuse me?"

"Those are clodhoppers, not feet, old son."

"Okay, right."

"Tomorrow, then. *Thirteen*. Ha! Ha!"

Larry placed the phone in its cradle. He sat alone in the living room. Vonda customarily went to bed early and played the evening news as background while she skimmed magazine articles. She and dearly-departed Lucy had gotten on well. Canasta and gardening buddies. Lucy loved her role as a wife and homemaker; Vonda wasn't as enamored. However, she'd either grown more accustomed to it or good at pretending.

The windows reflected the light of the floor lamp. He inhaled and listened to the house. Those decades in the city had conditioned him to neon and fluorescent rays, the low rumble of endless traffic. Nighttime here stole in on black wings and a breathless hush. Yips of hungry coyotes broke that stillness, as did the chorusing frogs. The small noises of animals merely emphasized that humans were visitors, lingering tourists. He felt nature pressing against the sides of the house, felt her in the chilly draft under the doors and window sills. A hunter searching for the weak point. An egg on the cusp of hatching?

Larry glanced upward and imagined the squirrel, lying in wait, saliva dripping from its incisors. Right on cue, muffled scuttling that abated momentarily. Later, swaddled in blankets, he dwelled upon sparking wires and the house consumed in a fireball. Tick bites that itched and bled for months. So many deer ticks in rural New York—a veritable plague. He recalled that sometimes, in the dark, a plastic shroud crackled near his face like webbing spun by some umbral horror, and his mother and father stood in silhouette, and the rumble of water falling upon itself became the wind punching the house.

"This is fascinating." *Fascinating* was Vonda's go-to multipurpose gambit. She said it in response to many things—news articles, an empty cereal box in the cupboard, the toilet seat left up, and so forth. "The Max Planck Institute reports baby owls' sleep activity is similar to that of very young mammals." She waved her magazine. A color photograph captured an owlet snoozing with its beak planted in straw bedding. Its fully extended legs were muscled like a weightlifter.

"I don't—there aren't any owls in the attic," Larry said. He considered how rarely one saw exposed owl legs. The sight was comical or uncouth. It also occurred to him that he'd left the toilet seat up more than usual. An uncharacteristic invitation to be excoriated.

"Too bad," she said. "Owls are killers. End of squirrel incursion. Assuming it's even a squirrel."

"It's a squirrel."

"How can you be certain?"

"Deduction."

She flipped the page. "Assumption occasionally finds congruence with fact."

"Deduction. I said deduction—"

"Historically speaking, as a rule, assumption leads to chaos."

"If not a squirrel, then I'm curious what else."

"Weasels. Chipmunks." Flip, flip. "Sparrows. Brownies. Who knows?"

"Excepting little people, I don't see how the specific identity of the critter fundamentally alters our problem. Something is there, which should not be, and it's raising havoc."

She smiled enigmatically.

"Roger will be along in a bit," he said to bridge the rapidly widening void.

"We're saved." Flip.

His skull ached. He walked outside to wait on the porch.

Roger arrived in a cloud of dust at the wheel of a Dodge. He wore a Yankees ball cap over remarkably thick, cropped hair. His coveralls were freshly washed. "Good grief. See that vent? That's plastic." He indicated a vent high on the north wall below the roof peak. Its dull gray paint had peeled, revealing a pale undersurface. A crack ran through the slats. Not large enough to admit a squirrel; although, if it worsened…

"I take it the vent should be metal," Larry said, mildly apologetic, as if he, and not the original owner, was responsible for faulty architecture. He too wore a ball cap (New York Mets), long sleeve shirt, pants, and boots. He'd always worn a hardhat while touring factory floors with other middle management suits. The habit of donning a costume to interact with the laboring class was ingrained.

"Heck yeah, it should be. Fooled me, and I've walked around this house plenty. See how they painted it gunmetal gray? We better replace the damned thing before it falls to pieces in the next big storm."

Roger lit a cigarette and strolled all the way around the house, examining the eaves and the siding for holes, without success. He unloaded an extension ladder and leaned it against the wall. He ascended the ladder and poked around the vent with a tape measure.

On the ground again, he lowered the truck's tailgate and dragged forth a skinny rectangular box of wire mesh. "Come here and have a look. This is a live trap. Cats, raccoons, skunks. Squirrels, we hope."

Larry walked over as bid. "No joke—it better not be a skunk!"

"You can set this baby up while I'm out."

"Out?"

"Gotta grab a replacement vent at the store. Not like I'm driving around with a spare on me." Roger gestured at the trap. "Anyway. Ever use one of these? Real simple." Whiskey fumes and cigarette smoke seethed from his pores, causing Larry to withdraw a step as the handyman demonstrated how to arm the trigger, which was a metal faceplate inside the trap. Squirrel bait would be laid at the far end. When the critter stepped on the plate, the box would snap shut.

"Don't we need to determine how the squirrel is getting into the attic?" Larry said. "Otherwise, it's an exercise in futility. Yes?"

"Easy, partner," Roger said. "Let me worry over the details. Your siding seems pretty tight So, we'll deal with what we can and continue the search later." He slapped the door panel and zoomed away.

Larry scrounged in Vonda's supplies for a handful of peanuts. Climbing partway into the attic, he whistled to calm his nerves, which were inexplicably frazzled. He placed the trap on a narrow causeway of planks, set the trigger, then pushed the contraption as far as possible with a broom handle.

"What was that tune?" Wanda emerged from the kitchen pantry as Larry washed his hands. "You were humming. What was it?"

"Uh, 'Dang Me'," he said. During the height of his era as a company envoy to overseas buyers, he'd become enamored of karaoke. Willingness to get piss-drunk, loosen one's tie, and slaughter beloved classics in front of a crowd of other inebriated slobs was international diplomacy 101. Especially in Japan, his most frequent travel destination.

"It's by Roger Miller," she said, naming the late-great 1960s country and western singer famous for "King of the Road."

"Yeah."

"That's funny. Ever happen to ask *our* Roger if he listens to the world-renowned Roger?"

"He wouldn't get the joke. Besides, five bucks says he's a Glenn Miller man."

"Shame about Glenn."

"That he died so young?"

"That he vanished."

"In a plane over the English Channel, in winter."

"Doesn't mean he died." She tugged the washcloth from his hand and folded it and hung it on its hook.

"I take the opposing view that dying is all Glenn Miller could've done."

"Sweetie, next you'll try to convince me that Amelia Earhart resides in the spirit realm too. Is death the worst fate you can imagine?"

He hesitated, aware she'd baited and primed a trap of her own. "No?"

"Name one fate worse than death. That doesn't involve your dick."

"I—hmm. Geez, Vonny, I don't know. Social disgrace?"

"Humiliation, eh? Would you sever the tip of your pinky to appease the boss man?"

"Probably not," he said.

"Or commit hari-kari to atone for an egregious faux pas?"

"Stab myself in the stomach?"

"Usually how it's done."

"Obviously. Again, no."

"So, we've established that, for you, fear of death supersedes shame or loss of face."

"Touché, my dear. Touché."

"Hark—Roger's back."

"Which one?" If he expected her to chuckle, he was sorely mistaken.

It proved a hotter than typical autumn afternoon. The sun angled toward the highest peaks and lent them the ominousness of a fairytale watercolor.

Roger unscrewed the old vent and swiftly replaced it with a shiny new metal version. He lingered, his ear pressed to the slats. Afterward, he sat on the bumper of his truck. Sweaty, flushed, and in obvious need of refreshment. "Man, that's odd."

"Odd?" Larry handed him an ice-cold bottle of cola. Probably not the kind of drink his friend wanted.

"Swore I heard…" Roger tipped his head back and swallowed most of the cola in a single draw. His hand trembled. He thanked Larry and got into his truck. "Hey, is Vonda here?"

"She's taking pictures down at the creek. Got the photography bug. All those magazines."

"Huh. When I was fitting the vent in place, I heard somebody call my name. Figured it was her, or the radio."

"The TV in the bedroom might be on."

"Early sign of dementia is hallucinating voices."

"About that squirrel…" Larry said.

"Did you set the trap okay?"

"No problems."

"Keep an eye on it," Roger said. "I'll touch base this week."

"You're a lifesaver."

Two days passed. Larry detected intermittent activity above—a sly rustle, a furtive scratch-scritching. He took the initiative to check the trap. To his chagrin, it remained empty and the bait untouched. On the third morning, Roger walked in, chit-chatted as he drank the last of the coffee, then strapped on a miner's lamp and disappeared into the attic.

Larry paced the hallway. Much as he detested the idea of a rodent lurking overhead, Roger's presence was almost equally unwelcome. There was no reason for Roger to mess with his boxes, no reason for him to pry. Nonetheless, that damned squirrel couldn't jump into the trap soon enough.

Somewhere around the ten-minute mark, Roger thumped against a plank or a beam. Then again, and a third and a fourth time. After an interval of silence came another series of thumps; softer, almost rhythmic. Roger uttered a muffled exclamation. Larry was more confused than worried. He stuck his head through the attic panel to see for himself what the hell was happening.

Partially illuminated by the miner's lamp and the light filtering through the vent, Roger sprawled atop a woman, his face pressed into the hollow of her neck. Jeans lowered; his skinny bare ass shuddered with exertion. She embraced him with slender, pallid limbs. Her eyes shone as she placidly wriggled her tongue through a hole in the side of his skull and removed brain matter the way a kid goes after an ice cream cone. Her tongue was long and sharp at the tip and as death cap-white as her clutching legs. Her funnel mouth caught every drop of blood.

Larry's arms gave way. He collapsed to the floor and then scooted backward until he smacked hard into a wall. His vision grayed and went dark around the edges. Time passed. Roger descended, pale and unsteady. He snugged his ball cap tight, and smiled glassily as he worked to buckle his belt.

"Hey, man," was all Larry could muster.

"No luck." Roger shuddered and his eyes animated slightly. "Tomorrow... We'll get that sucker tomorrow." He lurched to the door. Downstairs, he spoke briefly to Vonda. The front door opened and shut. The truck engine started and gradually dwindled. Meanwhile, Larry remained where he'd fallen, possessed by a horrifying sense of déjà vu.

The ceiling panel scraped and settled into place. Larry, galvanized by terror, leaped to his feet. Stumbling down the stairs, he caught a flash out of his peripheral vision. The hall light blinked twice.

Vonda listened to his panicky account, which he related through gulps of cold water. By the time he finished the glass, exhaustion drained him as well. Already, his description felt like snatches of a receding nightmare. He waited for her reaction.

She selected a copy of *Fortean Times* from a stack of magazines at her end of the table and regarded it. Her fleeting, sardonic smile cooled almost instantly. "I always knew you'd bring something back from one of your business trips." Before he could speak, she amplified her thought. "I was thinking of STDs."

"Sweetheart—"

"You've got a wandering eye."

"Vonny, I've never been unfaithful." His protestation sound desperate and tinny in his own ears. An actor reciting lines from a script.

"That's not quite the same as devotion, is it?"

Larry couldn't formulate a direct response. He set his hat on the table and absently massaged his skull. "We should call...someone." He almost said "Roger" by force of habit.

Her expression suggested *she* might be considering a call to a divorce lawyer or the boys in white coats. Instead, she tossed the magazine aside and stared into the distance. "I watched Roger stroll out the door," she said. "Whistling. Haven't heard him whistle since..."

"Since Lucy."

"Since Lucy."

"Yeah, but what now?" he said, trying to fill the void, as always.

She shrugged. "Who are we to do anything? As long as he's happy."

Larry's thumb found an unexpected softness above his right ear and dipped in. He flinched and uttered an involuntary cry.

"What's the matter?" Vonda said, startled.

"Nothing, sweetheart. Nothing." He gripped the edge of the table to avoid sliding into the abyss. Tears filled his eyes. "I'm happy too."

THE BLOOD IN MY MOUTH

"At first, the sight of death makes you want to puke," Dad said when I was eleven. Without looking, he worked the action of his rifle, chambering a bullet. We crouched in a blind near a swamp. We shared a six-pack of Pabst, waiting on a moose to wander into the killing field. Gnats were fierce, crawling into my collar and ears to bite. Our family hadn't eaten meat in nearly a week.

He'd served with the Marines who held Huế and lost some other places. He was accustomed to waiting and suffering. "Men cry and scream when they see their buddies shot. After a while you get used to it. Get used to anything. You'll be eating a sandwich in the foxhole and a mortar shell explodes nearby and you'll crawl out of the hole and wipe what's left of the guy next to you off your face to make sure all your own parts are still attached. Then you go right on eating lunch."

A few minutes later a cow moose and her calf ambled into view. He dropped them with his 7mm, bang-bang, and we got busy skinning and quartering amid the swamp stink and the swarming bugs. He whistled while he dragged the guts free into steaming piles as high as my knee and the blood overflowed and squelched underfoot. Said we had to work fast and make a lot of noise because a bear would likely come sniffing around the entrails and he'd forgotten to bring the shotgun with the heavy slug loads. Neither of us cared to meet a blackie without the shotgun.

Pop piloted a light cargo plane all across Alaska back in the 1970s. His older brother taught him on a Cessna. Uncle Mike was laid back; he stuck to the well-traveled air lanes and shook his head over Pop's increasingly daredevil exploits, his obsession with conquering the most dangerous airstrips he could find. Bush piloting in Alaska has always been an occupation with a high element of what the old timers call the "pucker factor." The graybeards also said a man had to know when to get shut of the trade because sooner or later he was bound to run out of chances and crack up for good. Didn't faze Pop, though. Nothing ruffled his feathers. He walked away from two out of three crashes and never had much to say. Two out of three ain't bad, am I right?

The only time he ever seemed shaken by something that happened on one of his many flights was after a trip over a certain region, remote even by Alaska standards. Pop swore there were monsters swimming in the depths of Lake Illiamna; a whole pod, big as whales—hell, as big as nuclear submarines. He'd seen them as serpentine blurs beneath the surface from his vantage at five thousand feet.

Pop's description of those pale silhouettes skimming between light and dark stuck in my head. He'd cracked the seal on a bottle of Jim Beam and propped his cowboy boots on the coffee table like Mom hated. His shaggy hair and mustache were black, his face burnt-copper from the glare, white patches around his eyes from his favorite set of amber-tinted aviator glasses. His teeth were bright white with a couple of gaps. A scar creased his brow. He'd fought a lot in his youth. Violence gave him a measure of joy that he'd lost after the war ended and only discovered again in wilderness flight.

That night I dreamed of paddling the lake in a canoe. I'd not been there in real life, never even seen a picture, so my imagination did the heavy lifting: an inland sea covered in swirls of mist from Arthurian legend, there was no end to it. The canoe sprung a slow leak and icy water sloshed around my ankles, then my shins, coming on fast.

A rotor whined and the shadow of a great bird floated across the void and the voice of darkness spoke into my ear, behind me as if from a distance, yet right there nonetheless. I don't remember what it said, not sure I *ever* knew on a conscious level. The voice boomed, a garble of alien tongues and electromagnetic waves, colder than the ice bobbing near the shore. It was in dialogue with my cells. The creepily adult thought occurred to me that I was receiving a message from myself beamed across a gulf between realities. A Bizarro Universe me resonating at peak potential. Maybe it was Pop's ghost a few years before the fact. Or maybe it was mine. They say, and I have little reason to quibble, that the universe cycles through itself. It is, as the Lake Illiamna of my dreams, endlessly repeating.

I told Mom the next day, that I was going to die on Iliamna when I got old. Mom laughed her nervous laugh and said not to be silly. Wasn't until much later as we were hanging around after Dad's funeral and she got plastered on scotch and confessed to having the same recurring nightmare during her own youth.

"You dreamed you were going to drown in Lake Illiamna?" I said, also pretty goddamned drunk.

"No, I dreamed my son would." She slugged another double and collapsed in the bathroom. We had to take the door off its hinges to get her out of there.

She returned to Plumtree, made famous by Robert Service, to be with her mother and sisters in the shade of the most baroquely majestic magnolia you ever did see.

O! Dark days followed with nary a ray of sun to shine on this dog's ass. I lived with one uncle or another until state law cut my traces and then it was cheap apartments and boarding houses, the bunk in a fishing boat or a tent on some gods forsaken remote surveying site. I slept under my share of pool tables and overpasses when times were lean. Slept under the cold, pitiless stars enough to have the sentimentality for god and nature and the great unknown seared from me. I think a little gangrene seeped in, though.

It's been a lifetime and I still hum "Killing an Arab" as I shuffle along the beach with a gun in my hand. When wrath moves me I hum Poe's "Angry Johnny" too, although the life-sustaining rage is gone, drained into the swamp whence it first came bubbling. I stare at the stars, the flat obsidian back of the sea rolling away toward the moon. The moon gets closer every night.

I died this evening. A hard, bad death. Not the worst thing that's ever happened to me.

Look, back in the day I was crazy too. Quite literally mad in the technical sense—undiagnosed Bipolar One disorder. That's from Mom's side of the tree. Mood swings like a motherfucker. High as a kite one minute, crashed on the rocks and sinking fast the next. Nobody understood what was going on, least of all me, hick kid from the utter north; holes in my Sorrel boots and chip on my shoulder and not an ounce of introspection to spare. Hate in all its black splendor was my gift. I put that slow-burning rage down to the natural order of things; my people were Scots-Irish with a bit of Comanche in the old pile somewhere. Poverty, stiff-neckedness, and wrath coursed in the blood. Champion grudge holders and enthusiastic brawlers; hard drinkers and hard luck cases, God bless us every one. Never occurred to me it might be something more purely chemical, or something invasive, cancerous. In any event, my youth was one long self-obliterating rampage.

At the nadir of this meteoric descent, the girl of my dreams swooped in for the kill. I was twenty-two, just like the caliber. You had to be careful where you pointed me.

First time I met Erica was a few minutes before my participation in a bare-knuckle boxing match in a deserted gravel lot behind the plant where we worked as seasonal labor packing frozen salmon into boxes and shipping them to Japan. The whole seething lot of us was drunk. Those of us who were residents had to be to get through the eighteen-hour workday, the 365 days a year soul-killing sojourn in Alaska. The hangers-on were drunk because it was the only way we could all speak the same language.

She watched me from the edge of the crowd of migrant workers and hobos and boggle-eyed college kids who'd flown up from the continental US to pay their tuition freight, get a bit of seasoning before scuttling back to their daddies' companies and beach houses. A chum rubbed my shoulders while I sat on a bucket and traded devil dog glares with my opponent across the way. Meanwhile, the dayshift foreman took wagers on the back of an envelope and occasionally conferred with his accomplice, the company QA, via walkie talkie. The accomplice lurked down the street of that industrial arena, on the lookout for airport police strayed from their normal cruising territory.

"Great anger I sense in this one," Erica said, sounding like our man Yoda on a bender, but I didn't care. She wore sweats and a tattered Blue Oyster Cult tee a size too large, yet snug nonetheless. Her tits mesmerized me, an anesthetizing image for the beating I was soon to receive. As a friend of mine commented later, her boobs were like two puppies fighting under a blanket. Thank God, Satan, the great Earth Mother, or whomever imbues certain nubile young women with gravity-defying double-dees and moral retardation. She chugged from a forty bottle of Steel Reserve and her eyes burned like the witchiest-bitchiest of Dracula's brides appraising the latest dinner guest.

Well.

Guy named Red from the loading dock had agreed to be my opponent. Nothing personal, the guy had a heart of gold; like everybody else, he needed the scratch. Red was a tough kid on loan from Miami; a survivor of gang turf wars. The scars on his barrel chest and pylon legs were thick as horse brands gone wrong. He slung two hundred and fifty-pound boxes of fish into shipping containers for his daily bread. A behemoth with fists the circumference and density of cinderblocks. Me, I was underweight, though wiry as a feral dog. The usual mismatch. I fought monsters in the pits. The brutes who were as mean as me, but bigger and better fed. There weren't any other takers. Nobody in his right mind willingly fights a man who's in it for the pain. The taste of blood in my mouth was an old friend.

On the other hand, money talks, yes it does, and to look at me was to underestimate the power of rage and primitive impulse. So Red and I went at it hammer and tongs there in the middle of the lot on a blazing-hot afternoon in July, our supporters shouting nonsensical encouragement while everybody else hooted and jeered and tried not to get splashed by blood and spit—most of the blood was mine. If not for the ring of truck grills I would've rolled out of there, a cartoon character shot from a cannon. Instead, Red settled for smashing me into the ground.

Luckily, the airport police received a tip about a street fight and a gathering mob and sent a patrol car to investigate. The QA lookout radioed the foreman and warned everybody to scram. Red stopped slamming my head against the bumper of a rusted Ford and took to his heels. Who would think a dude so girthy could flee with the agility of a deer? Our happy crew scattered, the match called on account of the fuzz. Final tally on my ledger was a missing tooth, rearranged nose, and a concussion that lingered for nearly two weeks. Also, minus the seventy-five bucks I'd put down on myself. Yeah, I was a little closer every day to remaking myself into Pop's image. All I had left to do was to make sure I died young.

Erica took me to her apartment and licked my wounds. I guess that put me in the black.

She strapped on the goggles, tipped the saké, and went kamikaze from day zero of our relationship.

Vodka, the cheaper the better. Microdot.

Ouija boards.

Tantric sex in a big way.

More vodka.

Choking games. The hard end of the belt.

Violence, yeah. Lots of violence. Feral or not, I was a pussycat by comparison to my new girlfriend. For her, drop of a hat and it was Go Time.

One cold September evening we packed a bottle of Stoli and a blanket that belonged to her late great dog Achilles and cruised to a bonfire/windsurfing party at Settler's Bay where she wound up beating the tar out of some poor surfer chick over territorial pissing. When the chick's boyfriend stepped in, Erica socked him too. Her fistful of death's head and gemstone rings made a sweet little knuckleduster that tore the guy's face wide open. I had to drag her back to the truck before the mob of surfer dudes and dudettes stomped us.

She slid aside her panties and fucked me on the drive home. No mean feat considering how cramped the cab of that half-ton pickup was. I almost flew my rig off the twisty road between Knik and Wasilla more than once. Girl was totally insane. Honky-tonk blues blasting on the radio, her nipple in my mouth, her face pressed into the roof of the cab, hands in my hair, both of my own hands clamped on her ass instead of the wheel, a hundred miles an hour in the dark.

I was young enough not to understand, arrogant enough not to care.

She dyed her hair so often I didn't figure out she was blonde for the first six months. Taller than me and curvy, but sort of muscular. She'd played soccer and rugby at college. Wouldn't tell me her major. I'm not going to say what school because it doesn't matter. College was over for her by a couple of years and I'd never gone. Her nose was a tiny bit crooked from getting broken during a scrum. Sexy, though, unlike my own near disfigurement.

Her family roots were Welsh and she had something of the moors about her; an aura of mystery. Pale as winter sand, she bruised easily. She favored rugby sweaters and track pants or old ripped jeans with bloodstains ground in most of the time; autumn colors. Funky glittery eye-shadow but no lip gloss, no perfume. I got to know her scent the way dogs do with one another. A soap and water girl. Mine, for a while, then through my fingers like the blood from my mouth after one of life's sucker punches.

Good thing pain is my thing.

Between and during marathon bouts of sex and booze we dropped blotter and listened to The Toadies, Poe, and The

Cure. A hell of a lot of The Cure, I remember that. "A Forest" was my theme in those days. Erica possessed eclectic taste in the arts. She jolted me out of my redneck roots with Bob Dylan, Procul Harum, Linda Ronstadt, The Clash. Bosch, Bacon, Dali, and Pollock at his maddest. *Don Quixote* was her novel of novels; *The Wizard of Oz* was her movie. *Oz* for the deleted scenes, the Hanged Man legend, the febrile luminescence of Judy Garland's flesh, the deep space chill of her eyes like something written by Clark Ashton Smith.

That fucking guy. Erica introduced me to Smith's work via a ratty paperback anthology she toted in her knapsack. Told me CAS had been her mom and dad's fave author since the Stone Age, that his baroque nihilism brought them together when they were undergrads at university. She preferred H.P. Lovecraft, although she didn't elaborate why.

Her little brother Isaiah died in a theme park accident. That was an off-limits topic. We talked about god, the cosmos, mankind's minute presence in the infinite sea of flaming gas and absolute zero, the meaning of it all, nothing really important.

Sometimes after pounding a boilermaker or two I'd dream again, a rare occurrence since my nightmares of Iliamna. In the distance reared a city with spires of dirty-black ice surmounted by clouds of gas that boiled upward through a hole into outer space. Others were of a Ferris Wheel on fire and rolling across a dawn plain like the wheel of the Death God's Chariot come loose. Erica loomed, tall as a skyscraper, watching the wheel go. Her skin glowed faintly, reflecting fire and flashes of distant lightning. A whip made of barb wire and logging chain hung from her fist. It gouged a furrow into the earth when she turned and strode toward me until the sun unfolded over her shoulder and struck me blind.

S he asked me once if I *ever* won any of my fights.

"All of them," I said. "Except the one against the Law."

"Moral victories are draws at best."

"What can I say? Pyrrhic Victories R Us. Masada is my handbook for daily living."

We were on the road to see her parents at their place in Moose Pass, a tiny town half an hour north of Seward. This was late March and bitter cold, making the journey a perilous one. Together for nine months and I still didn't know much. Such essential cluelessness would prove a recurring life theme.

All along Erica had been cagey regarding her family, choosing to change the subject whenever the conversation swung around to her childhood. Then, in a bolt from the heavens, after giving me an impassioned and impromptu blow job at the Wendy's drive-thru, she paused to stare at herself in the rearview mirror. Her expression was strange. She declared that perhaps the time was nigh to pay homage at court. Her eyes glittered with that light I'd initially attributed to mischievousness and booze. Full-on devilry, full-on insanity more like.

Thus, three days later, we were bundled into the cab of my old truck and slip-sliding along the treacherous Seward Highway while the wind buffeted and the snow whirled and The Fixx sang about how one thing leads to another. She gave me my mission briefing along the way.

Erica called her folks Rob and Willy (short for Wilhelmina) and seemed rather conflicted about them. I had the feeling she adored and hated them in equal measure. They were retired government workers who lived in a doublewide trailer at the Emperor Penguin Court, had once owned a mansion and a spread in Southern California but moved north due to job opportunities and fear of earthquakes. Of course, the Coleridges were to be disappointed on the latter front as Alaska got rocked by more earthquakes than any other state in the Union. Land of Ten Thousand Smokes, leading edge of the Pacific Rim's fabled Ring of Fire.

I wondered if she had any special advice for me—any inflammatory topics to veer away from? Any pet peeves to avoid petting by mistake? She laughed and told me to act however I wanted. Her parents didn't give a shit. Willy and Rob inhabited their own private universe. This was a day pass. She made me pull into a supermarket on the outskirts of Anchorage to snag steaks and salad. Her parents didn't keep food in the house, only liquor. She wasn't sure if they could stomach solid food, but it was worth a try.

We arrived at the Coleridge manse in one piece and I felt right the hell at home. A dead Christmas tree lay in the front yard where Rob had chucked it to make room for company. The wreath still hung on the front door, the cheap lights still twinkled in the eaves. Thick shag rugs in every room but the kitchen and bathroom; velvet hangings of voluptuous nudes reclining among prides of lions juxtaposed a black and white poster of Carl Sagan behind the television and a gaudy painting of a Mayan ziggurat enveloped in purple lightning made one hell of sensory-shocking triptych on the living room wall.

Erica wasn't kidding about the no-food situation. Liquor bottles crammed every cabinet. Empties overflowed the wastebaskets, milk crates of them were piled in the hall. When her parents weren't looking, Erica nodded at me and flipped open the oven. More empty bottles.

"Holy shit," I said, impressed.

Rob and Willy were moles recently emerged from a subterranean habitat: pale and soft and dressed in pajamas. Their thick eyeglasses reflected the meager light. The couple spent six months of the year at a timeshare condo Rob had finagled during happier times. Both were semi-expert blackjack players and haunted the Vegas Strip, guzzling comped booze and winning and losing meager fortunes until it was time to migrate north and hibernate again.

According to Erica, the pair usually woke around midafternoon and started drinking to kill the previous night's hangover and played innumerable hands of twenty-one, each armed with a mason jar of pennies and nickels to cover their wagers. The drinking and gambling ritual wasn't interrupted by our arrival. Erica sprawled on the couch and watched me sip tallboys and get snared into a marathon blackjack session. I took them for fourteen dollars in change. Willy scoffed when I attempted to decline the loot. She stuffed all those coins into a sock and made Erica put it in her purse. I didn't argue. Much as it pained me to exploit a couple of pickled geezers, I needed the gas money.

For a while nobody said much and I got the distinct impression Erica wasn't exactly in their good graces, nor had lugging home a ne'er do well such as myself done much to improve the climate. It was so frigid in the trailer we could've used the services of one of those icebreaker ships. A golf tournament played on TV and the clock radio was tuned to college basketball, both of which the Coleridges had money riding on. Willy dealt the cards, occasionally pausing to lean toward the commentary, swear under her breath, and scratch totals into a ratty notebook. Rob kept the booze coming and responded to Erica's queries about the recent blizzards and frozen water pipes with grunts and shrugs. He seldom lifted his bleary gaze from the table, studying the array of cards with tremendous intensity.

During a break in the action, while the couple exchanged monosyllabic insults over some point of contention, either regarding blackjack or the broadcasts, I wasn't clear, Erica spirited me away to her old room. I gathered it sat untouched since she originally left for college. Kind of dusty and cobwebby and it smelled stale, although not bad after the cigarette smoke stench that permeated the rest of the trailer. Admittedly, I was curious to learn more about my woman of mystery.

The fossil record of a typical childhood: Lite Brite and Etch a Sketch and stars painted on the ceiling; stacks of Cosmopolitan and Seventeen and a poster of Mick Jagger as a sweet young thing. A trove of costume jewelry gleamed atop the vanity and at the foot of the single bed was a dog pillow, leash and collar. The rabies vaccination tag on the collar said Achilles. She kept a picture of Achilles in a locket around her neck: a family scene in the woods—Erica ten or eleven, Rob and Willy in mackinaws and hip waders, and the dog at their feet. A brute with lots of teeth and a lolling tongue. Made me think of White Fang. No sign of brother Isaiah, oddly enough.

"Man, when did you move out?" I said, eying a parti-colored DNA model and slide rule gathering dust next to a stuffed panda that appeared to be a prize from some Alaska State Fair of yore. I edged away, paranoid she might try to make a move on me there in that musty tomb. The wheels were always turning in her brain, powering a carousel of agendas. Shagging me ten feet from the kitchen while her parents swilled liquor and squabbled over point spreads was her kind of kink, but a bridge too far for my taste.

"After Achilles died. A long time ago." That peculiar light inhabited her eyes again. She cocked her head in manner reminiscent of Willy's habitual gesture, listening to her parents' muffled argument, the faint exclamations of the announcers. "I went to college ahead of schedule. Full ride, so why not? Anything to get the hell away from here."

"Yeah, you and your full ride. What was it for, anyway?" I'd asked before; this time she humored me.

"I wrote a paper. Some stuffed shirts liked it. Voila."

I hefted the DNA model. "Must've been a hell of a paper."

"Yep. It detailed the effects of bong hits of Matanuska Thunderfuck

127

on the female libido. Where are you going? Why are you trying to escape?"

She was smart, that I knew, despite the fact she preferred to show the world a bruiser and boozer persona. Smart isn't even the right term—brilliant, genius, savant…Pick one of those and you'd be closer the mark. Erica had a photographic memory. List a sequence of phone numbers, book passages, whatever, she'd roll her eyes and recite them in a mechanical voice that sounded like the computerized time and temp recording. She could quote the entire dialogue of any film she'd ever seen, and did so on occasion when she was in the mood to drive me batshit. One of her favorite moods, in fact.

She had a will to self-destruction, was the problem. If not destruction definitely a kind of violent apathy. I was afraid to dig much deeper. Afraid and selfish. See, I liked how things were going between us for the most part. She didn't care that I was broke and without prospects. A low-maintenance chick in regards to material objects. Stupid, callow me, I thought that was a bargain. I recognized the Devil and the deep blue sea, but not that I was caught between them or that the water was rising like in that old Johnny Cash song or my dream of canoeing the lake.

"Did you know we're made of dead stars?" she said. "We're always sloughing off detritus and rebuilding ourselves. Every ten years you're basically a brand new person."

I admitted my ignorance of that factoid.

"Ah, so. Then you should also know I've done something to you. Not me, my electromagnetic field is kind of…Well it's kind of fucked up, I guess you'd say. My best bet is, yours is fubar too. CTD…cosmically transmitted disease. Osmosis, sweetie. We destroy the ones we love."

She caught me and stuck her tongue in my ear and had my belt mostly unlooped before I could react. Then she pushed me away, laughed and said, "What, you think I'd fuck you in my old bedroom while my parents are sitting outside? Get real, dude." She walked back into the kitchen, left me standing there with my pants down and a raging hardon.

Willy sobered enough to sear the steaks on a griddle and Rob found a mismatched set of glasses to fill with a nice Chablis they'd set aside for the occasion, and for a few minutes we sat around the rickety table in the 1960s kitchen and enjoyed a quiet dinner almost like a regular family. I got the feeling it was the first time in ages for any of us.

After the dishes were cleared, Rob turned his yellowed eyes on me and said, "So, kid. Any big plans?"

Erica clenched her knife and smiled at her dad. "Don't do it."

"She means it, Robert," Willy said, lighting a cigarette. Her dreamy tone sharpened into something menacing.

"Ah, come on. He's sniffing around my daughter like a hound dog. Be nice to know if his intentions are honorable."

"Your daughter can take care of herself," Willy said. "It's the boy we should worry about."

"What's to worry about? Erica, you break the news to Fido here? Bet not, judging by the sappy expression he's wearing."

Willy said, "Robert, shut your mouth. Honey, put the knife down."

Rob laughed a nasty drunken laugh, but he shut up and focused on his empty plate.

Erica set the knife aside. She stood and grabbed her coat. She said to me, "Let's go."

I didn't argue. Two feet of fresh snow piled on the road, and beneath that, black ice. A safer prospect than remaining in the trailer for the imminent brouhaha.

White-knuckled the one-hundred-plus-mile drive home. Made

it safe and sound, although, as Rob might've opined, that simply delayed the inevitable.

Spring came creeping on muddy little muskrat feet and we spent a long afternoon chucking crap from the apartment into the bed of my truck for a garbage run. When Erica tossed a box of her old journals and the high-powered telescope onto the pile, my ears pricked up. She kept the telescope near the sliding door to the back deck and used it to watch the stars on clear nights. She frequently jotted notes into a logbook. I asked what the notes were for and she ruffled my hair and told me to crack another beer like a good boy.

I couldn't help but feel her mood to purge was bound to include me sooner or later. Among the outgoing was a photo album. Pictures of the family in various California settings, one of Rob dressed in a suit giving a lecture at a packed assembly hall with the NASA seal on the wall behind his podium. He was lean and sharp, mouth twisted in wrath, index finger stabbing toward the camera. Definitely not the wasted, basted guy I'd recently met. I hid it in a footlocker with my old collection of pulp and western paperbacks. In the back of my mind I was thinking she'd be grateful someday. Even farther back, nearer my animal part, lurked some nameless motivation, a longing, and fear.

Alaska is a damned big, empty place bordered by Nowhere. Between frigid temperatures and snowfalls ass-deep to a giraffe, it has the weapons to kill anything more complex than a rock. Civilization exists in tiny, disenfranchised pockets surrounded by a howling void. Basically, it's the universe in microcosm.

There's always been plenty of tinfoil hat theories and superstitious legends to go along with all that frozen tundra—lost radar sites fronting for secret nuclear launch silos aimed at Russia; FEMA concentration camps for the inevitable apocalypse; UFO observation bases; etc., etc.

One day I was reading an article in the paper about the HAARP Project and the author's claim that how instead of improving communication or navigation systems the device was actually a bunker-busting ray being prepared for deployment against the various militia compounds scattered across the state. I laughed and pointed it out to Erica, hoping to josh her out of the funk she'd fallen into for the past several weeks.

Didn't have the effect I'd hoped for—instead, she stared at the article, then at me with that laser beam intensity she saved for her more sadistic moments. Her eyes were puffy. She'd abruptly stopped drinking and taking dope, which might've signaled a positive development under normal circumstances or with a normal person. Alas, this was altogether different with her; it heralded a deeper, more ominous stage of whatever she was going through. She said, "Well, of course that's bullshit. It's probably something worse. There's always something worse."

We didn't talk for nearly a week. I worked days at a construction site, hauling sheetrock and digging trenches. I'd drag ass home to a TV dinner and a six-pack of suds while she hunched at the opposite end of the couch, still dressed in her PJs, glued to NOVA. I didn't have a clue what to say, so I slumped in my work clothes and drank silently while fear burrowed ever deeper and made its nest in my brain. When feverish sleep enfolded me, I dreamed of drowning and of fire.

Finally, it came to a head. Erica kicked me out of bed before dawn and herded me to the truck while the sky was still slashed with stars. She refused to answer questions except to say we were going on a picnic; told me to shut my trap and drive. I did, still half drunk, eyes swollen mostly shut. Occasionally I stole glances at her—she was bundled in a dark flannel coat and a knitted cap and she wore a pair of wraparound sunglasses rendering her expression inscrutable.

Daylight burned away the shadows as we climbed onto the gravel access road that winds through Hatcher Pass. In the sourdough days there were hard rock mines and a series of tough and tumble camps. In my time the mines were long gone and the territory was deserted but for moose and fox and the ptarmigans that roosted in the crags and among the patches of tough alder and willow. Tourists from the Lower Forty-eight flocked to the hills in July to photograph the Dall sheep that capered along the cliffs. Magnificent beasts, those sheep. As a kid, I saw one of the poor fuckers, a big old ram ambling in the sun, trip on a loose rock and plummet into a crevasse and I wondered if any of the goddamned tourists had ever caught a pic of that side of Mother Nature. The Alaska they don't show you on the travel brochures.

She made me park on the shoulder of the road. From there we scrambled down and walked across a field of tundra and moss and blueberry bushes that wouldn't flower for a few weeks yet. The sun scorched us as it rolled over the peak and a sharp breeze whistled through the looming icecaps and reminded me that the deathly hand of winter never truly departed the northlands; it only withdrew up its own sleeve, biding for the short span of summer to end.

I was getting nervous. This being Alaska (and me a paranoid, delusional fuck), murder/rape capital per capita of the US, and famous for people blowing a fuse and whacking whole towns, my animal self went on red alert, not so casually scrutinizing her every move, half-expecting her to swing up the .38 auto I knew she stashed in her dresser and take a crack at me. Why would she do such a thing you might wonder? Didn't need to be a motive. Not in AK. Strange things were done in the Land of the Midnight Sun and only the Devil knew why.

Erica walked in front, a rucksack slung over her shoulder. Sack had a faded red hobo patch on the side. She'd packed chicken sandwiches and wine. The bottles clinked as she picked her way across an icy stream, hopping from rock to rock to keep her boots dry. She moved with the ungainly grace of a raven and when she glanced over her shoulder at me, her eyes were diamond cold as the eyes of the totem in front of Wasilla City Hall.

Atop a big flat rock that teetered near the precipice of a gulf into blue mist we made our stand and had the first bottle of eight-dollar wine, and after it was gone, or mostly, she scared me by suddenly cupping her hands to her mouth and shouting for Achilles over and over. "He's out here, somewhere," she said, taking my silence for inquiry. "Rob said a dog couldn't make the trip, that the chemical composition of the doggie brain made it a no go. I figured he was lying. Rob would definitely lie. He hated Achilles." She called for a long time.

For one giddy, hysterical moment her hollering for the ghost dog was too goddamned much to endure and I thought of pushing her over the edge. Quick boot to the ass was all it would've taken. Doesn't everybody have that thought, though? That morbid fantasy of how easy it'd be shiv a loved one in his or her sleep, to slip drain cleaner into his or her soup, to shove him or her off a ledge. Isn't it related to that freaky impulse to hurl ourselves off ledges, to spin the wheel of our sports car into the path of a dump truck? To fall in love?

Eventually I asked her what we were doing there on the side of the mountain. She rested her hands on her knees and regarded me. Her face was flushed. She said, "I'm trying to remember where it is."

"Where *what* is?"

"*Our* Plymouth Rock. *Our* Northwest Passage. My father's New

World. It's right around here, somewhere. Too early to hit the next bottle?"

"Your folks wouldn't say so."

"Cut the comedy. You ain't no Bill Hicks, boy."

I took the final swallow of the wine as a tribute to the departed legend. "Baby, what the hell is going on?"

"I'm trying to explain. Ever notice I spell Kalifornia with a K?"

"Yeah, and you cross your sevens like the Europeans. Kinda fancy for a chick from the trailer park, but who am I to judge, huh?"

"Um, hm. You think it's an affectation."

"I don't know what that word means."

"Rob and Willy were big wheels in Kalifornia. The government took care of everything—that's how important Mom and Pop were. Their brains were so powerful they could squash you with mind power. We were rich bitches back in Kal. Back in Kal I had a nanny, three tutors, a bodyguard/driver named Beasley, my own private rugby field. Back in Kal, Beasley drove me to an exclusive school in an armor-plated Cadillac. Back in Kal my pals were baby diplomats and shithead junior CEOs in training bras. The Secretary of State and a bunch of his cronies flocked to Rob's barbeques. I spelled my own name with a K. Erika. Oh, what a scene it was, in Kal. Only problem was, we were all doomed. Voyager broadcasting its dinner bell wasn't the brightest idea Mankind ever had. First contact didn't turn out so great. Turned out kind of like when driver ants march through the jungle munching every living thing that doesn't get clear fast. We didn't even get the fancy technological gifts or the fucking cookbook. Then again, what do you expect from a species that seeps down from cracks between the stars, huh?" As she spoke she loomed over me and a static charge built in the folds of my clothes and my hair stood on end.

I'd read a smidgeon of Nietzsche. I recognized an abyss when

I saw one. Her eyes gave me vertigo, scared me in that instant a thousand times to the power of ten more than anything CAS or HPL ever said. I was an animal in the presence of a dark wonder and all my masochistic resilience, my uncanny talent for taking a punch to the mouth, couldn't help me now.

"No, baby, nothing can help you now," she said. "Everything you believe is a lie. It's bullshit down to the quark. Come on. Let's keep walking."

We kept walking, and walking. Picked our way downslope until we arrived in the shadow of an overhanging cliff. Here was a hollow much obliterated by high school graffiti and shards of busted beer bottles from many campfire parties. Farther back was an aperture and a set of rusted metal doors thrown wide to reveal a moldy tunnel into darkness. It put me in mind of a bomb shelter, although I wasn't aware of any such structure in the region—the nearest bunkers were quietly crumbling a thousand miles south in the Aleutians.

"X marks the spot," she said and gripped my wrist with bone-crushing force. She gestured with her free hand, illustrating the scene: "Rob didn't invent the technology. Smart, not *that* smart. Uncle Kahart made the breakthrough—not really my uncle, he was just around so much, too bad the coot didn't make it through before…well, oh well. Nah, Rob is an opportunist, a two-legged coyote. He put apple and pi together and saw our way out of a super bad situation."

I didn't understand and told her so. Erica shrugged and said she didn't either except in the vaguest sense. Quantum physics wasn't her area of expertise like Rob, or particle physics like Willy. Blow jobs and lit theory, yeah. She said, "Isaiah died two weeks before Uncle Kahart threw the switch on his supercollider Tesla coil space and time machine. Two damned weeks. Yeah. What say we lay our coats down and do it on glass? You game?" Her diamond eyes were glossy. Had she ever cried in front of me? Hell if I could remember.

"Let me think on it—no." The bunker, the burned-out fires and spray paint scrawls reminded me of something. A legend or a curse that evaporated when I tried to haul it into the light. Something about a weird place the kids went to on a dare, an abandoned government lab where the ETs still visited in their saucers.

She said, "Oops, I forgot to tell you not to wear that watch. It's royally screwed. Now, lookee here. I've gotten closer and closer. I'm getting good."

And while I tapped the blank quartz face of my suddenly non-functioning timepiece, she walked right up to the threshold of the doors and bowed her head and spread her arms in a Jesus Christ pose.

Pebbles rattled and began to rise along with shards of glass and small sticks. This mass revolved around her in a funnel that continued to extend vertically. A shadow covered Erica's face and she slowly levitated until her shoe tips lifted from the ground. A black nimbus radiated from her like bad reception on TV sometimes causes images to distort and the entrance to the bunker warped and opened wider and I glimpsed flecks of stars turning and turning and got an impression that photocopies of my love were stacked atop one another and spiraling outward toward the galactic core. Then I shouted and she fell in a hail of glass and stones and the shadow whisked from her and she opened her eyes and stared at me. Blood made snail trails from her eyes, nose and ears. She was oblivious to that. "Do you see? Do you see?"

I couldn't speak. A foot between us, a million light years between us. The wind blew cold between us and a belt of coagulated stars sludged by. Whirling in *my* brain this time.

She swept her hand across her face and like a magician pulling a trick, the clouds parted and she smiled brilliantly, and oh it matched her eyes. "This was a stupid idea. Go ahead and assume I forgot to take my meds."

"Sure, baby," I said. In hindsight I should've said something else.

She left me a few days after the Hatcher Pass incident. Left everyone.

I crawled in from a ballbuster of a day and there was a note pinned to the fridge. *Going to get my dog. Love, E.* She left everything behind except her backpack and survival goodies, and the pistol. Probably hitched her way along the Parks Highway. None of our friends had seen her. Fortunately for me, a market video caught her buying bottled water and sundries in Palmer while I was miles away on a job. Because you know there were a lot of questions when she never returned. No answers but the tick of the clock in my room, the wind rubbing against the walls.

The Pixies spoke of a wave of mutilation. More like a wave of disintegration. The crack that runs through everything reaches across all time and space, travels jaggedly through all past and all potentiality. It is the slow fracture in the ice, the worm coring its way through the apple, coring the human heart. It is the following shadow.

I continued onward for years and years. Got married, if you can believe it. And to a wonderful woman who was far too good for me. It lasted longer than it had any right to, long enough that when the marriage collapsed with tears and recriminations, so ended my always tenuous connection to humanity. I wandered the earth, snarling, claws out.

My body was totaled by this point. Bad back, arthritis of

everything, tinnitus in one ear, bum knee, and chronic fatigue. I was scarred and scorched from sun and wind, the blows of daily travails. Crawling out of my bedroll each morning was a fifteen-minute session of alternately begging and cursing God. I started drinking in earnest, staggering from one series of dead-end labor jobs to the next. I withered until I became my essential self, a brute and a beast.

One night in a saloon in Dutch Harbor I got shanked while arguing with two locals over cards. A guy in a red and black lumberjack shirt stuck me with a serrated skinning knife, twice. Felt about the same as a light blow from a fist against my ribs, except so much deeper and colder. The joint was hopping, The Charlie Daniels Band booming from the speakers, sawdust and blurry strings of light, sloshing beer and my blood pouring down my leg and into my boot. Nobody paid me a lick of mind.

I walked outside and kept on going off the end of the boardwalk. This was late summer, so the big, rounded hills bordering the port were slowly vanishing beneath gauzy purple brushstrokes, but the sea and sky mirrored one another in a white blaze. I sat abruptly in a ditch, the tractor that dug it cold and still a few feet away, and gazed into the muck and scum that lay upon the bottom. The two fellows from the tavern came upon me there and kicked me until I lay face down in the mud. One of them held my ankles while the other stood on my neck.

I didn't struggle as much as you might suppose. Too weak, too sad, too sick of the whole rigmarole.

After what seemed an age, I climbed up out of the ditch and watched the murderers with their victim. As in the saloon, none paid me any heed. I turned west and moved like an arrow to the night water.

Yes, I searched for her all those years ago when she vanished into the ether. Of course, I searched. She was my love. I drove along dark and desolate highways and winding dirt back roads, checking every culvert, every ditch. I prowled unlighted paths among the black spruce of hill and marsh.

I returned to Hatcher Pass and retraced the steps that led us into the shadow of the mountain vault. Nothing inside except dust and guano, the remnants of hobo fires. I could've sworn the soot had crystallized upon one wall as the silhouette of a person in profile. My flashlight was dying and I had to leave.

Home again, I got wasted and lay around flipping through her photo album. The plastic was so cold it burned my fingers. Toward the back were several pages of pictures that obviously had been shot on a Hollywood film set; some kind of blockbuster fantasy-science fiction mashup. Hovercars, soldiers in bubble helmets toting elaborate ray guns, gargantuan and baroque structures. A weird-ass moon that dominated the sky in a sickening fashion.

The phone rang. Rob was on the line. He sounded way drunk, yet unnervingly lucid. "There's nothing back there where we came from. A skeleton world in a universe sliding toward heat death. It was the end of days. *They* arrived and they ate everybody. Kid, you hearing me?"

I was hearing him, unfortunately. I chugged booze right from the neck and that didn't help.

He said, "You gotta die to go back an' if you go back you die. She went back and she's dead." He was silent, then he sobbed and I heard the unmistakable clatter of glass against glass and ice cubes spinning like lotto balls. "This place doesn't possess the technology to build what we'd need…and the only man in this universe or the next who could put it all together had his brains vacuumed out a trillion light years from here. If I had the Machine, I'd go find her. Believe it, kid."

I waited him out. Then I said in a voice thick with grief and alcohol poisoning, "Could I do it?"

"Do what?"

"Could I…Walk to wherever she went? She thought I might be able to."

"Sure. Sure, you could. Gotta understand that your physical body won't make the trip. It's them twenty-one grams constituting the primal *you* that will pull the freight. Boy, just don't. You'll be dissolved like a tab of antacid in the guts of a whale. The real you, snuffed. Or worse, you'll make the crossing and reach where we fled from." He stopped and sobbed uncontrollably. Finally he said goodbye and hung up. We never spoke again.

I step onto the sea and begin to walk toward distant twin hemispheres cresting the horizon. One black, one white. They radiate fearsome energy and a sound—angels, devils, damned souls, singing and screaming. I am a seed floating within the grip of a current, capable of steering down one fork in the stream or the other, and little more.

I choose the black sun because it's a cavity in reality and it's where she went a billion years ago, thirty years ago, seconds ago. Passing through the portal is to step through a doorway into the violence of a blizzard, a blast furnace. The angels and the demons chorus and if I had blood and flesh it would surely boil from every millimeter of me.

Then for an eon there is the void, smooth and cool as the barrel of a rifle. I sail weightless at a velocity greater than the speed of light. I am a tachyon knifing through the fibers of space and time, a star hurled from the hand of a vengeful god toward the heart of everything. I am drawn with inexorable finality toward her spark in the endless gulf of night.

I fall from the sky with the impact of a meteor, and find myself trudging through the ruins of a forest. All is gray and cold. Ash swirls around me and lies in a thigh deep blanket upon the ground. Great trees have been uprooted and scattered. This is Tunguska, Siberia. Perhaps not my Tunguska, but someone's nonetheless. After a while I leave the forest and enter a plain. It too is covered in ash. Mountains rise in the distance, and the outlines of the city from my nightmares. No longer walking, I'm projected forward like a thought.

She awaits me atop a foothill in the shadow of the range. She is as I remember her. Her flesh is cold as arctic ice, her eyes…And the inimitable Achilles crouches at her side. The beast is red and black. His gaze is the gaze of the basilisk.

She smiles and reaches toward me. Her whisper carries across the gulf. "You made it."

I want to say that I love her, have always loved her, will always love her, here and in every universe. But the sky blackens directly overhead and I think of Damocles and of the man in red plaid, his boot descending to crush my life.

Her finger brushes my lips, shushing me. She embraces me and says, "Don't say anything and maybe it'll stay like this forever."

I'm a fool, but not a damn fool and I keep my mouth shut. So maybe it does.

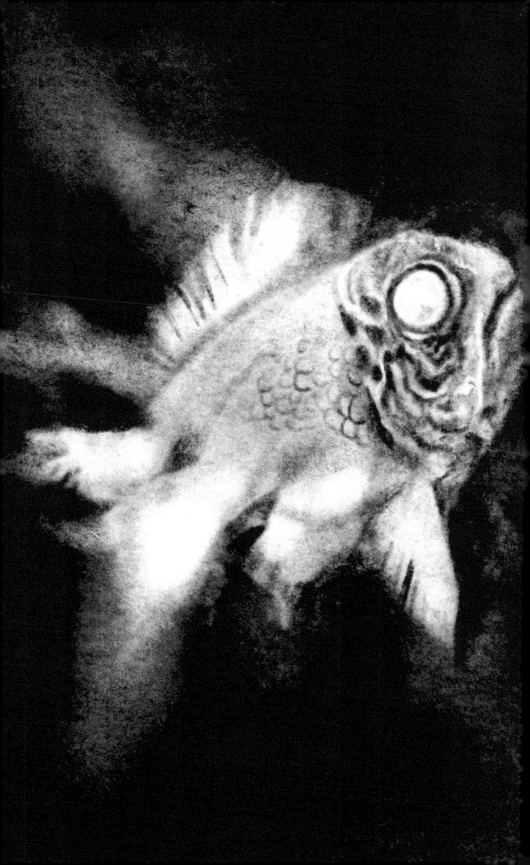

NEMESIS

P oe died of rabies, didn't he? Died raving, at any rate.
Here we are at end in a cheap motel along the lost
highway. You've been walking for a long time and the time
has come to rest. Your sandals are worn through to the bone. Your
beard could host sparrows. Your eyes have seen too much.

Sit in the armchair by the table. Here's a tumbler and an unmarked
bottle. The bottle should be green with electric lime, but it's black.
Pour a shot, set it aside. That's the hammer cocking back. That's the
muzzle and the bore of the universe bearing down; that's the naked
bulb in the eighty-dollar-a-night room snapping on. The window
frames the world like a television screen. That shadow flowing over
the tundra is the moon coming too close to its mother. While all
other points of fire wink out, a wandering star sparkles, black flame
from a black nozzle magnified by the whiskey glass bottom pressed
to your eye. Press RECORD. Time has come to get down to cases.

This room is a microcosm of everything that exists. You are
alone with the monkey that rides your back. DO NOT DISTURB
has arranged this tête-à-tête. There's no mirror, there's only you and

him and you aren't friends. There are, however, questions you've got to ask yourself here at the brink. Let's make it easy. These are yes/no questions. Be honest. Honesty is best.

For a moment back there you got to be a god. There were infinite possibilities. Look at what you did with that split second of omnipotence. Look into the mirror, if you are able. You open your mouth and the mirror shivers and somewhere a supermassive black hole dilates.

"But it wasn't that way at all," you say. "My father killed me when I was a boy."

You sound so sincere.

Despite what we thought the Mayans said, the world did not end in a fiery apocalypse last year and I am drunk as a lord.

The glow of the goldfish in its bowl greets me when I descend the twelve steps into the living room at oh-my-god-thirty in the a.m. intent upon finishing the vodka in the freezer. I'm dying of thirst. Dying of every lack.

The goldfish is named Hercules and it shines in the radiance of a wandering star that falls beneath the edge of icy peaks far to the west. Those peaks, serrated as a fillet knife, are millions of years in the making, as is the star's own brilliance. Hercules is older yet. You may wonder how this could be so, since goldfishes swell to match the dimensions of their confines. Surely such an ancient specimen could swallow a whale here on the eve of the last night of Anno Domini 2013. Hell, it should be enormous enough to gulp down a mid-sized city.

There you have it: I am the custodian of an infernal dreadnaught. I keep it in its tiny prison as a precaution. A check against unfathomable power. So far, so good. I unscrew the cap and drain the vodka dregs and that's better, I'm no longer a man crawling across the desert while vultures circle and circle. I'm rebuilt, remade, a millimeter closer to sanity. I'm in control. Nothing can go wrong.

I regard Hercules, hanging dead in the water like a tiny, unexploded torpedo. Something always goes wrong.

My twelve-year-old son Larry is convinced there's trouble. He knows from trouble. The left side of his face is mangled. Phantom of the Opera gruesome, he won't wear the mask Mom knitted him for polite company. The deed occurred two winters ago in the Northern Territories while we checked my trapline. A bonding expedition is how I sold it to Mom. Days and days of trekking through forests on bearpaw snowshoes, nights of heating pork and beans over cheery campfires; a real adventure.

But, damn, the ghost of Yul Brynner must've haunted the machine. It went wrong one afternoon on the shore of Great Slave Lake.

The gray wolf was caught fast in a leghold trap and had frozen to death. Or so Larry thought until it revived and sprang upon him and snapped its red jaws into his flesh. Destroyed his left eye, almost took his head off, but for me being Johnny on the spot with a shotgun loaded with slugs. Stupid kid should've waited for the all-clear before charging forward. My fault; I should've taught him better. I'll shoot the bastards from a helicopter from now on.

Anyway, the mauling unreeled before me with the slow-motion ineluctability of a high-speed car crash. The bite and the blast occurred two, maybe three, seconds apart. Fast ain't always as fast as we'd wish. Signal to nerve and my trigger finger twitched. Ka-fucking-BOOM and White Fang got taken in two while my boy, covered in blood, described a snow angel with his convulsions. I could see the circuitry of his brain through the gash where his lovely brown eye had been. He didn't cry. He stared at me with a dreadful calmness as complete and cold as the ice of the lake itself.

The stars came out while I sliced my long john sleeve and wrapped his skull. The rag soaked through, became his red bandanna of courage. The wandering star swung wide across the skinned heavens and filled his black iris with hell.

Larry said,

"**H**ercules is sick."

Dad's expression was remote as polar snow by the reflected luminance of his iPad screen.

"No, it's not sick. It's the Terror of the Deeps." He always referred to the fish as "it." He referred to all animals as "it." And babies.

"He swims upside down."

"Maybe it's bored."

Larry trained a penlight on the goldfish bowl.

"Oh, no. Leonardo da Fishie is gone! I thought he was hiding in the candy castle." A tear glittered in the boy's good eye. He took things like this hard, same as his mother.

"Ah, exhibit A. Hercules obviously devoured hapless LDF. Ergo, Hercules isn't sick. In fact, I submit that this is *prima facie* evidence that it is growing *stronger*."

"I put him in there because Hercules was lonely. They were supposed to be friends."

"Lemme tell you, son, this isn't such an unusual way for a friendship to end."

"His eyes…"

"Eh?" A latticework of diagrams and formulae shivered in Dad's glasses. He worked at the University of Fairbanks and was always bringing home some quaint and curious jag of arcane lore.

"Dad, his eyes…"

"Windows to the soul. Portholes, in the case of a fish."

"Damn it, John!" One half of Larry's face was livid, the other half dead as stone. All those severed nerves, you see. Spit flew when he got excited.

Dad set aside his notes. He made a steeple of his fingers and tapped his nose.

"You ever kill anyone?"

"No." The softness of the question sobered Larry right up.

"Interestingly enough, I have. With my bare hands, no less. The Marines trained me to do that. In light of this information, perhaps you'd care to reassess our relationship. Unless you prefer dancing on thin ice."

Larry and Dad were alone in the cabin. Larry's bothers, Mike and Sam, had gone into town with Mom for Christmas shopping. Larry didn't think his dad would risk murder, but the old man put the loon in loony and there wasn't much point in pushing his luck, especially without witnesses.

"Hercules's eyes are black. Pure black. Something is definitely wrong with him." Larry's voice quavered.

Dad thought about that for a few moments.

"There are two possibilities. Either Hercules is shining with the darkness of whatever abyss spawned it, or it acquired a fungal infection from munching Leonardo da Fishie. My money is on door number three: demonic possession."

Later, when Mom popped into his room for a goodnight kiss, Larry was still brooding. He informed her that he thought Hercules's strange behavior was an omen.

"An omen of what?" Mom said. The shadow of her head moved like a Medusa-coil on the wall.

Larry shrugged.

Mom smiled sadly and smoothed a lock of hair from his brow.

"Y'know, your father has owned a goldfish ever since we were in high school. Same bowl, same name. This has to be Hercules the Thousandth. There's something Freudian going on, I am sure. Don't antagonize him. He's not stable and he doesn't like you very much."

"Why does he hate me?"

"He doesn't hate you. You just annoy him terribly."

"Is it because of my face?"

"Oh, sweetie. Your father is a simple man. He's too dumb to feel guilty. You give him an inferiority complex."

"He's a world class scientist."

"Doesn't mean he isn't dumb enough to fear what he misunderstands."

"But why?"

"He thinks you're special. That frightens him. Brave men such as your father are frightened of the smallest things. Kind of like how elephants have a phobia of mice."

"That's just a myth!"

"Trust me on this. I'm giving you five dollars for your allowance, by the way."

"Oh. How am I special, Mom?"

"You're not, dear."

"Let me be clear, there is no Machine," Director Mallory said to close his remarks at the Star Chamber deposition. This emergency hearing was in response to an international crisis that appeared to be rapidly mutating into a global apocalypse. Blame had to be apportioned and attributed. Heads were going to roll, and how. The Director snapped his briefcase shut and strode out a side exit. He skipped lunch at the grill that day, became quite scarce indeed.

The Machine activated again six hours later and its effects were irreversible.

But by that time, when shit hit the fan for real, the Director was already aboard an emergency capsule speeding toward the moon. He and ninety-seven other bureaucrats, technicians, scientists, and prostitutes survived on a base hidden in a crater on the dark side for nineteen months. Eventually, they all perished of starvation, or mayhem induced by a cabin-fever-type syndrome. He went last— blew the station to smithereens with mining explosives and then unzipped his environmental suit to vacuum and watched his life boil away. He was lonely, not sorry. No one back on Earth cared. He'd been long forgotten.

We became aware that mischief was afoot long before it manifested into anything concrete. Much as I detected aberrations within my own body prior to the cancer diagnosis. What a life. Larry beats cancer and it bites me on the ass, among several other places.

Ah well. Where was I?

This colorless shroud had begun to spread beyond the simple colonies in the earth, contaminating the highest rungs of the ecological ladder. It had begun to creep into the collective consciousness of humanity. A psychic stain. We read this in the white gaps between the lines of news reports, heard it on the distorted short wave transmissions of my old ham radio. A farmer in Akron, an astronomer in Barrow, another week a Greenpeace scientist in Newfoundland. As yet, inchoate. Soon this would change.

Then, pandemonium. Then, endgame.

I had nightmares. The cancer intensified and so did the dreams. I suspected it might be a form of precognition, but reversed into the past. One night, Hercules broke his silence of decades and began to communicate with me via telepathy. He warned me and warned. I dragged my feet and upped my booze prescription. Who listens to a fish?

As weeks passed, the scenarios changed. In a panic, I called my boss at three a.m. to relay the latest from the psychic front.

The Director said, "What did you see?"

"It was grotesque. There was this primordial goo—"

"Goo?"

"Not actually goo, more of a jelly. None of us could decide if it was some kind of fungus, or an invertebrate. Slimy."

"Perhaps a snail without the shell, a jellyfish?"

"Jellyfish. This slime covered everything—the ground, highways, skyscrapers, mountains, everything. And it was… aggressive. Not intelligent, but definitely aggressive. Sensitive to light, sound, movement. People were fairly safe unless they started talking or moving around. Then this slime would crawl up after them, attracted to the commotion, and find them wherever they tried to hide. Horrible. This one scientist type kept saying the organism had been here forever, that it ate the dinosaurs, that it lived in a dormant state until something triggered its active cycle. That it represented evolution come full circle. We built this time machine, except it wasn't exactly a time machine, more like a machine that tapped different dimensional frequencies, and opened a gate to the end of the Jurassic and saw the slime appear. Dinosaurs were stampeding through an underground tunnel and it bottled them up and we heard them dying. Complete crap, I know, but damn if it didn't make sense. Parts are fuzzy, I don't remember all the details." I ran out of steam. "Pretty wild, yeah?"

"Yes. I want the truth. How did you—How could you know this?"

"Know what?"

"Drop the bullshit. Who's feeding you information? Don't give me anymore garbage about it being a dream."

"You wouldn't understand."

"Yes I will. We've seen everything, haven't we?"

I spilled, and man, it was a relief to finally tell someone about that damnable goldfish-cum-deathgod.

The Director let it hang for a long time. When he finally spoke, his tone was deadly calm. "John, I'm sending a car."

"Why?"

"You'll be taken into a field and shot. It's for the best."

"Ha, ha?" I said.

"Kidding. Emergency meeting."

The Director wasn't kidding, as it turns out. At least they made it appear to be natural causes. Poor Gladys had suffered enough.

"**B**ut it wasn't that way at all," you say. "My father killed me when I was a child. He shot me in the back while we were out moose-hunting. Watched me kick and squirm in the slimy leaves while I kept trying to catch my breath and eventually bled out."

You are nineteen. She is thirty and far from home, a Georgia peach who's taken it upon herself to divest you of your virginity. She's naked against the goose down comforter. Coals are banked in the potbellied stove. The blizzard is well into its third evening. The survival-shack is a vanishing speck on a vast snowy plain. Its windows are candy ice, its door frozen shut. The wick of the kerosene lamp burns low.

She places your hand against her sex, slides your fingers deep into her.

"Feel the shape of me."

You feel the shape of her, all right. Your body is green-lighted across the board, five-by-five, all systems go and awaiting the firing solution. However what blooms in your consciousness isn't an overheated reaction to her musky slickness, it's the howling void of the storm that opens from a pinhole to obliterate your rational thought, then overcome the solar system, the galaxy, and everything else.

The disjunction between flesh and thought only lasts a half-dozen ticks of the seconds-hand of the all-weather watch you wear on a string around your neck. Yet each infinitesimal pulse from its electronic braincase jangles the plexus of nerves around your heart and there's a bifurcation of reality. You are shattered and remade. Six beats over a span of sixty-million light years—your distilled consciousness elongated into a harpoon that pierces the corpus callosum of the universe. The wounded vista is a nightmare of nightmares; it is not dissimilar to gazing into the gaping pit of your own eye socket blown to impossible dimensions. And inside that cavern? A light that is darkness beams forth. Hideous red glow, disintegrating glare, death ray of the soul.

You will later discover that thousands of people across the world shared this precise experience at the precise same moment. Most of these people immediately resorted to graphic forms of self-annihilation.

Not you.

Your hair will go white from the vision, although when people ask what you saw out there, you'll only smile and change the subject. You'll have mastered the fine art of disassociation and forgetting. Booze will help. Insanity will help too. Mom lied—you are special.

You snap back to local reality and the woman drags you atop her. She doesn't notice that you've changed, been rearranged from the cells up. After you've made love, the Georgia peach kisses your cheek, tracing the old, bitter scar that marks the very core of you, just as a tree's rings spiral ever tighter. She asks how it happened. She's intoxicated with your imperfection.

You tell her about the neighbor who kept a kennel of racing huskies and how when you were ten your father made you enter the lot as the neighbor was hitching his team. Dad knew you were piss-in-your-pants-scared of dogs. He wanted to make a man of you, force you to confront your fear. Eighteen sled dogs, snapping and barking in madness to run as a pack across the tundra. You were small for ten and maybe a couple of them mistook you for prey and the others simply operated from instinct. You slipped, one of them nipped your arm, and then all devolved unto frenzy. They sank their fangs and pulled in opposite directions and there was a bucket of blood dashed upon the snow. Here came your dad's boots, and the mukluks of the neighbor, frantically jigging the way men will to stamp out a fire. They drove the enraged huskies away from your tattered ragdoll self. You remember observing the debacle from on high as a floating astral projection. Curious, yet detached from the moment.

Your Georgia peach listens attentively and when your words trail into nothingness, she asks what happened to the dogs, to your dad, to the neighbor. The lamp wick folds in upon itself and all is darkness.

"We went to hell."

Each day I begin with the basic facts of my existence: My name is Gladys. I am fifty-seven and a widow. Two of my three sons are also dead. It would be better if the eldest were gone, too. Poor aim is to blame. There'd been a flaw in the lens of the scope and the kill-shot went wide.

Larry is dead to me. Is that enough?

I am caretaker of a goldfish. His name is Hercules and he owned my husband until the day John passed away. The fish is all that I have left of my previous life. Won't be long until humankind in general can say that.

Red light comes through the window set high in the uppermost wall of the white room. Food is delivered on a tray through a slot in the metal door. There is a toilet, sink, and cot. Hercules in his domain upon a wooden folding table. My canvas and paints are long gone. My old books were spirited away as I lay in drugged stupor. The doctors don't visit anymore. Nor do the plainclothes policemen, nor the government agents. Once in a while, whispers filter through the intercom.

The voice says, *how could you?*

I lie on my cot and stare at the red light. I wonder what is left out there in the world. Why does anyone even bother with it? Humans are genetically predisposed to contest territory, even if the prize is irradiated tracts of scorched earth. We are born to fight, bred to kill. We are the makers of plague, the detonators of artificial suns.

Mike and Sam were perfect. Larry got cancer when he was young. Never proven, but we always suspected it had something to do with his father's tour of duty in Afghanistan. Maybe John didn't get the gas mask on in time and he unwittingly huffed a few breaths of some chemical agent or other, something that replicated itself through the blood and warped our firstborn. Yes, whatever it was, it came back for John. And now I'm alone.

We noticed the cancer only after it took Larry's left eye and began nibbling on his brain. The operation to remove the tumor was a gruesome success. The Elks Club paid for everything. Post-op, nothing was ever the same in our little Information Age family unit.

Larry's soul shriveled into to a wizened monstrosity. A cannibal gnome, invested and diabolical. I saw it in its reptilian elegance, peeping out from his heavy-lidded gaze. Gone was the sweetness, snuffed was the affection. He exhibited a sharp intellect that impressed teachers and doctors alike. They assumed he was bound for greatness. He fooled everyone—psychologists, teachers, friends, extended family—except for us. John and I recognized the coldness, the calculating edge to his new nature, and we were afraid. The kid became a liar and a manipulator. He made up a dozen convincing tales of how he lost the eye and deployed them with a conniving genius against suitable targets. He wanted to hurt us, especially his father. Why? I don't know. Perhaps he had something in common with all those assholes who climb mountains for the fuck of it. Perhaps the devil was in him. Perhaps my boy is the Antichrist.

I tried to keep the peace and failed. The feud between Larry and his father took on the spectacular excesses of the US/Soviet Cold War era. There were moments I feared John's temper would get the better of him and he'd smother the boy in his sleep. Dear God, now I wish he'd done it.

Red light keeps on creeping along the wall. Still no shadows, only the light. The intercom crackles and there is a long bleed of static. Someone begins whistling.

What year is this? I don't remember.

However, I *do* remember the instant it all crystallized for me: Halloween night, 2013. We put together a haunted house in the basement and invited the boys' classmates and a bunch of kids from the neighborhood. John played Dr. Moreau, decked in a ratty lab coat and a Panama hat, intent upon convincing the gaggle of "young entrepreneurs" to invest in his latest mad experiment. Meanwhile, I acted the role of an escaped bird-woman who'd enlisted the tykes to overthrow the good doctor and free the beast-people trapped in his laboratory. Twenty-five diminutive ghouls, goblins, witches, and Tinker Bells thumped down the stairs and piled into the drafty confines of the basement. After a brief tour of the various props (the radioactive scorpions and candy cockroaches were not to be missed!), Moreau gave his doomed spiel and was promptly slaughtered by his latest and greatest creation, the Alpine Wildman, a hybrid brute formerly known as Morris the Accountant. Reverend Custer played Morris with grandiose flourishes. The grizzled elder delighted in his slobbering and snarling role. He was a hell of a fellow, our right reverend.

Of course, Dr. M wasn't so easily defeated. Only by finding and destroying his brain, the phylactery of his evil spirit, could there be true peace on the Isle. The brain was a pink and black piñata John and the boys fashioned from newspaper, glue, and paint. Damned thing hardened into a cement block and none of the kids could perforate it with the beating stick (the doctor's cane) despite whaling on it with concentrated savagery. Happy young faces darkened and a few tears were shed until supermom Becky Champion, ever the quick-thinker, cried out, *That's not how ye attack a brain of quality!* and tore the piñata in twain so its sweet innards were cast to the ground. The ensuing scrum over butterscotch lozenges and chocolate raisins became so violent so quickly that the adults gawped in astonishment while tiny fingers were stomped and adorable pug noses squashed by bony little elbows. The children hissed and clawed each other with the ferocity of alley cats.

I spied Larry on the edge of the fray, smiling with the evil wisdom of an ancient puppeteer, hands clasped before him. He'd dressed as the Phantom of the Opera and the mask partially obscured his expression. He met my glance and nodded. Then he reached up and pried open the lid of his dead eye.

Hideous red light.

A few years before The Whimper (as some cheerfully allude to the apocalypse), Dad and you achieved détente. You started talking again, going to the bar during football season, barbeques in the summer, and that sort of thing. Should've guessed something was wrong. Cancer of the everything, in this case. But you didn't catch on.

He got trashed on boilermakers one night and told you about a camera he and some other scientists invented to take pictures of prehistoric Earth. Snapshots of the Cryptozoic? Absurd, right? Hell, that was only a piece of the puzzle. He looked around the bar real furtive-like and said that there was a sequence of photos cataloguing the entire solar system during roughly the same epoch. Black classification material; the sort of secrets men got themselves disappeared over if they spilled the beans. He'd drunk so much, he'd come around the mountain to a grim sobriety.

You said you couldn't get anywhere near understanding of the theory and he said that was okay, the eggheads didn't either. This was found art, son. Extra Terrestrial Technology abandoned during the last ice age. Geologists stumbled upon some funky equipment and semi-decipherable schematics at the heart of the Knik Glacier. The government swooped in to excavate and transport the works to a laboratory buried three quarters of a mile beneath Lazy Mountain. Dad's team spent eight years on the project. They were like the blind men and the elephant. It was big and dangerous, they could agree. There were unpleasant implications regarding humanity's link on the food chain. The eggheads agreed upon that too.

He mentioned nightmares. His eyes gleamed with tears and animal terror. Sinewy, gristly, fevered; he was at once the picture of a dockyard scrapper and fragile as tissue paper. Oppenheimer's cancerous ghost. He wept on your shoulder, apologized for letting you get your face chewed off, apologized for every miserly little crime he'd perpetrated against you, and you forgave him.

Here's the deal for all you finger-waggers and tsk-tskers: after the old man kicked, yes, you had a go at astral projection. You got fucked up beyond all recognition and staggered out past the Nome seawall and did your thing—sat like a yogi and meditated upon the destruction of the world. You visualized the worst possible shit your febrile mind could conceive of, and after a few fruitless minutes, dusted yourself off and walked to the Polar Saloon for a beer. Earth remained very much intact despite your efforts.

Didn't it?

Yes, the whole goddamned mess is my fault. Gladys knew there was something wrong with that boy. She begged me to have him locked away after the incident at his last school. The high-powered shrink we hired said as much. I wouldn't listen, wouldn't see, and wouldn't act on my conscience. I could've committed him, could've killed him, a hundred times over. She would've backed my play all the way to the bitter end. Hacked up the body and fed it to the chickens.

In retrospect, if I'd let the Big Bad Wolf eat him, everything would've been different. Sure, I'd still be dead. Some of you'd be around. Some of you'd have kids of your own by now. Grandkids, even. One thing in my defense: the little fucker was a lot brighter than I'd reckoned. Almost enough to make a father proud.

Oh, Gladys. You were right, although I'll be dipped if I ever saw his eye glow with hellfire. I mean, come on. We put you in the hatch for a reason. Worst part of it is, I knew what was going to happen. Unfettered access to the Project hath its uses, and—contrary to what some might believe—I'm not a total idiot. One night, I sneaked into the lab and calibrated the Machine to a much narrower set of parameters than we'd ever attempted, and it worked, after a fashion.

Compared to observing dinosaurs being consumed by tidal

waves of acid jelly, these images were prosaic: Larry was sitting lotus on an ice sheet—above it, actually; he floated two or three feet off the ground. Distortion occurred all around him. I figured it was quantum interference as the device sifted through infinite possible universes to home in on our future.

No. It was Larry in all his glory. He'd made the abstract leap that the Machine required to unlock the door and throw it wide. Anyone could've done it if they thought the right thoughts in the exact order. I don't understand why it had to be him. Outside of a couple of bad breaks, he had such a happy childhood.

I think the shithead killed my fish.

"**B**ut it wasn't that way at all," you say. "My father killed me when I was a child. He allowed me to be eaten a pack of sled dogs. I lived for three days on life support, then he gave the word and someone pulled the plug."

The Machine may or may not be a metaphor for our troubled times. Larry, its operator, is the everyman philosophers have dreamed of, warned us against.

What, precisely, did the Machine do? From the top: The Machine

A) Opened a doorway into prehistoric Earth/Signaled an alien invasion.

B) Activated a battery of satellites that bombarded the planet with X-rays and killed everyone on the West Coast, precipitating WWIII.

C) Activated a seismic occurrence that detached the West Coast from the continental USA and killed everyone, precipitating WWIII.

D) None of the above.

E) Something worse.

If you went with E, you are a gold star student.

"**B**ut it wasn't that way at all," you say. "My father killed me when I was a child. He pushed me over the bow of our riverboat as we floated the Yentna river. The muddy water is thirty feet deep and I sank without a scream."

It's a gorgeous fall evening in Palmer, Alaska. Hay dust hangs in the golden twilight. Blue clouds scrim the peaks of the Chugach Mountains. Scattered lights blink across the long sweep of the town. A soccer game is in progress on the high school field. The league championship is at stake.

Because there are inviolable rules regarding the temporal matrix, I won't tell you who I am. Nor shall I reveal the date, except to say it's the future. There are infinite futures, but only this one is yours. I can't tell you whether the invasion comes from outer space, or from the depths of the Earth. All I can tell you is that Mankind has eleven minutes and thirty-three seconds remaining in its geologically brief reign as terrestrial apex predator.

Boo, and hoo.

Flash forward ninety-nine years. Sorry to say no one is missing you. Any of you.

Somewhere in the middle of the chaos, Larry lugged Hercules down to Settler's Bay and dumped him into the water. The authentic Hercules, mind you. The goldfish that ended up in a bowl in Larry's mother's cell was a fake.

Naturally, the fish began to grow at an exponential rate, as Larry's dad always feared would be the case. And, naturally, when it achieved sufficient mass, it swallowed a Russian trawler on the Bering Sea. The first of many trawlers. This incident ultimately led to whole fleets being consumed. No maritime nation was spared.

Meanwhile, the rockets' red glare, and the miasma of chemical weapons, and so on. By the time Hercules got around to wreaking its vengeance upon the world, there was nothing around except millions of square miles of virgin forest. It opened its maw and gulped down the whole enchilada anyhow. Grabbed its own tail and swallowed hard.

Existence blinked into oblivion and that lasted for a couple billion years or a billionth of one second until a pinpoint of ultra-condensed matter in a sea of darkness cracked open and vomited forth the contents of a goldfish's last supper. Here we go again.

SOUL OF ME

You are Rex. You are dying.

Once, near dusk in late summer of Two Thousand and Something, you flopped in the tall grass. Shadows of clouds rolled across the field. You panted, pleasantly tired from chasing squirrels. You were seven, a German shepherd in your prime, or a nudge past it.

Often, you ran with your faithful companion, a female Siberian husky from the great white north. She'd changed since that romantic incident that resulted in a litter of puppies, had become more conservative and less of a hooligan. That day she remained in the house with the whining litter while you'd escaped through a loose screen door into the wild. Your own restlessness, your wanderlust, had only grown stronger as hers diminished.

You weren't really a shepherd, but a mixed-breed who loved to hunt, mainly for the chase. The kill didn't quicken your blood. Domesticated and pampered, you'd come far enough from the cave that the chase alone sufficed to quell the yearning of your soul.

Yes, you had a soul. In those days all animals did.

A woman called from the porch of the house. Her husband and son had gone away to war. The house was small in the distance, and the woman smaller, but the sound of your name snapped your head that direction. You didn't feel the bullet as it vectored through the back of your skull, much less sense the drunk neighbor in the plaid jacket who'd decided to sight in his rifle on a tree and missed the mark by a country mile. The neighbor was so near-sighted he'd escaped the draft and in doing so, killed you. That version of you, anyhow.

There are no accidents. Your once and future positronic brain will be aware of the totality of all recorded knowledge at the moment of humankind's extinction. It will understand that everything in the universe is in motion and that all of it, to the finest particle, is mated with something else. Stars, planets, waves of radiation, love, hope, despair, the whole shebang. In this case, your skull and a piece of lead traveling at a velocity of eight hundred and fifty-three meters per second.

You glimpsed a dilation of reality as the house and the woman were eclipsed by white light, a shimmer of dew burned by a sunray. You realized this was a dream of something terrible that had happened long ago. You also apprehended that "long ago" and "now" and "tomorrow" are roughly equivalent.

You'd been shot before, and worse. Your life had ended in violence dozens of times. You briefly perceived this fact, although you couldn't comprehend its meaning. Not with light and dark bending around you, not while the stars were falling from the sky, not when the ghosts of yourself were jetting from your body in a vapor trail of blood and bone. You were only a dog confronted with an infinity of potential that narrowed to one, post-singularity point:

Rex!
        The dream of yourself projects you forward past ages of domed cities, popular eugenics, limited immortality, and faster than light space travel and the resultant destruction of humanity, to an epoch that resembles the Paleolithic landscape of man and dog-kinds' prehistory. An arrival and departure point for your errant thoughts, your battered hulk of a body. This far-future world is a swamp, a rainforest, a vast savannah, an impending ice age. Red light suffuses the sky. Monsters walk the earth among the ruins of civilization.

You're in a fight. A spiked club smashes against your jaw. Another white flash. All you are pours down the funnel into the black.

One second, two seconds, three-hundred-thousand years, and then you're snapped back like a rubber band…

Wake up, Rex. Get up, boy.

This is the onboard computer exhorting you. Your overmind. Its tone is modulated to mimic the voice of a woman, a soldier, who handled you during your tour of some long-forgotten conflict. Like you, she'd been a fierce warrior. Before its gradual degradation over the eons, the computer could generate a million different voices to match a million different faces of men and women from your past. The female lieutenant's holographic ghost is the last human standing. She's a bit like you in that regard.

You've seen fire and you've seen rain, right now mostly fire, and if hell exists, James Taylor will sing an eternal set of his greatest hits. Your positronic brain is damaged; its systems are in the red, and you've been here before. But know this: this is the end, the real deal, end of the line unless you get moving.

A monstrous lizard wants your blood. It is a mutant with genes plucked from the Jurassic, fused with DNA by the same mad scientists who constructed true blue patriotic you. The creature was left to bubble on a Bunsen burner. Now it's evolved and loose like a fairytale dragon that's emerged from its mountain lair to annihilate the countryside. It is a destroyer; thirty times your mass and designed for mayhem on a grand scale.

The Gore King slaughters all comers, so far. When you leap, it swats you across the muzzle with its spiked and muscled tail. That's its go-to move. The tail lashes like a scourge. Five meters of armor plates, bone-splitting and envenomed; it is the hammer and the chain of a titan. It slew the old Spider God with that spiked mace. It clubbed Lord Guggtha and smote the brains from dire Haxx. It has leaned on this signature technique to ascend to primacy of the region. The Gore King also breathes fire. Flame spews from its maw in a stream of napalm. You remember napalm. The scientists baptized you in it, two million years ago, or so.

When the lizard is done with you, it'll slouch along the flank of the mountain to the honeycomb village of cave-dwelling hominids and devour them to the last. Going down for the count, you can't help but wonder if maybe the beast has earned its dinner.

In your final incarnation on this miserable, blood-soaked world, You are Rex. Spot, Fido, Roscoe, Yeller, Tramp, Rusty, Rin Tin Tin, Buck, and the others, the ever-popular others, yes, those too. But always and forever, Rex. The last of your kind and the kinds that came before.

Men made you with a drop of fossilized blood of a dog whose line descended directly from an Ice Age breed. They synthesized flesh and machine and you were the latest in a long line of milestones. Splitting the atom, penicillin, the Moon Landings, and then you. Your body and bones are reinforced with star metal. Your fangs are diamond daggers. Your hide is titanium alloyed with metal forged from a long-dead sun. Your heart is atomic-powered. Your acid blood is a cocktail that would've given Ponce de Leone the immortality he sought. Your canine soul is joined to a quantum computer that exists as a subatomic speck. The computer divides your consciousness with unequal precision between the simple, albeit highly-evolved canine brute, and the most powerful artificial intelligence conceived in its era. You contain the sum of human knowledge on that quantum hard drive. The millennia of lost music, art, philosophy, and culture exists as a tattered scroll in your mind's eye and it informs your decidedly non-canine thought processes; the yin to your doggie yang.

Muscle, sinew, and cell, down to the quark, is infused with nanotechnology that rebuilds your dead self from a bits of rag and bone. You can die, just like the old days, but it's harder now. You and death are uneasy comrades. Death beams from your eyes. Death erupts from your jaws in a sonic howl. Death is your companion.

Yes, indeed you were Mankind's best and most lethal friend and you protected them until the end. They're gone, Rex. An invasion of hollow beings from some dark star wiped them off the map in the year 2665. The war wiped the canine species out, too. Less of a war and more of an extermination, to be accurate.

During the final battle of Armageddon, you lost your handler, a human female soldier who operated twin .30 caliber miniguns from inside a titanium exoskeleton almost as durable as yours. Of all the humans with whom you'd served, she was the deadliest of the bunch; a real hunter. Then a hollow-thing breathed spores that ate into the joints of her armor, through the alloy, and she died screaming for God, her mother, and you, Rex. Meanwhile, a mountain fell on you, buried you for eons while the Earth rolled on and everything changed. The invaders slithered back whence they came. Forests, glaciers, and deserts overgrew all traces of humankind, entombed its cities and monuments. One fine day, an earthquake disgorged your hibernating self into the stark light. You woke by degrees over the generations and recalibrated yourself to patrol this strange new wilderness.

You call it Animal Heaven. Of course, animals hold dominion here. Earth and water teem with life: Terrible lizards and a plethora of murderous insects; hyenas, dingoes, wolves, and the most venerable of scavenger, coyotes, but no dogs. You are the last, the very last, and your howl echoes your loneliness and futility among the peaks and the tors of this happy hunting ground.

Don't quit, don't lie down. You're a warrior, Rex.
It's you versus all of them, as always. As for your humble beginnings, pick one, this one, retrieved from a snow crystal chipped off your memory core. It contains Whitman's multitudes. It will melt on your lolling tongue.

Remember why you fight.

Once, you were born in the winter of 1961, an emaciated mongrel runt. One blue eye, one brown. Your five brothers and sisters froze to death in a ditch in the Matanuska Valley, their guts picked by ravens. You remember the dirt-smell in the litter burrow, baby breath snuffled in your milky eyes as you puppies crawled over one another searching for a teat.

Mama went into the pound's gas chamber before you were weaned. You remember her scent too, musky and strong in your snout. The death cell would have been your fate, but you were reprieved in the eleventh hour. A farmer brought you home to be a companion of his youngest girl who'd gotten Polio and needed cheering-up something fierce. The family cured you of fleas, worms, and malnutrition. Despite their best efforts you didn't amount to much physically. Your spine didn't work right. You limped until the day you died.

The girl named you Rex. You and she were inseparable, quite a pair to draw to, the farmer said. You tramped the wild acres along Ruddick Creek together. Hobbled, really. Neither of you could go far without great effort. Mainly, you both lazed by the creek with her fishing line and cork dipped in the water, or lay on a hillside watching the clouds roll over the valley. At night you curled at the foot of the girl's rickety bed listening for her breath to hitch. When it did you'd lick her face to startle her awake. She'd gape at you, glassy-eyed and blue of lip, emerging from some deep subterranean well of consciousness like a diver who'd almost gone to the bottom for good.

Time leaked away.

You got old and went deaf. Your girl poked you in the ribs to get your attention, and sometimes it took a while for you to fade back into reality from wherever your spirit roamed when untethered from the yoke of consciousness. You dreamed of deer in the field, the bitch down the road, and of stranger sights—an apple-green sky, flinty mountain ranges, and vast glaciers blacked with the grit of a million storms. You dreamed of ancient men more brutish than the men of your day. These men dressed in skins and hunted caribou along the plains. You dreamed of men in armored shells who projected flame from sticks they carried, and you dreamed of darkness that filtered down from the sky and covered everything.

You were always bigger and stronger in these dreams, a real terror, like the Minoan Bull or the Nemean Lion, or Cerberus himself, but never big enough or strong enough to stop the destruction. After waking, you always forgot and the girl minced kibble and meat in your bowl.

The walks became more difficult as arthritis stiffened your joints. Sometimes the girl carried you the rest of the way home while your dozing head lolled against her shoulder. She didn't mind. She'd grown stronger over the years, or the years had taken less of a toll. Either way, you were in it together until the end.

One winter morning a stranger crept into the house. An escapee from the penitentiary out on Goose Bay Road. The law hunted this fugitive and his desperation knew no bounds. He carried a deer gun stolen from a neighbor's house. He caught the girl in the hallway and threw her to the floor. Who can say what lay in the convict's heart or what he might've done with that rifle? No one will ever know because you were there, roused from fitful dreams of apple-green skies and crimson sunrises, flying somehow, teeth bared, snarling. Time slowed and crystalized to an invisible point, the point of a blade, a tooth, your tooth. Sharp enough to travel through anything it touched.

Flash and boom.

The convict fled. They found him three days later, frozen on the Eklutna Flats, an empty bottle at his side. The ravens took his eyes.

The girl held your head while you died. As the lights within you began to dim, you recalled, for a moment, your purpose, and why you'd waited there all those years. Your gaze pierced the veil and you beheld the ghosts of yourself gathered round in an innumerable host that stretched back across eons to the time of tar pits and cats with saber fangs, back to the eon when there were no canines, only wolves. Only wolves racing in packs across the tundra and through the great forests of the earth.

You looked at her and your confused canine mind cleared. *Oh. This is why I am. This is what I do. But I loved her. I loved._*

For an instant you understood, then you were extinguished and reborn, as always.

Y ou are Rex, once again and forever more. But you have to get up.

What is your job, Rex? What is your sacred charge? To protect Man. Such is the programming of your computer brain, such is encoded within your very DNA. Ever has it been so. It doesn't matter that the hooting, long-necked savages cowering in their caves aren't quite Homo sapiens. This is the time of re-emergent dinosaurs and telepathic ants and a landscape littered with alien ruins. You long to hear a whistle, to hear your name called from a distant house. These savage hominids will have to do until they evolve. If they get the chance. And that's where you come in, Rex. You and your titanic capacity to absorb punishment, to endure, and to destroy. Your capacity for loyalty.

Flames engulf your body. The fire burns through you slightly faster than a trillion nano-bytes can repair the horrendous damage.

The crystalline flake with all those memories of the girl whirls away into the void and you howl after them, or the wind that also rushes into the void howls. You're a machine's machine, but the machine is malfunctioning so most of what remains is canine. A lost and lonely dog who's awakened to a world two million years separated from the one he best remembers. More flakes drift from black into black. Tiny fragments of memory flurry around you, through you.

A blizzard.

Remember why you're fighting the good fight.

There is fire everywhere. It revolves beneath you.

The sequoias are burning.

The old black mountains are burning.

Your fur is burning.

You are a torch ablaze and tumbling down the mountainside. Darkness recedes from your fiery glory. Your passage dislodges boulders and uproots small trees. Birds cascade into the night sky, seeking the void.

The vast and panicked flock is burning. Little stars, falling.

Earth and wood groan. You drop into an expanse of cold, black water. Plunge like the dying birds, like the dying stars. Flickering, flickering, gone.

You are Rex. Your systems are failing. Soon, your light will snuff in the depths. You will lodge in the sediment, among the bones of the terrible lizards and the bones of the ancient superstructures and the monstrous exoskeletons of the invaders who came from the rim of the known universe and perished in this place. The remains of your clones are here in their hundreds of thousands, annihilated wholesale by the enemy that crept down from the stars.

From the mud and the muck beneath the waves all life springs, and to that slimy bed all life will return when the sun finally swells too fat and too red. However, in your case, the return is premature. That icy mud envelops your fiery fallen star and snuffs the flames of the Gore King. Stitch by stitch, cells regenerate, tissue, bones, and ligaments reconnect.

Your eyes widen, shift to a new frequency that permits sight in the lightless depths. You struggle free of the embrace of the grave and shoot upward. You are a torpedo, a nuclear warhead. Your death rays build power for one more assault.

Once, during the spring of 9343 B.C., you dwelled in the forest near a village of mud huts. The village lay on the banks of a gray river. In those days, the wild packs had grown smaller and most dogs served at the heel of human masters. Not you, Rex. Not then. You were a prodigious brute, throwback to your wolf ancestors. The bulk of a steppe pony. White of fang and black of muzzle. You did not brook fools. The tribal hunters told legends of you and etched fantastical representations of your might and ferocity onto the walls of their abodes. Men feared you for on occasion you had crunched their bones and slurped their blood.

That spring you contested a massive bull elk for territory and because you desired the meat of his cows and their calves. You were gored through and through, trampled and mangled, and left dying in the high grass of the foothills where you'd been born. A young, unmated human female, an outcast from her tribe, discovered you in the throes of this most recent of deaths. She took pity upon you and nursed you from the precipice. When you regained some of your strength, you chomped off her hand. A hunting party of the tribe happened along shortly after this tragic incident. They beat you, bound you, bred you to their own domesticated mutts, and when they'd taken everything, they drove a spear through your heart and offered your flesh to their inchoately conceived gods. Apparently, the soul of you lived on in your progeny, never fully awakened to its provenance nor destiny. It didn't matter one way or the other. You have always respected strength. But, what a way to begin a relationship.

*T*he Gore King is bigger and stronger than you are. However, it's only an animal, only flesh and blood. It has limits. Limits to its cunning, limits to its strategic capabilities, limits of endurance. You are different. You accelerate while redirecting energy to lengthen your fangs and reinforce your armor, you double your mass with a trick of quantum co-location. The *auxiliary nuclear system deep in your innards whirs online and charges an array of combat protocols. Unlike the Gore King, which is compelled by its primitive urges, you are cursed with reason and a higher purpose.*

You throw everything at your enemy (from behind, naturally)—meson beams, plasma breath, sonic scream, your pointy and sharpened mass hurtling at one hundred and twenty kilometers per hour, jaws sufficiently powerful to shear metal, to rip apart stone. The Gore King's rear leg is clipped from the body and the body is barraged with innumerable fractures, tears, and ruptures. Your enemy is simultaneously burned, irradiated, and shredded. Its death shrieks are frightful.

You win again, Rex. Unfortunately, the Gore King got in a blow during its final spasms. Its spur opened you from stem to stern and your blood pours forth, rich and unceasing as you stagger down the mountain toward the hominid village where the monkey-men worship you alongside the sun, moon, and thunder.

Good work, Rex. Well done, old boy. You've saved the future of the human race. Your loyalty is a testament to all dog-kind.

The computer fades, its soothing voice full of crackles and pops, then gone. Systems are suffering a cascade failure. No coming back from this one, not this time. The computer is mistaken anyway. You loved Mankind, but Mankind had its shot. No, you battled for something bigger, something infinitely smaller.

You collapse on the riverbank by a cliff and listen to the wind moan among the honeycomb of rock caves. The inhabitants hoot, afraid to show their grimy faces. A mongrel mutt, odd of skull and possessed of overlarge ears, yet unmistakably canine, slips from the grass. She squats in the mud and observes you. The bitch cocks her head, confused by your scent. She is different from the kind you remember. Within a few generations that will change. Her mate is away, hunting. He has two brothers. They are a pack. Somewhere among the reeds, puppies whine for their mother. A sound you hadn't heard before yesterday for two million years; maybe longer.

You bear your bloody fangs and grin, and sleep.

III

ALAN SMITHEE IS DEAD

FEAR SUN

C lick.

Wow, this is exciting.

BOO-ooom! *goes the green-black surf against green-black rocks that jut crookedy-wookedy as the teeth of an English grand-uncle of mine.* FAH-whoom! Ba-room! *go the torpedoes bored into the reef like bullets from God's six-shooter (in this case a borrowed nuclear submarine). Then the dockside warehouses on stilt legs fold into the churning drink. Fire, smoke, death. On schedule and more to come in act two of Innsmouth's destruction. Daddy would have a hard-on for this action. Perhaps, in his frigid semi-after life, he does. I bet he does.*

The red light means it's on, lady. Let's hurry this along. All hell is breaking loose as you can see on the monitors. You don't need the gun, I'll speak into the mike. We've never met, but I know who you are and why you've come. I like you, chick, you've got balls. My advice, run. This won't lead anywhere pleasant. The Black Dog is loping closer. Gonna bite you, babe. Smoke on the water hides worse. Okay, okay, ease back on the hammer, girlfriend. I'll satisfy your curiosity even though you'll be sorry.

Speaking of, mind if I have a cigarette? Judging from your expression, it'll be my last.

Okay, let's start with last night and go from there.
Last evening went much the same as most of my nocturnal expeditions among the locals do: Cocktails and appetizers at the *Harpy's Nest*. Bucket of blood on the Innsmouth docks and the closest thing to a lounge within fifty miles. Lobster entrée, ice cream dessert cake. Karaoke night with the locals, oh Jesus. I totally abhor karaoke. I made fat ass Mantooth get up on the dais and sweat his way through "Dang Me." Not bad, not bad. Andi told me that Mantooth graduated from Julliard's drama division before he got into the muscle business. Huh. That goon has opened doors and twisted the arms of my stalkers since I escaped college. Surprising that I never knew.

My dress, a Dior original, cut low as sin. Better believe I danced with a whole bevy of rustic lads. The clodhoppers stood in line. Before the bar closed, my ass was bruised from all those clutching oafs and I got a rash from the beards rubbing my neck and tits.

For an encore, I balled a sailor in a shanty. A grizzled character actor named Zed whom the project team recruited from a St. Francis shelter and planted here in 2003. We shared a smoke and he recited the lore of this hapless burg and its doomed inhabitants.

"That's not the script I gave you." I stroked his dead white chest hair in warning. My nails alternated between red and black.

"It's the truth, missy. The devil's own." His tone made it evident he hadn't a clue with whom he conversed. Not a shocker—I eschew the public eye like nobody's business. It's also possible the drunken fool believed that theater had become life.

Zed's perversion of the project script offended me. Granted, I'd done the equivalent of visiting Disney World, fucking Mickey Mouse and getting offended when the dude in the costume refused to break character. Call me fickle. I whistled and the boys waltzed in and beat him with a pipe. Got bored watching him crawl around like a crab with three legs broken. They pinned his arms while I exorcised a few of my demons with a stiletto heel. The actor gurgled and cussed, but he won't tell. Know why? Because I stuffed a personal check covered in my bloody fingerprints into his shirt pocket. What was on that check? Plenty, although not nearly as much as you'd think.

That's it for last night. Oh, oh, I had a Technicolor dream. Dream may be the wrong word—I seldom do and anyway, I was awake at the time and staring at the motel ceiling, trying to connect the water stain dots and I closed my eyes for a few seconds and had a vision. I got shrunk to three inches or so tall and Dad's head loomed above me with the enormity of a Mount Rushmore bust. Icicles dangled from his ears and his flesh cycled from blinding white, to crimson, to midnight blue as the filament sun downshifted through the color spectrum. Dad said I made him proud and to keep on with the project. *The seas will swallow the earth!* And *All the lights are going out! Beware the ants!* His lips were frozen in place. He boomed his visions telepathically. Reminded me of my childhood.

Oh, Daddy.

Unless you're a well-connected investor or an FBI special agent, you probably haven't heard of my father. His personal wealth exceeded eighty billion before I got my hooks into it. Super!

Most of his projects weren't glamorous, and the sexy radio-ready ones have always operated through charismatic figureheads. Tooms?

What etymological pedigree does that connote? We've got relatives all over the place, from East India to Alaska—don't get me started on those North Pole, hillbilly assholes, my idiot cousin Zane especially. Anyway, he's dead. The Mexican Army shot him full of holes and good riddance, says I.

Daddy dwelt in an exalted state that transcended mere wealth; he was supreme. He created worlds: futuristic amusement parks, intercontinental ballistic missile systems, and designer panties. He also destroyed worlds: rival companies and rivals; he hunted tame lions in special preserves for dudes too smart to let it all hang out on safari. He aced a few hookers and possibly his first wife, I am convinced. The earth trembled when he walked. Cancer ate him up. All the money in the world couldn't, etcetera, etcetera. Per his request, the board froze his head and stored it in a vault at a Tooms-owned cryogenics lab—like Ted Williams and Walt Disney! Everybody thinks it's an urban legend. Joke's on them; I've seen that Folger's freeze-dried melon with my own two eyes—the hazel and the brown. What's more, he's merely the ninth severed cranium to adorn the techno ice cave. Every Tooms patriarch has gotten the treatment since the 1890s.

Come Doomsday, Daddy and his cohort will return with a vengeance, heads bolted atop weaponized fifteen-story robot bodies to make the Antichrist wee his pants. For now, he dreams upon a baking rack throne beneath a filament that blazes frozen white light. This private sun blazes cold *and* emits fear. His favorite drug of them all.

Yes, Daddy was a true mogul.

Mother came from Laos. A firebrand. Nobody ever copped to how she hooked up with Daddy. Some say *ambitious courtesan* and those some may be as correct as they are eviscerated and scattered fish food. Not sure if she was one hundred percent Laotian, but I'm a gorgeous puree of whatever plus whatever else. She hated English, hated Daddy, and virulently hated my older brother Increase (the get of the mysteriously late first Mrs. Tooms). She called him Decrease. Doted on yours truly. Taught me how to be an all-pro bitch. Love ya, Moms.

Mr. Tooms passed when I was sixteen. Mom died in a mysterious limo fire that same winter. The family business putters on under the tyrannical thumb of Increase. He knows what's good for him and leaves me to do as I please. No business woman am I.

My talents lie elsewhere. I revel with the merciless ferocity of a blood goddess. I settle for filthy rich, impossibly rich, which means *anything* is possible. Rich enough to buy a tropical island is rich enough to get a hold of a bag of Moon rocks on the black market is rich enough to turn this dying (dead) Massachusetts port town that time forgot into whatever I want. The people: sailors, peasants, moribund gentry, and their slothful cops, alder persons, zoning commissions, and chamber of commerce bureaucrats, mini moguls who measure up to Dad's shoe laces, if I'm generous. I own them too.

L et's step farther back to my vorpal teens.
Time was I aspired to be better than I am. Kinder, if not cleaner. Were I in the mood to justify a career of evil, I'd cite the head games (snicker) Daddy played with me and Increase, and that other one, the one who got away, the one we never speak of. I'd tell you about the Alsatian, Cheops, my best and only friend during adolescence, and how he drowned himself in the swan pond in a fit of despair. Took him three tries. I fished that waterlogged doggy

corpse out myself because the gardener got shitfaced and fell asleep in the shed.

Mostly, though, I'm the way I am because I like it, love it, can't get enough of it. Nature versus nurture? Why not some of both? It's impossible to ever truly know the truth. You have to dig extra deep to churn the real muck. You have to afford a person an opportunity to sell her soul. Gods above and below, did I have opportunity to aggrandize an overheated imagination!

The idea for the Innsmouth Project has incubated in my brain since I laid up with pneumonia at age twelve and somebody left a stack of moldy-oldies by the bed. The pinch-lipped ghost of HPL and his genteel madness made a new girl of me.

Great Granddad put ships in bottles. Dad made exquisite dioramas and model cities. Increase enjoyed ant farms. I read Lovecraft and a lot of history. Marie Antoinette's little fake villages captivated me. It all coalesced in my imagination. A vast fortune helped make the dream someone else's nightmare. Frankly, the US government, or a shady subdivision of the government, deserves most of the credit.

Six months after my father passed away I graduated from high school, with honors, and treated myself to a weekend at a Catskill resort that had been a favorite of the Toomses since the Empire State came into existence. No ID required for booze; handsome servants kept the margaritas coming all the livelong day for me and a half-dozen girlfriends I'd flown in for company. Andromeda kept a watch on us. With Daddy out of the picture, there was no telling if Increase or some other wolf might try to erase me from the equation. Ahem, *Andrew*. Andromeda was Andrew then, and not too far removed from his own youth. I read his, *her*, dossier on a whim. She'd majored in paleontology. When I asked why she'd thrown away the chance to unearth dino bones for a security gig, she smiled and told me to mind my business. Most intelligent bodyguard I've ever had, although not necessarily smart.

A guy approached me in the salon and Andi almost broke his arm I signaled. The dude, nondescript in a polo shirt and cargo pants, introduced himself as Rembrandt Tallen. He bought me a drink. I should have known from the ramrod posture and buzz cut that he was military. The next morning, upon coming to in a dungeon, blindfolded, chained to a wall, I also deduced that he was a spook. He removed the blindfold and made me an omelet. Pretty snazzy dungeon—it had a wet bar, plasma television, and the walls and ceiling were covered in crimson leather cushions.

Tallen kept mum regarding his team. The game was for me to assume CIA or NSA, and that's what I figured at first since our family was frenemies with those organizations. Black holes in the ocean was a topic I vaguely recalled. R&D at one of Daddy's lesser known companies looked into this decades before it became kinda-sorta news on a backwater science news site. The military and commercial implications were astounding.

My captor turned on the TV and played a highlight reel of various improbable atrocities that no citizen, plump and secure in his or her suburban nest, had the first inkling.

"Oh, my, goodness," I said as in crystal clear wide-screen glory, a giant hydrocephalic baby jammed a man in a suit into its mouth and chewed. Tiny rifles popped and tinier bullets made scarcely a pinprick on the kid's spongey hide. The action shifted to a satellite image of a village in a jungle. Streams of blackness surrounded the village as its inhabitants huddled at the center or atop the roofs of huts. The camera zoomed in as the flood poured over the village and the figures dispersed in apparent panic. Not that panicking or fleeing helped—the black rivulets pursued everywhere, into huts, onto roofs, up trees, and engulfed them.

"Beetles of an Ur species unknown to our entomologists until 2006. Vicious bastards. Although they refer to themselves as preservationists." Tallen smiled and his ordinary, bland face transfigured in the jittery blue glow. "Bad things are happening out there, Skylark. How would you like to help us make them worse?"

Would I!

The seduction progressed over the course of a couple of years and numerous clandestine rendezvouses. He quizzed me about Majestic 12, MKULTRA, and Project Tallhat. Had I ever met Toshi Ryoko or Howard Campbell? Amanda Bole? No, no, and no, I'd never even heard of any of these persons or things. That pleased Tallen, and seemed to relax him. He confided his secrets.

"It's not important, kiddo. Ryoko and Campbell are flakes. I'd love to see them erased, zero-one, zero-one. They have powerful friends, unfortunately. Forget I mentioned them. Servants of our enemies. Ms. Bole is open to an introduction, assuming you and I reach an accord. We think you're exactly the person to help us with a project."

"You mean my money can help with your project."

"Money, honey. You funnel the cash, we supply the technical know-how and the cannon fodder. You have a vision. We have a vision. It's a can't-miss proposition."

Tallen was so smooth and charming. I crushed on him. That corn-fed blandness really grew on me, or the Satan-light dancing in his eyes grew on me, or the fact he believed in elaborate conspiracies excited me (he claimed insects were poised to overrun civilization and that the Apollo explorers found a cairn of bones on the moon). At any rate, he broke out the maps, diagrams, and the slideshow prospectus. My jaw hit the floor.

His organization (I never did learn its name) had, sometime during the winter of 1975, allegedly established contact with an intelligence residing in a trench off the Atlantic shelf. As in an extraterrestrial intelligence that burrowed into the sediment around the time trilobites were the voting majority.

He laughed when I, unabashed Lovecraft enthusiast, blurted *Dagon! Mother Hydra!* and told me not to be stupid, this verged on Clark Ashton Smith weirdness. His associate in the deep requested some Grand Guignol theater in return for certain considerations that only an immortal terror of unconscionable power can offer.

Tallen, having researched my various childish predilections, proposed that we build and staff a life-model replica of Lovecraft's Innsmouth. Inscrutable alien intelligences enjoy ant farms and aquariums too. Some of them also quite enjoy our trashiest dead white pulp authors. He claimed that this sort of behind-the-scenes activity was nothing new. In fact, his superiors had been in frequent contact with my father regarding unrelated, yet similar, undertakings.

"Let me consider your proposition," I said. "Who is Bole? Why do I dislike her already?"

His smile thinned. "Mandy is the devil we know. It's tricky, you see. She came to us from across the street, on loan from her people. Her people are overseas, so she's here for the duration." Later, I learned that *across the street* was code for a foreigner who hailed from an extraordinarily far-flung location. Off-planet, say, but within a few dozen light years. *Overseas* meant something else that I decided was best left unclear.

I did ask once if Bole bore some familial relationship with the "intelligence." I was high on endorphins and bud.

So was Tallen. That didn't keep him from slapping my mouth.

"Are you trying to be funny? That's asinine." He relaxed and kissed away the bits of blood on my lip. "Let's not do that again, eh?"

I smiled, wanting him to believe I liked it, no hard feelings, while I privately reviewed all the ways to kill him slowly.

Surviving to majority as a Tooms heiress tempered my enthusiasm with a grain or two of skepticism. I hired world-class detectives—the best of the best. My bloodhounds tracked down scientists and sources within and without the government and from foreign countries. Results from this intelligence-gathering dragnet convinced me of Tallen's sincerity. Numerous reports indicated covert activity of unparalleled secrecy off the New England coast. The veracity of his most staggering claim would require personal investigation.

Meanwhile, my detectives and the scores of unfortunate people they contacted, died in mysterious accidents or vanished. I did the math one day. Okay, Mantooth did it on the back of a napkin. Four hundred and sixty-three. That's how many went *poof* because I asked the wrong questions. The number might be bigger; we were in the car on the way to a stockholder meeting.

"You gonna do it?" Only Andi would dare to ask.

Pointless question. She knew my capabilities. She knew I had to do it, because beneath the caviar slurping, bubblegum popping, jet setting façade throbbed a black hole that didn't want to eat the light; it needed to.

This town had a different name when Protestant fisherman Jedidiah Marshal founded it in 1809. Always off the beaten path, always cloistered and clannish, even by New England standards, afflicted by economic vagaries and the consolidation of the fishing industry into mega corporations, this town proved easy to divide and conquer. I retain an army of lackeys to orchestrate these sorts of stunts. Corporate raiders, lawyers, feds on the take, blackmail specialists and assassins.

First, we drove out the monied and the learned. The peasants were reeducated, or, as Tallen preferred, made to vanish. Gradually more actors were introduced and the infrastructure perfected. Necessary elements within the US government made the paperwork right. All it required was a nudge here and a bribe there from Tallen's operatives. The town was wiped from road signs, maps, from the very record. With the groundwork laid, Innsmouth, my own private economy-sized diorama, raised its curtain.

Assuming you're a casual observer, it's a humdrum routine on the surface.

Children ride the bus to school. Housewives tidy and cook while soap operas numb the pain. Husbands toil in the factories or seek their fortune aboard fishing boats. Come dusk, men in suits, or coveralls or raincoats and galoshes, trudge into the taverns and lounges and slap down a goodly portion of the day's wages on booze. At the lone strip club on the waterfront on the north edge of town, bored college girls and older women from trailer parks dance sluggishly. *The House of the Revived Lord* sees brisk trade Wednesday, Black Mass Friday, and by the numbers kiddie-friendly Sunday. I cherish the reactions of the occasional lost soul who accidentally detours through town: Some bluff day trader or officer worker tooling along Main Street with his uptight wife riding shotgun, her face scrunched in annoyance as she comes to grips with the lies the pocket map has fed her; and two point five kids in the back, overheated and embroiled in child warfare.

Annoyance gives way to confusion, which yields to revulsion at the decrepitude of the architecture and physiognomy of the locals, and ultimately, if the visitors prove sufficiently unwise as to partake of the diner, or gods help them, layover at one of Innsmouth's fine hotels, horror will engulf the remainder of their brief existence.

Even I, maestro and chief benefactor, can see but the tip of this iceberg. Scientists and men in black lurk behind the grimy façades of Victorian row houses—the scientists' purpose is to experiment upon the civilian populace as they might lab rats. Green lights flash through the murky windows, screams drift with the wind off the Atlantic. Ships and submarines come and go in the foggy dark. Andromeda and Mantooth worry about what they can't detect. I don't bother to order them to relax. Worrying is in their job description.

I acquired an estate in the hills. Fifteen minutes leisurely drive from town square. The gates are electrified, the house is locked tight, and guys with automatic weapons pace the grounds.

My first encounter with Miss Bole came when she wandered into my rec room unannounced. I sprawled across a giant beanbag while the news anchor recited his nightly soporific. I knew Bole to the core at first sight—kind of tall, black hair in a bob from the '50s, narrow shoulders, wide hips and thunder thighs. Pale and sickly, yet morbidly robust. Eyebrows too heavy, face too basic, too plastic, yet grotesquely alluring like a Celt fertility goddess cast from lumpen clay. She wore a green smock, yoga pants, and sandals. Sweat dripped from her, although she seemed relaxed.

"Hey there, Skylark Tooms. The Gray Eminence loves your style. I'm Amanda Bole. Call me Mandy." Her voice was androgynous. She gripped my small hand in her large, damp hand and brushed my cheek with cool, overripe lips.

"Gray Eminence. Is that what you call...him?" Pleasure and

terror made my heart skip, skip, skip. Sorry, Agent Tallen, but I think I'm in love.

"It, Skylark. *It*. I usually call it G.E. Confuses anybody at the NSA we haven't bought." Her wide smile revealed white, formidable teeth.

I'm usually an ice bitch during introductions. Feels good to keep the opposition on the defensive. Her? I looked into her sparkling frigid eyes and couldn't stop. Nothing in those shiny pebbles but my dopey face in stereoscope. "When will I meet it?"

"Assuming your luck holds? Never, my girl. G.E. has big plans for you."

Mandy pulled me to my feet. We had tea on the front deck by the swimming pool. The deck has a view of the ocean, hazy and smudged in the twilight distance. Lights of town came on in twinkling clusters.

"I think I've seen enough," she said, setting aside her cup.

She stripped and dove into the water. Reflections are funny—she kicked into the deeper end, her odd form elongating as it submerged. Ripples distorted my perspective and made her the length and width of a great white shark, gliding downward and gone as the tiles of the pool dilated to reveal a sinkhole.

Tallen called later. "I'm glad you're all right."

"Any reason I wouldn't be?"

"Ms. Bole told me that she'd decided to terminate your involvement. That would involve being shaken from a fish food can over the Atlantic. It seems she changed her mind."

"Uh, good, then?"

"Convenient! Now we can begin."

Some of what comes next, you already know. The cold death mask of rage, the pistol in your hand, what comes next is why you've returned and looked me up. Here's some context, some behind-the-scenes magic:

"Who gets to escape?" Mandy and I were revolving in the sex swing in the rumpus room. Mantooth hadn't seemed completely comfortable installing the equipment. I love that repressed New England prudishness about him.

"The narrator." Mandy's obsidian eyes reflected the light over my shoulder, or trapped it. Her eyes glazed, or shuttered (happened so fast), and reflected nothing from a patina of broken black vessels, a thousand scratches from infinitesimal webbed claws. "Our girl works for an amateur filmmaker. The source material is a trifle staid. Tallen made sure the filmmaker brought a camera crew, per G.E's request. Bubbly blonde, sensible, tough-as-nails brunette, strapping cinematographer, a weasel tech guy. That way there's a bit of sex and murder to spice up the proceedings. Our heroine, the sensible brunette, will escape by the skin of her teeth. Over the next couple of years, we'll shadow her, dangle the clues, and, ultimately, lure her back in for the explosive finale. Should be fun."

Hard to tell whether Mandy actually relished the impending climax. She remained disinterested regardless the circumstances. I relished it for the two of us.

Earlier, she'd given me a tour of a factory that covered for a subterranean medical complex. Her scientists were busily splicing human and amphibian DNA with genetic material from the Gray Eminence and subjecting that simmering, somatically nucleated mess to electromagnetic waves generated by some kind of Tesla-inspired machine. They'd been at it since the '70s, moving the operation from South Sea lagoons to secret bunkers such as this one.

According to the chief researcher, Dr. Shrike, the resultant test tube offspring teemed in the frigid waters along the coast. Allegedly, G.E. found them pleasing. It absorbed more and more fry every spawning cycle. That had to be a positive sign.

A few days later, I received an email. Man, I watched the footage of the pursuit and slaughter of that film crew (all but one) like a jillion times. The only downer, little miss tough-as-nails brunette stabbed the clerk at the wine shop through the eyeball. Too bad; he was sort of cute, and my god, what exquisite taste.

Point of fact, our heroine stabbed three guys, blew two major buildings to shit (with a few of our drone mercs inside), and steamrolled the Constable as she roared out of town in a wrecker. According to the goon in charge of the affair, at the end his minions weren't even pulling their punches, they were trying to get the hell out of the chick's way.

I was tempted to tell Mandy, sorry, babe, I've got the hots for another woman. Two reasons I kept my mouth shut—one, Mandy scared me oodles and oodles, and two, I suspected she didn't give a damn, which scared me worse.

How do we arrive at this junction? The explosions, the chatter of machine guns, screams, and death? Innsmouth crashing into the sea in a ball of fire? All according to the master plan, the Punch and Judy show demanded by the torpid overlord in the deep. This is what happened in the infamous story that HP wrote. I often wonder if he had help, a muse from the hadal zone, maybe.

Who can say where art ends and reality asserts primacy? Mandy's script, our script, called for you, our dark-haired girl, to return at the van of a fleet of black government SUVs. I hired a mercenary company to dress in federal suits and Army camo and swoop in here and blow the town and the reef to smithereens. Much as you did your first time through, except big enough to warm the heart of a Hollywood exec.

And here we are, you and I.

Certainly I believed my privilege would shield me, that I could gleefully observe the immolation of Innsmouth from the comfort of my mansion's control room. I figured when the smoke cleared and the cry was over, I'd pack my designer bags and flit off to the Caribbean for a change of scenery. Fun as it has been, nine months of cold salt air a year has murdered my complexion and my mood.

Guess you could say I was surprised when my guards were shot to pieces and an armor-piercing rocket blasted the front door. That's what Mantooth said they hit us with before you waltzed in here and capped him. Through the eyeball, no less. Don't you get it? All this destruction, Mandy and Tallen's betrayal, you glowering down at me, poised to shoot a bullet through my black little heart? A mix of prep and improve. Somewhere a dark god is laughing in delight, rapping his knuckles on the aquarium glass to get the fishies spinning.

The question is, do you want to live to see a curtain call. You're the heroine and if we're following the original plot, you have an unpleasant reckoning in your near future. I don't think this version of the tale will see you transforming into a fish-woman and paddling into the sunset. No, this is major league awful. G.E. awaits your pleasure. I doubt even God knows what's going to happen in the monster's lair. Got to be boring, lying there and emoting telepathically eon after eon. You'll make a pretty dolly, for a while.

Or, you could play it smart. My jet is fueled and idling at a strip just down the road. With my money, we can go damned near anywhere. Take your time and think it over. I'll give you until I finish this cigarette.

BANG! from a gun. A body thuds on the floor off-screen.

GODDAMNIT, *Andi! Why the fuck did you do that to the broad? It was under control. I had her in the palm of my hand. Shit. What do we do now? Mandy is gonna go nuclear. G.E. surely won't be amused. Where do we find a metaphorical virgin sacrifice at this hour? Andi..? Andi!*

You bitch. You almost had me going. No, I'm not sure if anywhere is beyond the reach of our friends. But let's hit the friendly skies and see, huh? Shut that down. I want to watch it later.

Click.

SWIFT TO CHASE

In medias res part II:

After a hard chase and all-too brief struggle, the Bird Woman of the Adirondacks loomed over me; demonic silhouette, blackest outspread wings tipped in iron; gore-crested and flint-beaked. Her thumbnail-talon poised to spike me through the left eye.

"To know itself, the universe must drink the blood of its children." Her voice cracked like an ice shelf collapsing; it roared across an improbable expanse of inches.

The talon pressed against my pupil. It went in and in.

Rewind and power dive from the clouds. Join the story, *in medias res,* part I:

Where in the world is Jessica Mace? That scene when the superlative secret agent gets captured inside the master villain's lair is where. Instead of a secret agent, here's little old me doing my best impression. Rather than a rocket station beneath a dormant volcano,

I'd gotten trapped on an estate (1960s Philip K. Dick-esque) nestled among the peaks of the Adirondacks. Cue jazzy intro music; cue rhinestone heels and a dress slit to *here*. My nemesis, billionaire avian enthusiast and casual murderer of humans, Averna Spencer, wasn't playing. Except she *was* playing.

First clue of my imminent demise (more like the fifth or sixth clue, but just go with it): a leather-bound copy of *The Most Dangerous Game* parked on the nightstand of my quarters. Second clue? The woman herself said over the intercom, "Fly, my swift, my sweet. When I catch you, I'm giving you a blood eagle."

Viking history isn't my specialty, but I know enough to not want one.

There I sat, dressed to kill or be killed. The loaner evening gown was a trap. Spencer had set it when she laid the fancy box across the sheets of the poster bed, and I sprang it as I slipped the dress on. Bird-of-paradise-crimson, gilded with streaks of gold and blue, a bronze torc to cover the scar on my neck (so thoughtful of my hostess), and four-inch rhinestone heels amounted to a costume worth more than I'd make in a lifetime unless that lifetime included a winning lotto ticket or sucking millionaire cock on the daily.

The ensemble transcended mere decoration; it reorganized my cells and worked outward like magma rushing through igneous channels. I'd stared at myself in the mirror and come face to face with a starlet. A tad hard-bitten. Close, though. Action heroine on the precipice of unfuckability by Hollywood's standard. Regardless, the illusion of fabulous me radiated heat—live-wire alive.

Yep, slipping into the dress had been to stick my head right through a dangling snare. Call it the price of admission. Too late to change a damned thing that was coming. I grinned like a prizefighter to keep my gorge down. I'd been here before and survived. Double-edged blade, the notion of past as prologue, and so forth. Resilience in prey excited Averna and made her want me that much more.

A girl on the run in a dress and high heels wouldn't run far is what Spencer bet, and why not? She owned the house. The house always wins.

The isolated mountain house of a high-tone serial killer isn't the kind of joint you accidentally wander into. I'd been recruited, seduced, and deployed. Dr. Ryoko and Dr. Campbell (more on my patrons—and their sexy, sexy bodyguard, Beasley—in due course), possessed a special interest in Averna Spencer's activities. My mission was to infiltrate her estate and conduct hostile actions on their behalf.

A few words about our mutual foe:

Averna craved the chase. She wasn't a slasher of (hapless) womenfolk or a sniper of unsuspecting coyotes. She didn't howl at the moon; hadn't been born under a bad sign or suffered childhood trauma. A hunter, nonetheless. Pure predator evolved to the job at hand. Sixty-three kills, if the cobbled-together records told it true. Sixty-three on US soil; only INTERPOL could speak for the body count in Europe where she frequently traveled.

The manifest of persons missing and presumed dead since 1988, included loggers, hikers, ex-military, a baker's dozen hardened criminals, and a former Olympic decathlete. These folks vanished across the US; law enforcement records established the deeds, but the authorities hadn't officially put it together. Unofficially, there were rumors. A retired FBI agent in Houston, a discredited private investigator in Wisconsin, and other assorted kooks, rocked the boat now and again. It came to nothing, as these situations usually do.

The track and field star haunted me. Strapping lad. Last known photograph taken at sunset, ice cream cone in hand (an athlete's notion of decadence), a tall, dark-haired chick hanging on his arm. Track and field dude—let's call him Rocky since he looked a hell of a lot like a Rocky I knew in high school—dressed nicely, smiled nicely. Only missed snagging the bronze medal by hundredths of a second. I imagined how he must've been later, after the kidnapping—alone, lost in a trackless forest. Pressed flat against the trunk of a pine, head cocked, every cord in his neck straining. Then, *slice*.

Rocky the Olympian's tragic story ended the same as the rest. Worm food.

Fast, strong, tough. Hadn't mattered, had it? Can't fight what you don't see coming, can't fight if you're prey. Dharma 101, friends and neighbors. The rabbit runs and the hawk dives.

Where do I fit into the grand scheme? I muck around in the rising tide of cosmic night. I'm hell on wheels. My totem animal is the coyote, the mongoose, my blazon a bloodied Ka-Bar in a clenched fist against a field of black.

Lest I join the dearly departed in their unmarked graves, the moment had come to make myself scarce. The original extraction plan struck me as sketchy at best—on the bright side of the equation, Spencer's houseguests normally returned to the world unharmed. The data led Campbell and Ryoko to theorize that those whom she kidnapped (and I qualified) were subsequently hunted across her estate grounds. Should the operation go pear-shaped, I was to flee Averna Spencer's home and rendezvous at a hunting cabin a mile past the estate's southeast boundary. My patrons had assured me they'd done the math forward and back—it wouldn't come to such an extreme. Bastards.

A grand staircase spiraled down into gothic gloom. Marble raptors guarded the way. I ripped the dress to upper-thigh, removed my heels, and transformed into a new creature; slippery and dangerous.

I hustled through the door and past a phalanx of artificial eggs arranged on the front lawn. Almost did a doubletake. The eggs were outsized and exaggerated, Andy Warhol style; waist-tall, maybe three feet in circumference, cast from milky-lucent porcelain that glowed in the porchlight. The one nearest my left was bisected at its apex, like a hollow rocket missing its conical nose. An egg and a coffin are antipodes of a closed circuit. Made it halfway across the yard before Averna's evil sidekick, Manson, shot me in the ass with a dart from a rifle. She waved when I glanced back. I flipped her the bird (ironic to the bitter end). Strength drained from me like blood from a tapped artery. Five more steps and I sprawled.

Averna rolled me onto my side. She moved her lips against mine in a not-quite kiss. Would've punched her in the throat except whatever Manson had loaded the dart with froze every muscle in my body. I tabled the impulse. She licked the salt of my tears and leaned back to regard me from the shadows. Eyes without a face. Yellow eyes with strange-as-shit pupils. Hawk pupils. I wanted to ask how she'd *known*. Maybe she didn't; and if she didn't, despite her rhetoric, I might escape with my skin.

This feeble hope persisted for less than five seconds.

"The doctors asked you to acquire a certain document, yes? They promised some grand reward for your service; appealed to your sense of honor. Couldn't you detect the evil in their black little hearts? Did you not whiff the deception?"

Had I been capable of speech, I'd have said nobody's perfect, and spat a gob in her eye.

She smiled. "I delivered the formula to them months ago.

Payment for your sweet self. I got the best of Campbell and Ryoko, as usual. The formula is worthless, lacking a specific strain of Jurassic protozoa, which, let us pray, no one ever resurrects. Blink if you can hear me."

I'm stubborn, so I glared, bug-eyed defiant. Impossible to tell if she was lying, and if so, how much. My "power" to behold the evil in the human heart doesn't work on women half as well as it does on men, and if she was telling the truth, it didn't work half so well on men as I'd thought.

A sociopath will say anything to make her victims squirm, which meant I dared not believe a word from her lips. Yet, and yet… I tried to speak; to scream, actually. Had my preparation and training been a ruse? Had those kindly eggheads really double-crossed me? Had their man-at-arms (and my lover) Beasley, participated in the con? Et tu, Beasley? Et tu, you handsome sonofabitch?

Averna said, "None of this is an accident. The doctors do not trade in coincidence and neither do I. We've observed you for many years. Something happened to your mother as a young woman. She met a friend of mine, a foreigner, you might say, who contracted with the CIA to enhance various programs. Lucius was part of an experiment, alongside many of her friends. She and the other surviving test subjects have been remotely monitored since the latter 1970s, as are their offspring. The…conditions that altered Lucius bloomed within you, yet skipped your brothers, Elwood and Bronson. Curses can be finicky.

"Did those old goats suggest they knew Lucius's fate? Spoiler alert: mother dearest isn't living in a trailer in Tennessee with a failed country singer. She didn't drink herself to death or get eaten by a bear. I am not privy to the machinations of Campbell and Ryoko. I *do* have my own brand of intuition. My intuition says they murdered

Lucius Lochinvar Mace. Did her in in the name of science." She rose and gestured to Manson who lurked nearby.

Manson hoisted me with her arms extended as if I were a crash test dummy. My field of view revolved off its y axis. I went bye-bye into the belly of night.

Backtrack, backtrack. Maybe you're wondering how a nice girl like me ended up in a place like this…

A pair of infamous scientists figured I might be game to solve a mystery and save the world. Unlikely, yet no less so than the rest of the improbable bullshit that increasingly defines my existence. My current boyfriend, the aforementioned Beasley, happened to serve as bodyguard, valet, and moral compass to the renegade doctors. He introduced us. This set the ball rolling. Happy (unhappy) coincidence? As I've come to mutter on a routine basis, there are no accidents.

Most people born prior to 1980 have at least heard of the inseparable duo, Toshi Ryoko and Howard Campbell (erstwhile academic favorites of every male-oriented pop magazine in existence). Renowned for death-defying expeditions, gauche stunts, and outré theories in their heyday; less celebrated of late. The naturalists retired (voluntarily mothballed, as Beasley put it) to a quaintly decrepit New England farm. Ryoko in his wheelchair, Campbell stooped to push. The inseparable duo as drawn by some virtuoso graphic artist; say Mile Mignola or Patch Zircher.

Prior to our first meeting, I did my homework and read the news stories (which traced back into the early '80s), watched myriad videos, and listened to radio programs devoted to their exploits (the *public* exploits; turns out the pair really and truly deserved the "mad scientist" appellation). Iconoclasts and apostates to the hilt. Neither man would go quietly to a nursing home. These two were fated for an exotic demise: they'd vanish in the Bermuda Triangle, or into the Amazon rainforest and leave behind a ravaged campsite, cryptic research notes scattered, a cursed Neolithic medallion dangling from a bush; or, an unmarked government van would whisk them to a black site for a final debriefing.

We got along swimmingly. Didn't mean I'd be a cheerful pawn in their schemes.

"The Shadow of Death slides across the floor," Dr. Campbell said, and nodded at his shoe in a sliver of sunlight.

"The Shadow of Death!" Dr. Ryoko struggled to light a cigarette. His palsy tremors came and went.

"Soon it will crawl onto us and dig in the spurs. Time yet…"

"…a few years yet. We can do some good."

"*You* can do some good, Jessica. Help us hold back the darkness."

What they wanted wasn't difficult. Hazardous to my health, yes, but not difficult. Some rich lady possessed a formula; a cure for a deadly strain of avian flu, or a recipe to weaponize the virus, nobody could be sure which. Campbell handed me an envelope full of notes and photographs and that's how I came to acquaint myself with the legend of Averna Spencer—AKA the Bird Lady of the Adirondacks, AKA (my addition) the Cuckoo Killer. She'd briefly made a public splash on nightly news programs when they profiled her participation in the emergent wingsuit craze during the late 1990s. As one of the few women rich enough and ballsy enough to leap off cliffs and sail like a flying squirrel, she'd represented a curiosity.

Averna kicked it old school, pre-Information Age—nothing left to chance in a computer database, otherwise Ryoko and Campbell would've enlisted a hacker and done the job by remote. She kept the formula locked in a safe at her residence; a cliff-side mansion-slash-fortified stronghold amid thousands of acres of wilderness. The aforementioned master villain's lair. Called it the Aerie.

The broad owned more land than Ted Turner in his Montana heyday with Jane Fonda and the Atlanta Braves. Closest road lay twenty miles southeast. Traffic came and went via a helicopter pad. Power derived from generators, turbines, and solar panels. Security? Ex-military goons provided by Black Dog; armed drones; bloodhounds and German shepherds. Land mines. The wilderness and its many teeth waited for scraps.

How did the doctors score this information? Dr. Ryoko claimed a contact on the inside. A spy in the house of love. While this shadowy individual didn't possess direct access to the formula, the person had provided a detailed description of the item and the combination to the safe where it currently resided.

My natural skepticism asserted itself. Setting aside reservations regarding the veracity of the alleged spy, why in the hell would Averna Spencer, noted recluse, grant me an audience?

"Never fear, we'll arrange it," Dr. Ryoko said. "You are the mistress of inevitability. The opener of the way. Occult forces magnetize to you."

"Spencer delights in taking things apart. Unbreakable individuals are her weakness." Dr. Campbell actually rubbed his hands when he said this.

"Oh, goodie," I said.

"If she isn't familiar with your résumé as a survivor of massacres and slayer of maniacs, we'll enlighten her. She won't be able to resist. You're a blue-ribbon prize."

"Nice as that sounds, I'd prefer to live a while yet."

Ryoko said, "The universe built you to destroy human predators as it built the mongoose to destroy serpents."

"Dang, as a little girl I adored Kipling's tales to the max."

I inquired at length as to what they meant by occult forces and got nowhere fast. Slick as politicians dodging press questions, they relentlessly pivoted to the matter of Averna Spencer and her formula.

Charisma, resourcefulness, and grit notwithstanding, *Mission Impossible* wasn't my bag. The doctors hung in there with the hard sell. Dr. Campbell said I owed it to the missing persons and their distraught families. Dr. Ryoko insisted I bore a patriotic duty to obtain the formula from Spencer. Heaven help us if the avian flu developed into a more lethal strain.

This dragged on.

"What's your decision?" Dr. Campbell tried on a hopeful, earnest smile. "Will you help us avert a global catastrophe?"

"Pass."

"You're a born meddler," Dr. Ryoko said. "Consider the stakes—mass extinction of multiple species…"

"Not for all the chickens in the world." I actually meant, sweeten the pot, you cheap sonsofbitches. They sweetened the pot.

Dr. Campbell said, "Twenty-thousand. Cash. Our entire rainy-day fund."

"Tempting, but no thanks."

The doctors exchanged a glance I'll take to my grave.

"We'll tell you what really happened to your mother," Dr. Ryoko said.

Ding-ding-ding. Winner-winner, chicken dinner.

The Aughts exacted a hell of a toll on the Mace family. It felt personal between us and the universe.

Mom took a permanent vacation to parts unknown.

My brother, Elwood, stepped on a landmine in Afghanistan.

Jackson Bane, love of my life, went down with his fishing boat.

Dad followed suit in a separate accident on the Bering.

A bunch of friends and colleagues got murdered by the Eagle Talon Ripper. The Ripper almost did me in as well, hence the scar on my neck. Melodrama galore.

Hindsight: Mom's final disappearance began the unholy countdown sequence. Unlike the many other instances where Lucius slapped Dad and hit the road for a week or a month, she didn't return. Didn't call, didn't write, didn't leave a hint where she'd gone and after a couple of years, her fate gradually became the stuff of legends.

Flash forward the better part of a decade. When the mad doctors offered to solve the nagging mystery of Mom's vanishing act, my instincts were to skip the whole middle part where I went off on a fool's errand into the den of a sadistic murderer. Quicker and more reliable to extract their information with a sharp stick.

Beasley presented a major obstacle. He watched over Campbell and Ryoko with zeal. The adorable brute exhibited a ruthless streak when it came to protecting the codgers. His bulging biceps and handiness with gun, knife, and hobnail boot, gave me pause.

It's seldom wise to tackle an irresistible force of nature head-on. I played it coy.

He implored me to forget the mission and slip away into the night. No amount of money was worth the risk, he adored me, et cetera. I informed him the old bastards had made me an offer I couldn't refuse—and then refused to tell him what the offer entailed. I asked if he'd ever met a woman named Lucius, real slick like. He shrugged and said yeah, she'd blown into camp a few years back, consulted with the doctors, then departed on an evening breeze.

Innocent, and I'm a decent judge of a man's soul if I gaze into his eyes long enough after a good hard screw. On the subject of screwing: I didn't have the heart to ask if he'd banged my mom.

"Spencer is a monster," he said as we smoked cigarettes in bed and slugged from a bottle of vodka. "She's protected by the powers of darkness. I've seen the file. I've seen all their files…"

"Who else are your bosses spying on?"

"Don't ask questions you'll come to regret. You're not a professional. The docs aren't either. Meanwhile, Spencer is queen of her little mountain fiefdom. Absolutely untouchable. The FBI knows. The Department of Defense knows. Everybody."

"The government is aware that she's a serial killer?" I feigned shock. Experience had taught me that we primates were capable of anything, everything. There ain't no good guys.

"Always room for one more creep on the payroll. Uncle Sam wouldn't give a shit if Spencer had Joseph Mengele's brain implanted. As long as she keeps her activities on the property and doesn't kill anyone important, she's golden."

"Golden," I said. "Reminds me of something…"

I loved Beasley, after a fashion. It isn't unusual, as Tom Jones might say. Big, sorta-handsome (he looked like a soap star who got smashed in the face with a shovel), mean guys rev my motor, and the Bease had it going on in spades. He loved me back, far as I could tell. Our mutual affection complicated matters; made what I had to do to get close to Averna a dilemma of scruples versus pragmatism. My scruples aren't what they used to be.

"Since I can't change your mind, I can show you what you've signed on for." He plugged in a laptop and ran three video clips.

Surveillance or home footage as shot by an anonymous someone with Ingmar Bergman's ice-cold aesthetic.

Clip one, black and white: *a man sprints along a seaside cliff toward the camera. The fuzzy shape of an enormous bird sweeps through the frame and plucks him in its claws. The man struggles as the bird cruises toward the horizon. They shrink to a distant blot—the smaller blot separates and plummets into the ocean.*

Clip two: *an actress clad in an elaborate costume (skintight suit pricked with gemstones; a demented mask with a red and yellow feather plume, a vicious iron beak, underarm webbing, and steely talons) glides the length of a vast solarium. She rebounds from the walls to alter course with horrible grace. Naked men and women scatter beneath her. Every pass, the performer decapitates a victim with the swipe of a talon or the slash of a spur. Viscera streams in her wake.*

I know from Wire-Fu. I can't find the wires.

Clip three: *Averna Spencer stands near a bonfire with her arms spread. An assistant (the woman in the photo with Rocky the Olympian) fits her into a wingsuit designed by Satan. Spencer's arms are harnessed to actual wings designed after some gigantic specimen—twenty feet, tip to tip. The feathers ripple, hinting at a color spectrum dulled by the black and white film. The fire illuminates queerly-hooked calf-high boots, steel (titanium?) talons strapped to her wrists, metallic panels across her breast, and a bronze helm crafted in the likeness of the god or devil of all avian-kind. Beneath the cruel beak, she grins.*

I stared overlong, evidently.

Beasley apologized, mistaking silence for dismay. Truthfully? The images had stolen my breath. A close race between disgust and awe. That's how much I'd evolved since Alaska. He figured I would react as any normal, rational person and tell the doctors to stuff their espionage mission. Quite the contrary.

Averna Spencer seldom emerged from her mountain fortress. She traveled in rarified company under various aliases and in disguise. Tracking her movements abroad proved a no-go. Campbell and Ryoko approached the finest detective agencies and were rebuffed without explanation. Beasley wasn't kidding when he said Spencer enjoyed protection from on high. Somebody ran major interference on her behalf, and I suspect that baloney had a first name, spelled CIA, and a second name spelled NSA, and a last name starting with Homeland Security. Spread enough money around and the baddest intelligence agency will act as your very own private concierge.

Since flushing out our quarry didn't seem a viable option, we needed to attract her interest. Birds appreciate shiny objects. The doctors devised a plan that involved getting me onto the guest list for an exclusive seminar featuring a famed ornithologist rumored to be an on and off again flame of Ms. Spencer. The doctors pulled strings and away I went to make the magic happen.

The lecture occurred in Kingston, New York at the home of a wealthy naturalist who reveled in this kind of groovy shit. Real nice place, if a tad stuffy. Kind of a museum, although the owner rarely opened for tours; he collected documents, weapons (a veritable shit-ton of knives), landscape paintings, and animal artifacts for his sole viewing pleasure. I've met a few guys with that particular pathology; the type who stored priceless art in bank vaults. Creepy bastards, the lot of them.

The ornithologist (Henry-something or other), on the other hand, seemed normal enough for a whack-a-doodle birdwatcher. We hit it off after I revealed my secret identity as a retired biologist. Dude gave his talk to a parlor-load of eminently bored stuffed shirts, then took my elbow and introduced me around. Scotch started flowing and I made tons of new friends.

One of these friends shook my hand and said to call her Manson. Manson stood tall and Amazonian in combat boots. She wore a bomber jacket (unzipped to flash DETROIT in block type across a stretched-tight T-shirt) and makeup fit to front The Cure. Cropped hair, heavy eyeliner, cherry-black lipstick, cherry-black nails. Yeah, I'd read her file too—born and raised in the Motor City, ex-con, worked as muscle for hire until Averna Spencer rescued her from the mean streets. I recognized Manson as the mystery girl in the last photo of Rocky, Mr. Decathlete, and in the video of her girding Spencer for mayhem. Guess that made her Oddjob to Spencer's Goldfinger, or Renfield to Dracula.

We adjourned to the veranda, admiring an autumnal blaze in the eye of the sunset. Manson reminded me of a female iteration of Beasley—big, tough, ruggedly attractive, and not overly gifted in chitchat. Manson came right to the point. She explained that her mega-rich, mega-private employer desired my presence at her estate for dinner and light conversation. The mysterious employer approved of my various exploits (especially the way I'd dispatched the Eagle Talon Ripper in Alaska). Should I be so gracious as to accept the invitation, my forbearance would be well-compensated. A helicopter waited nearby. No need to pack; my every need would be fulfilled.

Damn, the aforementioned forces of darkness moved in fast. Manson's Plan B probably involved a rag and chloroform, so rather than play hard to get, I acted tipsy and said, hell yeah, take me to your leader. What girl turns down a ride in a private helicopter? Not this girl! Manson ran a wand over my body from stem to stern and patted me down with more intimacy than a zealous airport security agent. Smart call, leaving my knives at home.

The helicopter carried us north for the better part of an hour.

Our pilot wore a snow-white uniform. His (or her) visor concealed his (or her) identity. I thought of Jonathan Harker's carriage-ride, Dracula at the reins, hell-bent for leather on the way to the castle. Dracula possessed a cold grip and the strength of twenty men. How strong was Averna Spencer's grip?

The answer—firm. That old saying about a velvet glove and an iron fist applies here. A few minutes after we touched down (and nope, I never saw her and the pilot together), the lady herself greeted me near the front lawn and its koi pond and assorted Greco-Roman statuary. Red dress and sensible shoes; she didn't wear any jewelry or makeup. She gently closed her hand around my throat and planted a lingering kiss on my cheek. Felt as if she could've torn my head off with a twitch. We locked gazes—her pupil molted yellow and back to black again, foreshadowing troubles galore. I gave not a shit. My legs trembled. Anxiety evaporated, replaced by thrill. Pheromones, mad pheromones.

The plan, such as it was, was to play hard to get, work the charm offensive, gain access to the Bird Woman's home and acquire the formula. Babies, those best-laid stratagems went out the window the instant I got a whiff of her scent.

No, man. Averna didn't have "sharp features," or a "cruel nose," or "talon-like" hands (usually), or any such shit. Dark hair, brown eyes (usually), athletic. The record put her well on the backside of fifty. Up close and personal, she felt a hell of a lot younger; ripped as a gymnast (a decathlete?), and nary a wrinkle or ha-ha, crow's foot. Averna understood how to walk, how to hold herself motionless the way politicians and models do, how to project her personality with kinetic force. Cool to the touch. Worth forty billion and enamored of esoteric scientific research. Spencer's corporations funded an assortment of crazy projects. Despite this massive wealth, her name seldom surfaced outside of highly insulated circles. A bizarre, protean vibe emanated from her and her retinue. Is evil (capital E evil) protean? That would explain much.

Invited me to freshen up (my quarters contained every amenity including evening wear in my size) and take a stroll with her resident PR man. Dinner at seven on the dot.

I toured the house. Bizarre and immense (immense even before factoring in a network of shops, garages, and the sector of hexagonal cottages where she stashed her off duty workforce and security personnel).

Envision a three-wing mansion of redwood logs and slate, mated to a giant bisected Bucky Ball on loan from the Martians—soaring, crystal-domed atriums with copses of full-sized pine trees and willows and a river falling over glass-smooth rocks; cozy parlors where fake flames danced inside hearths; steel bulkhead hatches concealed by cherry wood paneling and illustrated hangings that were sufficiently moth-eaten to indicate pricelessness; and an array of security cameras, some obvious and others less so. Most of the art was of the abstract genre. I didn't recognize anything.

Averna Spencer's PR lackey (a chipper guy named James who smiled like a hostage in fear of his life) took me in tow. According to my guide, the floorplan included a sauna, gymnasium, theater, bowling alley, discotheque, shooting range, and a spa. When his back was turned, I peeked inside vases and cabinets—no corpses, no skeletons. The circuit ended with a glimpse inside a museum gallery that would've made a nice addition to the Smithsonian. Dinosaur bones, suspended biplanes, and a two-story spire of glossy, radiant yellow crystal. The usual weird stuff one might expected to find in the trophy den of a megalomaniacal billionaire murderess.

When I craned my neck to get a better look, James became nervous.

"Ms. Spencer would prefer to show you these special exhibits herself. Someone accidentally left this open…"

"That's a huge chunk of crystal, Jimmy," I said. "Last I saw something like that was on the cover of a 1970s science fiction novel. And the bird skeleton…What's the wingspan? Twenty feet? Is it a pterodactyl?"

"No, ma'am, it is not a pterodactyl." James pulled a pair of brass-plated doors shut. "*Argentavis magnificens.* An extinct predator. Among the largest of her kind. She devoured prey whole. Shall we move toward the dining room?" He wiped his brow and checked his watch.

"The crystal. You simply have to give me the scoop, Jimbo."

"Ms. Spencer awaits." He led the way, and briskly.

"Does Manson handle the executions around here?"

He glanced over his shoulder, eyes glassy-bright. "Mainly, yes."

A woman spends her early adult years at hatcheries and aboard fishing trawlers doing the honest labor of tracking and cataloguing salmon (that great Alaskan export), and nobody cares. Americans want their food marginally harmless in a marginally attractive package; the fewer details, the better. A woman gets attacked by a mass murderer and lives to tell, everybody wants a piece of the action.

Type Jessica M into any search engine and the auto-form will suggest *Jessica Mace & Eagle Talon Ripper; Jessica Mace US Magazine;*

Jessica Mace Nude Photos; Jessica Mace Final Girl. Averna Spencer hadn't merely followed my career as portrayed in the media, she knew my whole origin story—how a while back, I'd barely survived an apartment complex massacre and fire; how I'd risen from near-death and killed the killer; how I'd bailed on my fifteen minutes and vanished (like mother, like daughter). She'd also obtained facts regarding my unpublicized excursions on the road. Averna confessed her fascination regarding people who had confronted the vicissitudes of existence in an intimate manner. I took it to mean she'd burned ants with a magnifying glass as a kid.

We finished supper and wandered through her hanging gardens and lesser aviaries. Flocks of tropical birds dwelled inside a dome of sparkly mesh that protected a lush jungle biome. It would take the gross national product of a small country to stock and maintain such a preserve.

Our path wound through an imported jungle. Paper lanterns (grotesque busts of birds of prey) cast our primeval surroundings in the light of an animated Kipling adaptation. Climate control simulated the tropics. Humidity soaked my clothes and I almost believed the sliver of moonlight peeping through leaves was other than a subtly masked klieg.

She said, "You're rather trusting for a woman who's had her throat slashed by a serial killer and lived to tell. Do you jump into a helicopter with any total stranger?"

"Manson isn't the kind of person you argue with." I raised my voice to compete with raucous chatter of birds and mating frogs.

"Manson is an extension of my will. I made her."

"Made her? As in Pygmalion?"

"Isn't that the idiom the cool kids are using?"

"Yes. Do me next, pretty please."

"I projected my life essence into her puny mortal frame and voila, a million-year evolutionary leap. It's a messy process. Not for weak stomachs."

Seemed an appropriate point to change the subject. "I read in an article that you employ a team of geneticists and zoologists. You want to protect endangered bird species." Campbell and Ryoko's dossier alleged that Averna Spencer hired mercenaries to shoot nest robbers and sabotage the infrastructure of land developers who operated in environmentally-sensitive regions such as South America.

"The science team pursues much grander designs," she said. "We work to resurrect a spectrum of extinct species. Avian, reptile, amphibian. I'm worried for honeybees. As our apian friends go, so go we."

"The research is conducted here, in house?"

"Yes, and in twenty-three other countries."

"Good thing you're loaded. Woman could burn through a fortune on fringe research."

"She could. Or she could manipulate a host of international political actors to foot the bill. Drug lords, warlords, bored industrialists...It isn't as difficult to separate them from their spare millions as you might think."

"Any luck raising the dodo from the dead?"

"Sixty-eight percent of this aviary system is populated by animals that no longer exist in the outside world."

I flashed to the giant bird skeleton in the private museum, and how the tall, crystal had seethed with a weird yellow fire. Decided to zip my lips. Averna's stride, long and graceful, reminded me of her unnatural strength. Her friendly smile hinted at savagery.

"My most prized work isn't specific to avian research," she said. "I hope to create a trigger of human evolution. A radically accelerated process."

"Mutation."

"After a fashion."

"Toward what end?"

"The ability to survive dramatic climate change. To withstand nuclear radiation and acid rain. To think faster. To dispense with antiquated paradigms of morality and ethics. To soar with the eagles and swim with the fishes."

"Things mad scientists say for five hundred, Alex," I said. "Any notable successes, a la *The Island of Doctor Moreau?*"

"Me, a scientist? Hardly. Certainly, I'm slightly bonkers and quite ancient. Old people acquire knowledge. We spread it around, for weal or woe. As to the matter of success, I'm banking on getting lucky tonight, at least. Let's swing by your room for a nightcap."

"Mine? Surely yours is more luxurious."

She took my arm rather possessively. "I sleep hanging upside down from a trapeze bar in Aviary 4. It's not a cozy rendezvous."

All I could see was the mask of the devil bird in the video clip, the feather plume; her victim's corpse tumbling toward the water; men and women screaming in a solarium, its walls splattered in gore. Averna, radiant and exultant as a blood god from the bad history books.

Half a magnum of 1928 Krug later:
     "Final girls are a necessarily rare breed." Averna studied my calloused palms, the yellow bruises along my shoulder. Her nails were trimmed close to the quick and unpolished. Dark specks of blood had gotten under some of them. "Your training regimen is fierce. No enhanced strength or ESP? No telekinetic powers?"

"I skate along on woman's intuition."

"No secret weaponry of any kind?"

"Apparently, I'm a mongoose. Natural weaponry. Rawr!"

"She kissed my (also bruised) belly. "I am curious what combination of pathology and trauma drives you to seek danger."

"This from Miss I-jump-off-cliffs-in a-wingsuit?"

"Pretend a normal person you'd like to fuck asked the question. The event in Alaska opened the world for you."

"Opened the world? Like I should be grateful? I never volunteered to get brutalized. I didn't tip that domino. The attack fucked me up royal." I resisted the urge to touch the scar on my neck.

"Or it awakened dormant DNA. Your latent adrenaline junkie gene."

"You know how it is—at first, it's about the rush, then the rush becomes a habit. After a while, you're basically screwed."

"Give it an eon. Who's your favorite superhero?"

"Let me think…"

"Don't think, tell me."

"Like tic-tac-toe?" I stalled.

"Cheating already."

"Okay. The Batman."

"Not Batgirl?"

"Defending my answer wasn't part of the game. I want every bit of power. You?"

"Captain Midnight."

"Who's Captain Midnight?"

"Seriously?" Averna cupped her chin and regarded me. "I'm reevaluating this whole relationship."

"All six hours of it."

"My time is precious, Mace. Bouquets of thousand-dollar bills could rain from the sky and it wouldn't be cost effective to stoop for the ones that didn't fall into my pocket."

"Okay, don't be rethinking anything. Give me a mulligan. Who the hell is Captain Midnight?"

"Ace World War One pilot. Could fly anything. Total badass."

"You're busting my balls over a cartoon from World War One?" She undid my bra and tossed it over the side. "Radio show."

"Seems like an odd choice for a hero," I said.

"Not if you knew me for more than six hours."

Ultimately, I told her my darkest secrets: Mom and Dad fought over the heavyweight title and it brought the Mace kids together; my first real love rescued me from the galley of a fishing boat right before it went to the bottom of the sea and a few happy years went by and nobody was around to rescue him; Mom ran out on us a hundred times, and finally, she stayed gone for good, either dead or reborn; when the Eagle Talon Ripper sliced my throat, I thought I'd died. Such a relief! The real reason I emptied the gun into the sonofabitch was because he'd done a half-assed job putting me out of my misery.

"At last I understand your motivation," Averna said. "It isn't thrill-seeking behavior. You experience suicidal ideation, probably stemming from survivor's guilt."

"I'm not suicidal anymore. Guilt? Not so much of that ether."

"Dying isn't easy for most people. Instinct is a real bitch and she wants to live. Sadly, those with a true death wish, suffer terribly. O cruel universe. It imbued you with unbearable misery and a rational mind. Care to guess what the mind says?"

"Let's fuck? Let's drink? Let's forget?"

"The mind says, no more, let's stop. The universe also imbued you with the genetics of a survivor. *Your* subconscious resists annihilation; it says, okay, you can die, but only after jumping through fiery hoops, only after completing an obstacle course in hell. Some people with your particular affliction drink themselves to death or go hunting for Mr. Goodbar. They take on risky jobs. You, my dear, follow this hard road. It led to my doorstep."

"The other shoe droppeth," I said.

"Just your panties, at the moment."

What's *your* motivation?"

Her long, cruel fingers dug into my hips. "I like it when my prey runs screaming through the forest. I like the idea that animals will inherit the earth. I like the idea that with a little push we could be apes again."

"Oh," I said.

On day two we buzzed the estate in the helicopter. Trees, tree-covered mountains, tree-covered valleys, and more trees. Averna piloted. She wore a shiny black flight suit that exaggerated her figure into comic book proportions. Manson sat in the rear, loose-limbed and heavy-lidded. Her suit and mine were dull gray.

My secret of the day: I'd seen this before. In the course of training for the mission, Dr. Campbell had put me into a hypnotic trance and shown dozens of satellite images of the territory. Military grade imagery that dialed right down to the individual acorn. He explained that a photographic memory wasn't necessary to retain this information—if I got lost in these woods, a certain phrase would trigger the implanted memories and I'd have access to a 3-D "mind map" of the surroundings.

I keyed the mike in my headset. "Averna, I read somewhere that you almost died testing a wingsuit in Finland."

"Norway. Bad landings happen. Fortunately, the crash appeared nastier than the reality."

Witnesses said she'd hit the turf at an estimated one-hundred and thirty-miles per hour. The article also claimed it required a team of surgeons four operations and a roll of duct tape to put Humpty-Dumpty together again.

"Tycoons evidently score the world's greatest docs. I know women with C-section scars that could've been done with a boar spear."

"Flawless skin was a gift from my mother. Hold on." She banked hard right and put the helicopter into a shallow dive toward the foothills. We shot through a notch in the tree line and she leaned back on the yoke into a near vertical climb to hop over the rocky crown of a hill, then pushed hard and dropped hard to skim several feet above a lake, and steeply up again at the last second as a wall of evergreens closed in. My heart remained where it had leapt from my chest, a couple miles back.

Upon our return to the house, I retreated to my room and pondered the implications. Eighteen hours with Averna Spencer convinced me she didn't possess a scintilla of spontaneity. Her brain functioned on a beautiful, cold algorithm that perfectly mimicked human thought, human desire, yet possessed the nascent spark of neither. Rich folks often exhibit outsized egos and a narcissistic compulsion to impress the peasants. Averna didn't give a damn. She'd taken me on the flyover to demonstrate the geography and parameters of her estate for a practical purpose. In retrospect, the message was no less subtle than if she'd leaned over and whispered that I should get my track shoes laced. It's on like Donkey Kong, girlfriend.

The second message was delivered much later in the evening as I prowled through the house, casually testing locks and poking my nose where it didn't belong. Happened to peek into an antechamber and Lo! Averna (naked and gleaming) straddled Manson (naked and gleaming) atop a couch. Averna swallowed grapes from a prodigious clump. She regurgitated into Manson's wide-open mouth and sealed it with a kiss. She winked at me. Her yellow eye reflected the epoch when scales and dagger-length talons were king (queen).

I backed away slowly, as one does when menaced by a large and partially satiated predator. Propelled by unreasonable jealousy, I strode to Averna's quarters, temporarily dismantled the security feed with an electromagnetic device disguised as an earring (in addition to zoology, exobiology, physical anthropology, and several other disciplines, including hypnotism, obviously, Doc Campbell dabbled in experimental engineering), and went straight for the safe. I'd memorized the combo and the doctors assured me that all I needed to do was glance at the documents; vital contents would be retrieved via hypnosis during my debriefing. Campbell assured me the mind operated like a camera and everything it experienced was undeveloped film.

The safe lay empty but for a piece of paper that read, *Bluebeard is a cautionary tale, lover,* and signed with a lipstick kiss.

I decided to hoof it, mission be damned, and take my chances in the mountains with the bears and the wolves and the inevitable pursuit. Two guards were posted on either side of my bedroom door. Stony-faced guys in military uniforms, assault rifles at port arms. So much for sneaking off, stage left.

Day three, several guests emerged to join the fun. Averna behaved as the convivial lady of the manor. We played games of the mundane variety. Mini golf and horseshoes in a horseshoe pit worthy of the Roman Coliseum. Manson caught my attention and casually straightened an iron horseshoe with her bare hands.

Then supper.

While gnawing on a pheasant wing and swilling fancy imported lager, I rubbed elbows with the new folks. Three of them had arrived at the estate a week prior; two others had gotten flown in that morning. Young men, down at the heels, but strong and athletic. Army guys who hadn't readjusted to life stateside; a boozy ex-cop; a kid maybe six months clear of high school where he'd wrestled varsity; and a couple cop/soldier wannabes. Each of them hoped to score a permanent security gig or at least a free ride as long as it lasted. I chatted the boys up—no close family; they were at loose ends. Nobody back home would notice, much less care, when they went missing. I won't bother with names; simpler to think of them as Hapless Victims #1 through #5.

Manson stood next to me at the bar. She wore a dark gown and a star pattern of heavy purple eyeshadow. "We don't usually entertain more than a couple of guests. This is special."

"What's the occasion?"

"It's Tuesday. Go back to your quarters. Ms. Spencer left you a gift."

"Because it's Tuesday?"

"Because there will be entertainment later this evening and you may wish to dress appropriately."

This is where you came in…

Averna kept me stewing (quite literally) for forty-eight hours, plus or minus; a fact I estimated by the phase of the moon and an above average internal clock.

Why giant synthetic eggs? The design of the incubators was strictly symbolic. The contents—a contemporary primordial soup chock full of vitamins, proteins, and assorted mystery elements intended to cleanse her chosen, to heighten our reflexes and provide sufficient high-test nourishment for a proper hunt—could've done its work in a tank. She preferred elaborate theatrics; a consequence of eternal life. Have to wonder which came first: murderous rage or immortality. Since I could only hazard a guess, I guessed the eggs were deposited at various predetermined sites on the estate. We prisoners "hatched" and were subsequently hunted by our hostess and her majordomo.

During incubation, my dreams were psychedelic and fantastically, Lucio-Fulci-strength, macabre. Visions, perhaps. I beheld the male guests pelting through a night forest roiling with phosphorescent mist. Averna glided down on stiff, black wings. Her wingsuit defied physics. She tilted vertically and her toes dug into the soil every third or fourth gigantic stride and beheaded each of the fleeing men with a casual swipe of her metallic talons. She accelerated in dizzying curlicues through gaps in the trees.

Averna crooned to me through an intravenous drip. She spoke of evolutionary slippage, of natural mutation and genetic manipulation.

I die and live again and again. My soul regenerates into new flesh.

I have broken the hearts of countless men. I have eaten the beating hearts of countless men. I have devoured so many beating hearts, I shit and piss black heartblood.

I am a fountainhead of raped vitality.

I am a supplicant of the gods of eternal return.

I mean to devour you as I've devoured the rest in their multitudes.

You'll regenerate as I have done since the dawn of hominids. We'll meet again in a hundred million years at the dawn of the hominids. We'll meet again between one scream and the next.

Wake up, wake up, wake up…

I love and hate *The Vanishing.* The Dutch version by Sluizer; don't bother with the American remake, hunky Jeff Bridges notwithstanding. In a previous life, I made my bread as a marine biologist. I survived many a tedious night aboard fishing tenders on the Bering Sea with a stack of paperbacks and VHS tapes while the rest of the crew was drunk or unconscious. Somewhere in the middle of *The Vanishing* a character describes a nightmare of being trapped in the darkness of a golden egg. Love it because the image got to me on a primal level and stuck. Hate it for the same reason.

These many years later, waking to fluid blackness three thousand miles east of Alaska, tubes up my nose and down my throat, body coiled like an embryo inside a golden egg of my very own? Must be the abyss everybody talks about.

I kicked, one-two, and dove deep into a sea of blood. Crimson light churned. The shell cracked and broke and the universe spilled me onto a carpet of pine needles. Out came the rubber tubes with a yank; then a bout of projectile vomiting—pheasant, sorbet, and copious amounts of whiskey and synthetic amniotic fluid. The blood in my eyes seeped down and dried into scales. Tears dug diamond furrows through caked-on grime. My convulsions subsided. I stood and leaned like a drunk against the bole of a hemlock and assessed the fucked-upedness of my situation.

A mild evening in the early October. Mosquitos whined; could have been worse. Clouds rolled over a crescent moon. Had to think fast, had to move. Standing still would get me dead. *Moving* would get me dead. Where was Rikki-tikki-tavi in my hour of need? An owl screeched. The bird glided past; the very shadow of death itself.

I'd trained for the direst scenarios—spent the previous several months jogging barefoot to toughen my feet; I also worked on traveling in New England forests at night to sharpen my lowlight vison. An affinity for rough and tumble notwithstanding, no way, no how am I a martial artist. I sparred with Beasley, who agreed (after I walked into his right hand three or four times) keeping it simple would be for the best. He honed my bag of dirty tricks and taught me a couple new ones.

Should've done more. Should've stayed in bed.

For all the roadwork and psychological preparation, and despite my alleged "purpose" and indomitable resolve, it was a psychological body blow to wash up on the proverbial lee shore: naked in the middle of the woods in the dead of night, pumped to the gills with experimental juice and on the run from Elizabeth Bathory II and her army of mercs. I intoned Dr. Campbell's mnemonic phrase (*the mind is a camera*) that would supposedly trigger a pseudo-holographic image of the surroundings. It worked, too.

I waded down a stream to confuse tracking dogs, then dug a hole near the roots of a tree and covered myself in clay, pine needles, and sap. I hadn't worn hair products or used scented soap or perfume in months. The docs put me on a regimen of an experimental, military grade antiperspirant.

Smeared head to toe in muck, I ran like hell through the dark, dark woods like a doomed slasher heroine. I angled southeast for the extraction point (would Beasley await my arrival?); kept right on trucking until daylight and then burrowed into a deadfall and slept. Night came around. I slurped brackish water from a puddle and set forth again, skulking from tree to tree with a wild animal's determination to survive. For a while, I believed I'd successfully evade and escape. Hope makes fools of us all.

Contrary to the cliché, I didn't trip and sprain an ankle, didn't sob or shriek to give away my position, and didn't glance over my shoulder every ten feet. Perversely, that last detail proved my downfall.

She hit me the way a hawk or an owl does an unsuspecting squirrel. Instead of severing my spine on impact, Averna merely snagged my long, luxurious mane and ascended vertically, yanking me off my feet. Similar to those rides at the State Fair—the ones where a scabrous, hungover carny straps you into a harness that dangles from a big metal wheel and up your sorry ass goes, with nothing between your sneakers and sod but a sheer drop.

The radiant sickle moon gashed the clouds; first above, then below. Averna clutched my hair in her left fist and skimmed treetops at a precipitous velocity, dragging me several feet lower like the tail of a kite. We dipped and swooned; accelerating, decelerating. If she had a jet pack strapped on her back, I didn't hear it. The only sounds I heard were the hissing breeze, and the clatter of branches when she swung me viciously against the canopy. Each blow knocked the breath from me and tore my flesh.

God knows where the bitch's flight plan would've taken us. I didn't stick around for the surprise. It required a metric fuck-ton of grit to recover from the initial whiplash and saw through my hair with a shard of the designer egg I'd carried (and managed not to drop) this entire time. Sliced my fingers and palm, but it got the job done—half a dozen convulsive hacks later, the last strand parted and I bailed. She cried my name.

Momentum hurled me in a broad arc. I caromed from leafy boughs and they snapped beneath my cannonball passage. Five seconds? Five thousand years? Those few heartbeats stretched across multiple lifetimes. Don't remember hitting the earth. Black stars cleared and I lay in a pile of dead, slimy leaves, oxygen smashed from my lungs, gaping at the moon.

A circling shadow blotted the light. I caught a glimpse of Averna in her radiant glory and realized the mysteries of the universe dwarfed my comprehension. She didn't need a wingsuit. She didn't need wings. She didn't need anything.

Manson strode from the depths of the forest. She didn't put a bullet through my skull as I might've logically assumed. She scooped my battered self (broken ribs, lacerated hand, and a world class concussion) into her arms and lugged me half a mile to the cabin. I don't recall a hell of a lot about the next couple of days except that the place was empty. No phone, no Beasley. Pretty clear my fate had been sealed from the beginning.

Manson played nursemaid by firelight from a decrepit hearth. Stuffed me into a sleeping bag and got an I.V. drip pumping fluids into my veins. Everything went blurry after the adrenalin wore off.

I dreamed that Averna, garbed in her horror show suit, shattered the cabin door and loomed over me as I lay helpless. Her wingtips scraped furrows in the walls. *Behold. I am the apex. I stand where humanity begins and where it will end.* She lovingly popped my eyeballs with her claws.

Woke screaming to beat the band.

Averna, dressed in a natty jacket, tenderly stroked my brow with a damp cloth. She revealed I was merely the second person to ever make it across the finish line. For me to plummet from the treetops and bounce instead of splat, represented a bona fide miracle. I didn't argue the point. Fell unconscious for however long it took for my injuries to mend.

Jessica, you must understand we're all meat and blood for the slaughterhouse. Regardless, we should learn until the very end. Sapient beings exist to acquire experience. The beasts of the wilderness kill and eat us. The wilderness itself kills and eats us. Every scrap down to our quintessence reduces and divides among maggots and dirt and adds to the sum.

Go in peace, dear girl. You and the world have unfinished business. Far be it from me to stand in the way.

Could've been a fever dream, could've been legit; either way, Averna and Manson let me live. Eventually I roused from blind sleep, aching, traumatized, and swaddled in gauze. The girls left clean clothes, pain pills, and an envelope with a few bucks inside a knapsack. Also, a loaded pistol and keys to a Jeep parked by the front porch.

Time passed. I bided it with grim patience.

Beasley the vigilant had to sleep sometime. I waited to make my move until he embarked upon one of his not infrequent drunks. Walked into the New England farmhouse around dawn. The doctors were seated at a table in the den, bickering over a pile of research papers. They registered surprise at my appearance, although less than one might expect. Fuckers had seen everything at least once, I suppose. Dr. Ryoko reached for a drawer, then noticed the pistol in my hand, and sat back with a resigned sigh.

"Hello, gentlemen," I said. "Tell me about my mother."

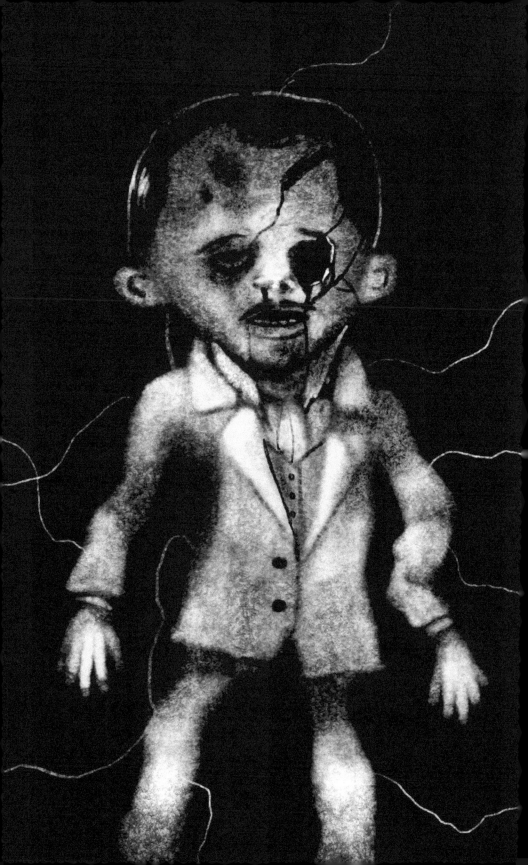

DON'T MAKE ME ASSUME
MY ULTIMATE FORM

POLYCHROMATIC MERCY

Before you become Dee Dee Gamma, before the Black Kaleidoscope takes over your existence, you are Delia Dolores Andersen and you specialize in knocking over jewelry stores. Today will be your last day on the job. Your head swivels and that serves nothing, spares you nothing as your partner, a brute, points her gun at the jeweler and squeezes the trigger. A bullet punches into the jeweler's forehead. The pistol vibrates. The frame drags, almost disintegrates into cigarette burns, and then steadies. Words and sound synchronize

What you're thinking at this moment is primitive and inchoate as the explosion of electrified chemicals and neurons through your system. The thought is as elastic as all of time and space, and like the contrail of the reflexive act, it hangs in your mind in the gulf between, *Don't touch that alarm, you stupid sonofabitch,* and, *Sweet*

Jesus, oh, fuck. Willa killed him. That's right, you forgot for a moment, your partner's name is Willa. An Iowa girl, a Star Wars action figure collector, overweight and undereducated, childlike in her emotional incapability. She appears baffled at the report and the jeweler sprawled on the floor.

Now you've got the case with the diamonds and are cat-footing through the ghost-lighted lobby for the doors. You stepped in blood to collect the prize and you leave a trail.

The driver rolls up to the curb in a Maserati. She pegs it zero to sixty before you get buckled. The vista of glass shop fronts, sidewalk cafes, alleyways, and cross streets blurs, reverses into sequoias, swamps, the mists of prehistory and bubbling lava. Keep rewinding. An old star burst into a fountain of gamma rays about a hundred million years ago. That cosmic lance has crossed an infinity of cold and darkness to pierce the sunroof, the dome of your skull, and your brain. Cells roil and transform in squamous panic. Decades of your allotted mortal span are reduced to a handful of years. Every tick of the second-hand is emphasis.

Your consciousness untethers from its flesh and rises above the car for a fraction of a millisecond that lasts closer to an eon. The universe fractures into a blizzard of eternally replicating slivers of ice. Images are imprinted within the slivers. You see men in uniforms with automatic weapons. A wound drips in a magenta sky. You behold with the searing clarity of an X-ray the new ravenous companion that has taken root in your gray matter. Cancer, malignant with a capital C.

You will never be alone again. That realization should be terrifying. You feel nothing, however. You remain numb, even when it all begins to come true.

Mrs. Shrike

Seven months into a twenty year stretch in a Spanish prison, a chick from way back in high school visits your cell. She apparates between skull-shattering migraines.

Norse: "Hi, I'm Indra Norse. Mrs. Shrike thought a friendly face might cheer your gloomy ass up." Afro, shooting glasses, gold jumpsuit, utility belt with a black sunburst buckle, and combat boots. She looks different than the demure schoolgirl you knew in Alaska. Faster.

You remember her instantly because she'd been the smartest girl in the room. Her names fascinated you. Indra is a male god and Norse seems an odd surname for an African American family. You also recall that speculating on the subject is a sure-fire way to get punched in the mouth.

Norse: "Two options, Dee Dee. Run away with me to the circus, or rot here. Option one, I return in twenty-four hours with all the papers to make you a free woman. Only catch, you gotta repay the debt. We'll talk about that later. Option two, I hope you are happy with the roaches."

You don't require twenty-four hours to weigh the merits. She gives them to you anyway. She asks how the migraines are as she watches you dress in clean traveling clothes. No fancy jumpsuit for you. Later, perhaps. Your own questions are deflected—who, what, why?

Norse: "The spirits aren't cooperating? Ask the magic eight ball again later. Eat these pills. Take the edge off those headaches."

Clean clothes, clean record, passport, and tickets home. Norse's reference to your heightened powers of perception, which is a secret you've not bothered to share with anyone. The FBI is running a game, has to be. *Somebody* is running a game. Life is rigged.

It's true—pain pills are addicting when you gulp them in bunches.

An inoperable brain tumor grows fat and you've resigned yourself to the worst. The pills fog your mind too often. Although once details begin to reveal themselves, you're actually grateful for the respite from reality. What passes for reality, at any rate.

You: "Where are we going?"

Norse: "The Nest."

THE NEST

The Nest is located in western Washington. *Mrs. Shrike's Home for Wayward Girls* is how it hits you after you mingle with Norse and the others at Liz Lochinvar's Bellingham residence. Set among old-growth fir trees and straight out of the 1960s with lots of glass and lots of shag. Jacuzzi, steam room, a wet bar, etcetera, etcetera. Lochinvar, another of your long-lost high school comrades, inherited it from some rich relative and this is where Mrs. Shrike keeps you sharp and ready as a box of knives. You have access to food, weapons, and discretionary funds. Everything except capes and domino masks. Those will come later.

Several women form the heart of the sorority itself. Introductions occur around a coffee table while a grand Pacific Northwest thunderstorm rumbles overhead.

Norse: "Naval Intelligence. Profiler. Authority doesn't give a damn about ridding the world of evil. I want to burn things down."

Lochinvar: "Ex-Army. Olympic Judo champeen. Too many rules. Wasn't suited for it. Not at all." She smiles at the knife in her calloused fist.

Sloan: "Ex-housewife. Alcoholic. Addict. Antisocial. Shrike taught me how to manage my assets. By the way, fuck Judo. Krav Maga all day and all night." She smiles at Lochinvar. A couple of sweet-faced calendar girls who can tear phonebooks apart with their bare hands.

Mace: "Professional final girl." Her voice is rough, her neck is scarred. She smokes the living shit out of cigarettes. She wears a bunch of fighting rings. A tattoo of binary code runs along her left forearm. The Zeroes and Ones spell REX. He's dead.

You: "I'm a career criminal. I'm dying."

Norse: "Dying? Dying? Bitch, we're survivors."

Sloan: "Survivors—for now."

Lochinvar: "It doesn't matter a rat's ass what we *were*. Now we're the point of the spear. Now we are the first cohort. What scales you ain't shed from your old life, will fall real soon."

Sloan: "The legionary first cohort of ex-girlfriends." She whacks her bottle of Rolling Rock against Norse's.

You: "Groovy digs, to be sure, and the company is pleasant—"

Mace: "She wants to know why we've gathered here today…" She's half in the bag, which proves to be a routine condition.

You: "Point of the spear? That's not phallic or anything."

Sloan: "We're down with phallic metaphors, and phalluses."

Norse: "*Some* of us are down."

Lochinvar: "We are a privately funded clandestine civilian agency. Certain elements within local and federal law enforcement and military organizations are aware of our existence. Some of these tolerate us, assist us on occasion. Mostly we're on our own."

Norse: "We fight evil."

You: "Specifically?"

Norse: "We rescue kittens from trees."

Sloan: "We help old ladies cross the street."

Norse: "No job is too large, no need too small."

Lochinvar: "The other day I personally annihilated a cult that wanted to revive mass sacrifice to open a wormhole to deep space in somebody's basement. Next week it could be some asshole has figured a way to construct a pocket-sized death-ray."

Mace: "Or the kitten will be up another tree."

Sloan: "We ennoble the downtrodden and defame the wicked. We set fires, we bat our eyelashes, and we get the last word. Whatever it takes."

Norse: "You just never know what will happen when you jump out a bed in the morning. Shrikes have all kinds of fun."

You nurse your near-beer and search their faces for the joke or the con. None of them give a damn about your skepticism. The easy camaraderie and devilish smiles aren't the kind a woman can fake. Their gallows humor and haunted glances are sharp enough to cut right through your cynicism. These are condemned souls hatching doomed escape plans while the firing squad assembles. If your foot wasn't already in the grave you might worry more. You wonder about frying pans and fires.

Norse squeezes your hand and your apprehensions are overcome.

X

The stories are similar for the others who inhabit the Nest, the girls who come and go on mysterious errands and sometimes disappear without a forwarding address. Each of you has a purpose, a function within a great complicated pattern. Nine is the current magic number of the roster of your all-girls club. There were eleven as recently as last week; circumstances are such that membership fluctuates. Although the core of the team hails from Alaska, none of you calls it home for one reason or another. The last frontier is a magnet that draws against the metal in your blood and you'll head back soon enough, ready or not.

Cryptic histories and gallows humor to the contrary, not all of you are damned. Far less melodramatic. However, *you* are and that's why everybody smiles like you're a puppy with cancer, except you're a thirty-something ex-con with cancer. You're happy to have a job. Each of you has one individual to thank for this newfound lease on life.

You refer to your benefactor as The Old Woman in the Mountain. The connotations are evident upon consideration of your group's favorite problem-solving methods. You also refer to her as Mrs. Shrike because that's the long defunct company name graven into the serial plate on the underside of the midnight blue phone. Shrikes are beautiful and cruel. The universe, blind, insensate, and implacable, understands perfectly.

The Old Woman represents an enigma. The fact you can't turn the Black Kaleidoscope her direction is troubling. Who is she? A do-gooder tycoon? The mouthpiece of a multinational corporation? A government shill pulling strings for murky objectives? Lochinvar and Mace allegedly have the most insight. Too bad they aren't talking. The name of the game is trust, although blind faith seems more apt. Bottom line, you placed your bet. Let it ride.

You and Norse aren't present when Lochinvar unlocks the sacred gun safe (a rusty and verdigris-stained Diebold hulk with cutsie skulls and crossbones painted on the side) and makes the ritual call on the midnight blue rotary. You get an earful soon after. Lochinvar convenes an emergency session to discuss the options. She drops the blinds and puts on the lamp with the crimson shade; transforms the furnished basement into a bunker where generals have gathered to decide between DEFCON 2 or DEFCON 1.

Word is, X must be retrieved or else. *Or else* could indicate the assassination of a world leader, the end of an era, or the fiery demolition of planet Earth. *Or else* covers a spectrum of unpleasant possibilities.

Once X is secured, further instructions will follow. The main problem confronting the group is that none of you know what X represents. The basic idea seems to be this person or item currently resides in a ghost town in Alaska and that you'll recognize X when you see it. Are missions always this ambiguous? That would explain why Lochinvar brought you into the fold despite your violent misdeeds and how much fixing it took to cover your tracks.

The other girls want to draw lots, throw dice, or knives, go two out of three falls. This case is special. *You* are uniquely suited for the business at hand—the mind control lessons are paying off. Most importantly, the Old Woman in the Mountain informs Lochinvar and Sloan that it must be you, no substitutions. This is your trial by fire, Gamma. The first mission is a blooding and it is traditionally done solo. Mace and Lochinvar explain that they'll run interference and direct the opposition's attention elsewhere and give you the best chance possible. However, this first go-around, you're on your own with everything to prove.

To be accepted by the team, to become part of something larger than yourself…You need it to fill your hollow core. Time surely isn't on your side. In the face of imminent extinction, no risk is too great for a shot at redemption. Whatever threat lurks in the great white north can't be worse than the miserable existence you've put in the rearview nor the malignancy of your traitor cells. The others laugh at this naiveté. Mace and Lochinvar, despite their scars and their notoriety, laugh the loudest. Their bitterness raises the hair on your neck. In that moment your friends aren't soft or warm or jocular. No longer are they sarcastic ex-college girls gone a little wrong, lounging in bathing suits, indolent from wine. They are druidesses, naked but for antlers and red ochre, obsidian daggers raised high against the black supermoon, as they loom over the sacrificial slab and you squirming there.

You smile as the fantasy bursts. A weak smile because you're never sure anymore. Could be in another reality, a previous incarnation, wherein Mrs. Shrike's crew ate human hearts and trilled Aztec death whistles.

Sloan believes the effort is fruitless and that it will end in all your deaths. She's a gleeful pessimist. Mace says it doesn't much matter, win or lose. She's even more of a pessimist. Neither of them are talking about your impending trip into the north, they're referring to the big picture.

Norse: "May as well be me. Spare new girl the pain."

Sloan: "Nuh-uh." She flexes her biceps. "It should be me *and* thee. Could be an occasion for violence. Home girl's soft. We're the violent ones."

Lochinvar: "You smack-talkin' bitches need to stifle yourselves." Her cool glare shuts them right down. She takes her orders directly from the Old Woman. The Old Woman calls the shots and she has spoken. That makes you the It Girl.

Plans are laid. The point of no return zooms past.

GO NORTH, YOUNG WOMAN

The going-away ceremony is a barbeque on a beach near the Nest. Lochinvar's a disco fanatic. She lugs a record player and a portable generator to the event; broadcasts the hot '70s beats on scratched vinyl. Neither KC nor his entire Sunshine Band help to dispel the mood of impending doom. The driftwood blaze isn't merry either, it's a Roman Legion bonfire on the eve of a massacre.

Everybody kisses your cheek, except for Norse who goes for a little more. Mace hugs you and says to check the drop box in Palmer; she's sent ahead her second favorite holdout knife. In the morning you're gone and the cabal of kick-ass bitches, the voice on the midnight blue rotary in the gun safe, and all the rest, recedes into the province of dream and delusion.

There's a four-hour flight from SeaTac to Anchorage, Alaska. The easy part. From Anchorage, you drive. The rental is dinged in all four panels, its windshield is cracked. Duct tape on the gear shift.

You swing through Palmer and visit the apartment of your contact, a sympathizer. A bland woman in a red bathrobe with a heron stitched to the breast mutes her soap opera to answer the door. She doesn't ask questions. She hands you a key and points to a metal box in her shoe closet. Inside that box there are three burner cell phones, an atomizer of compressed acid (with Mr. Yuck stickers plastered to the barrel), a set of topographical maps, and, tucked into a manila folder, fifteen hundred dollars in assorted bills and a nine inch commando knife attached to a sticky note emblazoned by a lipstick kiss. Thanks, Mace.

The real driving begins.

Alaska is emptiness ringed in prehistoric fangs. This is the season of mosquitos and thunderstorms. The sun never completely sets. Red skies. Wetlands, peckerwood forest, and mountains keep going and going whichever way you turn your head. The sea gleams harsh as chipped glass, but you haven't seen it since you pushed inland. Mace claims sleeping on a boat brings the weirdest dreams. She'd know.

Green earth gives way to tundra and shale. Towns lie in strips. Roads are geometric slashes radiating from the carven visage of a forsaken god's skull. Summer is eighty-seven days long. Dust cakes the windows of the shops and of the cars. Beams of sunlight and headlights through the dusty windows intersect as rays of mud.

You pop a ball of chocolate caffeine. Trucker-strength, goddamnit. Onward and onward.

Poor men are made of mud. Said Tennessee Ernie Ford. He also said a rich man has blue in his blood. When the blue is black and black is mud that pours from incandescent clouds and caged filaments and oozes like tar from opened flesh, you will have arrived at the great X burned into the map. You will stand in the mud-light, buried like a flint arrowhead, in the heart of the X. Eventually the habitations of men fall away and there are no other vehicles. The land aches. It doesn't want you around either. You're the grain of irritating insignificance in the flesh of the oyster.

Onward and onward until the radio grinds static and ravens glide overhead. Signs warn against trespassing before they disappear.

Murdockville is the ghost of a mining town a corporation laid out seventeen years ago at the height of a boom. No one has lived here in fourteen. Sadly, the mine went bust and the brand spanking new facilities were evacuated overnight. Tundra and earthquakes and relentless north winds are returning the place to dirt, one roof tile, one brick, one smashed window at a time. Summer, and thank the powers for that much. This will be no place for a human being when winter howls down from the snowy range.

You've traveled through dust and darkness to claim your prize, to grasp Fate by the throat. Yours is the gift of second sight. Premonition, clairvoyance, telepathy, woman's intuition. Whatever it is, it's not reliable enough to break the bank in Vegas. Weak and intermittent as a radio broadcast that can only be received under perfect atmospheric conditions, it has led you in fits and starts to these modern ruins lost within the ancient wilderness.

The Old Woman in the Mountain says the prize will be subtle, yet obvious. Your choices inside this shelled out room in an abandoned rec center boil down to either a jukebox, a buckshot blast pattern through a corkboard bulletin board, or the bundle of rags and wooden sticks cast aside in the corner. The bundle proves to be an Edgar Allan Poe puppet. Two feet long; the puppet's colors are faded bronze flecked black, its skull is deformed, and its prim black suit hangs in cerement tatters. Its strings are clipped and its mustache is clotted from a nosebleed. One cockeye peers, cold as the permafrost. The other eye is a ragged hole. Behold a simulacrum of Poe, dead from booze and rabies and after the vermin have had at his face.

You don't want to believe that you've seen this puppet. Your sister, Harmony, owned several marionettes when you were girls. Poe, an astronaut, a Punch puppet, and others. Harmony wasn't skilled in puppetry; she enjoyed flailing her troupe across makeshift stages in skits she learned while watching *Mr. Rogers' Neighborhood*. Teen years (boys, cliques, and a new car!) arrived and those puppets went into a Salvation Army bin. Yet here Poe is, the once pallidly morose creature who resided on a shelf above Harmony's bed. Pallid moroseness has progressed to disease and horror.

First prize, indeed.

POE BOY

*P*oe: "Humans are not inevitable, Annabel. You used the Black Glass to find me. An unwise course. Exceedingly." The puppet's voice is educated, yet rough, and far from the mannered Victorian accent your subconscious might be expected to affect. This is closer to your grandfather's voice, or how you imagine it after these many years.

A lesser soul would scream and hurl the puppet aside. You are made of heavier metal; one flinch and a strangled cry of surprise is the extent of your concession to civilian frailty. The puppet's lips don't move, the first clue this is a hallucination or a miracle. You would love to believe you've acquired super powers manifesting as psychokinesis or full-on telepathy, however it seems more probable that the brain tumor is finally impinging upon something vital, as promised. Migraines, nosebleeds, hallucinations; none of it is promising. Puppets don't speak of their own accord and that means you've elevated the art of the interior monologue to a new level.

You: "The Old Woman says that." You set Poe in the passenger seat. The trunk would seem more plausible, except you decide to keep the puppet near, like a proper enemy. "And my name isn't Annabel.

Poe: "Isn't it, Ann? Does she? Lochinvar *claims* to speak to her."

You: "Maybe I should tape your mouth."

Poe: "I've seen hell, Ann." He pronounces *Ann* with a sneer.

You: "My friends will want to hear all about it."

Poe: "It is not inevitable that you will meet them again."

You turn the key in the ignition and nothing happens. You unwrap another caffeine pill and eat it, slowly crumple the foil and its hornet graphic. Wind pushes against the car. Directly before you, the skeletal frame of a radio tower trembles. To your left, lies a row of low buildings with boarded windows and tan doors, sealed tight against the elements. On your right, across a tussock field, spreads a disjointed landscape of alder thickets and marsh. Hills rise and rise. It is late afternoon and the sun is a blade stabbing toward the mountains. You dial the special number and let the machine record, then disconnect. Waiting is the hardest part is right.

The burner phone hums. It's Lochinvar.

Lochinvar: "What you got, girl?" After you describe the situation and your acquisition, she says to hang tight. Minutes pass. "Has it said anything?" Her tone is different.

You: "The puppet?"

Lochinvar: "Has it spoken? This is important."

You: "It's not that kind."

Lochinvar: "All puppets are that kind. This...puppet was abandoned in New York State ten years ago. Now it's hiding out in Tumbleweed Alaska. Hell of a migration."

You: "Someone obviously—"

Lochinvar: "Someone obviously my ass. Has it spoken or not?"

You: "No." You massage your skull even though the pain hasn't started. You don't need second-sight to detect the edge in her voice. She's been on the horn with the Old Woman, getting the signals.

Lochinvar: "All right. Thank god."

You: "Why thank god?" You straighten in the seat and regard your little buddy.

Lochinvar: "Mrs. Shrike says if it's quiet, you're still in the green."

You: "Oh. I probably don't want to explore the implications."

Lochinvar: "Correct, you do not. Keep X under direct supervision. Get home."

After Lochinvar has gone you chuck the phone and hit the ignition. No joy.

Poe: "Scary music and car troubles mean only one thing."

You study the surroundings. The hand of darkness is slipping ever closer.

You: "We've got the place to ourselves, Eddie. We're in the green."

Poe: "Why'd you lie to your pal?"

You: "I didn't lie."

Poe: "You lied your lips off."

You: "We aren't having this conversation. You're an aural hallucination precipitated by my terminal decline. And shut up."

Poe: "Please, put me back." The puppet's head slips, so its remaining eye fixes on you.

You: "I've driven all this way. C'mon."

Poe: "You've never killed. You're not the same as the other girls. You don't have the guts. Please put me back. *It's* going to get me. You led it here. Please, please, please."

You: "Nevermore."

Poe: "Fool! The car isn't going to start. I'm dead. The Eater of Dolls is coming."

You: "Shut up, Eddie." After a deep breath, you try, try again and the engine catches, praise the powers above and below.

Poe: "Oh no oh no oh no." Then the puppet laughs.

You've heard that sound. When the doctor called to say your

mother's cancer, and now *your* cancer, had done its work. You heard it again when your old golden retriever cried once in the night as she was going, gone. You heard it during an adventurous youth, moments before the thin ice of a lake cracked beneath your boots. You heard it last when a kid from Indiana, a Star Trek fanatic, cocked the hammer of a pistol.

You gun the engine and roll.

BLACK KALEIDOSCOPE

C hocolate speedballs can only take a woman so far and no farther. Pricks of fire float upon the eternal Alaska summer twilight and resolve to the streetlamps and illuminated shops of a town. You fuel the car at a Tesoro and roll into a flophouse motel. Your watch says it's a quarter until nine. Exhaustion weighs your skull like an iron ball. Three or four hours sleep to recharge the batteries, then you'll hit the trail again and press on to Anchorage. Food can wait, a shower can wait. Sleep is what you yearn for.

Poe: "Dear Ann, this isn't a good idea." The puppet tries to sound reasonable, avuncular. "Keep trucking, sister. It wants you to stop. It wants to catch us."

You tuck Poe under your arm and go into the cheap, claustrophobically narrow room. Mold, sweat, smoke, a hint of whorish perfume. Water stains and AC on the fritz. TV works fine, though.

You: "Hey, *Lamb Chop* reruns!" You click and click the remote, hunting for some porno.

Poe: "Stopping is bad." The puppet lies primly in its nest on the opposite bed. The table lamp bathes it with a cancerous glow. "In these situations, stopping is always the worst thing you can do."

You: "Short of fucking outside of wedlock, right? Does masturbation count? Because I plan to rub one out and cash in for the night. I can't see straight enough to avoid the ditch. Free skin flicks and a soft mattress win."

Despite your bravado, you lock the door and block it with a coffee table. A peek through moth-eaten blinds apprises you that the parking lot is mostly empty, and no one stirring except a drunk in shredded fatigues collapsed near the PEPSI machine by the manager's office.

You: "There. You're safe from The Eater of Dolls. Wake me up if he, er, it, comes knocking."

You swallow pills to dull the spike traveling through your skull, dim the lamp, and lie propped against the headboard while spray-tanned actors undulate perfunctorily on the television screen. The next click of the remote takes you back and back to a shirtless Danzig performing "How the Gods Kill."

Poe: "You're a doll." *Its tone is petulant and sinister.* "It will like you too."

You: "Be quiet. You're pissed because somebody snipped your strings. For a marionette that's like getting turned into a eunuch, right?"

Poe refuses to dignify that crack with a reply. You feel the puppet's anger seething.

You haven't dreamed in years. When your eyes close and your consciousness dissipates, it funnels into the barrel of what the eggheads, Toshi and Campbell, who work for Mrs. Shrike, call the Black Kaleidoscope. Quantum location and temporal fragmentary acquisition and dilation is a mouthful. Itty bitty time molecules get snagged in the sieve of your ultra-powerful, ultra-sensitive subconscious and translated into occasionally useful psychic imagery. It feels a hell of lot like astral projection from the way generations of hippies and crystal-loving earth mothers have described gliding along at the whip end of a silver cord. The main difference is, you don't zoom through a gulf of mist and light; you submerge into the black tar between blazing stars, the infinite Lagerstätte where consciousness goes to die. The ichor of the cosmos drowns your senses.

...*Your father folds his arms and stares into the sunset. He never hugged you, never hugged your mother or sister. He backhanded you once, for coming home after curfew with your hair mussed and lipstick smeared. He apologized and apologized and pressed an icepack to your cheek. Last time he ever touched you...*

...*The Maserati careens into a cow pasture. Spanish cops with automatic weapons fill the car with holes, your accomplices with more holes. You surrender peacefully, like the coward you are...A Spartan cell, iron cot, a corroded toilet, trained cockroaches to keep you company...*

...*Norse caresses your cheek.* "Did you have the sight when you were small, or did it develop after you got sick?" *You can't remember not possessing some form of the sight. You don't know if non-memory is true memory. The Black Kaleidoscope has a tendency to overwrite your mind. For example, it helps you forget that Harmony, not some chick from Iowa or Indiana, was driving the getaway car and how, after the third or fourth bullet, her face relaxed until it assumed a puppet's perfectly lifeless expression.*

...*Lochinvar drags on a joint, although her expression remains severe. She struggles to explain how the team receives assignments; it's cryptic—Mrs. Shrike is a facilitator; she doesn't tell her girls everything. Some of it they must learn for themselves.* "We use auguries," *Lochinvar says.* "Tea leaves, pigeon guts, the stock market. Tarot cards. Fortune cookies. Crazier than that."

"Brute force," *you say and decline the joint when she tries to pass it to you.* "What's it all about?"

"Survival. Living to fight another day. We'll see where it goes from there..."

...*Ants mobilize in the depths to invade rival colonies. The quiet slaughter that ensues dwarfs all the wars of men combined…Giant wasps float down from the spreading shadows of the canopy to assault a honeybee fortress, and again, the carnage is numbing…*

… In the rearview as you ball out of Murdockville, the doors of the deserted buildings swing open, one after another in a domino chain…

…Poe tumbles through darkness, limbs jostling, wrapped in a feeble halo of light, dissolving. "Oh dear Annabel. It's your fault she's dead. She was the good girl." *You want to defend yourself. Harmony was a grown woman. She chose to roll the bones and they came up snake-eyes. Words remain impossible. You howl in grief instead. Poe can't hear you. Your sister can't hear you either. They're out there, zipping farther into the great dark…*

…Meanwhile, something is coming up from behind. You glance over your shoulder…

THE EATER OF DOLLS

Y ou come to around midmorning. No one murdered you in the night and that wipes the slate. You check in with Lochinvar. She's unhappy, says to decamp and get driving. Pain pills and breakfast are in order. Your head and stomach conspire to heap misery upon you.

There's a lounge three blocks from the motel. The lounge is arranged similar to those rococo establishments that were popular in the '60s and '70s when your parents dragged you along for breakfast before church. Heavy paneling and dark, heavy furniture that invite gloom. Thick glass ashtrays. The host herds you into the smoking section despite your muttered protestations. He seems fearful.

Pancakes, eggs, coffee. Your waitress is haggard. You wonder if she stayed up late watching porn too. You have to wonder because your talent is more remote-viewing than ESP. Her nametag says CRO. She stares at your forehead, your shoulder, Poe canted against the opposite side of the booth, everywhere but your eyes.

The coffee is bitter. It's daylight, barely, and the place is half full of truckers and the jocular plaid and Carhart workaday set.

Two young women occupy a booth closer to the entrance. Tourists like yourself. Unlike you, the pair wear slinky dresses glittering with sequins, long white gloves (more sequins), and expensive hairdos. The brunette faces the door. The nape of her neck curves most shapely. The blonde is sharp-featured in a way that some find repulsively attractive. Her lipstick lends the illusion she's been slurping at the neck of a slaughtered gazelle. She smiles and sips orange juice, extra-large. She isn't wearing jewelry. Hmm. What to make of that?

The Black Kaleidoscope grinds inside your skull. Crystalline flakes of potentiality quiver, seeking to coalesce into concrete knowledge—all the knowledge that exists exists in the cosmic tar of your subconscious, if only you'll stare deeper... You fight the compulsion. Too much pain this early in the morning.

Poe: "Oh." It has remained inert until this moment. "No. No."

The blonde peels the glove from her right hand. Her hand hasn't seen the sun in a while. It belongs to an older, emaciated person or an albino crocodile. Still smiling (the painted sneer of a manikin), she reaches under the table and you freeze with a premonition of impending awfulness—she's going to whip out a gun or a bomb or some other lethal device. If only you'd brought one of your own; if only Norse or Sloan were here. Either of them would be ready for an action scene. Mace would've, as the group's wise Odysseus figure, plotted an escape route and a plan to burn the lounge to cinders in her wake.

Instead of a submachine gun or a grenade, the blonde retrieves a dummy clad in a lumpy silver spacesuit and balances it on the edge of the table. The dummy's face is white and mottled as boiled flesh, lacking ears, eyes, and nose. Of course the dummy is faceless; without a helmet, one unguarded glance at the sun burned it away. Its mouth makes a tiny sphincter about the size of a woman's fingertip. Its left arm rises and gauntleted fingers waggle a greeting.

Poe: "The Eater of Dolls." The puppet speaks with awe.

You: "What the hell is going on?" Surely it would be nice to ask someone other than a puppet. The waitress moves among the tables, she and her patrons apparently oblivious to the Moulin Rouge hot chicks and the world's most hideous dummy.

Poe: "As You Know Bob. What in the name of the Dark have they done? Bob used to be a marionette. Bob was my friend."

Bob: "Edgar. Edgar. Edgar. Edgar. Edgar. I'm still your friend. Edgar." Bob's sucker mouth dilates. Its voice is husky and feminine and carries intimately—or, as must be the case, the blonde's delivery is theater-caliber. "I've searched and searched for you. I'm your friend, Edgar. I'm." As the dummy speaks, soft material bulges and darkens where the eyes should be. Yes, darkens like blood seeping through cloth.

Poe: "Oh no oh no oh no." Again with the jagged laugh.

Bob: "Oh yes, Edgar. Together. You and me. Me."

You're impressed. The dummy's voice is in your ear, yet the blonde's lips don't twitch. She's a master of ventriloquism.

The waitress's head snaps around. She lurches to a halt near your booth. Her expression is going through changes.

Waitress: "Yes, a master of ventriloquism. Yes." Her voice too is husky and feminine and soothing. "Dee Dee Gamma. Leave. Leave the puppet. Leave."

Bob: "I want Poe, only Poe." Its voice harmonizes with the waitress's. "You may leave unharmed if you leave at once. Thank you, Mizz Gamma. Thank."

Patrons continue their routines. A trucker tries the door handle several times before he unravels its mystery. Three burly dudes who've traded raucous insults for the past twenty minutes lapse into meditative silence. Two of them are poised, cups raised midway. The third drools through a grin, enchanted by some vison.

You intuit what they're experiencing. The pressure in your head changes. Your nipples stiffen. Warmth suffuses your belly. The harsh dimness of the lounge softens as your mind softens. Your tumor responds to the siren call. That insensate malignancy wants to enter the blonde.

Poe: "—in your mind, Ann!" The puppet's voice cuts through the drone of your colliding thoughts.

It is enough to snap you back to earth. Around the room, glasses and cups shatter. Cutlery and fragments of porcelain levitate and drift in counterclockwise spirals. The floor trembles. A low rumble begins in the earth.

You rise and snatch Poe and stride toward the entrance. Bob and his two bimbos are between you and the door. The blonde manipulates the dummy, or maybe the other way around. The brunette rises to block the way. She's as pretty as a rabid fox. You palm the atomizer in your left hand. She's wearing sunglasses, but her nostrils flare when you jam the nozzle in her face. She quickly sits again.. Good girl.

Ten steps gets you inside your car and the doors locked. As the key turns, you sense a malevolent presence traveling through the wires. You exert your will. The engine fires on the first try.

You: "Ed, what do I win if I get you back to civilization?" You drive across a concrete divider and smash through a ditch onto the road. Your mother raced Baja in the late '70s. She taught you how to handle a car.

Poe: "A tattoo of a shrike somewhere inconspicuous and the satisfaction of a job well-done."

Ninety degree left, and you sideswipe a street sign. The passenger window cracks. Needle pegs eighty-five.

You: "Satisfaction, huh? Well, I always meant to get a tat before I died."

Poe: "Your girls think I know details about the enemy. They're wrong. Bob can't be stopped. Bob's master can't be stopped. I can't save any of you. I'm sorry, Annabel. I'm sorry it's going to eat us."

You: "The dummy isn't going to eat us."

Poe: "Bob isn't a dummy. Bob is a shell that contains awfulness."

You locate the last burner phone and dial Lochinvar. Ring, ring, ring. You attempt to project your mind's eye two thousand miles east where your comrades doubtless gather at the Nest. Two problems—first, serious meditative concentration is difficult under these circumstances; second, poisonous psychic vapors roil around the car. You own personal acid rain cloud, courtesy of the dummy and its girls.

Full tank of gas, mountains on every side. You're traveling through a valley, perhaps the original Valley of Death the Good Book made famous. Inside an hour this surface road will intersect a major highway and from there it's three hundred and twenty miles to Anchorage. At the moment, those times and distances feel as if you're in a space capsule plotting a course for Alpha Centauri. Long, long way and the landscape creeps by too slowly.

You make it another seventeen miles.

KISS OF THE PSYCHOPOMP

Every light and dial on the dashboard goes bonkers. A whisper tickles your inner ear. Marilyn Monroe speaking from the grave? Guttural and alluring and incomprehensible, although the sense of threat is plain, the voice intimates you should pull over before it's too late. *This* is why the Old Woman sent you. She'd known the tricks the enemy would deploy. The other Shrikes possess a capacity for violence that dwarfs your own. You're a thrill-seeker, not a killer.

Yet, you are the only one who can access the Black Kaleidoscope, and that is the ace of spades in your back pocket.

The devil's breath is hot in your mind, but you push the whisper aside and block the image of a giant silver figure striding across the hills to squash the car into a blob. You also block corresponding images of everyone you've ever loved dying hideous deaths, of the Earth blackening as a leaf blackens in a flame.

Your enemies decide there are other ways to skin a cat.

The radiator boils over. You forge ahead in a cloud of steam and smoke. The trunk springs open, then shears away and bounces on the pavement. The rear passenger door goes next. The rear passenger tire blows and you do some fancy steering to keep from wrecking. You know it's over but for the crying.

So does Poe. The puppet moans prayers in what you guess to be Old English.

A metallic glint appears in the rearview and begins to chew the gap; it's a black Lincoln roaring at one hundred and twenty, easy. Late '80s model. Heavy as a tank. Intuition suggests the blonde is driving, sneering as she closes the distance.

That last high-speed pursuit in Spain is on your mind. It didn't end well. They seldom do. You grit your teeth and spin the wheel one hundred and eighty until the other vehicle is in the bull's-eye of your hood ornament.

You: "Guess what, bitches? I'm the last person on Earth you want to play chicken with." You drift into the left lane and gradually press the pedal to floor. Euphoria, better than any dope, carries you away in the split instant that the enemy driver loses her nerve and tries to veer aside and your bumper annihilates everything in its path.

Hell of a crackup. The airbag does its thing, although there's a lot of blood leaking through your pants leg and from your busted nose. Your car lands in the ditch. It's totaled. You escape the wreckage,

Poe tucked under your arm like a football. The black sedan has flown off the road and flipped onto its roof near a deserted T intersection. Pieces of metal and glass are scattered along the pavement.

Poe: "Run run run." It chants in a monotone. "Run, your sister is not far ahead."

Flight is not an option. You're light-headed from blood loss. You hobble to the centerline and take a stand. High noon minus a six-shooter. Mace's knife is strapped to your ankle. The thought of bending to draw the blade wearies you. You've misplaced your purse and the atomizer. A tiny part of you dares hope someone will drive by and report this clusterfuck to the cops. Waves of psychic static break against the bulwark you've raised to protect your will. Animals within the radius of that emanation are curled whimpering in their burrows; any human approaching within a mile is sure to find themselves parked and missing a block of time. Whatever Bob and its bimbos are, they've cleared the decks to ensure this is a private affair. It's down to you and a maimed puppet here at the crossroads.

The driver door crushes outward until it clangs wide. The blonde (you think of her as Betty) unfolds and shuffles toward you. Same routine on the other side, and here comes the brunette (Veronica). They stand shoulder to shoulder, twenty feet from where you and Poe grimly await what must transpire.

Their dresses are perfect—the blonde in black, the brunette in white, neither so much as smudged. Dresses perfect, hair un-mussed, the duet did not escape unscathed. Their sunglasses are lost. Both women are lacerated and bruised. The blonde's left leg is shattered. Bones protrude. The brunette's lower jaw hangs by bloody tendon strands. She sways as her comrade sways and that gory jaw is a slow-arcing pendulum across her chest.

This should surprise and horrify you. You chuckle and maybe that's the same.

The Brunette: Leave the puppet, Ms. Gamma. Her telepathic voice scratches at your brain. She winks. *Don't make* him *come out of the car.*

The Blonde: "Leave the puppet, Ms. Gamma." Chipper as hell.

Bob (muffled): *Give me the puppet, Mizz Gamma. Give.* It murmurs these sweet nothings into your other ear in the blonde's voice except accompanied by a split second image of a thorn tree upon a blasted field beneath a carnivorous red sky. Many severed heads dangle from the tree, their many mouths dripping crimson pulp, the hideous red light of the sky reflecting in their eyes.

The offer is tempting. Hand over Poe, turn away, and limp across the tundra toward the sun that never completely sets during this time of season. Demonic smirks to the contrary, possibly the Muppet sisters are on the level and you'll actually go free. Your mother didn't raise a sucker and it doesn't matter. Walking away is a fantasy. In a few seconds you'll keel over like road kill. Suck it up, Gamma, this is your moment of truth. You're standing in the fire.

You: "Poe, this is the end of the road, I fear."

Poe: "Gamma, don't. I was born in a studio in New York City in 1929. My father was a carpenter. He emigrated from Poland. He had many children and grandchildren. I was the only marionette he created. His daughter carved Bob in 1970."

You allow Poe to slip from your hand. The puppet goes quiet. Its expression is inanimate. There is nothing of your sister nor yourself within the eroded face, nothing of life in the tangle of disjointed limbs. Still, a pang shoots through you as your boot descends on the puppet's cranium. You stomp twice, to be certain. Murdering the final vestige of your childhood, or brutally putting it out of its misery. Either way, the act drains most of what's left in your tank. You crumple and your pose isn't much different from the ruined marionette.

The women exchange a glance. The blonde covers her mouth.

Her grin slides past her fingers. The brunette makes claws of her gloved hands and rakes her hair. Hanks tear free and she gesticulates. She hisses and burbles. It dawns upon you that they approve of your choice.

The Blonde: "There are mistakes, then there are colossal, life-altering blunders." She lowers her arm to reveal a cold, dead expression. "Guess which one you've made?" She gestures at her partner.

The brunette walks to the upended car. She crouches and disappears inside. You think, how phallic, how quiet it is without Poe's company. You wish you weren't falling asleep. Seconds pass. The sky shifts magenta; swaths are rapidly melted through by undulating cigarette burns. Your hands are magenta and covered in amoeba shadows. Your vision grows fuzzy. You rest your head on the centerline, watch the stripe stretch into the magenta gloaming. The asphalt is as soft as that goose-down pillow you had as a kid.

You mistake the screams for a siren. Soon, the screams end and a figure slithers from the wreckage. The figure reflects the colors of this subarctic wasteland and hurts to gaze upon. It expands and contracts, dragging itself across the road to where you are pawing, too late, for the commando knife. The brunette follows close behind.

Bob is missing parts; its mantle is perfect. Bob is coming for you with what its got. The dummy is no longer a dummy, it has evolved into something old and unspeakable to match its skinned and boiled visage. Right arm torn off in the crash, the sinuous left works fine to lever itself over your body until its sucker lips are poised near your own. You fight. The blonde and brunette step on your wrists.

The Blonde: "Inoperable isn't an obstacle for Bob. He'll fix you, good as new. Ever had psychic surgery, little girl? Get ready."

Bob: "My brother iz spared the worzt. Worzt." Fingers grip your chin and tilt your head. "Inside you iz what I really want. Want. Alwayz wanted *you*, Mizz Gamma. Gamma. Iz why we brought you here. Here. Away from your nezt. Nezt."

Its mouth opens and a blood-slick tendril uncoils and descends and penetrates the corner of your eye. Bob licks your right eye out of the socket, crushes and devours that red grape. Magenta brightens and incandesces in a blast of white phosphorous.

Your mind leaps from your thrashing self, breaching sunward. Gravity seizes you, drags you backward. Voices call to one another from the distance, *Inbound, weapons hot.*

—*Too late, goddamnit.*

—*Ninety seconds. She's alive.*

—*Remember, concentrated fire on the visitor. Burn him down, everybody survives.*

—*If the dampeners hold. If she's alive.*

—*Cut the chatter. Eighty seconds.*

A wave of screeching static overwhelms your fleeting escape and you plummet to earth.

The wriggling, piercing tongue burrows. The real delicacy is your faithful tumor, uprooted and teased into daylight and sucked segment by necrotic segment into an eager maw. The dummy whipsaws its head, attacking the extrusion of malignant flesh as if it were a string of saltwater taffy. At last the tumor pops free and is devoured. Bob relaxes its death grip on your jaw and your skull bounces on the pavement.

Bob: "Fear. Guilt. Pain. Ecstazy. Your strength. Your weaknez. Manifezt in cannibal organizm. Thank you, Mizz Gamma. Thank."

You aren't fully conscious for this experience. Unfortunately, the Black Kaleidoscope spins wildly of its own volition and you witness these horrors from multiple perspectives.

The blonde lifts Bob into her arms and cradles the dummy with mechanical tenderness. The brunette extends her index finger and examines the long, sharp nail she means to insert into your brain. She smiles and leans toward you, and her torso disintegrates and the rest of her is batted away. The blonde says something to Bob. The dummy is sated and sluggish and too slow to respond.

The blonde inhales to scream. Bob's mouth dilates. Laser dots dance against their bodies, then those bodies are shredded to sawdust and a mist of scorched blood.

A half-track clatters through the hills and rolls up. Sloan is on the .50 caliber gun. Norse and Lochinvar emerge. The women are clad in jumpsuits and headsets. Lochinvar carries a heavy rifle with a scope. She inspects the remains and nods with satisfaction. Apparently, this is a triple-cross. The dummy and its entourage were the targets all along—the Black Kaleidoscope confirms this, a day late and a dollar short, alas. You'd applaud Lochinvar's ruthlessness if you could muster the strength to raise your voice.

Norse presses her cheek against yours. She smells of grief and adrenaline, but she hasn't shed a tear. She says she's got you, promises it's over. You laugh because you know the secret. It's always only beginning, always only transforming into something worse.

MRS. SHRIKE'S GIRLS

A video cassette is locked inside the Diebold gun safe. The video features various Shrike women in candid shots. An off-camera voice greets each woman by name and asks, "Why? Why have you come here? Why have you pledged yourself to Mrs. Shrike?"

You: Pale from months in the cell, scrawny, apprehensive. You wince and rub your temple. Pain radiates from your eyes. "Time is short. I want to make amends. Redemption? Yeah, sure."

Liz Lochinvar: Seated on a stump, surrounded by evergreens, her nose broken and bloodied. Her left forearm is slashed vertically to the crook of her elbow. Exposed metal glistens within the wound. A broadsword rests across her thighs. "Revenge. Man."

Robin Sloan: Luxuriating in a Jacuzzi, fine as a movie starlet in her string bikini and sunglasses. She raises her left fist to reveal raw and swollen knuckles. "I pulverize cinderblocks with my bare hands. Mrs. Shrike lets me pulverize faces. Boom!"

Indra Norse: Leaning against the hood of a '68 Mustang. Her jumpsuit is crimson. "Because, there's a war on. It's as tiny and savage as colonies of insects going at it. I'd rather not be on the side that gets annihilated. But yeah, we're gonna lose. Wanna fuck?"

Jessica Mace: Bruised cheek, blazing eyes, wild hair, torn jacket. A car is on fire in the background. A large dog presses against her leg, its thick fur plastered in gore. One eye gone, the other yellow as hell. Instead of speaking, Mace takes a long, insolent swig from the neck of a whiskey bottle. Her glare holds until the video cuts to black.

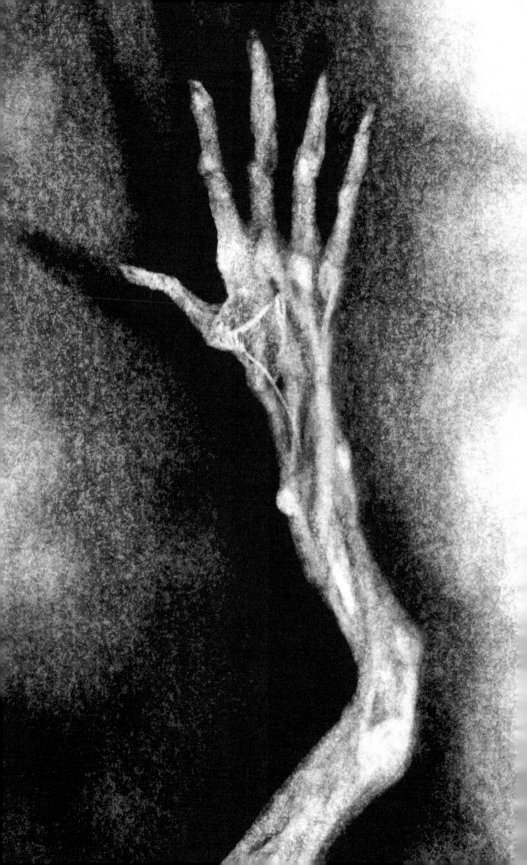

AMERICAN REMAKE
OF A JAPANESE GHOST STORY

I've become intimate with a curse in folklore known as a geas. That's when a witch, or a fairy, or the supernatural entity of your choice, compels a hapless mortal to undertake duties on the creature's behalf. Woe betides the mortal who shirks the quest; increasingly worse calamities befall them until they relent or die.

Somebody, somewhere, laid one on me.

A much younger, blissfully ignorant, Jessica Mace would've glibly asserted that fairytales are bullshit hoodoo made up by gullible peasants. Problem is, when I neglect to investigate the various mysteries in my path, I get epic migraines and nightmares. The more I rebel, the more intense my misery until it becomes debilitating. "Debilitating" sounds dry—I suffer projectile vomiting induced by the sense fire ants are hollowing my skull. Exactly as the legends describe, right? Call it a form of madness or a kind of placebo effect. Odds are Hamlet told Horatio the truth about the denizens of his undreamt philosophy. Whatever, whichever, however: the world shows you its dark side, you take notice. That fucking needle starts skipping, you're a true believer.

Beasley, a boon comrade and sometime lover, once questioned my motives. We were dumping the corpse of a serial killer down a mineshaft in eastern Montana. The killer, a Richard Ramirez lookalike, had picked me up at a roadside tavern. RR Jr. chauffeured me to his favorite dump site while I batted my lashes and stroked his thigh. Thank whichever patron saint is in charge of such details that I'd managed to open the passenger door and light the cab for Beasley to take his shot. I'd only been half-strangled before the bullet came through the windshield. As the late, great Al Davis would say, *just win, baby.*

In the aftermath, we recovered with a bottle. Beasley said, *Jessica, you're a bright woman. You got an education. Why schlep all over the continent looking for horrors to battle? Why live your life as bait in a trap?*

I recall pouring another healthy dose of whiskey into our glasses and lighting a cigarette. I drank the booze and smoked most of the cigarette before coming up with a succinct answer. *If I don't, the horrors tend to come looking for me.* Bless him, he caught my drift.

Ever consider the possibility you're cursed?

Halfway into the bag, it was probably a throwaway comment. I had, in fact, never entertained the notion. A pit opened in my mind. A pit with all manner of darksome surprises at the bottom.

Shortly after wrapping the horror mockumentary, *Torn Between Two Phantom Lovers,* which was based on archival footage of a tragedy in Japan's Sea of Trees circa 1977, director Gil Finlay and his wife Rikki bought a farm near the Catskills. The way I heard it, the previous owners, a retired couple, passed away unexpectedly and their lawyer unloaded the deed for a song. A big American Gothic structure updated to resemble something Argento might've used as a set in the heyday of vinyl and exploitation cinema. Gil invited a few of us to the housewarming. I rode along with a sound tech and a gaffer. Cold and starry, but not quite winter. Basically, my mood writ large.

The creepy part was when we pulled into the yard and the place perfectly resembled my recent bad dreams right down to the peaked roof, nearby shed, and fields and woods. The dreams themselves were vague and disjointed as dreams are wont to be. I recalled wandering fields by moonlight, then an endless maze of dim hallways. Occasionally, someone or something on my periphery plucked at my hair…

"Jessica, baby!" Rikki hugged me on sight. Almost didn't recognize her in a cocktail dress, her hair done up and face put together. Bowie-level glam. She usually dwelt in the background, organizing Gil's life and dousing fires as his unofficial publicist. She was a genius at it, too. Otherwise, I sincerely doubt he would've remembered which direction his pants went on in the morning.

She apologized for the mess. Renovations were behind schedule—carpenters had knocked down a wall here and there, drop cloths covered half the furniture, and a crew of electricians hadn't finished rewiring the house. Lamps shone in the main areas while outlying rooms were either strung with plastic bulbs or left utterly dark. "A housewarming isn't a party, it's a get-together, right?" she said. "Like casual Friday, but for a house."

I advised her not to worry—as long as she kept the booze flowing and nobody fell into an open pit, guests would let the decor slide. She nodded gratefully, then dashed off to holler at Gil who'd tramped in from the muddy backyard (in reality, a pasture) while still wearing a pair of clodhoppers. Plenty of his homies had made the scene, including assorted C-listers and a couple of LA suits. The suits in particular seemed bemused by the rustic location.

It promised to be a long grind of an evening. I lurked on the stairs, not far from the front door, weighing the pros and cons of abandoning my mission and doing a French leave even if it meant trudging down the dirt road that led here. This dude in a starched shirt handed me a can of beer and said running wouldn't do any good—he'd tried it once or twice. I introduced myself and waited for him to recognize me; either from my striking features or the jagged scar on my throat. His expression remained neutral. Apparently, enough years had passed people didn't recognize me on sight. Twenty-four-hour news cycle was erasing our collective memory like California shoreline. I popped the top (ensuring the seal hadn't been violated) and drank to the continued decline of civilization and my own celebrity.

"I'm Lee," Starched Shirt said. "How are you associated with Mr. Big Shot Film Director?"

Instead of a wiseass response like *Where do ya think he gets his blow?* or *I'm the entertainment, bitch!* I played it straight. "PA for *Phantom Lovers*." Not a lowkey brag so much as a confession. Production assistant was a polite showbiz definition of lackey. Fetch doughnuts, tote equipment, hold a character actor's hair back when she puked after a bender; whatever old job came along. "You?"

"We've been through the wars."

"Which wars?"

"I scouted locations for Gil on *Bleeding Mansion* and *The Ornithologist*."

"*The Ornithologist*, huh? Nasty."

"You screened the whole thing? Impressive."

"Between my fingers."

"The critics did too," he said. "An eight-minute scene of a dying naturalist getting his asshole pecked out by vultures is a bridge too far for normies. Great writing, nonetheless."

"Okay, my burning question: was *The Ornithologist* an homage to Hitchcock or snide commentary?"

"Snide homage. Getting even on behalf of Tippi Hedron, maybe. Should ask him yourself. Or Rikki. Saw her squeezing the literal shit out of you earlier."

"She's a sixteenth grizzly bear." Another swallow of cheap, warm beer and then I slipped it in. "Somebody said the old owners died. That true?"

He nodded with sagacity borne of incipient drunkenness. "Gil says the husband dropped dead in the yard. Brain aneurism? Heart attack? I don't know. Wife clicked her heels and went back to wherever. Gil and Rikki were looking for a country retreat…"

"That explains the frantic renovations."

"Rikki needs to make it her own—"

"She *needs* to exorcise the ghosts."

"Well, again, the guy died in the yard… Does that count toward a haunting?"

"If you're the kind to put stock in hauntings, then yep. It counts."

He nodded the way one does when one doesn't mean it. Then he stiffened with his mouth quirked oddly. "Weird, I wanted to say something. It's gone." He shook himself and his eyes unglazed. "Maybe it'll hit me in a minute."

"Five minutes after you get home," I said. "That's how it always happens."

Lee nodded another polite nod and raised his beer and sipped. His eyes darted with an animal's dismay.

We stood there as the silence grew awkward. Because I was suffering a combo of boredom and edginess, I said, perhaps a trifle stridently, "My opinion about *The Ornithologist?* Gil's subconscious was broadcasting a public service message: leave Mother Nature the hell alone. Fuck them loggers. Fuck them tourists and farmers. Fuck them David Attenborough types, too. She didn't ask for any of it."

"Okay, then," he said, glancing toward the other guests as if one might beeline over to rescue him.

Meanwhile, I'd already drifted miles away, scoping the layout once more and reassessing avenues of escape. Yeah, pulling stakes for town was tempting. I wouldn't do that; not while afflicted with a geas, or my compulsion, or call it what you will. What were my options? The aforementioned stairs at my back, climbing into the unknown. Front door and farmland. Brightly lit kitchen through an archway where the hardcore extroverts instinctively gathered. Dark passage on my left, a cluster of green bulbs glowing at the far end.

"Adios. Gotta powder my nose." I handed Lee my mostly empty and left him mildly befuddled with longing. Beasley could've, would've, commiserated.

Something was wrong. My plastic divining ball had decreed it so. Divining ball, you ask? Best way to describe it would be as an off-brand Magic 8 Ball, way smaller than the original. I could palm it, easy. Several years ago, a circus strongperson named Mary stuck it into my pocket; a parting gift at the conclusion of a harrowing adventure. She'd inherited it from a fortuneteller who'd met an unforeseen demise. Mary warned me to restrict myself to a couple of questions per week. *You fight the forces of darkness with forces of darkness. Beware, kiddo. This is a portal to the void.* Previously I'd relied upon chance to guide my quixotic journeys as a professional final girl. These days, the mini-oracle and my innate gifts combined to ensure I never missed the chance to become embroiled in the most bizarre and dangerous circumstances.

To that point: upon receiving the housewarming invitation (and subsequent nightmares), I'd casually rattled the ball and said, *Dear Oracle, is anything fucked up happening at Gil's house, and if so, should I be concerned?* Which, I presume, is how the petitioners at Delphi phrased their entreaties regarding love, life, and invading Spartan armies. The pocket oracle generally responded with yes, no, or maybe. Occasionally, it escalated to cryptic phrases and symbols. This time, its little window fogged over and red-limned letters coalesced to spell SHE WAITS. A bit disquieted, I pressed my luck and asked if people were in danger. Upon shaking the ball, a skull bobbed to the surface.

Damn. I should've asked if *I* personally was endangered. It probably went without saying.

After ditching Lee, I ducked outside and smoked a cigarette. The stars were still twitching; the moon had made some progress. Their supreme indifference to the insignificant horrors of human drama was pleasant, emotionally stabilizing. Back indoors, I began my tour of the premises by skirting the living room. None of the clustered guests struck me as a round character much less a serial killer. I've an unerring sense regarding these matters. Two girls were bumping and grinding to classic era Depeche Mode. I recognized them from craft services; they'd dutifully arranged sandwiches and refilled carafes day and night, rain or shine. Illumination was funny here; it made bands across their eyes. Straight out of an Argento joint.

I left them, too.

Prickling neck hairs and the queasiness in the pit of my gut acted as faulty Geiger counters—the physical manifestation of hyperactive intuition. Lacking clues, besides a vague, but escalating sense of danger, all I could do was bumble around waiting for one or more of my alarms to trip. Dowsing for evil, more or less. I moseyed along the hall toward the rear of the house, projecting myself into shadow. Part of the weirdness was a natural consequence of transition—white patches on the walls where old photos once hung, not yet covered by the new. To walk through an abandoned home is to traverse the confines of an open grave. The floor lamp beckoned me with its wan light. I ignored doors on either side. This was a mundane adult party, which meant unlike the barn burners we had in high school and college, people hadn't gathered to do keg stands, nor paired off to fuck on piles of coats.

Swim to me, swim to my shoal, the lamp said. A metal door let onto the back porch. Half-bath on the right—I peeked inside. A bearded guy camped on the toilet, pants around his ankles, chin cupped a la *The Thinker.* Candles burned on the sink. He nodded. I reversed with a quickness. Another door, on the left, ajar. A chain of plastic bulbs twisted in descent, nominally illuminating old, grooved steps that had weathered the drag and scrape of many feet.

Down, down into a brick and beam cellar because what goes up, and so on. Three women sat on the floor near the furnace, each haloed in crawling green light. They hunched over a homemade Ouija board. Which figured. Two men perched on a matched washer-dryer set, sharing a joint. Looked like bros to me.

"Shh! It's a séance," Dryer Bro shushed me before I could even get my loud mouth in gear.

I don't know why some people assume raised voices are antithetical to communing with spirits while others are full speed ahead with hymns and hosannas. "Oh, that's stupid." I lit a cigarette. "You don't screw around in a house where somebody recently kicked."

"I thought you didn't screw with the *infinite*," Dryer Bro said.

Washer Bro apparently hadn't heard the news. He almost dropped the joint. "Somebody died here? Totally uncool. Hey, Shelley. Maybe you should ixnay—"

The brunette leading the "séance" was probably three or four years past her high school goth peak. She opened her smokey eyes and shot daggers at Washer Lad. "Maybe you should cram it, Ashton."

"Shelley," I said. "Your boy here is on the money. Ixnay."

"Who the hell are you?" Smokey Eye Chick said.

"Last of the red-hot Samaritans. I'm curious. Where'd you call?"

"Huh?"

"Activate a witchboard, you're making a call to a random payphone across the veil. Could be a bad neighborhood. Anybody can pick up. Scary part is, whoever's on the other end has deluxe caller ID." I tapped my head. "Mr. Ghost of a Psycho Killer's got your name, number, and home address." True as far as it went, although I might've overstated the danger a wee bit.

"There's a psycho in here, for sure." Her smirk reminded me of every foe I'd dreamed of socking in high school and a couple I'd actually punched.

"See? This shit is already going sideways, kid." My heart wasn't really into yanking her chain. Didn't have to consult the oracle to confirm I'd hit a dead end. The sense of dread had faded to a dim background thrum. "Your funeral," I said with as much menace as possible while exiting the basement.

Back in the living room, somebody lowered the stereo volume and cued *Bleeding Mansion*, Gil's debut feature film, on a wall screen.

As the title credits rolled over a still of the eponymous *giallo* mansion, I realized it was a ringer for this very house. Gil's mansion possessed slightly different angles, yet the spirit of it unnerved me. The house in my nightmare was a composite of both; I didn't like that, either.

Bam! Dread restored to one-hundred percent. An impression spiked into my brain, a vision, if you will, of a slack-faced man being pulled by his hair up through a hole in the ceiling. I leaned against the wall, playing it casual as a wave of dizziness receded. This kind of destabilizing, traumatic sense of collocation rarely occurred, but when it did, boy, howdy. The image faded like a pop flash, imprint wavering, wavering, gone. The room I'd glimpsed was small and lighted by afternoon sun. Second floor bedroom or office? Only way to know was to poke around, even though I really, truly, abso-fucking-lutely wanted to do anything but.

"Yo, lady."

I pivoted, left hand resting on the knife under my jacket. A formidable blade; slim and easy to conceal. Smokey Eye Chick had apparated out of the shadows on my six. She stared an owlish, luminous stare as if trying to drink my soul.

"Lady," she said again with a flat affect. "I was supposed to tell you something. You should go upstairs now." Her lips kept moving after she finished. She regarded the ceiling, turned, and walked off; neck craned so far backward her head flopped as if the vertebrae had come undone. Our inverted gazes locked as she wobbled down the hall.

Frankly, I was at a loss. The million-dollar question: how much did I care for the fate of Gil and Rikki? Followed by: will you wind up wearing adult diapers if you defy the curse and bail? The answers were, a lot, and, probably even worse.

We, the cynical audience, hunker in seats of a darkened theater and mock the heroine who fumbles around, shining a feeble light into corners while meekly calling, *Who's there?* Where's that cynical movie-going wisdom for those who reenact variations of that scene in scores of homes every evening? Yeah, we scoff at heroines and then stumble into our own fates at the first point of crisis. It's because we've trained ourselves to ignore the little warning voice that says, *Don't investigate the noise that woke you. Don't cross the empty parking lot after hours. Don't be a fool.*

Speaking of fools. The second floor was dark. Party echoes were muffled; a warning that I'd drifted from shore into deep waters. I tried a wall switch to no avail. Then, before I resorted to my penlight, fifteen or twenty feet directly ahead, a floor lamp (cousin to the one downstairs) snapped on. Off. On. Off. On. Faster and faster until it strobed. I approached and crossed into a small office—desk, file cabinet, bookshelf, couch. Another wall switch, also dead. The strobing lamp eroded my composure. I glanced up and saw the inevitable ceiling panel partially ajar. An invitation.

I pushed a footstool beneath the gap and, penlight clenched in my teeth, levered myself into the attic. Warm and musty. Cobwebs, exposed rafters, and fiberglass insulation. Stacks of cardboard boxes and bundles of magazines and newspapers. Home for mice. Home for termites. Home for something else, too.

My feeble penlight probed edges, traced contours of a larger, obscured geography; a midnight continent waited for its latest pilgrim to venture a step too far. Among the detritus, a wooden placard lay propped against boxes. I gleaned just enough kanji to deduce someone had smuggled it from Jōren Waterfall in Japan. Jōren Falls, famous for its natural beauty, was also the origin of the legend of a beautiful spider demon who, in bygone days, lured travelers to their doom. Occasionally, the gods dispense with omens and hand you an actual fucking sign.

A millisecond after I shined my light on that placard, metaphorically speaking, the piano music ceased mid-note. Someone sighed, followed by a sound like cartilage separating. A shape developed like a photographic negative among the rafters—broad, softly angular. Bulky, but nimble. She. Nothing else to call her except she. Her pale visage glimmered against the black frame of her hair, the black of her body. Her eyes were enormous like those of Smokey Eye Chick last I glimpsed her in the hall.

"What do you want?" I said. As if I didn't have a good guess. As if I wasn't stalling, hunting for a crucifix, some magic words of protection. Could I take her on with a knife? Could I take on a bear with a knife? May as well ask, could I leap off a cliff with a knife in my teeth and survive?

"Final…girl," she said. "My dream." Her voice was mine by way of a child's mimicry. "Dream…"

"Same. You summoned me. Why?" I sensed the only thing keeping me alive was our shared uncertainty. Some power, perhaps the one that cursed me to unravel mysteries, had brought us together. On this occasion, perhaps she craved an answer as much as she craved other forms of sustenance.

Her long, segmented arm that was not an arm unfolded. She brushed my cheek (chitinous, tickly), once, then withdrew. "Sad," she said. "Hungry."

I froze. Everything in my bladder wanted to escape. The flesh of my cheek felt abraded and raw. And yet. Years before, I'd seen news footage of a man in a hot, dusty village, extending his water bottle to a cobra dying of thirst. A gesture of humanity in a moment of tremendous peril. I clung to that notion of compassion now. I clung to the notion that even in this impersonal, inscrutable universe, there exists a purpose. "You're lonely."

"Alone." A correction or confirmation. Her bloodless expression gave nothing back. Pitiful, tiny me reflected in her eyes.

"Is this really where you belong?" I said as an idea bloomed. "Hidden away in an attic?"

"Waterfall," she said and gave me another jab with her psychic stinger.

A falling curtain of water misted me; it boomed against stone. I glimpsed the silhouette of a lovely woman enfolding weary passersby to her bosom. Men, usually. Faithless, straying men.

"We could find a new waterfall. Would that make you happier?"

She leaned forward. Roofbeams creaked and sagged. "Happier."

The face of the killer back west floated in my mind's eye, attached to a mobile of a bunch of other creeps cut from the same bolt of cloth. Men who'd tried to do for me and failed. Stranglers. Shooters. Slashers. She regarded my thoughts and saw them too.

I raised my arm a bit. This took more resolve than I can properly convey. Instinct more than courage, honestly. "So you know, I meet a lot of assholes in my travels."

Didn't take long for her to decide. She crawled across the beam, contracting, diminishing from colossus to a speck, from an imminent hazard to a vague threat, and alighted on my palm. Soft, yet deadly sharp, she weighed as much as a breath, a guilty conscience. Everything and nothing. I gently nestled her into my coat pocket. She curled around the oracle.

Trembling, I shut off the penlight and stood in the heart of the void. "Are you a force of darkness?" I asked my new friend.

"Darkness," she whispered.

"It was a rhetorical question." I smiled with the euphoric dregs of terror and lowered myself into the land of the living.

IV
LAKE TERROR

STRIDENT CALLER

Languid days of fucking for rent didn't faze rambling man Jesse Craven. One summer he witnessed death on tidal flats in Alaska. A blonde woman and a sorrel horse doing that romantic canter near the surf as seen on the cover of many a bodice-ripper. Mud caught them fast. They'd screamed as the sea rolled in. Nobody could do a damned thing. Later in his youth he'd blown a state trooper to avoid a possession rap. After a few homeless months in winter, he'd gratefully eaten a roadkill coyote that a big Aleut chopped in half with an ax. He'd done worse. Done what was necessary, same as anyone.

A hell of a long way from the Last Frontier, his dark curls specked gray, and granite abs gone a tad soft, he'd done it *all*. Unlike many of his friends and fellow travelers, he hadn't gotten hooked on liquor or addicted to dope or caught an embarrassing, career-ending disease. Jack of a dozen trades and possessed of not half-bad looks, his mutably convivial personality proved sufficient to excel at the job of survival. His sole motivation at this stage of the game? Three square meals a day, a roof overhead, and minor pleasures where he found them.

Craven discovered the secret to longevity. He tended to roll with life's punches, such as his mistress Deborah's unpredictable moods and strange demands. *People like you disappear every day, Princess,* she'd murmured when they first met after a literary reading at the Kremlin Lounge in New York City. Craven might've been a rootless drifter, yet he'd read his share by campfire light and the electric shine of dirty bulbs in flophouses from Seattle to Poughkeepsie. He knew his way around the Beats and better still the women who frequented the cafes and bars made famous by reprobate poets and other lettered scoundrels.

They'd slipped upstairs to the jazz club and gotten loaded. Deborah licked his earlobe while they shared a dance. *Pretty lost boys disappear and nobody cares. Better come home with me to be on the safe side. I live out in the country, far from prying eyes. We can do anything we want.*

He'd accepted both the widow's pet name and her offer of protection. She took him to her big house, a couple of hours north in the shadows of the Catskills. Cow country. Field, stream, and darksome forests populated by decaying farms and rural estates. Like a grateful stray, he made peace with the monthly dinner parties that saw him banished to his chamber at the end of the hall where he flopped on a poster bed and listened to muffled conversation and raucous laughter until dawn. No problem. Eccentric socialites weren't his crowd. He didn't dig sséances or any of that weird shit either. The routine had begun to chafe mainly because it defied his nature to put down roots. Eight months so far. How much longer could he play Midnight Cowboy?

A familiar wanderlust called his name. Craven fantasized about the open road as he rinsed away Deborah's cloying musk. The water hit in cold pellets. No electricity since the storm first broadsided that morning. He dried himself with a fluffy towel on the landing before the half stained-glass window. Late, late sun emerged in a brief glory of lambent redness. The squall had ended. Another approaching storm mantled the mountains in the west; a front the color and texture of smoke from a great fire. Pieces of the neighbor's sycamore scattered the yard. A branch speared the camper shell on Craven's '82 Datsun. The marble fountain frothed—twin columns of nymphs supported a basin carved into the improbable likeness of a bloodthirsty ape. Twigs bobbed like skeletal fingers clawing from the turgid depths.

The driveway went for fifty yards through sycamore and pine. The dairy farmer across the rural blacktop road had wisely called in his cows. Odors of tramped soil and cow shit persisted in the empty pasture, green and powerful after the downpour. A tiny mother-in-law cottage nestled on the far edge of the property—this was the abode of groundskeeper Andy. Gardener, handyman, and sentry, Andy was a late-career Boris Karloff-looking sonofabitch who stalked the grounds while wearing the scowl of an ax-murderer on vacation. Craven hadn't exchanged two words with him. Gardener Andy kept a low profile, appearing and disappearing in a swirl of dead leaves.

"Dude, you are morbid as hell today." Craven spoke to hear his own voice echo in the foyer. Were he to leap into the Datsun and drive, the bright lights of Kingston awaited him twenty minutes east. He wouldn't leave quite yet. First, because he enjoyed the kinky pleasure of balling Deborah, and second, there wasn't enough gas in the truck to reach town.

Artemis crouched at the end of the hall by the bedroom door. Craven rescued the brindle pit bull during his hippie-at-large days in the Pacific Northwest. Time and cynicism had rendered the wriggling puppy an inscrutable grand dame. Sunlight came through a rain-dappled pane and fitted a glowing band across her eyes. The rest of her bulk sank into shadow. Eyes without a face, man. Something Saul Bass or Fulci would film.

Craven went into the amphitheater-style living room where Deborah napped on the couch with a travel magazine spread open on her breasts. Her belly and thighs were caressed by the wavering lines of a prism as it revolved in the skylight from a string. Seventy-fifth birthday coming next month, she possessed the florid sumptuousness one might expect of an aged yet ageless scream queen. Beloved by Italian horror film aficionados, ignored in the USA; the manse served as a shrine and a living tomb.

"Vic, Vic," Deborah said, stroking herself. She talked in her sleep. Crazy shit, too. Claimed to not remember her dreams. Probably a lie. She was cagey like that. Free with her body, yet coolly impersonal. "Don't bother. Don't. Come here, baby. Don't open the hatch. It's too late. Oh, well."

He touched her foot. Canary yellow toenails, canary yellow fingernails. Bobbed gray hair, a trimmed bush with a brunette dye-job. Heavy on the eye shadow and mascara. Violent violet lipstick. Her habit was to remain stock still for a few seconds upon waking in order to gain her bearings. He knew she'd revived because he could see her eyelids flutter behind the smoky lenses.

"Jesse. Where am I?" She had a hell of a voice, its richness cultivated by dint of studio lessons and a few thousand "little-pick-me-up" snorts of coke from her snuff box.

"Home," he said. "Snug as a bug in a rug."

Deborah propped herself against a cushion. Her gaze shifted to his legs and tracked upward. "Put some clothes on. No son of mine walks around in the altogether." Usually, it took a few seconds for her to recall her son was a rock journalist named Erik who lived in

Chicago. She never registered embarrassment at her lapses. At least she hadn't yelled *Erik* while they were getting it on.

He grasped his cock and gave it a twirl. "Perhaps it has eluded your notice that you too are decadently naked."

"No power?" she said.

He shrugged. "Life in the country."

"Be dark soon."

"Hint taken." He slipped into a silk robe that had belonged to Deborah's husband. Crimson with a cowl bunched around the shoulders and embroidered by gold stars. Craven strolled around the house and lighted candles and oil lamps and wall lamps in cloudy antique glass bowls. There were a lot of lamps and bowls. Deborah suffered from mild nyctophobia. This marked the third major power outage since Craven moved in, thus he knew the routine.

Artemis stoically shadowed him. He paused to let her do her business in the backyard, then resumed his circuit, eager to complete the task before sundown. While night and darkness held no special dread for him, neither did he relish the idea of traipsing the house during a blackout. The place was creepy enough in broad daylight.

Big? The pad almost qualified as a mansion, a Hammer Film hybrid of American Gothic and Mission Revival that rich kooks once built atop cliffs with primo views of the ocean. A three-story maze of narrow passages, thick carpet, and a plethora of mismatched rooms. The décor skewed toward the macabre. Rooms were straight out of occult movies of North America's hippie era—garish yellow curtains, fisheye mirrors, heavy wooden furniture, liquor cabinets, lava lamps, gargoyle light fixtures, and oval doorways hidden behind psychedelic velvet hangings. The perfect place to host a dinner party and then watch the guests vanish one by one.

Dearly departed husband Victor earned his bones as an

entertainment lawyer before he and Deborah retired to the mid-Hudson Valley. He'd made his gorgeous young wife a raging success for a mayfly's span—long enough to set them both up nicely. A connoisseur of Roman-Greco and Medieval European art, he'd possessed the means to acquire plenty of it. His library shelves creaked with leatherbound tomes of esoteric lore. In the den, an oil painting of seven hooded magician apprentices supplicating Satan hung above an abandoned mahogany rolltop desk. Someone had carved a Latin phrase into the hutch.

Craven didn't read Latin. Victor had mastered it, Craven knew because he'd spent a long evening on the internet, panning for gold. Nothing was hidden in the digital age. Victor passed away at home seven years ago. Obituaries always say "passed away" if the details are prurient or scandalous. Brief mentions in *Variety* and *The Hollywood Reporter* also played the death coyly. Craven figured it *had* to be an OD or suicide.

Framed photographs of young, lush Deborah in the buff were salted here and there throughout the house. A smaller photo was tucked into an alcove—Deborah, perhaps thirty-five, in a string bikini on the deck of a sloop. White ruins dotted a distant, hazy shoreline. Victor clutched her waist. He wore a Hawaiian flower print shirt and grimaced at the camera, tongue protruding; a comedian strangling on an invisible noose. Someone knelt on Deborah's other side. A man with large hands (his head was cut off by the frame) and wide shoulders under a linen tunic. The bisected man pinned the shiny corpse of a squid to the deck with a spear from a spear gun. The squid's tentacle lifted slightly; forty years frozen in mid-convulsion.

Craven once jokingly asked her if Victor practiced black magic. She took it seriously, or pretended to. *He tried. He committed fully. We had another child, you know. But she... Victor was a disappointment to our father.* Whatever she meant by that—Deborah had a mind full of cats. Her games and her delusions were often inseparable.

Dusk claimed the land as Craven finished. The wind picked up and a hard rain started in. Thunder boomed, closer and closer. Artemis slunk away to hide under the bed. The dog feared few things except storms. She developed that dread back when Craven hiked the Olympics during late summer and high winds lashed the trees. Man and dog cowered inside a flimsy tent. Men rationalize forces beyond their control. Dogs do not.

Craven experienced a pang of nostalgia as he fetched a camp stove from the garage. He boiled tea for Deborah and they sat at the island in the kitchen. Large black skull candles flickered between them. Tall shadows climbed the walls.

She poured cream from the mouth of a pewter faun. "I dreamed I went to a café in a small town. A girl in an apron came around and poured complimentary tea for the mornin' customers. Everybody drank tea and either died or fell into a coma. I did *not* drink the tea. On the next table lay an old book with gilt letterin'. Part of the title read—*Conversing with a Barbed Tongue.* Someone behind me said, *Yes, that one. Pick it up.* The horrible whisper frightened me. I leaned over and picked up the book. It smelled like a piece of soft wood that had lain in the muck of a swamp. The pages were gummy with mold. My hand went numb. I woke to ya standin' there like a slowly spreadin' Adonis." She waited for him to respond. Finally, she said. "What would ya say it means?"

"Dreams never mean jack shit." He gulped hot tea. She had revealed a dream, which represented a first in their relationship. He should feel some sense of closeness, of bonding. He felt uneasy instead. A taboo had been broken, a line crossed.

Lightning hissed near the yard and its blue stroke cast Deborah's face into a death mask. He jumped. She smiled patronizingly. *"Conversing with a Barbed Tongue.* That's suggestive, don't ya think? Like a rare tract an exorcist would stash in his files with a bottle of good wine for a paperweight. Or a tract the Witchfinder General keeps in his traveling satchel of horrors."

"It also sounds like a chapter some fallen angel would dictate to a Franciscan monk," he said, smiling to let her in on the joke. "The Apostles got theirs. I'm sure a demon would jump at the chance to say its piece for the record."

"The weather channel forecast this storm on Tuesday." She apparently disliked it when he spoke more than one sentence at a go.

"I suppose that means your dinner party is canceled." He tried not to sound smug.

"Yes and no. There might be a gatherin'." She took his hand and kissed his fingers. Her eyes gleamed with tears, although her unkind smile remained. "I hope not. But if they decide to visit, I am sorry."

"Hey, your place, your rules. Kind of weird to come over in this weather." He laughed and squeezed her hand in a gesture of cheap graciousness.

She pulled away and stared into the skull flame. "I minored in music."

"Oh? Makes sense. Useful skill for an actress." Craven lifted the cup to his lips. Empty.

"Aspirin' actress then. I dabbled in so many things durin' college. The world didn't truly open for me until I met Victor." Deborah reached into a drawer and brought forth a flute and delicately held it to the light. The instrument glinted, dull, loveless, and the color of dried blood. "This is *Strident Caller.*"

"Your flute has a name. I knew a coal miner who played a harmonica. Every single night after supper. He didn't name it or anything."

"His wasn't an object of power."

"No. It was a plain old cheap harmonica."

"Objects of power are always named. *Strident Caller* is a recorder, not a flute. My family has passed her down through generations. Hollowed from a child's radius in the days of antiquity, she belongs to a set of nine. A recorder, lyre, didgeridoo, hichiriki, drum, whistle, sitar, violin, and a horn." Deborah went to the center of the kitchen. She breathed notes through the recorder. Her black silk robe clung to her breasts and hips as she swayed to a harsh, discordant melody. Thunder served as her metronome. Her playing was terrible and compelling.

Craven's stomach felt odd. "Uh, wow. Does your family own the other instruments?"

She stopped playing, although she didn't lower the recorder. "That would be utterly mad. Nobody owns such instruments. We are stewards."

"Sorry. I didn't realize."

"I am not terribly accomplished. Victor trained as a pianist in childhood. Law school stripped that joy from him. He became cruel after our honeymoon. He showed me the world, for a price. I was his slave. Our son too, until he fled home and lived with my sister in Alaska. To think a cold, hostile land would prove more nurturin' than his own home." She rotated, bent at the waist and shook her buttocks with the aplomb of a burlesque dancer. The recorder notes climbed a notch.

"A slave?"

Three long notes that bled dry. She looked over her shoulder at him. "Ya think I'm melodramatic."

"Deb, your ass is dramatic. That's all I know."

"Men enslave women in a thousand small ways. Victor's possession of me was simply more overt. Early on I defied him. I only complied half the time. He decided fifty percent wasn't adequate."

Down the hall and slightly muffled, Artemis howled. She snarled and then fell silent. Craven didn't enjoy the shrill fluting either. Or the rolling thunder. The cacophony set his teeth on edge.

Deborah ceased playing mid-note. "Not all music soothes the savage breast." She straightened and remained motionless for several seconds. "The great dark gathers around us. *Strident Caller* is like a needle that pierces the black membrane and sucks ichor of the devil gods. It will begin in a moment."

The flame of the skull candle bent to the left and licked the wax rim.

Deborah! Someone shouted from downstairs. Deep and authoritative and angry. *Bring him to me!*

"Who's that?" Craven stage-whispered. He'd almost fallen off his stool.

She finally turned and sighed theatrically. "Take a guess."

"I don't have a clue. Although, I am sure I just pissed your old man's favorite robe."

You sorry sonofabitch! a different angry voice cried from the same direction as the previous.

Craven pinpointed the roaring to the billiards room. He'd locked the exterior doors and seen no one during his sweep of the premises. An intruder could've hidden in a closet or under a table. Unpleasant explanation. Although, every explanation was unpleasant.

The stranger said, *Deborah! Deborah! Deborah! Deborah! Deborah! If I have to come get him…*

"Ya'd better go," she said. Her tone was mild. "He'll come up here. He'll come, and then…"

Craven snatched the biggest butcher knife from the block. "The fuck I will. Is this a joke? Where's your cell? Get Five-Oh on the horn." He whistled for Artemis. Normally a dependable watch dog, the sound of a stranger's voice should have brought her running.

"Jesse, calm yourself." Deborah smiled. Unctuous and facile. Flies and honey and so forth.

"The fuck I will. Artemis!"

"Jesse—"

"The phone. Give me the goddamned phone." He realized he'd pointed the knife at her and tried to rein himself in. "The phone, Deb." He followed her chin gesture and took the pearl-case cell from where it lay upon a knick-knack shelf. He hit 911 and as the circuits did their thing, he watched the stairs that spiraled downward into gloom.

The angry voice boomed through the speaker, *YOU SMARMY BASTARD! NOW YOU'VE DONE IT! PUT DEBORAH ON!*

Mushrooms, peyote, acid, nitrous, glue, melted Styrofoam… at one time or another Craven tripped balls on pretty much every substance that could take a man for a ride. Looking into Deborah's luminous gaze, a madman on the cell in his left hand, cleaver clutched in his right while thunder crashed and lightning blazed, he entertained the notion she'd slipped something into his tea, because the moment stretched and his emotions felt too unstable. "Deb, are you screwing with my mind? Why?"

She played a treble note. Yellow eyes gleamed in the shadows. Artemis padded into the kitchen and sat next to Deborah, head pressed against the woman's leg. They stared at Craven. He stepped forward, not entirely clear in his head what he meant to do, and the dog bared her fangs. Artemis didn't growl and that was far worse.

"Shit." He remembered nursing her with an eyedropper and how she'd looked at him as if he were everything in the universe. The sting of tears surprised him almost as much as Artemis offering to take his hand off at the wrist. He backed to the top of the stairs and listened. Ceiling timbers creaked and wind chimes sang. "Whoever's down there, better run. I'm gonna put the hurt on you, pal." He sounded convincingly rough and ready—the command voice he'd learned from listening to cops. He'd summoned this voice in the past when confronted by fellow vagrants vying for a patch of ground, or intimidating teenagers who thought a seedy dude hitching along the highway would make excellent sport.

He went to his room and dressed with the haphazard efficacy of a man in a hurry to escape before an angry cuckolded husband arrived on the scene. Pants and shoes make a world of difference when it comes to prowling through a dark house. No use wasting precious mental energy in a vain attempt to sort the situation beyond his grasp of the apparent facts—Deborah was a kook (old news) and she'd put one of her whack-job socialite buddies (or her weird gardener) up to shenanigans. He didn't give a flying fuck at a rolling doughnut as to who, what, or why. The cleaver went tucked into his belt and he selected a nine iron from Victor's golf bag in the closet. It swished reassuringly as he executed a few practice swipes.

A flash of orange light caught his attention. He peered outside. Fire engulfed the Datsun. Andy stood nearby, naked but for Wellingtons, and inked with kraken tentacles. The gardener, oblivious, or immune to the elements, smoked a cigarette, his head tilted to regard Craven's window. The sycamores and the grass of the lawn reflected the blaze. Hooded figures lurked amid the undergrowth, obscured by darkness and whipping smoke.

Deborah's recorder bleated from the kitchen. Its melody rapidly descended through a complex sequence of stops and blats, then ceased. The storm died at that moment as well, and the house fell silent.

Craven hustled back, yet she and Artemis were already gone. Two choices presented themselves to his tunnel vision—bolt through the front door and make a break for the road, or venture into the basement and attempt to collect his turncoat dog as that's where the crazy widow must have taken her. Probably only had a few seconds to decide before the cultists, or whomever skulked in the woods, busted through the door to drag him away for ritual sacrifice or gods knew what.

Really, no decision at all. He followed pale, shifty lamplight down into a passage. He glanced into a succession of rooms—billiards, guestrooms, bath, storage—each empty. At the end of the hall double doors painted white and black let into a home theater. The doors parted. Reddish light dripped.

Deborah knelt at the threshold. Her hair lifted, as if pulled by a strong wind. "Ya wouldn't come. Ya wouldn't submit. The membrane is tender, but resilient. It always seals. He takes blood with him. Always blood."

Past her, within the room itself, a disk of watery red light shimmered on its edge like a freestanding mirror. An entire vista of hellish landscape suggested itself—a lunar maw and jagged, mountainous fangs; a sea of crimson, rolling vertically. A man's silhouette receded toward the heart of the disk, slightly hunched and dragging an inert, possibly canine-shaped object. The front door crashed in above. Deborah covered her eyes and bowed her head. Craven simply reacted. He ducked into the spare bedroom, wriggled through the window, and ran until he reached the highway. A guy in a BMW eventually gave him a lift to Kingston.

The police took his report with straight faces. Two cops visited Deborah. A young cop and a much older cop. All the old cop said upon their return was that she'd decided not to press charges. Craven was not welcome at the house and his meager belongings were in a box in the trunk of the patrol car. The young cop handed over the box with a bland expression of professional disdain.

The box contained spare pants and shirts, socks, and Artemis's vaccination tags. Craven had no idea what to do next. The old cop told him there was nothing to do except get gone while the getting was good. He did.

A couple of years later, Craven hopped a train chugging through California. He shared a cold boxcar with a hobo who'd done a tour in the Persian Gulf. The men drank a bottle of Knob Creek and talked about their lives as the engine traveled through haunted industrial star fields.

He told the hobo about the time he'd escaped a bunch of Satanists. After a long silence, the hobo asked him, *why are you crying, man?* and he rolled over and dreamed of being hunted through the primeval forests of the Olympic Peninsula, Artemis a fleeting shadow— sometimes ahead, sometimes behind, always near.

Craven lurched to his feet. Still drunk and half in the dream, he went to the gate and screamed her name, "Artemis! Here, girl!" He clutched the gate and leaned precariously into the wind. The train rushed onward and carried him farther and farther away.

Dawn splintered at the rim of galactic nothingness. He left the train and ambled to a park near a withered forest. The forest decayed beside a river that had slowed and stopped. He slept with his face pressed against a picnic table. The rough wood smelled of acid rain and whiskey and his own bile. The edge of the sun broke through the crust and burned white as the eye of an acetylene flame. He raised his head and watched a mutt wandering listlessly among busted glass and scraps of paper. Pigeons scattered from its ragged path. Craven whistled. The black dog swung around unsteadily. Collarless and skinny as a stick. Its matted sides heaved. One eye drooped shut. Dry foam caked its muzzle.

Craven took a hank of beef jerky from his pocket. He shook the jerky and whistled again. His lips were cracked and it sounded feeble. The dog limped toward him, whining. He dropped the jerky. He held his hand the way a man does over the heat of a barrel fire, shifting it this way and that. The dog whined again, yawned frightfully, and bit him with seeming diffidence. One chomp of green fangs, sunk in good and deep. The dog thrashed as instinct commanded, and finally released. It wheeled stiffly, like an automaton, and moved away and eventually disappeared into some underbrush.

Dark blood oozed and filled the punctures in Craven's hand. Blood slithered down the back of his arm; its tributaries dripped onto the table. He wrapped his hand in a bandanna. The bandanna had been with him for a while, but he couldn't recall where he'd picked it up. Wearied beyond repair, he rested his forehead against the wood and left it there. The sun kept rising, kept drilling through the icy shell of night and burned the back of his skull like it might thaw him out.

Nobody ever came to the abandoned park except for hobos, scavengers, and birds. In a while, sparrows began to flit down from the dry branches and peck around the bench and atop the table. Much later, one alighted upon Craven's shoulder. It plucked at his hair. He didn't mind.

NOT A SPECK OF LIGHT

One 3 a.m. of the soul, I suspected I didn't love my wife anymore. This bleak realization surfaced from twilight depths, seeped into the desolated world, and battened upon me like a demon straddling its victim in a gothic oil painting. The nightlight guttered, casting strange shadows across the blanket. Wind scratched at the eaves and coyotes yipped in the nearby hills. Was my loneliness, my sense of estrangement and regret, an insidious form of vastation? Was the hairshirt suffering of domestic ennui a kind of purification of my past evils? Findlay reciprocated my lack of tender emotion; her shoulder was mighty cold in bed. Neither of us would've copped to such a brutal truth during the daylight hours of our status quo. But the reality lurked, the kind of nagging disquiet one's body or subconscious mind generates to warn of dire trouble. Gravity being what it is, our relationship kept limping along, battered, riddled with knife wounds, leaving a trail of blood. What to do? Some couples go to therapy or embark upon a madcap international voyage. Some get pregnant in a last-ditch attempt to bail out a failing marriage. Some cheat. Some go mad.

We adopted a dog.

I rescued Aardvark as a bedraggled yearling pup from the shelter. He was gawky and shy, the kind most people walked past without a second glance. Not me—he may as well have crouched under a halo as bright as an arc welder. Didn't consult Findlay, but she forgave the trespass five seconds after the little bugger skulked through the door. *Aardvark* was an unusual choice; we figured a kid named him and let it ride. Half hound, half something else (something shaggy), mournful and loyal. Shy in the beginning; he slept in a corner of the apartment and refused to eat or drink while either of us were present. Coaxing him for daily walks proved a monumental task. Noises frightened him—cars, people, other dogs, and especially raised voices. If a man shouted, he'd cower until I lifted him and lugged him to safety. Matters improved over the course of months. He gained confidence, bit by bit. We bought him many, many chew toys, although his favorite thing to ravage was inevitably my grimiest pair of tennis shoes. Findlay and I took turns sleeping on the floor to be near him. One night, a thunderstorm crashed over the town; Aardvark leaped onto our bed and burrowed under the covers, his icy paws pressed into my spine. We couldn't shake him after that. Took a while for him to grow into his clunky, angular head. His irrepressible joy at riding in the car caused us to extensively travel the Hudson Valley just so he could stick his weird head out the window. Weekend camping trips became a staple. Findlay bought a camera to photograph him romping the hills and dales of lost summer days. Aardvark finished the interlocking puzzle of our lives, temporarily cemented the bond in a way I hadn't realized was possible. Fair to say, the three of us were inseparable.

For better or worse.

When our New Paltz apartment complex abruptly changed hands, the new realty company nixed pets. Findlay said screw it, let's take the pooch and buy a house closer to the Catskills. She adored that good boy so much, she would've moved into a tent in the woods to keep him around. I felt the same.

She said to me, a bit drunk on wine, "Wanna know why I wasn't extra pissed when you brought him home?"

I admitted to wondering at my fortune.

"My folks always had dogs when I was a girl," she said. "My favorite was a huge black lab. Mom and Dad named him Errol after old-time actor Errol Flynn. Smelled terrible. Musky. Might've had some Newfie in him; they have that oily fur. I picked his collar. Thick leather, almost as wide as a belt strap. Heart-shaped ID tags. They jangled as he ran around the yard or shook himself dry. He romped in the sprinkler every chance he got. You always knew he was coming closer because of those tags. Years after he died, sometimes I'd wake up in the night and hear his tags jingling in the hallway outside my bedroom, clear as hell. Like he'd never left, was just sleeping on his bed near the door. I wasn't ever sure how to feel. Comforted or afraid…"

Occurred to me that was why she disdained mysticism—it struck a raw nerve.

She managed an office for a Kerhonkson plumbing contractor. She also studied karate three days a week at a local basement dojo; second-degree black belt. Whatever needed to get fixed around the apartment, she fixed. Including wagons, should some fool step out of line. I served as an associate editor and designer for a company that specialized in tabletop roleplaying games. Decent pay; remote work, except for biannual trips to the Pacific Northwest to endure staff meetings and the occasional seminar or conference.

Findlay and I pored over listings and soon found a sweet deal on a renovated farmhouse attached to twenty acres within sight of the mountains. Money wasn't an issue; we'd stashed a modest nest egg and Findlay's parents wrote a check to cover closing costs. Boomers to the hilt, they crossed their fingers, taking it as a sign of nesting and that grandchildren might finally be en route even as the clock ticked down to zeroes. Suckers. The sellers, whom we never met, were a movie director and his manager wife. In turn, they'd snagged the land from a retired New York couple with a vague, tragic backstory. The realtor didn't recall offhand who owned it before that. Probably a farmer. The Hollywood couple decided country living was for the birds. What about the retirees who preceded them? The realtor grimly disclosed that the husband had keeled over in the yard. Did we have a problem with purchasing a home where someone died? Folks might reasonably feel a certain way about such details. Findlay said if it wasn't an axe murder, she didn't give a shit. I asked if both had died or only the husband. The realtor wasn't sure. Probably just the dude? We closed a week later, superstitious dread be damned.

The house was in decent shape, requiring a slate of minor repairs typical of an aging structure. Roof patching, gutter upgrades, some electrical work. I installed security cameras on the front and back porches; deployed a couple more on the far perimeter of the property near a dilapidated shed that sheltered the original well; a colonial antique now long defunct. I had a vague ambition to capture wildlife in action and parlay that into a podcast—an industry writer reporting from the country, something along those lines.

As for the neighborhood: Go left and Millgore Road (tar lane, no centerline) climb a steep hill toward the highway. Hook a right and you can follow it into the Catskills. The house is encircled by cornfields and woods. The Shawangunk Ridge hunches its lengthy spine to the south. Kingston (former state capital until the British burned it in 1777), Stone Ridge, and Accord (hamlets both) lay a hop, skip, and a jump along 209. Country suburbia. Neighbors were scattered up and down Millgore. One lady illustrated children's books; another guy surveyed for Ulster County; a struggling generational dairy visibly declined a bit more every day. Farther off, peeking between boughs of a magnificent pine copse, were the gables and dormers of a decaying manse tenanted by an honest-to-God scream queen, or so claimed the clerk at the mom-and-pop gas station. Traffic, seldom heavy, petered out after nightfall. Oppressively quiet but for owl hoots and the aforementioned coyotes. The neighborhood got what locals called country-dark. The dairy barn's lamp and the scream queen's porchlight way out across a field, and a sprinkle of lonely stars, were pretty much it.

Maybe that change from city apartment life to a woodsier setting got into my head. Odd occurrences kicked off almost immediately. Inexplicable odors, weird creaks in the attic, and dark spots in corners where lamplight should reach, but didn't. The closet door in the den frequently stood ajar. Inexplicable isn't quite accurate. Any number of rational things cause smells or sounds. Acoustics can be finnicky and wood paneling infamously sucks light. It wasn't the Amityville Horror, but it felt like *something*.

Longtime friend, John Dusk, a counselor at the Northeast Military Academy (a high school for rich ne'er-do-wells), had recently turned us on to feng shui. The fact someone had died there intrigued him. He invited herself to dinner and brought a bottle of wine to pair with my spaghetti. None of the vino was for me—I'd climbed onto the wagon after a tumultuous college experience and ridden it since. His housewarming gift was a paperback on feng shui, naturally. John D toured both floors and the basement, identifying strong points and trouble spots. He'd waved at the sunroom: *Okay, Lars, this is your luck room. Close doors to channel positive energy, especially closets and bathrooms. Closets are portals. Toilets drain luck. Mirrors are also portals and shouldn't hang in opposition to one another.* He spent two seconds on a ladder with his head stuck through the opening into the empty attic before retreating. *Don't go up there,* he said. I asked why not. *Bad feng shui.*

Meanwhile, my wife tolerated the proceedings with a maternal eyeroll. Findlay wasn't keen on hearth magic or mysticism in general—her mother was a fundamentalist Baptist, her father some sort of druid, and she'd consequently rejected the metaphysical realms with prejudice. Contrarily, my beliefs have always been intense, yet inchoate, born of intuition and a handful of odd experiences. Corner me and I'd put five bucks on reincarnation, genius loci, and the existence of extraterrestrial visitors. I mean, ponder all those crop circles and cattle mutilations. Yes, Uri Gellar could really bend spoons and the Warrens chatted with genuine spirits—why do you ask? During moments of introspection, John D used to spark a j and remark that the sum of earthly data routinely doubles and redoubles. Yet, everything humankind learns merely digs a deeper hole, proving the universe is large and unknowable.

Tell it on the mountain, brother. Any animal could've told it, too.

We endured that first winter with its big storms and frequent power outages. The area got above average snowfall due to the surrounding mountains; alas, Ulster County took its sweet time clearing backroads. That following summer, I devoted more time to exploring the environs. The rear pasture was thick with wild grass. Thornbushes and bittersweet tangles choked the woods on other side of the house. During walks, I carried a machete to kill invasive vines wherever I found them strangling native flora and to chop a jungle path to the creek.

Our schedules worked out so one of us was always home with Aardvark. Usually me. I suspect doggo would've preferred Findlay's company, but he politely accepted the situation and my bribes of his beloved turkey jerky. Aardvark's best pal in the world was Sleestak, the grizzled black tomcat who haunted the grounds. He wheezed and sneezed and his eyes were enormous; reminded me of the villainous lizard men from the '70s show *Land of the Lost.* Could've gone with the Death Maker in parody of ye moldy oldy Mentos ads.

Sleestak rebuffed my efforts to lure him inside, preferring to make a nest in the ramshackle equipment shed near the back porch. Sorry mice, sorry birds. Twice a day, I bussed kibble and canned tuna to his enclave. I scratched his ragged ears while he chowed down and warned him to watch out for the Cooper's hawk that roosted atop a ginormous pine. *Watch out for Mr. Hawk. Watch out for Mr. Fox, too.* According to a clerk at the post office, feral cats were scarce due to the prevalence of roving coyote packs. *Beware the coyotes, little cat!* This idyllic domain was a throwback to darker, Bambi and Old Yeller era Disney. Mourning dove feathers from Mr. Hawk's daily predations kind of set the tone. I also stumbled across a fresh deer carcass in the overrun pasture.

"Life is cheap on the outskirts of Stone Ridge," I'd warned curious Aardvark as he rammed his snout into a pile of green exploded doe guts. Sleestak, shadowing us as usual, hissed in agreement. Had a feather stuck to his chin, a mean glint in his feral eye.

See, life is cheap *everywhere* and the cat wasn't so much a fan of roughing it in the outdoors as he was terrified of the house. The layout was vaguely suburban Gothic redolent of Italian and Spanish influences slapped over a traditional Northeast farm manor. Four bedrooms and a master suite, two-and-a-half baths, kitchen, pantry, office, den, storage, sunroom, attic, and a cavernous basement.

Paul Wooster, another close friend I'd known since high school (he wrote instruction manuals for several popular board game companies and a bunch of obscure ones), saw photos of the layout and suggested I renovate a man cave—someplace cozy to paint wargame miniatures, organize my comic book collection, and set up a writing desk to plink away at a crime novel as I'd threatened to do for years. Preferably isolated from everyday concerns, such as my doting wife and her honey-do lists. Initially, I had designs on the basement because the second-floor office was too high profile; the den was a den; kind of stuffy in a 1960s fashion, only suitable for relaxing in silk pajamas or drinking cocktails with the neighbors, if we ever had any over. Problem was, the basement gave me the creeps. Never could shake the silly, yet persistent, impression that it was a maze of barrows extending past the washer and dryer at the bottom of the stairs.

Proceeding with the best intentions, I secured a desk and a manual typewriter. Fancied myself Darren McGavin as Kolchak, *The Night Stalker*, except instead of pursuing confessional occult journalism I was spinning an occult crime yarn. The weight of the earth that oppressed me and a sense that an inimical presence loomed over my shoulder collaborated to end the experiment after several weeks. Oh, and Aardvark drew his line in the sand at the stairs; he wouldn't descend with me for love or turkey jerky. When

I physically encouraged him, he clung to my leg and peed. A dude can't chill without his best friend. Understandable, right?

Leaves turned gold shortly after our first anniversary in the hinterlands. Triumphant upon completing my latest editing project, I indulged in a day off to enjoy the glorious autumn weather. Walking behind the house, I noticed a tall, older man standing in the overgrown field on the opposite side of the stone fence. His broad shoulders stretched a pair of grimy white coveralls. His presence was that of an apparition, a gothic revenant come to roost.

Aardvark whined. Sleestack demonstrated the better part of valor and vanished into a bush. A small cyclone of fallen leaves whirled around us, then dissipated.

"Hi," I said. A weird impression hit me that the guy had been waiting a long while, motionless as a scarecrow, pine needles snagged in his Caesar cut.

"I am Andy," he said with a heavy accent. His craggy features were molded into an all-or-nothing scowl. "You are the neighbor." *Neighbor* was enunciated with the inflection of a medieval hetman confronting the spear-wielding representative of an invading tribe.

"Right! Lars. My wife is Findlay. And this is Aardvark." We shook over the fence. His was the forceful grip of a man who labored with pick and shovel. Aardvark stopped whining, but his scowl matched Andy's in tight-lippedness.

"I labor for Ms. Infante." The big man wiped his hand on his opposite sleeve, took a pack of cigarettes from his pocket, and lighted one. He gestured toward the mansion across the field. The home of the reputed scream queen. "She requests the pleasure of your company." His gaze shifted to Aardvark. "And the company of your hound."

"She likes dogs? Big, scruffy dogs? That's commendable." In my experience, too many wealthy folks disdain canines that don't fit into a handbag.

"The mistress *adores* all dogs. Shall I inform her you will be over for cocktails imminently?"

Several feeble excuses to beg off flashed by. Under his pitiless gaze, none felt remotely sufficient. Trapped, I said, "Sure, Andy. Say an hour?"

He nodded stiffly and walked away. I watched him slog through dying grass toward the mansion as if there was a windup spring in his back. Findlay wouldn't get home until evening. No reinforcements for me and Aardvark. Doggo's hackles were still bunched—a mood usually reserved for delivery drivers or cops. Some dogs hate uniforms; my money was on the serial killer coveralls. My lip curled in a snarl.

I changed into a dress shirt reserved for video conferences. Kept it on a hook on the office door. Considering his skittish behavior, I briefly considered leaving the dog. Told myself I was being a ninny. He obviously needed *more* socialization now that he'd languished in the boondocks for a year—seven years, by canine reckoning. Ran a comb through his coat to purge the worst tangles. Did the same for myself. We took the long way—out to the street then down to the Infante mailbox. The sign at the entrance of the long, bumpy lane said PRIVATE DRIVE. Formerly paved; now worn to dirt and roots. Apparently, B movie bucks don't last forever.

At the house proper, a fountain divided the circular drive—a grotesque marble ape supported by a harem of verdigris-stained nymphs, none of them happy. Borderline enormous house; front porch roof supported by colonnades; smoky amber windows; cracked plaster siding and numerous flowers in urns and hanging planters. Front door bands were riveted like the entrance of a fortification.

Andy (in a fresh, crisp, white utility suit) opened the way before I could rap the iron knocker. He walked us through a gallery of tiled flooring interspersed with sections of hardwood or deep, ivory shag. Passages branched. The joint might very well have represented the labyrinth of a posh minotaur. Somebody sure liked lamps—electric, oil, and salt, glowed rosily from the recesses of various nooks and crannies. He silently deposited us in an amphitheater parlor and took his leave. Anemic light fell through tall windows. The carpet's funky geometric design made me queasy. Italian sofas and the subtle concavity of eggshell plaster exuded the vibe of a Giallo film set. I half expected a black-gloved serial killer in a motorcycle helmet to jump into the frame brandishing a razor.

"Darlin'!" Through a doorway slithered Deborah Goodwin Infante, famed B actress in the flesh. Draped in a clingy purple gown, she undulated from light to shadow and into light. Lost a few years (but not all of them) with each swing of her hips. One of those people who ripen into graceful middle age then stay that way, more or less, until the casket lid drops. A spiky bronze pendant of an occulted sun glinted amidst impressive cleavage.

"Nice to make your acquaintance, Mrs. Infante." I side-eyed Aardvark—he shrank from her boisterous presence, but wagged a default wag of greeting. His cautious way of asking, *new friend?* The magic eight-ball would answer, *Unclear. Try again later.*

"It's Deborah. Deb. Ya met Andy, my manservant." Her voice was rusty, faintly slurred. Long Island by way of more cosmopolitan climes. Her tone suggested she relished referring to him as manservant as much as she savored her collection of lamps.

Hoping she appreciated the connection to her career, I said, "Quite a character. He resembles a Hammer walk on."

"Ya mean Amicus." She smiled; a bit long, a bit yellow. Sharpish. "Despite my winsome charms, he's as close to Karloff or Christopher Lee as I ever managed. Andy and his people served my husband's family for ages. Victor died, the last of his name. On this continent, at any rate. So, Andy's debt transferred to me. We're alone now in this house, but he remains Vic's man at heart. Sometimes, it's difficult to tell who's the master and who's the servant in our fucked-up relationship. What's yer poison, handsome? Wait, lemme me choose."

"As long as you choose something non-alcoholic. I'm, well, I don't partake."

"That's Vic, my dearly departed." She indicated a row of photos on the mantle— the late Victor Infante, a slick fella wearing different ensembles against various exotic locales; same sinister smile and impressive sideburns that silvered, then whitened, from left to right in the sequence. She swayed to a fancy liquor cabinet, added ice to an even fancier glass. Splashed cola over the top and pressed it into my hand. A double bourbon was her preference. Definitely not the first of the day. She poured water from a carafe painted with white flowers into a white porcelain dish and carefully set it on the floor before Aardvark, who hesitated, then lapped with slobbery gusto.

"G' boy, g' pooch. You're a guest. We mus' each sup. Remember— Imdugud saves. C'mon, Lars." She led me to a couch and we sat with her thigh entirely too close to mine. Before us lay a marble slab of a coffee table. Barren except for a wooden bowl of fruit that gleamed seductively as a Vermeer. It was only upon second glance that I noticed a housefly sluggishly trundling across the weeping skin of a pear.

"Yer a writer?" Something of an accusation.

"Games," I said.

"Board games? Please tell me it's not those dreadful video games. Utter brain rot. My son got hooked on 'em after he lost his way. Awful."

"No, ma'am. Narrative storytelling. Players sit at a table and assume the role of detectives, secret agents, or wizards, and have adventures of the mind."

"Ooh, I love roleplay, Lars. So does sweet, sweet Andy. How I punish him." She flicked her wrist, cracking an invisible whip. Three rings—opal, ruby, gold band. "That's what ya do, eh? Ah, to play games for a living. Much like acting. Dress up. Kissy-face. Violence…"

I swallowed fast to hide my expression. Said, "Playing is fun. Writing less so. And proofing. And wrangling distribution. I'm a man of many hats."

"Written any scripts?" She leaned closer. Her perfume slapped me silly. What the hell was that scent? "Screenplays are a passion of mine."

"Well, I'm working on a novel."

"Ain't everyone?" Another smile, but it dimmed even faster. Her glass was already depleted. She recharged it. Her hands were soft, liver-spotted, shaky. "In my youth, I met loads of screenwriters. Vic was a famous entertainment lawyer, knew everybody. Had 'em over to our villa all the time. Scurrilous rodents. The novelists were worse. Paunchy, opinionated layabouts. Inveterate drunks. Always moochin' off their patrons. Fuck ya in the ass and say, *it's research, baby!*"

Not sure whether to laugh or not, I sat perfectly still.

She said, "I studied abroad. Modeling classes, voice acting. Music. Toured the casting couches of the great cities. I developed an embarrassin' obsession with Machiavelli and especially the Borgias. Those rotten sonsofbitches knew how to treat an enemy. Their ancient methods came in handy durin' my time in Rome. Had my share of rivals in love and as an actress. Cinema is a cutthroat world."

"I assume modeling is competitive as well."

"The fuckin' worst, m'friend."

Aardvark whined and whapped his tail against the floor. Mrs. Infante cooed something damnably close to Latin as she bent and patted his head. He took a cue from me, freezing in place.

"Such an unusual combo of attributes. Snobs malign mixed breeds. I'm rather fond of mutts." She sighed melancholically. "Vic murdered the last dog that came 'round. Its owner humped more than my leg, ya see. My husband, a jealous bastard here and in the hereafter."

"Excuse me?" I did a doubletake.

"He *enslaved* the pooch is closer to the truth. Same difference, considerin' where Vic resides. Dark urges and peculiar desires ruled him."

I envisioned a pharaoh and his slaughtered retinue in the afterlife, except instead of a pharaoh, a smarmy attorney to stars of schlock. Then I glanced at my nervous Aardvark again and the image was less amusing.

She said, "The dog's name was Artemis. O, sweet canine, beloved of the goddess. Whaddaya think of my home?"

"Reminds me of a movie location. It's nice. Classy."

"Truly? Some find it ominous. Or gauche. I keep the tackiest stuff in a trophy room under glass. The cheesecake photos and goofy props are amusing until ya hit a certain age, then it tends to curdle like sour milk."

I tried not to reflexively ogle the nearest of several photographs of her younger self in the buff. Tan lines and tautness. Whatever lay in the trophy room must've been super-duper salacious.

She continued, "Victor bought this house because of the location. Stone Ridge is a colonial settlement. The Shawangunks are riddled with mines and natural caves. There's a black bear den near the creek on yer property. Did ya know? Andy and Vic considered smokin' the sow out with a bonfire."

"What would they do that for, Mrs.—Deb?"

"Vic had this fantasy about fuckin' on a homemade bearskin rug. I nixed the idea. Filthy creatures, bears. Besides, fur belongs on animals. But, caves and caverns. Not to be overly woo-woo, this area is a conflux of power. Genius loci coupled with the juju manifested by natives and white settlers. Esopus, Dutch, Germans, Irish. Each with their particular lore and superstitions. Care to freshen that, Lars?" When I shook my head, she made a face. She rose, swirling her drink as she sashayed to the liquor cabinet. Dumped in more ice, more booze, returned to my side and had at it. "Vic's idea of a two-martini lunch was a four-martini lunch. I did my level best to match him, blow for blow. Nobody could. Gods forgive me, I'm still tryin'." She leaned over precariously and brushed the fly from the pear. Took a bite and chewed while juice dribbled down her chin. Plenty of eye contact. She moved to feed me, but I'd already retreated to the other end of the sofa. Mrs. Infante dabbed her sticky flesh with her index finger. "Yes, caves and caverns and haunted houses. This entire neighborhood, possesses a psychic history that would straighten yer curls. A bloody, dripping wound." More smacking and gulping. She discarded the gnawed pear amongst an apple and a bunch of green grapes. The fly returned with greedy eagerness.

"Permit me to broach a delicate subject," she said. "I fancied meeting you in person—we should always endeavor to know our neighbors. However, my ulterior motive…"

"Sure." I was not, by any stretch of the imagination *sure* of anything except wanting to vanish into a hole in the earth.

"Would you be willin' to sell yer dog to me?" She licked her stained lips. The light abruptly changed so all of it gathered around her shoulders and behind her head while the rest of the room dimmed. Her face submerged into shadows except for her eyes, her long, glittering lashes.

"I don't understand."

She slid across the sofa and clutched my knee. Her yellow-lacquered nails dug in. Quite possibly a stronger grip than ham hock Andy. "I gotta have him. I gotta. He's exactly what I've sought. You can see his perfect lil' soul shinin' like a halo. Never mind the scruff, the impurity. Mud on a diamond."

"Ma'am. Aardvark isn't for sale. He's a member of our family."

"Oh, tosh. People make such ridiculous comparisons. *My dog is like a child! My fur baby!* Et cetera. Absolute tripe. Animals are animals at the end of the day. Not babies, not real family. They live short lives devoid of higher purpose. No connoisseurs of art among 'em. No nuance or intuition. Lovely creatures, yes. Simple creatures, yes. What did Herzog say of bears? Their smiles are devoid of empathy or love. They are cruelly indifferent, like nature herself. Dogs are the same. The fuzzy scoundrels wear masks of domesticity. Conditioned to perform. Certainly, we can come to a suitable accommodation. I'll give ya…" She closed her eyes as if concentrating. "Hmm, five hundred dollars sound reasonable? Perhaps I could throw in a bonus.

A piece of erotic memorabilia? I've an ivory phallus of a satyr you and yer woman might enjoy—"

"No, ma'am." I stood, Aardvark's leash in a death grip. "That's a kind offer, really. Sadly, my gentle wife would strike off my head with her authentic bespoke katana. No questions asked. C'mon, boy." I tugged the leash and we bailed on that scene.

"Should ya reconsider." Mrs. Infante called. Or, "Ya should reconsider…"

A fly landed upon my neck. Tickle, tickle. I crushed it without a thought.

That night our house was dark except for the protective bubble of the bedside lamp. I lay atop the covers, scrolling the news on my phone. Aardvark snuggled at my feet, twitching occasionally as he chased dream rabbits or fled lascivious crones. Findlay leaned over the bathroom sink removing her makeup. She'd received a hell of a shiner at karate. Through the half-open door, she listened to my tale about how the scream queen propositioned me over the dog. Afterward, she asked why I agreed to visit Mrs. Infante considering my and Aardvark's misgivings.

"Material for the novel," I said rather than admit I'd wussed out under Andy's withering gaze. "Why not, right? She's a hell of a character. So's the gardener."

"The novel. Uh-huh. In another life, you would've told the handyman to fuck himself and socked him in the jaw if he didn't like it."

"You have me confused with a different fella. The boy who thought he was gonna be a private eye."

"Miss that boy. Now I'm stuck with one who writes about them."

Fictional detectives fit into convenient archetypes: The Tough Guy; The Dandy; The Brain; The Drunk; The Narcoleptic; etcetera. I'd be the gumshoe who gets punched a lot. I said, "Infante suggested our house is haunted. Said 'horrors' occurred in the attic."

"Wait, John got a bad vibe in the attic…"

"You don't believe in vibes." A tactically stupid comment.

"Just making conversation, honey." Findlay's tone suggested she'd clenched her teeth.

I tried to retrieve the situation. "So, uh, wanna guess what kind of horrors?"

"Okay. What kind?"

"Unclear. Seemed to excite her, though."

She emerged, left eye dramatically black and blue, cheeks scrubbed and flushed, clad in her most no-nonsense nightgown. The gown, complemented by her icy stoicism, informed me there'd be no funny business. She said, "Here's my intel on Infante—"

"You have intel?"

"Yep. The scream queen is a rich, pampered headcase. Ask anybody. Never worked a day in her life, unless you count flashing your tits on camera and shrieking for effect. Gets off on the notion of mayhem. One of my company's plumbers did maintenance for the late great Victor Infante. Vic and Deb gave him the creeps. He swears they were into hinky shit."

"Swingers?" I said.

"*Hinky*, not kinky, but maybe that as well. Occultism. Rituals. Bad touch New Age hoodoo. The plumber claims a buddy of a buddy dipped a toe in their midnight circles until the whiff of perversity overwhelmed him. Hinted about nasty stuff. Piss drinking. Animal sacrifice. Like that."

"Animal sacrifice." I flashed back to Mrs. Infante's cryptic comments regarding Vic and the dog he'd harmed. Grown man or not, twenty-first century or not, my skin prickled. "Sounds positively druidic. Goats, chickens…?"

"Dogs." She climbed into bed and pulled the covers to her chin. "Turn off the light, would you? The whole thing bothers me. You visiting the wicked witch. Me happening to chat with a guy who knew the lowdown about her and her dead husband. Plus, I had a nightmare."

I clicked off the lamp. The room contracted. We were inside a capsule tumbling through outer space. "Last night?"

"Last week. Forgot it until just now."

"How'd it go?"

Findlay sighed. I thought she wouldn't answer, but after a while, she did. "I dreamed Aardvark was in the kitchen at the back door. Door was torn off its hinges. I mean there was some other shit, my dad kicking my brother's ass, the boss yelling about missed calls, you refusing to eat takeout I brought home, you know how dreams are, but all that crystallized into this spooky deal with puppers. He wasn't right. Longer, heavier. Silhouetted, eyes of white flame. He led me outside into the shadows across the field. No moon, no stars, no nothing. I could make my way because his eyes beamed that hideous red light and it illuminated the grass and bushes. We reached the scream queen's house…Went in through the storm doors to the cellar. Down a tunnel that reminded me of the French catacombs. Bones embedded in the walls, the weight of rock and oppression. At the end was a portal. A conduit to the void. The void of voids. He barked at me, then bounded across. I couldn't decide what to do. Follow him or run. A voice said to me, *All who enter here: there's no way back.* So I woke up and you were sleeping. Aardvark was missing."

"Wasn't part of the dream?" I said around a yawn.

"No. For real vanished. Took a powder. Five a.m. I had a small panic attack. Aardy stays glued to the bed until I drag my ass downstairs to let him run. I can't quite explain except to say it felt wrong. Like he'd slunk off to be sick. The air was heavy. Charged."

We'd hired a carpenter to install a pet flap in the kitchen door; locked it after sundown to repel wild animals and burglars. Aardvark's first trip of the day meant one of us had to set him free—Findlay, more often than not. He wasn't prone to wandering the house at night; him being AWOL in the a.m., was unprecedented.

"Where was he?" I was fading fast.

She said, "I checked the living room and kitchen. Then I heard him whining in the hall. You left the basement door open. Again."

I didn't protest that I always shut the basement door on account the stairs were steep and because of that ominous aura. Instead, I patted her arm and mumbled an apology. How could I be so dumb, et cetera.

Her arm was stiff as wood. "He crouched on the threshold, growling. His fur was poofy. Fierce as hell, our boy."

Dimly occurred to me Aardvark's discontent might be a trend, a doggy crisis. Could doggy valium be in order? A doggy psychotherapist? Unlike Findlay, I hadn't been raised with animals. Despite a keen adolescent longing for a dog or cat, my parents adamantly refused to add a member to our nuclear family. Impossible for adult me to anticipate the emotional needs of our furry friend.

Something startled me. Sleep apnea, saliva down the wrong hatch, who knows, but I woke, choking, afterimages of a hellish, cackling Deborah Infanti cavorting in her diaphanous gown. Aardvark's familiar lumpen weight was missing from the foot of the bed. I went groggily downstairs and found him pointed at the basement stairwell, shivering, his fur on end. The doorway cut into utter blackness that could've led anywhere, even the void of voids. I stroked his knotted shoulder. A faint odor of sickness lingered. Might've emanated from him or the foundation. I shut the door and then coaxed him upstairs. Like all journeys home in the dark, the walk took longer than it should've. Halfway up the stairs I heard a faint thump and the unmistakable creak of hinges. I resisted an overpowering urge to look over my shoulder at what might've been gaining.

In the morning, Andy awaited me and Aardvark at the mailbox. He stood rigid as a tree. His coveralls were metallic gray. He smoked a cigarette. Same rigamarole as our last meeting—the cat split for high timber, Aardvark performed the role of an uptight asshole, I fidgeted.

"Good day, Lars." Complete flat affect.

"Good morning, Andy. Geez Louise, pup. Calm your tits." The pup would not, in fact, calm his tits. He uttered chainsaw-revving growls.

"Mrs. Infante directed me to inform you she's willing to pay two-thousand dollars for your noble cur. Other benefits to be specified later."

"No." My own brusqueness surprised me. Hungover from the previous visit to Mrs. Infante, this entire bit had gotten under my skin. Now with Aardvark snarling and pulling against the leash, my patience was at low ebb.

"Twenty-five hundred dollars." Andy ignored the jaws snapping in the general vicinity of his groin. "More than fair, yes?"

"Cur isn't exactly a compliment, Andy."

"*Noble* cur."

I regarded him, confused and hot under the collar, wondering if this was how Findlay felt at any given moment—a volcano percolating.

"Three-thousand dollars," he said. "I can proffer no higher."

"Look, guy. I need to get my mail. You might want to step aside…Ardy is in a mood."

The grizzled sonofabitch did *not* step aside. He blew a cloud of smoke, then opened the mailbox and extracted a bundle of rubber-banded envelopes and Findlay's monthly subscription of *Ka-Pow! Magazine*. He handed them to me. "The mistress makes her offer in good faith, sir. You are well-advised to accept."

"Well-advised!" I snatched the mail while struggling to control my frothing dog who seemed increasingly intent upon chomping the handyman's balls. "He's not for sale, dude. I don't get what you mean by well-advised. Sounds threatening."

"Sounds threatening because it is threatening." He stood somehow taller. A stagecraft trick; the way Christopher Reeve had Clark Kent remove his glasses and straighten his spine to transform into Kal El. "Do you have even the slightest inkling of who I am? Were you to apprehend my exalted lineage as a servitor and agent of unspeakable powers, you would loose your bowels in abject terror. Your ignorance is no matter, as I am of scant significance compared to those whom I supplicate. My master, Lord Infante, mercy upon his wandering soul, was a disciple of the Salamanca Seven, devotee of the Undulant Gods, annotator of the Nocturnal Grimoires. He dwells now as an infernal phantom, yet we feed him from time to time by the ravening shine of Old Mr. Moon. The crackle-spark of waning souls are his provender to sup as the cycle draws nigh here in autumn's gathering shadow. Your noble cur would amuse our fallen master, sustain his lambent shade as it ravels on the chaos plane. Or so my mistress believes. Once she sets her eye upon someone or something, the matter is decided. You can accept fair payment and deliver the animal sacrifice, or I will seize the animal sacrifice over your mewling objections. I care not. Not a jot, not a whit, not a flying rat's ass."

I was stunned. What to do with such a deranged monologue? Growing rage jolted me into action. Dragging Aardvark backward, I said, "Do me a favor? You and your lunatic mistress." I nodded toward the field. "Stay on that side of the fence."

The tall man sneered. "Imdugud steal your tongue. The die is cast. Night lurkers will visit you anon."

I made a note to purchase a shotgun at the earliest opportunity.

Findlay's response upon hearing of the encounter with Andy: "What the fuck? Sonofabitch comes anywhere near Aardvark I'll cut off his arms."

The forces of darkness converged the next weekend.

Paul Wooster drove down from Boston to spend the night. John Dusk lived nearby in Rosendale. His wife had departed on a ten-day trip to visit relatives in Europe, so it didn't require much arm-twisting to get him to join us for the last barbeque of the season. I broiled ribs and we ate dinner in the back yard while the sun set behind the mountains. It grew chilly; John D and Paul did battle in an impromptu (and ill-advised) pushup contest, which Jazzercise-loving Paul won handily. I shrugged into a coat and Findlay slipped on a sexy turtleneck she hadn't worn since a birthday of yore. The three of them got crocked on imported beer while I nursed a tall glass of ginger ale. She stuck a cherry in it and kissed my forehead with more warmth than usual. As I said, they were drunk. Everybody swapped tales of woe regarding our jobs. Dog and cat patrolled, on the make for discarded crumbs. John tossed Aardvark a chunk of meat then ducked as Findlay menaced them both with a carving fork. Scraps were a no-no due to the dog's indelicate reaction to human food. *Now he'll crap for a week, you sonofabitch!* she yelled. Oh, well, the damage was done. While John D was distracted, I dropped some gristle at my feet and gave Aardvark the high sign. That's why we were best friends—I bought his loyalty at every turn.

Later, as a surprise to honor recent neighborly encounters, Findlay dredged up one of Deborah Infante's giallo films; a 1978 offering called *The Pack Master*. Badly edited, awfully dubbed-over Italian, drolly performed by a minimal cast. Radiant, nubile Deborah spent much of her screentime combing her hair, talking on the phone to breathless suitors, eating cereal, and screaming at various jump-scares. While topless. She (a painfully obvious mannequin) was torn apart by wolves (in reality, run of the mill dogs) in the final frame. The eponymous pack master, a hooded villain, stood by and laughed as the credits rolled.

"Damn!" John D said. "Your neighbor is a smokeshow."

"In 1978." I'd squirmed throughout the movie, recalling the actress's unctuous demeanor, her gray teeth ripping into that overripe pear.

By then it was good and dark with a chance of frost. Paul retired to the spare bedroom dressed in the burgundy pajamas he brought on every overnight trip. Too blitzed to drive home to his empty house, John D faceplanted on the couch and began to snore.

In bed, I clicked off the light and pushed my feet against Aardvark's warm bulk. He snored almost as loudly as John D "I'm sorry."

"For what?" Findlay's voice was muffled by a pillow. She'd rolled onto her side, facing the wall.

"For accepting Deborah's invitation."

"Shut up."

"Feels like I started something. Shouted at the devil. Opened a cursed tomb. I dunno what."

"You didn't start anything that wasn't already in motion. *She's* the curse. Probably ruins it for everybody who moves into this place. Besides…"

I waited. Then, "Besides?"

"Katana," she said, dreamily. "Those bastards cause any trouble, my blade will descend as if swung by the Shogun's own headsman… snicker snack."

I fell asleep. Bad dreams. When I roused at first light, Findlay breathed steadily, her arm draped over my chest; an old comfortable intimacy I'd nearly forgotten. Aardvark was gone.

We frantically scoured the premises for our dog. Zilch. Paul offered to stay and join the search party. We convinced him to go—he had a long drive ahead.

John D, cantankerous when the mood struck, dug his heels in. "Nobody's waiting on me at the casa. I'll cruise around the neighborhood, see what I can see." Upon which, he jumped into his car and zoomed away.

Findlay took the path along the creek; I the back forty. Heart sunk, guts congealed, filled with dread. Worst feeling I can recall in my entire life. I knew in the very fiber of my being who was responsible. After a fruitless search of the brown field, I jogged over to the Infante residence and knocked. Heart beating fast, nerves jangling in anticipation of a showdown. The prospect of physically handling Andy if matters went sideways wasn't promising. No wilting flower, I'd nonetheless shaken the brute's hand and possessed an inkling of his terrible strength.

Deborah answered wearing enormous sunglasses and a plush yellow towel and stained moccasins. "Lars, hon. Thirsty?" She waggled a glass of booze.

"Our dog is missing." My voice sounded eerily flat. The calmness of a man severed below the waist in an industrial accident, adrenaline and endorphins delaying onset of panic and pain.

"Oh, sweetie. Ya won't find him in this realm. He's gone where the freezin' wind of night blows, roamin' Stygian fields with Artemis, never to return." She stepped aside and gestured indolently. "Andy acted of his own volition, whatever threats he may've leveled, whatever high-flown monologue he recited. Silly fucker swears fealty to a shade. As I said, yer pooch isn't here. Have a look if ya think it'll ease yer mind. It won't."

What the spider said to the fly notwithstanding, I brushed past her and made a circuit of the premises, whistling and yelling for Aardvark as I trotted. Kind of expected Andy to leap from a closet with a spade. All the closets and cupboards I flung open were empty. The confusing array of rooms too. Spent the better part of an hour combing that mansion, cellar to attic, and found nary a dog hair.

Deborah said, "Feel better? No?"

I wanted to throttle her. To shake her until her teeth rattled and she revealed Aardvark's fate. Instead, I clenched my jaw and withdrew.

"Go on home, regroup," she said. "Vic's the source of yer troubles and mine. He can't be killed, my dead hubby. Yet, if ya can devise a method to destroy him, I won't complain. Think of it as one of yer roleplayin' games. Yer goin' on a quest."

I relayed this to my wife when we rendezvoused back at the house.

She said in an icy tone, "Infante is a liar. Nothing on the security feed. Almost forgot the trail cams. I downloaded them. Look." She tapped the keyboard of my desktop PC and played footage recorded overnight. A few minutes after 3 a.m., a gangly figure, which bore a suspicious resemblance to Andy, crept to the sunken wellhouse and disappeared inside.

I agreed this was a horse of a different color.

"Let's go over your conversation with them the other day," she said. "And that shit at the mailbox."

I dutifully recounted my visits to the Infante manse and Andy's unhinged threats. The evidence was thin in a legal sense, yet sufficiently concrete to justify a blood feud if human history was prologue.

Her eyes crackled. She grabbed a bottle from the cupboard and poured. Straight rye down the hatch. No chaser. She wiped her mouth, ready to hop onto the warpath. "Obviously, we're going to get him. We can't leave a faithful soul where the fuck ever he is."

"Honey," I said.

She gulped another three fingers of bourbon. "Honey nothing. The bitch sent her minion into our home. He walked in and stole our dog. That won't stand."

"Honey," I tried again. "It's not certain he came into the house. Lurking at the edge of the property is hardly the same."

"Trespassing is a crime."

"Let's think this through. Better not to go off half-cocked—"

"Fuckin' watch me."

"Aardvark wasn't at Infante's. I searched high and low."

"While you were searching, did you see the gardener?"

"No."

"Then you *didn't* search everywhere."

"Everybody around here has a gun," I said. "The smart move is to call the cops, right? John?"

John D had walked in moments before, frowning. "No way on God's green earth Mrs. Infante or her handyman will admit to stealing Aardvark, so the cops won't do anything. Alleged dognapping isn't a high priority unless you live in Beverly Hills." He gestured toward the hallway. "Been in the cellar recently?"

"Why?" I said.

"I checked a minute ago. Figured Aardy might've crawled into a cool, dark corner if he was sick or scared. And…you'll want to see this."

He led us into the basement, past the washer-dryer combo and my unused desk. At the far end where the rough, unfinished ceiling slanted downward, a tunnel mouth gaped and past it, bored a passage of fitted stones. Kept going beyond the fragile beam of Findlay's phone light.

"Holy shit," she said.

"It's always been a blank wall," I said to John D. "You toured the whole building when we moved in. Notice this?"

John D shook his head. "In fact, I did not. A secret door?" He poked and prodded for a hidden switch like an archeologist in a black and white horror flick, to no avail.

After a short period of gawping uselessly, we reconvened upstairs in the kitchen. *Yer goin' on a quest,* Deborah had said, splashing booze. *If ya can devise a method to destroy him, I won't complain.* Victor Infante was certifiably deceased, so why did she speak of him as one might a mythic figure, an immortal bogeyman? And why did her echoing words stir such dread in my heart? None of this seemed real; I'd sunk into a lucid dream.

Findlay said, "I don't understand what we're dealing with, and I don't goddamned need to understand. Facts are facts: those whack jobs next door tunneled under our house. Tunneled under our house and stole Aardvark."

"That tunnel isn't fresh," I said. "Notice the mold, the shade of the stone? Somebody cored it decades ago. Longer, maybe."

"A distinction without a difference," John D said.

"Fresh or old, what do you want to do about it?" I naively said to my wife. Should've known she'd have plenty of ideas.

"We'll be like three little ninjas and follow the tunnel back." Findlay went into the bedroom and pulled on loose-fitting clothes (unzipped jacket over a cool T-shirt featuring a skeletal ouroboros entwining the Earth) and hiking boots. She slipped a tanto into her boot. Seven-inch carbon steel blade. Sharp enough to shave off your freckles if you weren't careful. Then she belted on her katana so it hung Samurai style. By no means an expert, she'd nevertheless taken several years of instruction at her dojo. Until this moment I'd considered her obsession with ancient weaponry and ritualized violence as essentially harmless, a nerd's preoccupation; kind of cute even. What an asshole.

Outvoted, I succumbed to the moment and brought Aardvark's leash and a flashlight. John D possibly knew something we didn't. He grabbed one of my hiking knapsacks and tossed in bottled water, trail mix, and road flares from the trunk of his car.

I said, "Hey, Pizarro, we're not headed into the South American jungle."

"You don't know where we're headed," he said.

We trooped down into the basement and across the crumbling threshold. A murky passage stretched on and on. The farther we walked the more convinced I became that despite Findlay's suspicions to the contrary, this tunnel wasn't of recent construction; it had existed for centuries. To what purpose, only the gods could say. Dripping fractured brick curved around us not unlike the ribcage of a petrified leviathan; archways every few paces, dead dirt and mouse bones underfoot. Smelled of dankness and decay. The gloom reddened like furnace coals burning through a coke glaze; just ahead stood metal double doors beneath a lintel scriven with angular symbols, their granite channels soft with mold. An oil lantern dangled off a wall hook. Beneath its dull glare waited the gardener, Andy, head cocked, smoking. Dressed in black coveralls today. His eyes were lustrous stones in the lamplight. He cast aside his cigarette butt. His towering, multiarmed shadow cracked its knuckles.

"Hello, lambs. Lamb chops. Grateful you came."

"Step aside, friend." John D shuffled forward. Affable as ever, but also grave with conviction.

Laughing, Andy pushed him over and kicked his ribs. A resounding kick too; the likes of which belonged to a four-color comic panel with a jaggedly lettered KAWHUMP! The air left my friend in a godawful wheeze. He writhed on the ground, squashed, neutralized. Amazed me, I won't lie. John D was no child—270 with a lot of muscle from yard work and grade A genetics. I'd once seen him pull a stump out of the earth with a rope. Findlay rushed in kamikaze and the gardener clipped her with a short, piston-fast straight right to the mouth and she dropped like she'd been clotheslined. Chivalry demanded I swing, which I did, in an ungainly, top-heavy fashion that swished a hair wide. I stumbled into Andy. He latched onto my right shoulder, the way Dad might when you're a kid and it's time for a man-to-man chat, and squeezed. Felt like a pair of iron tongs cranked tight. Not ashamed to say I cried. I was still crying as I sank to my knees. Findlay, lips bloody, popped up, a vicious jack-in-the-box, white-knuckling her tanto. She stuck that dagger right to the hilt in Andy's heart. I segued into amazement again as his grip slackened on my shoulder and relieved the crushing agony. He fell backward off the knife and slid down the wall into a seated position, clutching his chest. His expression was that of a man puzzling over a set of instructions written in a foreign language. Findlay hesitated, possibly weighing whether or not to stick him again. No need—his chin sank and he went still.

John D struggled to his feet. I unscrewed a water bottle and gave him a sip. He hissed manfully when Findlay checked his ribs. Dented and already blackening. Fractured for sure. The heavy doors were forged of corroded bronze. She and I leaned on them hard before they rolled open, groaning. Chill air. We crossed into a rough-hewn chamber that gradually widened until walls and ceiling fell away and revealed a sweep of night sky. At our back, the ruined wellhouse, but altered to resemble a medieval woodcut. Before us, a photo negative of our neighborhood environs. Details were fuzzy; a stone here, a tree there, misaligned, or perhaps, completely reversed. How would I know? Who keeps track of such trivialities as the placement of a dead branch, a tumbled rock? Sepia twilight drizzled from the horn of a too-near crescent moon, its pitted visage straining against a softly illuminated burial shroud. Fields of scrub spread before us. Ash powdered the earth; remnant waste of a vast conflagration. Tasted of fire and metal. To our left, a paved road and canted powerlines. Blackbirds perched the wires, pellet eyes judging. Past the vista of field and wood, the shadowy bulk of a mountain range was familiar, yet alien. Trunks of scorched trees that leaned exhaustedly in Charles Heston poses of imminent death. John D spotted two sets of dog tracks, one normal, the other enormous, looping toward Deborah Infante's distant mansion.

We followed.

A bundle of furry darkness moved among the trees—Sleestack, though changed, a panther in miniature, and white-gazed. His yowl echoed tinnily as he bolted into deeper gloom, lost to view. Distances were exaggerated or foreshortened and so too the passage of time. The crunch of our shoes upon bleached tufts of grass and brittle dead leaves didn't carry far. Nor did our voices. The atmosphere lay thick as a heavy blanket upon our shoulders; the spectral light played tricks. I uneasily noted how our shadows crept like stalking beasts, and how my wife and friend were transformed to silhouettes with shining cutout eyes radiating moonlight, twins to the evil blackbirds.

"Possibly a dumb question," Findlay said through a balaclava she'd repurposed as a handkerchief. "Is this nighttime?" Blood dried in unsettling Rorschach patterns on her neck and shirt collar.

"I don't think so," John D said.

Me neither. My rational mind observed the moon and a couple of lonely stars and calculated the obvious solution. My deeper self, the cave dweller, knew better. There was no day or night in this place. Purgatory didn't go by an earthly clock.

The Infante mansion existed as a stain upon the severely curved horizon, seeming to remain at a distance for hours while we marched across the ashen fields, until it loomed before us of a sudden: sharp-angled, its many windows dead and blind. The tracks led up the front steps and through the open door.

"The den of the dragon." John D breathed raggedly, his mouth crimped in pain.

For his sake, I really hoped we wouldn't encounter a dragon, a minotaur, or any other mythical monster. Unfortunately, nightmare logic had infected objective reality and it seemed certain that a hellish challenge awaited.

Inside was the mansion I'd visited twice previously, but now reminiscent of a faintly lighted mausoleum. Another photo negative of the mortal world. Torches of white fire sizzled in iron sconces, emitting no heat. Skulls embedded the smooth granite walls. Our warped images blurred against polished tiles. A trio of leering ghouls advancing toward their fate.

"Cozy," John D said.

In the cathedral parlor, Deborah Infante reposed upon a throne of obsidian. Naked save for a silvery diadem and a purple boa, she fairly gleamed, flattered by the omnidirectional light—younger and lither than last we met. Heavy-lidded eyes narrowed in pleasure, she sipped from a skull chalice. I realized even as she spoke in rich, sultry tones, revealing her fangs, that this was merely a simulacrum of the actress, a doppelganger spawned by the outer dark.

She said, "Ah, the guardian is slain. Here you stand, gallant at the rim of oblivion. I am the Psychopomp. You seek my lover, the invidious lord of this Lagerstätte."

"Wrong." Findlay drew her katana. It shimmered silver to match the scream queen's diadem. "We seek our dog. Maybe you've seen him—yay long, scruffy, bad breath, winsome."

"Yes." Deborah Infante whistled. Two dogs padded into the room. Aardvark, muddy, head hung, tail tucked, refused to meet our glance or acknowledge Findlay's calls. The other was a pit bull mix—brutish and massive and dreadful of aspect. My wife was likely tempted to reach for him, but something in the Psychopomp's demeanor commanded us to hold fast. Infante continued, "He and Artemis rove the north shore of the River Esopus. They belong to Victor. Go forth hounds." She whistled again and the dogs silently loped through an archway. She smiled at me over her chalice. "Lucky for you, the master is abroad in the territories, else he'd have your skins to line his cloak. Unluckily for you, you cannot return to the sunlit world. The way was closed upon your entrance and sealed by the blood of the guardian which you gleefully shed."

I said, "Gleeful isn't quite the way I'd—»

"Are you familiar with Aardvark's true history?" The Psychopomp's feathery purple boa flexed and shimmered; its crimson eye cracked open, revealing a hint of extradimensional horror, of collapsing galaxies and cindering stars. Then it shut again. "He survived a housefire. Human mother, father, twin girls, and a cat. Rescuers discovered him under debris, unconscious. Everybody else succumbed to smoke inhalation. A nice fireman revived him with an oxygen mask and two-finger chest compressions as one would an infant. Family perished, none to claim the pup, he went to the pound. Slated for euthanasia."

"The shelter never said anything," I said.

"Those charnel houses hold vile secrets dear. Technically, your furry companion died until his little ticker restarted." Her serrated grin expressed hunger rather than amusement. "I'm certain Aardvark, stranded for a few moments in purgatory, witnessed the Valkyries swooping to bear him to Valhalla and a comfy spot near the hearth. Now he resides in hell. As do we all."

"Thanks, lady," I said, turning to leave. "We'll be on our way."

"You cannot depart this chamber lest it be over my corpse."

"Music to my ears." Findlay settled into a killing stance.

Deborah Infante's chalice clanked upon the floor as she rose with uncanny alacrity. Her talons were long and curved. She flew toward us, a wire-fu acrobat, arms outflung, jaws agape. Findlay swung three times and finished with a reverse thrust.

"Jesus Hopfrog Christ," John said.

"Yeah," I said.

The Psychopomp's last words gushed forth on foamy blood bubbles: *Victor shall return to wreak his vengeance. You shall be aware of his approach for the whole of the moon and stars shall be snuffed until not a speck of light remains in this benighted land.* Whatever else she muttered was lost as her head rolled away.

Afterward, we simply tracked Aardvark's muddy prints through the house and to an open door at the far end. As we exited, John D knocked over a pair of braziers, igniting furniture, drapes, and everything else.

The River Esopus wasn't far, although we trudged one hundred years and a day to reach its banks where Aardvark sat hunched and disconsolate. Artemis paced the far shore. She howled. Aardvark howled. Mist thickened, erasing the underworld, stone by ancient stone, tree by withered tree. I carried our dog as he kicked and yelped. Eventually, he went limp in my arms, muzzle pressed hard into my armpit.

We passed the Infante house. Popping and crackling, the mansion smoldered at its joints. Smoke roiled, shot with licks of white-black flame. Window glass shattered. Eventually, the structure folded inward in a grand whoosh, painting the bloodless land in a flare of unlight. We turned from the mountain of rubble and trudged the path home, our way lit by the diminishing glare of the pale inferno.

The wellhouse had collapsed, blocking the way we'd originally come. None of us dared speak aloud what that meant. John D nodded farewell as he walked into the woods in the general direction of Rosendale.

I don't know what became of him.

Together as a family, forever. Was it worth it? This muttered query echoed in my brain when I awakened after a long, fitful doze, inhaling frigid dampness, exhaling soul smoke.

Our good boy abandoned his post in bed and slept near the door. He only ate or drank when I brought his dishes to him. Time passed, as it always does; seamless as an eggshell. I became nocturnal. No choice, really. The darksome moon rolled through the clouds, trailing a mare's tail of fire over our unlighted house. Dimmer and dimmer, though. Fewer and fainter stars. Sooner or later, there'd be none.

Aardvark hunched at my feet while we kept an interminable graveyard watch. On those endless evenings, collapsed in a wingback, I'd regard my hand, washed in a ghastly bluish haze upon the armrest, contemplating its disconnectedness, a phantom limb on the verge of dissolution. Sleestack, or a lumpen shadow imitating Sleestack, scratched at the window, then fled before I summoned the energy to respond. A man's screeching laughter boomed in the mountain valleys, drawing nearer and farther, erratic as a fast-moving thunder storm. On those occasions, we cowered and waited for the cessation of reality. But the evil laughter receded and reality went on.

Sometimes Findlay drifted in from wherever she lurked to join us, hair done up, her eyes large and mysterious as the waning starfields. She wore the same bloodied shirt and carried her katana in its scabbard. Once, after an eternity of silence, she said, "That day you visited Deborah's house…Do you ever wonder if she poisoned your drink?"

A second eternity passed while I chose to ignore the question. Occasionally, Artemis bayed on the moors; a knell of death that rattled the shingles and caused mice and bats to scuffle in their hidden places. Aardvark moaned a low guttural response such to raise the hairs on my neck. I didn't begrudge him his melancholy. Humans shouldn't be the only souls entitled to doomed romances.

I patted him and he licked my hand with his cold, dry tongue.

TIPTOE

I was a child of the 1960s. Three network stations or fresh air; take your pick. No pocket computers for entertainment in dark-age suburbia. We read our comic books ragged and played catch with Dad in the backyard. He created shadow puppets on the wall to amuse us before bed. Elephants, giraffes, and foxes. The classics. He also made some animals I didn't recognize. His hands twisted to form these mysterious entities, which he called Mimis. Dad frequently traveled abroad. Said he'd learned of the Mimis at a conference in Australia. His double-jointed performances wowed me and my older brother, Greg. Mom hadn't seemed as impressed.

Then I discovered photography. Mom and Dad gave me a camera. Partly because they were supportive of their children's aspirations; partly because I bugged them relentlessly. At six years old I already understood my life's purpose.

Landscapes bore me, although I enjoy celestial photography—high resolution photos of planets, hanging in partial silhouette; blazing white fingertips emerging from a black pool. People aren't interesting either, unless I catch them in candid moments to reveal a glimmer of their hidden selves. Wild animals became my favorite subjects. Of all the variety of animals, I love predators. Dad approved. He said, *Men revile predators because they shed blood. What an unfair prejudice. Suppose garden vegetables possessed feelings. Suppose a carrot squealed when bitten in two…Well, a groundhog would go right on chomping, wouldn't't he?*

If anybody knew the answer to such a question, it'd be my old man. His oddball personality might be why Mom took a shine to him. Or she appreciated his potential as a captain of industry. What I do know, is he was the kind of guy nobody ever saw coming.

My name is Randall Xerxes Mortimer Vance. I tend to leave Mortimer out of the equation. Friends tease me about my signature—RX and a swooping, offset V. Dad used to say, *Ha-ha, son. You're a prescription for trouble!* As a pro wilderness photographer, I'm accustomed to lying or sitting motionless for hours at a stretch. Despite this, I'm a tad jumpy. You could say my fight or flight reflex is highly tuned. While on assignment for a popular magazine, a technician—infamous for his pranks—snuck up, tapped my shoulder, and yelled, *Boo!* I swung instinctively. Wild, flailing. Good enough to knock him on his ass into a ditch.

Colleagues were nonplussed at my overreaction. Me too. That incident proved the beginning of a rough, emotional ride: insomnia; nightmares when I *could* sleep; and panic attacks. It felt like a crack had opened in my psyche. Generalized anxiety gradually worked its claws under my armor and skinned me to raw nerves. I committed to a leave of absence, pledging to conduct an inventory of possible antecedents.

Soul searching pairs seductively with large quantities of liquor.

A soon-to-be ex-girlfriend offered to help. She opined that I suffered from deep-rooted childhood trauma. I insisted that my childhood was actually fine. My parents had provided for me and my brother, supported our endeavors, and paid for my education; the whole deal.

There's always something if you dig, she said. Subsequent to a bunch more poking and prodding, one possible link between my youth and current troubles came to mind. I told her about a game called Tiptoe Dad taught me. A variation of ambush tag wherein you crept behind your victim and tapped him or her on the shoulder or goosed them, or whatever. Pretty much the same as my work colleague had done. Belying its simple premise, there were rules, which Dad adhered to with solemnity. The victim must be awake and unimpaired. The sneaker was required to assume a certain posture—poised on the balls of his or her feet, arms raised and fingers pressed into a blade or spread in an exaggerated manner. The other details and minutia are hazy.

As far as odd family traditions go, this seemed fairly innocuous. Dad's attitude was what made it weird.

Tiptoe went back as far as I could recall, but my formal introduction occurred around first grade when I got bitten by the photography bug. Greg and I were watching a nature documentary. Dad wandered in late, still dressed from a shift at the office and wearing that coldly affable expression he put on along with his hat and coat. The documentary shifted to the hunting habits of predatory insects. Dad sat between us on the couch. He stared intently at the images of mantises, voracious Venezuelan centipedes, and wasps. During the segment on trapdoor spiders, he smiled and pinched my shoulder. Dad was fast for an awkward, middle-aged dude. I didn't even see his arm move. *People say sneaky as a snake, sly as a fox, but spiders are the best hunters. Patient and swift.* I didn't give it another thought.

One day, soon after, he stepped out of a doorway, grabbed me and started tickling. Then he snatched me into the air and turned my small body in his very large hands. He pretended to bite my neck, arms, and belly.

Which part shall I devour first? Eeny, meeny, miny moe!

I screamed hysterical laughter. He later explained that tickling and the reaction to tickling were rooted in primitive fight or flight responses to mortal danger.

Tiptoe became our frequent contest, and one he'd already inflicted on Greg and Mom. The results seldom amounted to more than the requisite tap, except for the time when Dad popped up from a leaf pile and pinched me so hard it left a welt. You bet I tried to return the favor—on countless occasions, in fact—and failed. I even wore camo paint and dressed in black down to my socks, creeping up behind, only for him to whip his head around at the last second and look me in the eye with a tinge of disappointment. *Heard you coming from the other end of the house, son. Are you thinking like a man or a spider? Like a fox or a mantis? Keep trying.*

Another time, I walked into a room and caught him playing the game with Mom as victim. Dad gave me a sidelong wink as he reached out, tiptoeing closer and closer. Their silhouettes flowed across the wall. The shadows of his arms kept elongating; his shadow fingers ended in shadow claws. The optical illusion made me dizzy and sick to my stomach. He kissed her neck. She startled and mildly cussed him. Then they laughed and once more, he was a ham-fisted doofus, innocently pushing his glasses up the bridge of his nose.

As with many aspects of childhood, Tiptoe fell to the wayside for reasons that escaped me until the job incident brought it crashing home again. Unburdening to my lady friend didn't help either of us as much as we hoped. She acknowledged that the whole backstory was definitely fucked up and soon found other places to be. Probably had a lot to do with my drinking, increasingly moody behavior, and the fact that I nearly flew out of my skin whenever she walked into the room.

The worst part? This apparent mental breakdown coincided with my mother's tribulations. A double whammy. After her stroke, Mom's physical health gradually went downhill. She'd sold the house and moved into a comfy suite at the retirement village where Grandma resided years before.

The role of a calm, dutiful son made for an awkward fit, yet there wasn't much choice considering I was the last close family who remained in touch. Steeling my resolve, I shaved, slapped on cologne to disguise any lingering reek of booze, and drove down from Albany twice a week to hit a diner in Port Ewing. Same one we'd visited since the '60s. For her, a cheeseburger and a cup of tea. I'd order a sandwich and black coffee and watch her pick at the burger. Our conversations were sparse affairs—long silences occasionally peppered with acerbic repartee.

She let me read to her at bedtime. Usually, a few snippets from Poe or his literary cousins. *I've gotten morbid,* she'd say. *Give me some of that Amontillado, hey?* Or, *a bit of M.R. James, if you please.* Her defining characteristics were intellectual curiosity and a prickly demeanor. She didn't suffer fools—not in her prime, nor in her twilight. Ever shrewd and guarded, ever close-mouthed regarding her interior universe. Her disposition discouraged "remember-when's" and utterly repelled more probing inquiries into secrets.

Nonetheless, one evening I stopped in the middle of James' "The Ash Tree" and shut the book. "Did Aunt Vikki really have the gift?"

Next to Mom and Dad, Aunt Vikki represented a major authority figure of my childhood. She might not have gone to college like my parents, but she wasn't without her particular abilities. She performed what skeptics (my mother) dismissed as parlor tricks. Stage magician staples like naming cards in someone's hand, or locating lost keys or wallets. Under rare circumstances, she performed hypnotic regression and "communed" with friendly spirits. Her specialty? Astral projection allowed her to occasionally divine the general circumstances of missing persons. Whether they were alive or dead and their immediate surroundings, albeit not their precise location. Notwithstanding Dad's benign agnosticism and Mom's blatant contempt, I assumed there was something to it—the police had allegedly enlisted Vikki's services on two or three occasions. Nobody ever explained where she acquired her abilities. Mom and Dad brushed aside such questions and I dared not ask Aunt Vikki directly given her impatience with children.

"I haven't thought of that in ages." Mom lay in the narrow bed, covers pulled to her neck. A reading lamp reflected against the pillow and illuminated the shadow of her skull. "Bolt from the blue, isn't it?"

"I got to thinking of her the other day. Her magic act. The last time we visited Lake Terror…"

"You're asking whether she was a fraud."

"Nothing so harsh," I said. "The opposite, in fact. Her affinity for predictions seemed uncanny."

"Of course, it seemed uncanny. You were a kid."

"Greg thought so too."

"Let's not bring your brother into this."

"Okay."

She eyed me with a glimmer of suspicion, faintly aware that my true interest lay elsewhere; that I was feinting. "To be fair, Vikki sincerely believed in her connection to another world. None of us took it seriously. God, we humored the hell out of that woman."

"She disliked Dad."

"Hated John utterly." Her flat, unhesitating answer surprised me.

"Was it jealousy? Loneliness can have an effect…"

"Jealousy? C'mon. She lost interest in men after Theo kicked." Theo had been Aunt Vikki's husband; he'd died on the job for Con Edison.

I decided not to mention the fact that she'd twice remarried since. Mom would just wave them aside as marriages of convenience. "And Dad's feelings toward her?"

"Doubtful he gave her a second thought whenever she wasn't right in front of his nose. An odd duck, your father. Warm and fuzzy outside, cold tapioca on the inside."

"Damn, Mom."

"Some girls like tapioca. What's with the Twenty Questions? You have something to say, spill it."

Should I confess my recent nightmares? Terrible visions of long-buried childhood experiences? Or that Dad, an odd duck indeed, starred in these recollections and his innocuous, albeit unnerving, Tiptoe game assumed a sinister prominence that led to my current emotional turmoil? I wished to share with Mom; we'd finally gotten closer as the rest of our family fell by the wayside. Still, I faltered, true motives unspoken. She'd likely scoff at my foolishness in that acerbic manner of hers and ruin our fragile bond.

She craned her neck. "You haven't seen *him* around?"

"Who?" Caught off guard again, I stupidly concluded, despite evidence to the contrary, that her thoughts were fogged with rapid onset dementia. Even more stupidly, I blurted, "Mom, uh, you know Dad's dead. Right?"

"Yeah, dummy," she said. "I meant Greg."

"The guy you don't want to talk about?" Neither of us had seen my brother in a while. Absence doesn't always make the heart grow fonder.

"Smart ass." But she smiled faintly.

In the wee hours, alone in my studio apartment, I woke from a lucid nightmare. Blurry, forgotten childhood images coalesced with horrible clarity. Aunt Vikki suffering what we politely termed an episode; the still image of a missing woman on the six o'clock news; my father, polishing his glasses and smiling cryptically. Behind him, a sun dappled lake, a stand of thick trees, and a lost trail that wound into the Catskills…or Purgatory. There were other, more disturbing, recollections that clamored for attention, whirling in a black mass on the periphery. Gray, gangling hands; a gray, cadaverous visage…

I poured a glass of whiskey and dug into a shoebox of loose photos; mainly snapshots documenting our happiest moments as a family. I searched those smiling faces for signs of trauma, a hint of anguish to corroborate my tainted memories. Trouble is, old, weathered pictures are ambiguous. You can't always tell what's hiding behind the patina. Nothing, or the worst thing imaginable.

Whatever the truth might be, this is what I recall about our last summer vacation to the deep Catskills:

During the late 1960s, Dad worked at an IBM plant in Kingston, New York. Mom wrote colorful, acerbic essays documenting life in the Mid-Hudson Valley; sold them to regional papers, mainly, and sometimes slick publications such as *The New Yorker* and *The*

Saturday_Evening Post. We had it made. House in the suburbs, two cars, and an enormous color TV. I cruised the neighborhood on a Schwinn ten-speed with the camera slung around my neck. My older brother, Greg, ran cross-country for our school. Dad let him borrow the second car, a Buick, to squire his girlfriend into town on date night.

The Vance clan's holy trinity: Christmas; IBM Family Day; and the annual summer getaway at a cabin on Lake Terron. For us kids, the IBM Family Day carnival was an afternoon of games, Ferris wheel rides, running and screaming at the top of our lungs, and loads of deep-fried goodies. The next morning, Dad would load us into his Plymouth Suburban and undertake the long drive through the mountains. Our lakeside getaway tradition kicked off when I was a tyke—in that golden era, city folks retreated to the Catskills to escape the heat. Many camped at resorts along the so-called Borscht Belt. Dad and his office buddies, Fred Mercer and Leo Schrader, decided to skip the whole resort scene. Instead, they went in together on the aforementioned piece of lakefront property and built a trio of vacation cabins. The investment cost the men a pretty penny. However, nearby Harpy Peak was a popular winter destination. Ski bums were eager to rent the cabins during the holidays and that helped Dad and his friends recoup their expenses.

But let's stick to summer. Dreadful hot, humid summer that sent us to Lake Terron and its relative coolness. Me, Greg, Mom, Dad, Aunt Vikki, and Odin, our dog; supplies in back, a canoe strapped up top. Exhausted from Family Day, Greg and I usually slept for most of the trip. Probably a feature of Dad's vacation-management strategy. Then he merely had to contend with Mom's chain-smoking and Aunt Vikki bitching about it. Unlike Mom and Dad, she didn't do much of anything. After her husband was electrocuted while repairing a downed power line, she collected a tidy insurance settlement and moved from the city into our Esopus home. Supposedly a temporary arrangement on account of her nervous condition. Her nerves never did improve—nor did anyone else's, for that matter.

We made our final pilgrimage the year before Armstrong left bootprints on the Moon. Greg and I were seventeen and twelve, respectively. Our good boy Odin sat between us. He'd outgrown his puppy ways and somehow gotten long in the tooth. Dad turned onto the lonely dirt track that wound a mile through heavy forest and arrived at the lake near sunset. The Mercers and Schraders were already in residence: a whole mob of obstreperous children and gamely suffering adults collected on a sward that fronted the cabins. Adults had gotten a head start on boilermakers and martinis. Grillsmoke wafted toward the beach. Smooth and cool as a mirror, the lake reflected the reddening sky like a portal to a parallel universe.

Lake Terron, or Lake Terror as we affectionally called it, gleamed at the edge of bona fide wilderness. Why Lake Terror? Some joker had altered the N on the road sign into an R with spray-paint and it just stuck. Nights were pitch-black five paces beyond the porch. The dark was full of insect noises and the coughs of deer lurching around in the brush.

Our cabin had pretty rough accommodations—plank siding and long, shotgun shack floorplan with a washroom, master bedroom, and a loft. Electricity and basic plumbing, but no phone or television. We lugged in books, cards, and boardgames to fashion a semblance of civilized entertainment. On a forest ranger's advice, Dad always propped a twelve-gauge shotgun by the door. Black bears roamed the woods and were attracted to the scents of barbeque and trash. *And children!* Mom would say.

The barbeque set the underlying tone; friendly hijinks and

raucous laughter always prevailed those first few hours. Revived from our torpor, kids gorged on hotdogs and cola while parents lounged, grateful for the cool air and peaceful surroundings—except for the mosquitos. *Everybody* complained about them. Men understood shop talk was taboo. Those who slipped up received a warning glare from his better half. Nor did anyone remark upon news trickling in via the radio, especially concerning the Vietnam war; a subject that caused mothers everywhere to clutch teenaged sons to their bosoms. "Camp Terror" brooked none of that doomy guff. For two weeks, the outside world would remain at arm's length.

Mr. Schrader struck a bonfire as the moon beamed over Harpy Peak. Once the dried cedar burned to coals, on came the bags of marshmallows and a sharpened stick for each kid's grubby mitt. I recall snatches of conversation. The men discussed the Apollo Program, inevitably philosophizing on the state of civilization and how far we'd advanced since the Wright Brothers climbed onto the stage.

"We take it for granted," Mr. Mercer said.

"What's that?" Mr. Schrader waved a marshmallow flaming at the end of his stick.

"Comfort, safety. You flip a switch, there's light. Turn a key, a motor starts."

"Electricity affords us the illusion of self-sufficiency."

"Gunpowder and penicillin imbue us with a sense of invincibility. Perpetual light has banished our natural dread of the dark. We're apes carrying brands of fire."

"Okay, gents. Since we're on the subject of apes. We primates share a common ancestor. Which means we share a staggering amount of history. You start dwelling on eons, you have to consider the implications of certain facts."

Mr. Mercer shook his head as lit a cigarette. "I can only guess where this is going."

"Simulation of human features and mannerisms will lead the field into eerie precincts," Dad said.

"Uh, oh," Mr. Schrader said. "This sounds suspiciously close to op-shay alk-tay."

"Thank goodness we're perfecting mechanical arms to handle rivet guns, not androids. Doesn't get more mundane."

"Mark it in the book. Heck, the Japanese are already there."

"Whatever you say, John."

"Researchers built a robot prototype—a baby with a lifelike face. Focus groups recoiled in disgust. Researchers came back with artificial features. Focus groups *oohed* and *ahhed*. Corporate bankrolled the project. We'll hear plenty in a year or two."

"Humans are genetically encoded to fear things that look almost like us, but aren't us."

"Ever ask yourself why?"

"No, can't say I've dedicated much thought to the subject," Mr. Mercer said. "So, why are we allegedly fearful of, er, imitations?"

"For the same reason a deer or a fowl will spook if it gets wind of a decoy. Even an animal comprehends that a lure means nothing good." Dad had mentioned this periodically. Tonight, he didn't seem to speak to either of his colleagues. He looked directly at me.

"Shop talk!" Mom said with the tone of a referee declaring a foul. Mrs. Schrader and Mrs. Mercer interrupted their own conversation to boo the men.

"Whoops, sorry!" Mr. Mercer gestured placatingly. "Anyway, how about those Jets?"

Later, somebody suggested we have a game. No takers for charades or trivia. Finally, Mrs. Mercer requested a demonstration of Aunt Vikki's fabled skills. Close magic, prestidigitation, clairvoyance, or whatever she called it. My aunt demurred. However, the boisterous assembly would brook no refusal and badgered her until she relented.

That mystical evening, performing for a rapt audience against a wilderness backdrop, she was on her game. Seated lotus on a blanket near the fire, she affected trancelike concentration. Speaking in a monotone, she specified the exact change in Mr. Schrader's pocket; the contents of Mrs. Mercer's clutch, and the fact that one of the Mercer kids had stolen his sister's diary. This proved to be the warmup routine.

Mr. Mercer said, "John says you've worked with the law to find missing persons."

"Found a couple." Her cheeks were flushed, her tone defiant. "Their bodies, at any rate."

"That plane that went down in the Adirondacks. Can you get a psychic bead on it?"

Aunt Vikki again coyly declined until a chorus of pleas "convinced" her to give it a shot. She swayed in place, hands clasped. "Dirt. Rocks. Running water. Scattered voices. Many miles apart."

"Guess that makes sense," Mr. Mercer said to Mr. Schrader. "Wreck is definitely spread across the hills."

Mrs. Schrader said under her breath to Dad, "Eh, what's the point? She could say anything she pleases. We've no way to prove her claim." He shooshed her with a familiar pat on the hip. Everybody was ostensibly devout in those days. Mrs. Schrader frequently volunteered at her church and I suspect Aunt Vikki's occult shenanigans, innocent as they might've been, troubled her. The boozing and flirtation less-so.

The eldest Mercer girl, Katie, asked if she could divine details of an IBM housewife named Denise Vinson who'd disappeared near Saugerties that spring. Nobody present knew her husband; he was among the faceless legions of electricians who kept the plant humming. He and his wife had probably attended a company buffet or some such. The case made the papers.

"Denise Vinson. Denise Vinson…" Aunt Vikki slipped into her "trance." Moments dragged on and an almost electric tension built; the hair-raising sensation of an approaching thunderstorm. The adults ceased bantering. Pine branches creaked; an owl hooted. A breeze freshened off the lake, causing water to lap against the dock. Greg and I felt it. His persistent smirk faded, replaced by an expression of dawning wonderment. Then Aunt Vikki went rigid and shrieked. Her cry echoed off the lake and caused birds to dislodge from their roosts in the surrounding trees. Her arms extended, fingers and thumbs together, wrists bent downward. She rocked violently, cupped hands stabbing the air in exaggerated thrusts. Her eyes filled with blood. My thoughts weren't exactly coherent, but her posture and mannerisms reminded me of a mantis lashing at its prey. Reminded me of something else, too.

Her tongue distended as she babbled like a Charismatic. She covered her face and doubled over. Nobody said anything until she straightened to regard us.

"Geez, Vikki!" Mr. Mercer nodded toward his pop-eyed children. "I mean, geez-Louise!"

"What's the fuss?" She glanced around, dazed.

Mom, in a display of rare concern, asked what she'd seen. Aunt Vikki shrugged and said she'd glimpsed the inside of her eyelids. Why was everybody carrying on? Dad lurked to one side of the barbeque pit. His glasses were brimmed with the soft glow of the coals. I couldn't decipher his expression.

Mood dampened, the families said their goodnights and drifted off to bed. Mom, tight on highballs, compared Aunt Vikki's alleged powers of clairvoyance to those of the famous Edgar Cayce. This clash occurred in the wee hours after the others retired to their cabins. Awakened by raised voices, I hid in shadows atop the stairs to the loft, eavesdropping like it was my job.

"Cayce was as full of shit as a Christmas goose." Aunt Vikki's simmering antipathy boiled over. "Con man. Charlatan. Huckster." Her eyes were bloodshot and stained from burst capillaries. Though she doggedly claimed not to recall the episode from earlier that evening, its lingering effects were evident.

"Vikki," Dad said in the placating tone he deployed against disgruntled subordinates. "Barbara didn't mean any harm. Right, honey?"

"Sure, I did…not." From my vantage I saw Mom perched near the cold hearth, glass in hand. The drunker she got, the cattier she got. She drank plenty at Lake Terror.

Aunt Vikki loomed in her beehive-do and platform shoes. "Don't ever speak of me and that…that fraud in the same breath. Cayce's dead and good riddance to him. *I'm* the real McCoy."

"Is that a fact? Then, let's skip the rest of this campout and head for Vegas." Mom tried to hide her sardonic smile with the glass.

"Ladies, it's late," Dad said. "I sure hope our conversation isn't keeping the small fry awake." Maybe he glanced my way while stretching.

His not-so-subtle cue to skedaddle back to my cot left me pondering who was the psychic—Aunt Vikki or Dad? *Maybe he can see in the dark,* was my last conscious thought. It made me giggle, albeit nervously.

Greg jumped me and Billy Mercer as we walked along the trail behind the cabins. Billy and I were closest in age. Alas, we had next to nothing in common and didn't prefer one another's company. Those were the breaks, as the youth used to say. The path forked at a spring before winding ever deeper into the woods. To our left, the path climbed a steep hill through a notch in a stand of shaggy black pine. Mom, the poet among us, referred to it as the Black Gap. Our parents forbade us to drink from the spring, citing mosquito larvae. Predictably, we disregarded their command and slurped double handfuls of cool water at the first opportunity. As I drank, Greg crept upon me like an Apache.

He clamped my neck in a grip born of neighborhood lawnmowing to earn extra bucks for gas and date-night burgers. "Boo!" He'd simultaneously smacked Billy on the back of his head. The boy yelped and tripped over his own feet trying to flee. Thus, round one of Tiptoe went to my insufferably smirking brother. Ever merciless in that oh-so special cruelty the eldest impose upon their weaker siblings, I nonetheless detected a sharper, savage inflection to his demeanor of late. I zipped a rock past his ear from a safe distance—not that one could ever be sure—and beat a hasty retreat into the woods. Greg flipped us the bird and kept going without a backward glance.

The reason this incident is notable? Billy Mercer complained to the adults. Dad pulled me aside for an account, which I grudgingly provided—nobody respects a tattletale. Dad's smirk was even nastier than Greg's. *Head on a swivel, if you want to keep it, kiddo.* He put his arm around my brother's shoulders and they shared a laugh. Three days in, and those two spent much of it together, hiking the forest and floating around the lake. The stab of jealousy hurt worse than Greg squeezing my neck.

Near bedtime, we set up tents in the backyard, a few feet past the badminton net and horseshoe pit. The plan was for the boys to sleep under the stars (and among the swarming mosquitos). Mrs. Schrader protested weakly that maybe this was risky, what with the bears. Mr. Schrader and Mr. Mercer promised to take watches on the porch. Odin stayed with me; that would be the best alarm in the world. No critter would get within a hundred yards without that dog raising holy hell. And thus it went; Odin, Billy Mercer, a Schrader boy, and me in one tent, and the rest of them in the other. We chatted for a bit. Chitchat waned; I tucked into my sleeping bag, poring over an issue of *Mad Magazine* by flashlight until I got sleepy.

I woke to utter darkness. Odin panted near my face, growling softly. I lay at the entrance. Groggy and unsure of whether the dog had scented a deer or a bear, I instinctively clicked on my trusty flashlight, opened the flap, and shined it into the trees— ready to yell if I spotted danger. Nothing to corroborate Odin's anxious grumbles. Scruffy grass, bushes, and the shapeless mass of the forest. He eventually settled. I slept and dreamed two vivid dreams. The first was of Aunt Vikki spotlighted against a void. Her eyes bulged as she rocked and gesticulated, muttering. Dream logic prevailing, I understood her garbled words: *Eeny! Meany! Miny! Moe!*

In the second, I floated; a disembodied spirit gazing down. Barely revealed by a glimmer of porchlight, Dad crawled from under a bush and lay on his side next to the tent. He reached through the flap. His arm moved, stroking.

These dreams were forgotten by breakfast. The incident only returned to me many years later; a nightmare within a nightmare.

Over blueberry pancakes, Dad casually asked whether I'd care to go fishing. At an age where a kid selfishly treasured an appointment on his father's calendar, I filled a canteen and slung my trusty Nikon F around my neck and hustled after him to the dock. Unlike the starter camera I'd long outgrown, the Nikon was expensive and I treated it with proper reverence. Film rolls were costly as well. Manual labor, supplemented by a generous allowance and a bit of wheedling, paid the freight. Mom, a stalwart supporter of the arts, chipped in extra. She encouraged me to submit my work to newspaper and magazine contests, in vain. Back then, the hobby was strictly personal. I wasn't inclined to share my vision with the world just yet, although I secretly dreamed big dreams— namely, riding the savannah with the crew of *Mutual of Omaha's Wild Kingdom*.

The sun hadn't cleared the trees as we pushed away from the dock. Dad paddled. I faced him, clicking shots of the receding cabins and birds rising and falling from the lake and into the sky. He set aside his paddle and the canoe kept on gliding across the dark water.

"This is where we're gonna fish?" I said.

"No fishing today." After a pause, he said, "I'm more a fisher of men."

"I don't get it."

"Time to begin reflecting on what kind of man *you* are."

"Dad, I'm *twelve*." I inherited my smart-Alec lip from Mom.

"That's why I don't expect you to decide today. Merely think on it." He could see I wasn't quite comprehending him. "Ever since you showed an interest in photography, I had a hunch…" He cupped his hands and blew into the notch between his thumbs. Took him a couple of tries to perfect an eerie, fluting whistle that rebounded off the lake and nearby hills. He lowered his hands and looked at me. "I planned to wait until next year to have this conversation. Aunt Vikki's...outburst has me thinking sooner is better. Sorry if she frightened you."

"Why did she fly off the handle? Are her eyes okay?" I hoped to sound unflappable.

"Her eyes are fine. It's my fault. The Vinson woman was too close to home. Anyhow, your aunt is staying with us because she can't live alone. She's fragile. Emotionally."

"Vikki's crazy?"

"No. Well, maybe. She's different and she needs her family."

"She and Mom hate each other."

"They fight. That doesn't mean they hate each other. Do you hate your brother? Wait, don't answer that." He dipped his paddle into the water. "What's my job at the plant?"

"You build—"

"Design."

"You design robots."

"I'm a mechanical engineer specializing in robotic devices and systems. It's not quite as dramatic as it sounds. How do you suppose I landed that position?"

"Well, you went to school—"

"No, son. I majored in sociology. Any expertise I have in engineering I've learned on the fly or by studying at night."

"Oh." Confused by the turn in our conversation, I fiddled with my camera.

"Want to know the truth?"

"Okay." I feared with all the power of my child's imagination that he would reveal that his *real* name was Vladimir, a deep cover mole sent by the Russians. It's difficult to properly emphasize the underlying paranoia wrought by the Cold War on our collective national psyche. My brother and I spied on our neighbors, profiling them as possible Red agents. We'd frequently convinced ourselves that half the neighborhood was sending clandestine reports to a numbers station.

"I bullshitted the hiring committee," Dad said. He seldom cursed around Mom; moreso Greg. Now I'd entered his hallowed circle of confidence. "*That's* how I acquired my position. If you understand what makes people tick, you can always get what you want. Oops, here we are." Silt scraped the hull as he nosed the canoe onto the shore. We disembarked and walked through some bushes to a path that circled the entire lake. I knew this since our families made the entire circuit at least once per vacation.

Dad yawned, twisting his torso around with a contortionist's knack. He doubled his left hand against his forearm; then the right. His joints popped. This wasn't the same as my brother cracking his knuckles, which he often did to annoy me. No, it sounded more like a butcher snapping the bones of a chicken carcass. He sighed in evident relief. He removed his glasses and became unrecognizable for a moment. Then he put them back on and all was right again. "Son, I can't tell you what a living bitch it is to maintain acceptable posture every damned minute of the day. Speaking of wanting things. You want great pictures of predators, right?" I agreed, sure, that was the idea. He hunched so our heads were closer. "Prey animals are easy to stalk. They're *prey*. They exist to be hunted and eaten. Predators are tougher. I can teach you. I've been working with your brother for years. Getting him ready for the jungle."

"The jungle?" I said, hearing and reacting to the latter part of his statement while ignoring the former. "You mean *Vietnam*?" There was a curse word. But he promised Mom—"

"Greg's going to volunteer for the Marines. Don't worry. He's a natural. He's like me." He stopped and laid his hand on my shoulder.

Heavy and full of suppressed power. "I can count on your discretion not to tell your mother. Can't I?"

Sons and fathers have differences. Nonetheless, I'd always felt safe around mine. Sure, he was awkward and socially off-putting. Sure, he ran hot and cold. Sure, he made lame jokes and could be painfully distant. People joke that engineers are socially maladjusted; there's some truth to that cliché. Foibles notwithstanding, I didn't doubt his love or intentions. Yet, in that moment, I became hyperaware of the size of his hand—of him, in general—and the chirping birds, and that we were alone here in the trees on the opposite shore of the lake. Awareness of his physical grotesqueness hit me in a wave of revulsion. From my child's unvarnished perspective, his features transcended mere homeliness. Since he'd stretched, his stance and expression had altered. Spade-faced and gangling, toothy and hunched, yet tall and deceptively agile. A carnivore had slipped on Dad's sporting goods department ensemble and lured me into the woods. *Let's go to Grandma's house!*

Such a witless, childish fantasy. The spit dried in my mouth anyhow. Desperate to change the subject, perhaps to show deference the way a wolf pup does to an alpha, I said, "I didn't mean to call Aunt Vikki crazy."

Dad blinked behind those enormous, horn-rimmed glasses. "It would be a mistake to classify aberrant psychology as proof of disorder." He registered my blank expression. "Charles Addams said—"

"Who's that?"

"A cartoonist. He said, 'What is normal for the spider is chaos for the fly.' He was correct. The world is divided between spiders and flies." He studied me intently, searching for something, then shook himself and straightened. His hand dropped away from my shoulder.

Such a large hand, such a long arm. "C'mon. Let's stroll a bit. If we're quiet, we might surprise a woodland critter."

W e strolled.
Contrary to his stated intention of moving quietly to surprise our quarry, Dad initiated a nonstop monologue. He got onto the subject of physical comedy and acting. "Boris Karloff is a master," He said. "And Lon Chaney Jr. The werewolf guy?"

"Yeah, Dad." I'd recovered a bit after that moment of irrational panic. The world felt right again under my feet.

"Chaney's facility with physiognomic transformation? Truly remarkable. Unparalleled, considering his disadvantages. Faking—it's difficult." One aspect I learned to appreciate about my old man's character was the fact he didn't dumb down his language. Granted, he'd speak slower depending upon the audience. However, he used big words if big words were appropriate. My deskside dictionary and thesaurus were dogeared as all get-out.

While he blathered, I managed a few good shots including a Cooper's hawk perched on a high branch, observing our progress. The hawk leaped, disappearing over the canopy. When I lowered the camera, Dad was gone too. I did what you might expect—called for him and dithered, figuring he'd poke his head around a tree and laugh at my consternation. Instead, the sun climbed. Patches of cool shade thickened; the lake surface dimmed and brightened with opaline hardness. Yelling occasionally, I trudged back toward where we'd beached the canoe.

He caught me as I rounded a bend in the path. A hand and ropy arm extended so very far from the wall of brush. A hooked nail scraped my forehead.

Look, son! See?

Instead of pausing to peer into the undergrowth, I ran. Full tilt, camera strap whipping around my neck and a miracle I didn't lose that beloved camera before I crashed through the bushes onto the beach.

Dad sat on a driftwood log, serenely studying the lake. "Hey, kiddo. There you are." He explained his intention to play a harmless joke. "You perceive your surroundings in a different light if a guardian isn't present. Every boy should feel that small burst of adrenaline under controlled circumstances. Head on a swivel, right, son?"

I realized I'd merely bumped into a low-hanging branch and completely freaked. By the time we paddled home, my wild, unreasoning terror had dissipated. It's all or nothing with kids—dying of plague or fit as a fiddle; bounce back from a nasty fall, or busted legs; rub some dirt on it and walk it off, or a wheelchair. Similar deal with our emotions as well. Dad wasn't a monster, merely a weirdo. Aunt Vikki's crazed behavior had set my teeth on edge. The perfect storm. My thoughts shied from outré concerns to dwell upon on Dad's casual mention that Greg planned on going to war and how we'd best keep on the QT. Not the kind of secret I wanted to hide from Mom, but I wasn't a squealer.

He remained quiet until we were gliding alongside the dock. He finally said, "Randy, I was wrong to test you. I'm sorry. Won't happen again. Scout's honor."

It didn't.

Toward the end of our stay, the whole lot of us trooped forth to conduct our annual peregrination around the entire lake.

We packed picnic baskets and assembled at the Black Gap. Except for Dad, who'd gone ahead to prepare the site where we'd camp for lunch. Another barbeque, in fact. Mr. Mercer brought along a fancy camera (a Canon!) to record the vacation action. He and I had a bonding moment as "serious" photographers. Mr. Schrader, Dad, and a couple of the kids toted flimsy cheapo tourist models. Such amateurs! Mr. Mercer arranged us with the pines for a backdrop. Everybody posed according to height. He yelled directions, got what he wanted, and joined the group while I snapped a few—first with his camera, then my own. I lagged behind as they scrambled uphill along the path. Odin stuck to my side, occasionally whining, but nothing dangerous appeared.

We trekked to the campsite. Hot, thirsty, and ready for our roasted chicken. Dad awaited us, although not by much. None of the other adults said anything. However, I recall Mom's vexation with the fact he hadn't even gotten a fire going in the pit. She pulled him aside and asked what happened. Why was he so mussed and unkempt? Why so damned sweaty?

He blinked, pushed his glasses up, and shrugged. "I tried a shortcut. Got lost."

"Lost, huh?" She combed pine needles out of his hair. "Likely story."

That winter, drunken ski bums accidentally burned down the Schrader cabin. Oh, the plan was to rebuild in the spring and carry on. Alas, one thing led to another—kids shipping off to college, the Mercers divorcing, etc.—and we never returned. The men sold off the property for a tidy profit. That was that for our Terror Lake era.

Greg skipped college and enlisted with the United States Marine Corps in '69. Mom locked herself in her study and cried for a week. That shook me—she wasn't a weeper by any means. My brother sent postcards every month or so over the course of his two tours. Well, except for a long, dark stretch near the end when he ceased all communication. The military wouldn't tell us anything. Judging by her peevishness and the fact she seldom slept, I suspect Mom walked the ragged edge.

One day, Greg called and said he'd be home soon. Could Dad pick him up at the airport? He departed an obstreperous child and returned a quieter, thoughtful man. The war injured the psyches of many soldiers. It definitely affected him. Greg kibitzed about shore leave and the antics of his rogue's gallery of comrades. Conversely, he deflected intimate questions that drilled too close to where his honest emotions lay buried. Dumb kids being dumb kids, I asked if he killed anyone. He smiled and tapped his fingers on the table, one then another until both hands were drumming; hypnotic and horrible. That smile harked to his teenaged cruelness, now carefully submerged. More artful, more refined, more mature.

Greg said, *The neat thing about Tiptoe? It's humane. Curbs the ol' urges. Ordinarily, it's enough to catch and release. Ordinarily. You get me, kid?* We didn't speak often after he moved to the Midwest. He latched on with a trucking company. The next to the last time I saw him was at Dad's funeral in 1985. Dad's ticker had blown while raking leaves. Dead on his way to the ground, same as his own father and older brother. My brother lurked on the fringes at the reception. He slipped away before I could corner him. Nobody else noticed that he'd come and gone.

Aunt Vikki? She joined a weird church. Her erratic behavior deteriorated throughout the 1970s, leading to a stint in an institution.

She made a comeback in the '80s, got on the ground floor of the whole psychic hotline craze. Made a killing telling people what they wanted to hear. Remarried to a disgraced avant garde filmmaker. Bought a mansion in Florida where she currently runs a New Age commune of international repute. Every Christmas, she drops a couple grand on my photography to jazz up her compound. I can't imagine how poster photos of wolves disemboweling caribou go over with the rubes seeking enlightenment. Got to admit, watching those recruitment videos shot by her latest husband, my work looks damned slick.

And full circle at last. My coworker startled me; nightmares ensued; and creepy-crawly memories surfaced. Cue my formerly happy existence falling apart. 2 a.m. routinely found me wide awake, scrutinizing my sweaty reflection in the bathroom mirror. I tugged the bags beneath my eyes, exposing the veiny whites. Drew down until it hurt. Just more of the same. What did I expect? That my face was a mask and I peered through slits? That I was my father's son, through and through? If he were more or less than a man, what did that make me?

On my next visit, I decided to level with Mom as I tucked her into bed.

"We need to talk about Dad." I hesitated. Was it even ethical to tell her the truth, here at the end of her days? *Hey, Ma, I believe Pop was involved in the disappearances of several—god knows the number—people back in the '60s.* I forged ahead. "This will sound crazy. He wasn't…normal."

"Well, duh," she said. We sat that there for a while, on opposite sides of a gulf that widened by the second.

"Wait. Were you aware?"

"Of what?"

Hell of a question. "There was another side to Dad. Dark. Real dark, I'm afraid."

"Ah. What did you know, ma'am, and when did you know it?"

"Yeah, basically."

"Bank robbers don't always tell their wives they rob banks."

"The wives suspect."

"Damned straight. Suspicion isn't proof. That's the beauty of the arrangement. We lasted until he died. There's beauty in that too, these days." Mom's voice had weakened as she spoke. She beckoned me to lean in and I did. "We were on our honeymoon at a lodge. Around dawn, wrapped in a quilt on the deck. A fox light-footed into the yard. I whispered to your father about the awesomeness of mother nature, or wow, a fox! He smiled. Not his quirky smile, the cold one. He said, *an animal's expression won't change, even as it's eating prey alive.* May sound strange, but that's when I knew we fit perfectly."

"Jesus, Mom." I shivered. Dad and his pearls of wisdom, his icy little apothegms. *Respected, admired, revered. But replaceable.* A phrase he said in response to anyone who inquired after his job security at IBM. He'd also uttered a similar quote when admonishing Greg or me in connection to juvenile hijinks. *Loved, but replaceable, boys. Loved, but replaceable.*

"He never would've hurt you." She closed her eyes and snuggled deeper into her blankets. Her next words were muffled. I'm not sure I heard them right. "At least, not by choice."

Mom died. A handful of journalist colleagues and nurses showed to pay their respects. Greg waited until the rest had gone and I was in the midst of wiping my tears to step from behind a decrepit obelisk, grip my shoulder, and say, "Boo!" He didn't appear especially well. Gray and gaunt, raw around the nose and mouth. Strong, though, and seething with febrile energy. He resembled the hell out of Dad when Dad was around that age and not long prior to his coronary. Greg even wore a set of oversized glasses, although I got a funny feeling they were purely camouflage.

We relocated to a tavern. He paid for a pitcher, of which he guzzled the majority. Half a lifetime had passed since our last beer. I wondered what was on his mind. The funeral? Vietnam? That decade-old string of missing persons in Ohio near his last known town of residence?

"Don't fret, little brother." Predators have a talent for sniffing weakness. He'd sussed out that I'd gone through a few things recently, Mom's death being the latest addition to the calculus of woe. "Dad *told* you—you're not the same as us." He wiped his lips and tried on a peaceable smile. "Our parents gave me the good genes. Although, I do surely wish I had your eye. Mom also had the eye." The second pitcher came and he waxed maudlin. "I've thought about things a lot, these past few years. Apologies for being such a jerk to you when we were kids."

"Forgotten," I said.

"I've always controlled my worst impulses by inflicting petty discomfort. Like chewing a stick of gum when I want a cigarette so bad my teeth ache. I needle people. Associates, friends, loved ones. Whomever. Their unease feeds me well enough to keep the real craving at bay. Until it doesn't." He removed a photo from his wallet and pushed it across the table. Mom and Dad in our old yard. The sun was in Dad's glasses. Hard to know what to make of man's smile when you can't see his eyes. I pushed it back. He waved me off. "Hang onto that."

"It's yours."

"Nah, I don't need a memento. You're the archivist. The sentimental one."

"Fine. Thanks." I slipped the photo into my coat pocket.

He stared at a waitress as she cleared a booth across the aisle. From a distance his expression might've passed for friendly. "My motel isn't far," he said. "Give me a ride? Or if you're busy, I could ask her."

How could I refuse my own brother? Well, I would've loved to.

G reg's motel occupied a lonely corner on a dark street near the freeway. He invited me into his cave-like room. I declined, said it had been great, etcetera. I almost escaped clean. He caught my wrist. Up close, he smelled of beer, coppery musk, and a hint of moldering earth.

"I think back to my friends in high school and the military," he said. "The drug addicts, the cons, and divorcees. A shitload of kids who grew up and moved as far from home as humanly possible. Why? Because their families were the awfullest thing that ever happened to them. It hit me."

"What hit you?"

"On the whole, Mom and Dad were pretty great parents."

"Surprising to hear you put it that way, Greg."

"Yeah?"

"We haven't shared many family dinners since we were kids," I said. "You weren't around to know one way or the other."

Instead of a scowl, he smiled the way a wild animal does. All teeth and no joy. "Take my absence as an expression of tenderness. Consider also, I might have been around more than you noticed."

He squeezed. "That keen eye of yours has to shut sometimes, right? They were great parents. The best."

As I mentioned, despite his cadaverous appearance, he was strong. And by that, I mean bone crushing strong. My arm may as well have been clamped in the jaws of a grizzly. I wasn't going anywhere unless he permitted it. "They were good people," I said through my teeth.

"Adios, bud."

Surely was a relief when he slackened his grip and released me. I trudged down the stairs, across the lot, and had my car keys in hand when the flesh on my neck prickled. I spun, and there was Greg, twenty or so feet behind me, soundlessly tiptoeing along, knees to chest, elbows even with the top of his head, hands splayed wide. He closed most of the gap in a single, exaggerated stride. An impossible stride. Then he froze within spitting distance and watched my face with the same intensity as he'd observed the waitress.

"Well done," he said. "Maybe you learned something, bumbling around in the woods." He turned and walked toward the lights of the motel. I waited until he'd climbed the stairs to jump into my car and floor it out of there.

A long trip home. You bet I glanced into my rearview the entire drive.

Later, in the desolate stretch that comes along after 3 a.m., short on sleep due to a brain that refused to switch off, I killed the last of the bourbon while obsessively sorting those photographs one more time. A mindless occupation that felt akin to picking at a scab or working on a jigsaw. No real mental agility involved other than mechanically rotating pieces until something locked into place.

Among the many loose pictures I'd stashed for posterity were some shot on that last day at Lake Terror in '68. The sequence began with our three cheerfully waving families (minus Dad) assembled at the Black Gap; then a few more of everybody proceeding single-file away and up the trail.

I spread these photos on the coffee table and stared for a long, long while. I only spotted the slightly fuzzy, unfocused extra figure because of my keenly trained vision…and possibly a dreadful instinct honed by escalating paranoia. Once I saw him, there were no take backsies, as we used to say. Dad hung in the branches; a huge, distorted figure hidden in the background of tree trunks and heavy canopy. Bloated and lanky, his jaw unslung. Inhumanly proportioned, but unmistakably my father. Gaze fixed upon the camera as his left arm dangled and dangled, gray-black fingers plucking the hair of the kids as they hiked obliviously through the notch between the shaggy pines. His lips were frozen mid-squirm.

Eeny. Meeny. Miny. Moe.

(YOU WON'T BE) SAVED BY THE GHOST OF YOUR OLD DOG

The man dreamed of his gray, rheumy-eyed dog, lost for many years now.

"I always loved you!" the dog said. "Even when I did wrong!" The dog did not speak as men speak, of course. His notched ears crumpled and he howled. But it meant the same thing.

"I always loved you as well, you incorrigible asshole," the man tried to answer. He could not speak because it was a dream.

The man awoke and waited a while for the strength to rise. No more water, no more hardtack or jerky. His snowshoes had gone up as kindling smoke. He leaned his pack and rifle against a tree. He buttoned his coat and tightened the laces of his boots. He kicked dirt over the ashes of the fire.

Sky and the earth were the same deep matte. Cold as the metal of his broadhead axe. Icicles snapped from his beard. Tiny icicle tears snapped from his lashes when he blinked.

The man was no scout, although he'd lived in the woods and

knew how to survive. He limped in ever widening circles along the slope of the mountain and eventually cut across the dog's trail. Blood glittered in the paw prints. North.

As ever, he'd followed the tracks for a short time when it began to snow.

AFTERWORD

"Let me tell you about the time I almost died." So go Denzel Washington's infamous words at the opening scene of *Fallen*.

Well, let me tell you about the most recent time I almost died. Not from cancer when I was a toddler, not the thirty-six hours I spent in a blizzard in Alaska as a young man, but the summer of 2022 when I developed a nagging cough that developed into vomiting pieces of my lung, dropping 80 pounds, undergoing major surgery, and spending five weeks immobilized in a hospital bed by midwinter. It was, to paraphrase Roger Zelazny, a close thing. A matter of hours, according to one of my surgeons.

Two nights before the big operation to remove a mass in my lung, and a substantial portion of the organ itself, I was at the human equivalent of ebb tide. Unable to eat or drink, unable to do much more than lift my hand. In and out of consciousness; I dreamed the hospital bed transformed into a glass coffin. The coffin drifted in an interstellar gulf of stars. The cornucopia of stars melted to slag and crushing darkness absorbed all light and heat until I hung in a void.

The coffin shrank around me, so I crawled into that unlight, the heat death of a condensing universe slowly flattening me into atomic dust. It wasn't such a bad feeling in the moment; it reminded me of that time on the ice near Nome and how after a certain point, mind and body begin to divest of pain and suffering. In great extremis, you let go—like a rabbit in the jaws of a fox finally accepts the finality of its predicament and ceases the good fight.

Then I woke, still groggy, still dying, but faintly afraid and regretful. Regretful I hadn't spent more time with Jessica M and Valentina, that I hadn't called my friends more often. That I would never finish this book, or the next one, the dark fantasy collection I've dreamed of writing for so many years.

At the time of this note it's spring of 2024. I'm still in recovery and likely will be for a long time. Some conditions are improving; other damage was permanent. Regardless, my situation is vastly better than it was in early 2023. I have many people to thank—the doctors, nurses, and staff at the Kingston, Westchester, and Mid-Hudson hospitals, my partner, Jessica M, and the well-wishes and kindness from close friends, colleagues, and readers around the world. The community at large extended a hand; you bolstered my determination to survive to write more books and to reunite with the people I love. Thanks isn't enough…But thank you.

These stories were over the past decade and change, culminating with the novelette, "Not a Speck of Light," which is original to this collection. It was an eventful stretch that saw me publish multiple books, including the Isaiah Coleridge series; Phil Gelatt adapted my story "—30—" into a feature film; I endured the passing of my dear companion, Athena, and celebrated the arrival of another wonderful dog, Valentina. Much changed, and of course much remained the same as it ever was. *Not a Speck of Light (Stories)* is tonally similar to its predecessor, *Swift to Chase,* in the sense that *Occultation & Other Stories* reflected an evolution from my very first collection, *The Imago Sequence* all those years ago. The pieces herein represent my current take on the contemporary weird and horrific, mixed with a bit of thriller and noir. Familiar, yet different, a serpent shedding its skin, an insect transitioning into something new and terrible.

For me, every collection is a battle fought in a war of attrition that we all lose in the end. Our best hope is to leave something of ourselves behind; a token of the joy, suffering, and turmoil that make up a life. Literature is my gesture against the dark.

I can't say where this is all headed—only that I'm grateful to be here and have a chance to travel with you a little farther down the trail.

—Laird Barron
April 7, 2024
Stone Ridge, NY

ACKNOWLEDGMENTS

My deepest gratitude to the following:

Family and Friends: Jessica Maciag; Mike Davis; Ed Maciag; John, Fiona, and David Langan; Timbi Barron; Paul Tremblay; Ellen Datlow; Livia Llewellyn; Jeff Ford; Kris Dikeman; Martin Garner & Vitskär Süden; Phil Fracassi; Stephanie Simard; Norm Partridge; Brian Keene; Mary SanGiovanni; Mark Tallen; Kelly Link; Scott Lynch; Elizabeth Bear; Priya Sharma; Elizabeth Hand; Corey Farrenkopf; Gage Prentiss; JD and Lara Busch; Christopher Coke; John Ryan; Jane Rideau Demuth; James Frauenberger; Deborah Engel-DiMauro; Eric Judson; Phil Gelatt; Victoria Dalpe; Lou Pendergrast; Jason, Harmony, Oksana, Julian, and Quinn Barron; William Barron; Mrs. Gray.

Special thanks: my agents Sarah Gertson, Pouya Shahbazian, and the team at New Leaf Media; Trevor Henderson; Todd Keisling; Yves Tourigny; Greg Greene; Janet Reid; Jordan Hamessley; Sara Minnich; Roger Miller; Slow to Chase; Laird Barron Reddit community; my fans who've stuck with me since 2000.

Editors who originally published these stories: Douglas Coen; John

Joseph Adams; Christopher Golden; Robert S. Wilson; Steve Berman; Theresa DeLucci; S.T. Joshi; G. Winston Hyatt; Greg Kishbaugh; Lois H. Gresh; Darren Speegle; Ross Lockhart; Jess Landry; Aaron French; Kat Rocha; Ellen Datlow.

Extra Special Thanks to Doug Murano and family at *Bad Hand Books*.

ABOUT THE AUTHOR

LAIRD BARRON spent his early years in Alaska. He is the author of several books, including *The Beautiful Thing That Awaits Us All, Swift to Chase,* and *The Wind Began to Howl.* His work has also appeared in many magazines and anthologies. Barron currently resides in the Rondout Valley writing stories about the evil that men do.

Milton Keynes UK
Ingram Content Group UK Ltd.
UKHW041827130824
446844UK00001B/134